Quench the Moon

Walter Macken, author and dramatist, died in April 1967 in his native Galway at the age of 51. At 17 he began writing plays and also joined the Galway Gaelic Theatre (the now celebrated Taibhdhearc) as an actor. In 1936 he married and moved to London for two years, returning to become actor-manager-director of the Gaelic Theatre for nine years, during which time he produced many successful translations of plays by Ibsen, Shaw, O'Casey, Capek and Shakespeare. To enable him to have more time for playwriting, he moved to the Abbey Theatre in Dublin. Macken acted on the London stage, on Broadway and also took a leading part in the film of Brendan Behan's *The Quare Fellow*. Many of his plays have been published, and of his novels the first two, *I Am Alone* (1948) and *Rain on the Wind* (1949), were initially banned in Ireland. Several other novels followed, including *The Bogman*, which first appeared in 1952, and a historical trilogy on Ireland, *Seek the Fair Land*, *The Silent People* and *The Scorching Wind*. *Brown Lord of the Mountain* was published a month before his death.

Walter Macken
Quench the Moon

Pan Books in association with
Macmillan London

First published 1948 by Macmillan & Co Ltd
This edition published 1974 by Pan Books Ltd,
Cavaye Place, London SW10 9PG
in association with Macmillan London
6th printing 1982
ISBN 0 330 23894 9
All rights reserved
Set, printed and bound in Great Britain by
Cox & Wyman Ltd, Reading

TO MY MOTHER
AGNES MACKEN
THIS BOOK
AS THE FULFILMENT OF AN AMBITION
AND AN INADEQUATE TRIBUTE
TO HER COURAGE AND
FIDELITY

You took east from me and you took west from me –
  You quenched the moon and took the sun from me –
You took the bright heart within my breast from me,
  And great great my fear that you took God from me.

(Translation from the Irish song 'Domhnall Óg'
from *Ceól Na nOileán* collected by
An tAthair Tomás Ó Ceallaigh)

CHAPTER ONE

The seagull soared in the sun-misted air, high, high over the village of Killaduff, and far from his comrades resting lazily on the weeded rocks, or planing languidly over the summer-warmed seas of the Atlantic.

The boy lying stretched on his back, cradling his head in his arms, regarded the seagull and thought that it would be a good thing to be able to fly effortlessly like that, if you could get used to keeping your wings outspread. The boy was dressed in the coarse white 'bainin' coat, an open-necked, striped shirt and homespun 'ceanneasna' trousers stopping short at the shin. His build made him look much older than his ten years, and the big chest and well-filled coat arms gave promise of great strength and bigness. His eyes were as blue as the cloudless sky, but it was probably the yellow colour of his fair hair which attracted the seagull. From his great height he may have mistaken it for a patch of the Ourish sand, planted miraculously on a brown Connemara hillside.

However it was, he came down from the vault of the sky like a star falling from the firmament, and then climbed again screeching shrilly as the boy rose to his feet. Stephen O'Riordan laughed, because he thought it very funny to see the flooster that descended on the frightened gull, who had indignantly spread his wings, turned his tail on the human being, and headed back to his usual haunts.

Stephen stretched himself and then looked back at the schoolhouse to see if there was any sign of his friends. It was a very ragged-looking schoolhouse lying there under the colossal shadow of the mountain that was known as the Brooding Hen. It was one-storeyed and you could clearly see where the two slates were missing from the roof. The roof had been patched up with something, but not sufficiently well to stop the rain-water from percolating and staining the wall inside a dirty green, like the colour of Ireland on the map that graced the opposite wall. The interior of the schoolhouse was very shabby and decrepit, like an old grandmother who is living alone, waiting to die, and existing on a hand from the neighbours now and again. But indeed the teacher, Andrew McCarthy, was as decrepit as the school and was the reason why Stephen was waiting, quite patiently, for the release of his friends Paddy Rice and Thomasheen Flannery.

Ten years ago when he had first come to Killaduff, McCarthy had been a much different man. Fortunately for himself he had no photographs of himself as he was then, or, looking at the dapper, small, neatly-dressed young man in a blue pin-striped suit, with glossy black hair and a friendly smile, and comparing this with the very fat, sloppy, badly-dressed unshaven edition of today, he might have been tempted to end it all, or to become a worse boozer than he was at the moment. It was a pity about McCarthy in a way. He might have gone places, because he was a well-read man. He had married unfortunately, more because his wife had a large family of fierce brothers who, when he had committed an indiscretion, insisted on an early wedding, than from love. His wife was probably the most stupid woman in Connemara, and that's a great boast, and she bore children with amazing regularity, so that before poor McCarthy was properly aware of it, he was bound to Connemara with chains he didn't have the courage to break; so he settled down to go to seed, drinking fairly heavily, when he could afford it, and beating the devil out of the scholars at school as an outlet for his repressions. But he was wise enough and he never beat them indiscriminately. He would judge what their status in local society was and hammer them accordingly. Paddy Rice now, was the son of Rice the man with the pub and shop in Killaduff, so, although everybody knew that Paddy was the devil himself on two legs, he got off fairly lightly. Thomasheen suffered more but not too badly, because everybody was aware that he was his father's favourite, and since Thomas Flannery was a very big man with a temper to match, McCarthy thought discretion in his case would pay dividends. If it had been any other two who had done today what they had done, they would have found it difficult to sit down for a week. They had annoyed McCarthy's eldest son Padneen, a big stupid lout who took after his mother, had become involved with him, and, while Thomasheen held the school-bags, Paddy had delivered a sound trouncing in a fair fight. McCarthy was secretly delighted that his son had taken a beating, because he had one day heard the Padneen, who gave promise of turning into a strong man like his uncles, say that he only wanted to grow up so that he could hammer a job on his oul fella. Instead of beating the combatants McCarthy had kept the lot of them in after school to do extra lessons, thereby punishing himself more than them, because his throat was parched and he was longing for a pint.

Poor old Bigbum, thought Stephen, turning away from the school to look down into the valley, I wonder if he knows that we call him that. Only too well did McCarthy know, since Padneen had called it to him to his face one day after he had been severely beaten.

Looking at the land spread at his feet, Stephen felt dimly that he was looking at something that could not be put into words. The road on his left was a yellow ribbon meandering down into the valley. You could see Ourish Island way out in the distance, separated from the mainland by a two-mile stretch of sand, coloured like ripe oats. Below, at the bottom of the Brooding Hen, lay a small tree-dotted lake which drained the silver streams coming down from the mountains. The floor of the valley was dotted with other lakes and streams, broken up by the interlacing flint roads, brown cultivated patches of earth, and some small green pastures clinging desperately to the sides of the brown rocky mountains. Away in the distance Stephen could see his own house at the side of the road leading to Ourish Strand. It looked like a toy house down there, long and white with a yellow thatched roof, and the green fields around it which had been

9

carved with courage and tenacity from a reluctant and stony earth.

Looking at his house made him think of his mother, Martha, who was the reason that the people thought that the young Stephen O'Riordan fella was different – talks just like the mother, not a Connemara woman at all, a Dubliner, if you don't mind. Martha had told Stephen how she had come to Connemara, and it sounded good to him although a bit sorrowful in spots. She had been educated in an orphanage in Dublin by nuns, and the chaplain to the orphanage had been a certain Father O'Riordan, a most unorthodox priest by all accounts, who had taken a great interest in Martha. He had set out to educate her, starting her on the most peculiar books about pirates and robbers, with bad fellas who were very bad indeed and good fellas who were sickeningly perfect. From those he had progressed her to better books, to histories and classics and plays and poetry, so that when her time came to leave the nuns she had a better education than a first-year university student. She had formed the habit of grading people according to her early reading, and if a person wasn't a Pirate with her, he was a Hero, or a mixture of both was a hybrid known as a Piro. Stephen gathered that Father O'Riordan had a very poor opinion of the world in general and of mankind in particular, and since he moved such a lot amongst mankind he ought to have known.

Anyhow, he had got a few jobs for Martha in Dublin, and then one day his brother from Connemara, Martin O'Riordan, had come to the big city looking for a girl who would come back and work in his house for him.

Father O'Riordan had allowed Martha to take the job, reluctantly, because he was not very sure of his brother. They had seen little of each other since the day they were born, and what little they had seen they were not so keen about. Martin had been in America for many years, and when their father had died, returned to run the farm in Connemara, and appeared to have amassed plenty of money in the meantime. But Father O'Riordan thought that Martin was carrying something in his mind that was weighing him down. In the end, Martha, who was keen on seeing Connemara, won the day and she came to work for Martin, and according to the rest of her story, which was always short, she had fallen in love with Martin and married him and lived happily ever afterwards. Stephen wasn't so sure. All he knew was that his mind always shied away from thoughts of his father.

What Martha didn't tell him was that she no more loved Martin O'Riordan than Martin O'Riordan loved her. When he had met her at the station at Galway and taken her to Clifden in the train, which at that time plied a leisurely course through the most beautiful scenery in the world, she had been attracted by the bigness and the silence and the good looks of Martin. It had not taken her long to realize that that was all that lay between them, a physical attraction that vanished almost overnight. She might never have been content to remain if she had not fallen heavily in love with Connemara, with its barrenness, and its strength and cruelty, because there are no half-measures with this place. You either loathe it or love it, and that's that, and whether or which, you are going to have a fight on your hands, a fight for existence with your body, or the fight of your lungs against the air and the weather. It seemed to suit Martha. And then Stephen had been born and that clinched it for her. He had not been born without trouble. She had had to have an operation, as a result of which Stephen could be her only child. This seemed to alienate Martin further from her. She had found out that he drank quite a lot, but that he was better humoured when he had taken a drop. He was a surprisingly good reader of good books, and had built up a respectable library. He did not seem to be very keen on his only child. With a consequence that Martha lavished on Stephen everything that she had in herself, but even so life with her husband was not easy. Eleven years ago, when she had come to Connemara first, she was a tall girl with jet-black hair and regular features. She was still tall, and her features were still regular, but the hair at each side of her head was as white as the inside of a cloud and her face was not free of lines.

Stephen turned back to look at the school again and saw the figures of the two boys chasing out of it as if the devil was on their heels. He picked up his school-bag from the ground and waved at them. This served to increase their speed, so that when they approached him they were breathless.

Paddy Rice was low-sized, with a mop of unruly black hair and the restless eyes and limbs of the true harum-scarum. He was dressed like Stephen, and kept shifting impatiently from one foot to the other.

Thomasheen was an engaging youngster. He was tall and thin, and woefully untidy. Instead of a bainin he wore a knitted jersey, which was rent here and there to show the clean striped shirt he wore underneath. His trousers, despite the best efforts of his mother, seemed to be always needing buttons. He had a great tuft of red hair, and fair eyebrows over wide innocent eyes which gained him forgiveness from all for the most heinous crimes.

'Ora, Stephen,' said he breathlessly now, 'oul Bigbum had a rale grind on today, so he had. I was afraid a me life he was goin' t' clatter the divil out 'f 's.'

'Don't mind 'm,' said Paddy, throwing himself on the grass. 'Anyhow, I'll be lavin' 'm after the summer. The oul fella is sendin' me to a secondary school somewhere.'

Stephen and Thomasheen were dismayed.

'You mean you're goin' to leave Killaduff?' Stephen asked.

Paddy was uncomfortable.

'Yeh,' he said, 'I'm afraid I am.'

'Jay, that's terrible, so it is!' said Thomasheen.

'It's me oul fella,' said Paddy, in explanation. 'What can I do? He's makin' me go, so he is.'

'Ah, jay!' ejaculated Thomasheen again.

'Arra, cheer up, Thomasheen,' said Paddy, slapping him on the back, 'I'll be comin' home on holidays, won't I, an' we'll kick up murder like always.'

12

'School won't be the same,' said Stephen, 'with you out of it.'

The school will be a very flat place without Paddy all right, he thought. Nobody with the courage to cheek McCarthy or to stand up to him, tempering the other children's great fear of him. Stephen himself was not in the least afraid, and McCarthy treated him decently enough, but he could never wave an invisible banner of revolt like Paddy, nor restore the scholars' self-respect with a well-aimed Paddy Rice jibe. Then another aspect of Paddy's departure struck him suddenly.

'Look, Paddy,' he said, waving a hand in front of him, 'won't you miss all this when you go away?'

'All what?' Paddy asked, surprised.

'I mean all this down there, the mountains and rivers and things . . . well . . . it's hard to say . . . just all that . . .'

'God, that's a quare wan,' said Paddy. 'Miss that dirty oul mountain is it, and thim oul streams and a few oul houses that should 'a' been knocked down years ago. No fear! It's me for the big towns, boy! I was in Galway once, remember? Jay, they's somethin'! Talk about people and boats and big houses, an' pictures an' thin's an' trains an' motor cars an' everythin'. Jay, that's where I want t' go always, not t' be stuck in an oul hole in the wall like here.'

'Will yeh see all thim thin's?' Thomasheen asked, his eyes wide.

'Yeh, sure,' said Paddy, starting to strut. 'Jay, wait'll I get at 'm! Just wait'll I get at 'm! Come on, an' I'll chase ye down to the ind a the road.' With a whoop they started off, Paddy having taken an unfair advantage.

The road was dusty and their bare feet raised clouds of it in the air. They approached a turn in the road, their school-bags floating out behind them, and Paddy started to imitate a motor car, turning an imaginary wheel and making honking noises. They flew around the bend of the road close together and burst like an exploding bomb on the figure of a man who was trudging up the hill. The four of them collapsed, the man with a shout of fear that was strangled as he fell. The three boys were quickly on their feet and they retired to a suitable distance so that they could beat a hasty retreat if their victim turned nasty. They looked at him very warily. They saw a smallish man, dressed in a bainin coat, ceanneasna trousers, and a high-necked blue jersey, the whole topped by a black Connemara hat which he was now dusting carefully. He had a small wizened face, creased with wrinkles and tanned by the suns of fifty years to the colour of old mahogany. He looked at them with one of his eyebrows raised.

'Well, the curse a the seven blind bastards on ye!' he said in a low, clear, venomous tone.

The boys remained completely unmoved.

'So is your oul mother!' Paddy answered rudely, and the three of them prepared for flight, but to their amazement the man on the ground laughed and started to haul himself to his feet.

'A chip of the oul block, hah,' said he. 'Now I bet you're oul Paddy Rice's son from over beyant.'

'Mebbe yer wrong now,' said Paddy, visualizing the hard hand of his father descending on him.

'I couldn't mistake that oul dial,' said the other. 'What in the name a God are ye chasin' over the country like that for, knockin' down oul men left, right, an' centre?'

'We didn't know you were coming,' said Stephen.

'And I bet you're a son a Martha O'Riordan's, are yeh?'

'Yes,' answered Stephen. 'She's my mother.'

'Fair enough,' answered the man, 'and a damn fine woman, too, and I'm ashamed teh see a son 'f hers committin' assault an' battery on a poor oul man.'

'You're a quare poor oul man,' said Thomasheen. 'I know yeh well. Yer Michilin Fagan from Crigaun an' me father says yer the toughest oul ram this side a the Twelve Pins.'

Michilin laughed loudly.

'Ah God, isn't that something! Outa the mouths a babies. Is that a nice way for yer father teh be talkin' about a Christian?'

14

'Ah, he likes yeh all right,' said Thomasheen, looking at him in wonder, as if trying to find out why on earth his father should like an old reptile like this.

'Ah,' said Michilin, 'yer father an' mesel' had great times long ago. We had indeed, Thomasheen Flannery. I never thought he had a big fella like you. Tell me,' he said, seating himself on the green bank at the side of the road and pulling out an old briar pipe, 'where are ye off to now?'

'Ah, we're goin' home after school,' said Paddy, closing up a little.

'Is that so now?' said Michilin.

'What do you do?' asked Stephen, also coming closer.

'What do I do?' reiterated Michilin. 'Oh, well, I fish mostly out on the sea near Crigaun.'

'Me father,' said Thomasheen, 'says that yer the biggest poacher this side a the Maam valley.'

Michilin let a great laugh out of him again.

'Ah,' said he, 'wait'll I see yer father, sayin' things like that about me. He oughta teach yeh teh keep yer mouth shut, me boyo.'

'Don't mind Thomasheen,' said Paddy. 'He's always shovin' his foot in it like that. Nobody can tell 'm nothin' that he doesn't tell.'

Thomasheen was indignant.

'Well, I didn't tell yer oul fella,' said he, 'that yeh whipped a tin a biscuits outa the shop last Saturday.'

'Now, for God's sake, shut up, Thomasheen, will yeh! D'ye want teh ruin me, d'ye?'

'Ah, I'm sorry,' said Thomasheen. 'I oney wanted teh show that I could keep a secret, that's all.'

'Do you do any poaching?' Stephen asked Michilin, with interest in his eyes, and sitting down beside him on the bank.

'Well, now, it depends what you call poaching,' Michilin answered.

'He means,' said Paddy, coming over and sitting down as well, 'do you be stealin' salmon an' sea-trout outa the lake and the river beyant.'

'Look,' said Michilin, 'they's no such thing in Ireland as stealin' salmon an' sea-trout. Now lissen, ye do history at school, don't ye?'

'We do,' they answered in unison.

'Well,' said Michilin, 'if ye had any sinse ye'd realize that it's all a pack a lies from beginnin' t' ind, and that the rights a the common man is bein' jilted on 'm left, right, and centre. Let me tell ye somethin'. The good God didn't make the world and put salmon and sea-trout and brown trout into the lake and river down there so that some oul shenanager from England 'd be comin' over an' takin' it from the people that has the rights to it be justice and humanity. Whin God med Connemara He med it for the people, an' when He said t' the oul salmon and sea-trout t' flock into the lakes at the proper season He never told nobody that you have t' have a licence t' grab a few a them, or that some fella from the back a beyond 'd be able t' stop yeh from takin' a fish out oo a river that passes be yer own front door. No bloody fear He didn't!'

'But sure,' said Stephen, 'it isn't a man from England that owns the fishing at all. Isn't it some man from Dublin that owns it?'

'Some oul maker a tin cans, with more backside than brains, *says* he owns it,' said Michilin furiously. 'But how in the name a God can yeh own somethin' that belonged t' nobody in the first place? It's like the haws on the trees, I tell ye, or the blackberries plucked from a bush at the side a the road. God put thim there because they were necessary for the birds and the people, so that they could have a stab at them whin they're hungry, and it's just the same with the fish in the rivers as the fish in the sea, and don't ever let anybody tell ye any different.'

'Ah, but jay, that's stealin',' said Thomasheen.

'Look, will yeh have a bitta sinse?' said Michilin. 'It isn't stealin' t' take what belongs t' yersel' be rights, and let me tell ye that any man in the whole a this diocese that had a bitta sinse 'd be down there whippin' an oul salmon any time he felt like it.'

16

'Will you take me fishing with you sometime?' Stephen asked gravely.

'Heh, Steve, they'd put yeh in jail!' said Thomasheen.

'On bread and water,' added Paddy.

'Have you ever been caught, Mister Fagan?' Stephen asked.

'No,' said Michilin judiciously. 'I have never been caught with a salmon in me possession.'

'You see!' said Stephen to the others. 'What's the harm if you won't be caught?'

'Ah, that's the story,' said Michilin, amused, and rising to his feet with a laugh, 'that's the Tin Commandments biled down to a nutshell. Don't be caught! Well, goodbye, lads. For God sake look where ye're goin' anymore, will ye? The next fella ye run inta'll kick the guts outa ye.'

'You never said,' insisted Stephen, 'whether you'd take me fishing with you or not.'

'Well, now,' said Michilin, rubbing his chin, 'I'll see about it. Most of me fishin' is done at night, yeh see, and little boys don't be up and about the time a night that I do. What time do yeh go to bed now?'

'Oh, about nine or so,' said Stephen.

'There, yeh see,' said Michilin, 'you'd be a poor partner for me, because I'd be oney startin' me business about that time. We'll wait a little longer until you grow up more. What about that, hah?'

'But you won't forget,' said Stephen.

'No,' said Michilin seriously, 'I won't forget.' Then he swung on his heel and commenced the climb up the hill. The three boys followed him with their eyes.

'I never heard that kinda history in school,' said Thomasheen.

'That's a bitta Irish history he med up himself,' said Paddy.

'Maybe his is the true version,' said Stephen.

'Ah, come on with your law-dee-daw,' said Paddy, recommencing the charge down the road. Thomasheen took up the chase. Stephen turned once more to look after

Michilin, who, he found, had turned around. Stephen waved a hand at him before turning to follow the two lads.

They were almost breathless when they came to the end of the hill and turned off for the road home.

'Jay, I'm hungry,' said Paddy. 'I could ate a bullock.'

'Me too,' said Thomasheen.

'Would you really go out with me man?' Paddy asked.

'Yes, I would,' Stephen said. 'I like him.'

'Ah well, every dog likes another dog. Look, lads, what'll we do after dinner?'

'Ah, I have t' go out an' give a hand on the bog,' said Thomasheen disgustedly.

'Nobody *has* t' do anythin',' said Paddy.

'You don't know my oul fella if y' say that,' said Thomasheen.

'All right so,' said Paddy, 'you can go to your oul bog. What will we do so, Stephen?'

'I don't know,' said Stephen. 'Sure we'll do something or other. Call around to my house, will you. Maybe we would go into Ourish. The tide will be down by then.'

'All right so,' said Paddy, 'I'll call around for you.'

'I'll see ye tomorra, lads, won't I?' said Thomasheen hopefully.

'Yeh might,' said Paddy, 'if yer oul fella doesn't be makin' yeh do somethin' else.'

'Ah, no he won't,' said Thomasheen breathlessly. 'On me word, I oney have t' go t' Mass. That's all.'

'Right, we'll see yeh after Mass so. Maybe we'd go over a bit a the road an' bate up the Crigaun fellas.'

'Ah, jay, that'll be great,' said Thomasheen.

'Well, I'll be lavin ye here so,' said Paddy, turning to swing up the by-road. 'I'll whip a couple a fags outa the shop afterwards, Stephen, an' we can have a few pulls.'

'Ah, lads, keep an oul drag for me, won't ye?' implored Thomasheen.

'We might,' said Stephen, 'if you don't get sick like the last time.'

'Ah, no I won't, on me word,' said Thomasheen. 'I've

been practising with turf mould in a bitta paper since an' I can put it through me nose now. Honest I can, fellas!'

The both of them laughed at this picture.

'All right, Thomasheen,' said Paddy, 'we won't forget.'

Stephen and Thomasheen turned on their own road.

'It'll be kind of lonely without Paddy, won't it, Stephen?' Thomasheen asked.

'It will, all right,' Stephen said, 'and when he goes away once, he won't have any time for us when he comes back.'

'Ah, no, he wouldn't do that,' said Thomasheen. 'I hope Mister O'Riordan won't send you away to a school, Stephen.'

Stephen looked at Thomasheen's wide-eyed face and laughed.

'No, I don't think I'll be going to school, Thomasheen,' he said.

He was almost sure he wouldn't be sent away to school because he thought that there was not enough money in his family to let them send him away. Apart from which, Stephen thought, looking around him, I don't think I'd like to be sent away from here even for a short time. He couldn't imagine waking up in the morning and not being able to see the Brooding Hen outside his window and all the familiar things about him. Although it might be nice for a while to see what a big town was like. He'd like to see the Dublin that his mother talked about to him, even though she didn't seem to like it much. But then he wouldn't like to leave his mother, even for a short time. It was funny that he could just think of his mother and he saw her before him, her features exact, and she smiling always because she never seemed to do anything else but smile at him, and then she would smile with her whole face. He automatically quickened his pace when he thought of her, and slowed it again when he thought of his father.

Stephen did not know what to make of his father. He was used to other boys' fathers. He saw Bigbum in school beating hell out of his four chickens, and he appeared to hate them. That was real enough. You knew where you stood there. Your father hated you, and he knew that Padneen McCarthy hated his father, and that the one ambition of the child was to grow up big and be able to wallop his father.

Then Thomasheen was a great favourite with his father. You couldn't but help liking Thomasheen anyhow, but it was obvious that Mister Flannery had a great gradh for Thomasheen, the way he was always fighting with him and threatening every five minutes to take off the belt and give it to 'm. But he never seemed to have time to take off the belt, and it was not unusual to see big Thomas Flannery rolling in the field with his little son Thomasheen, tickling the life out of him, and both of them laughing helplessly. Then if he saw you looking he'd get real rough with Thomasheen and he'd say, 'Get up outa that! What are yeh doin' wastin' yer father's time like that for?' and he'd walk away from him to whatever he was doing. But everyone knew that he was soft about Thomasheen.

Paddy Rice's father was somewhat the same, only Stephen didn't think there was as much affection between them. Paddy's father would be strong and weak betimes. Sometimes when he lost his temper he'd raise his hand to him, but Paddy always fought back. Then at other times he would be very weak with him and Paddy would make hay. Stephen thought that that was why Mister Rice was sending him away, because he thought that Paddy was wild and he was not able to control him, since Paddy's mother died when he was a child. The father never married again and Paddy was the only son. Stephen felt he understood, in a dim childish way, the other fellows and their fathers, but he was at sea when it came to his own father, Martin O'Riordan. Martin hardly ever spoke to him, except to say now and again, 'Hey, hop off to bed, you now!' or 'Hurry up now; do you want to be late for school?' or things like that. Stephen just saw him at meal-times really and sometimes on a Sunday when he wasn't working about the farm. There was something about the silence of his father that stopped him from making overtures to him. When he was younger he remembered hazily trying to say 'Look, Daddy!' when he found something interesting, and he remembered being hurt or surprised when all he would get was an impatient 'Yes, yes!' before his father went back to reading a book or a paper maybe, and then his mother would come and say, 'Show me. Isn't that grand now, and weren't you the great fellow to find that all by yourself?' He had learnt to leave his father alone, but it would be a great thing to have a father like Thomasheen who would do things with you.

Thomasheen's father was waiting outside the gate.

'Didn't I tell yeh before, Thomasheen, not t' be dawdlin' comin' home from school. Hurry up an' get yer dinner before I take the belt t' yeh!' he shouted.

Thomasheen remained unperturbed and ran up to him.

'Hey, father, we ran inta Michilin Fagan,' he said breathlessly, 'an' he was tellin' us great yarns, an' he's goin' teh take Stephen fishin', an' Paddy Rice is goin' away t' school after the summer an' sure y' won't sind me away teh school?'

'Divil a fear a me,' said Thomas, laughing, 'not unless yer oul aunt dies in America an' laves us a fortune. What did yeh think a Michilin, Stephen?'

'I liked him very much, Mister Flannery,' said Stephen.

'You were right, too,' said Thomas. 'Michilin is a great lad. Hey you, get inta dinner teh hell before I knock sparks off yeh! Don't yeh know we have t' go t' the bog, don't yeh?' He said this giving Thomasheen a gentle kick on the backside.

'So-long, Stephen,' said Thomasheen, running in.

'Goodbye,' said Stephen, and watched them into the house before he turned down the road where his own house lay. He paused there at the wooden gate, which his father had made last autumn. The pony and cart were not there so his father was not home from the bog yet, or Danny. Just then he saw his mother's face at the window. She waved a cheerful hand at him, so he raised the latch of the gate and raced up the path.

CHAPTER TWO

Martha was waiting at the door for him, and as usual, when he had been a time away from her, he felt the bubbling that always came up in him when he saw her at the door. It was very seldom that she would take him in her arms or kiss him, because she seemed to know instinctively that that was something ten-year-old boys could not abide. But she embraced him with her eyes. He liked the look of her, because in comparison to other fellas' mothers in Connemara she was up at the top of the class. She was always so clean, and she always smelled of the scented soap that lay on the saucer by the side of the washing-table in the kitchen. Not for her the big, dung-stained boots that other Connemara women wore in the fields or feeding the pigs, nor did she stride around as the others did in their big bare feet, red and raw from the weather. Of course, he thought, she could afford to be different, because they were, for Killaduff, comparatively big farmers.

'Is there any sign of your father, Stephen?' she asked him.

'I don't see the car coming, Mother,' said Stephen.

'Well, how did you get on at school today?' she asked, following him into the kitchen. You could see Martha in everything in the kitchen. To quote some of the less lucky neighbours, 'you could eat your dinner off the floor, so you could'. The open fireplace was painted a startling white like the walls. The fire always seemed to be tidy, despite the all-pervading ashes of a turf fire. The delf on the dresser shone with cleanliness. The chintz curtains on the window were bright and cheerful.

'Oh, the same as usual,' said Stephen, throwing his bag of books on the table which was laid for the dinner, and sitting on the wooden stool in the far corner of the fireplace. Martha reflected that she was probably spoiling Stephen, as she took the bag and left it on the table near the dresser, where basins and milk-pails lay in orderly rows. Maybe, she thought, it's because he's the only one, and because I love him so much. He is like myself then, and anyhow I had no mother to spoil me when I was his age; and as well as that, she comforted herself, if your nature is bad, it's bad and that's the end of it, but if you are good, then there's nothing on earth that can make you bad.

'Mother,' Stephen said suddenly, 'do you know a man from Crigaun called Michilin Fagan?'

'I do indeed,' answered Martha, 'and he's a Pirate if ever I met one.'

'Do you mean that he's a bad man, Mother?' queried Stephen.

'No,' said Martha, laughing, 'but I mean he's what you'd call a good-bad man. Did you meet him or what?'

'Yes,' said Stephen, 'we saw him today coming home from school and he was saying most funny things about salmon belonging to the people, and that you couldn't call poaching stealing because you were simply taking back something that belonged to you. Is that true?'

'As far as Michilin is concerned, it is true,' said Martha.

'But do you agree with that?' Stephen persisted.

'I'm afraid that I do,' said Martha; 'but that doesn't mean that the other side is wrong either, because I have always been on the side of the filibusters, and then I have always liked men that hold certain beliefs and that are willing to do anything on earth to uphold them, even though they may be wrong ones. Isn't that a terrible thing for a mother to say to her child?'

'I don't think so,' answered Stephen judiciously, 'because I'm not sure that I understand it. I suppose that Father Michael out there would say that Michilin is a thief, would he?'

'I'm not sure,' answered Martha, 'because it is well known that the Father often has a plump salmon for his dinner on a Friday in season, when his only source of supply could have been the brave Michilin; but if it was your uncle the priest in Dublin now!'

23

'What would he have said?'

'It isn't what he would have said, but what he would have done. He would have been out at night with Michilin learning the ropes, if I know him rightly, and then preaching sermons on a Sunday about the rogues that went around stealing salmon at night.'

'When will I see Father O'Riordan, Mother?' Stephen asked.

'Oh, I don't know,' said Martha. 'He doesn't like leaving Dublin.'

'He came to marry you, didn't he?'

'Yes, but that was different,' she answered. And so it was. He would never forgive his brother Martin for having married the little orphan child whom he had sent to him as a servant. It was obvious that he and Martin did not agree. When he had heard about the wedding, he had come down on them like a roaring white-headed lion, and had called his brother for everything in the calendar. He had done his best to persuade Martha to come back to Dublin, but she had made her choice and she was obstinate enough to stick to it. He had to agree in the end, but he had said to Martin:

'I know you, Martin. You're a brooding dog. There's been something laying on your mind ever since you came back from America and I know you have an indulgence for the black bottle; but look, be good to this Martha, do you hear, or you'll have to account to me for her; and remember, Martha, there's no backing out of marriage. When Connemara finally gets you down and you begin to hate the sight and sound of everything to do with it, you can't run away from your husband. You'll have to stick to him, come hell or high water. Have you thought over all that, have you?'

She had thought over it, and as she had said to him, not only was she marrying his brother Martin, but she was also marrying Connemara, because she knew that it had got into her blood, everything to do with it, and that anaemic existence in the cities or plains of Ireland no longer held any appeal for her. She wasn't sure of her husband, but she was sure of Connemara.

24

'Did you know, Mother,' said Stephen, 'that Paddy Rice's father is sending him to a college somewhere after the summer?'

'Yes,' answered Martha, 'Mister Rice was telling me. He finds Paddy is a bit of a handful and he's going to let the priests have a shot at moulding him.'

'I suppose there's no chance of me going, is there?' Stephen asked.

'Do you want to go?' said Martha, as something caught at her heart.

'Well, not exactly,' said Stephen, 'but I'd like to be more educated when I grow up and Mister McCarthy can only teach us so much, and I wouldn't like after that just to have to stop and never learn anything any more.'

This surprised Martha, because you never stop to think of ten-year-old boys worrying about higher education. But then she supposed that she would be partly to blame for sedulously pouring these thoughts into his head since the day he was born. Maybe she had treated him the wrong way. She had talked to Stephen always as if he had been her own age. She thought she had been right, but then again maybe she had been wrong. Maybe she should have given him some of the soft talk that children expect, because now, to her, he seemed much older than his years. But, she consoled herself, it would have been very hard to have soft-talked to Stephen when her husband was around. She could imagine the silent contempt and impatience it would have aroused in him, the deliberate exit he would have made.

'Look, Stephen,' she said, 'I'm afraid, we are not like the Rices. I'm afraid that your father would not have enough money to send you to a boarding-school, but you will have your education.'

'How, Mother?' he asked.

'Well, this is how it is. Because you go to colleges and do exams is no reason to say that you are educated. Suppose you leave the secondary school and go higher to the university and become a professional man. That is no guarantee that you will be educated at the end of it. There's many a

25

doctor, many an engineer turned out of universities and they are as ignorant, educationally, as bull's feet. Because a man has been through a university is no guarantee that he is educated, and some of the greatest writers and thinkers that ever lived never saw the inside of a university, unless they were on a conducted tour. So what? So you educate yourself. You wouldn't call me an ignorant person, would you?'

Stephen considered this, with his head on one side.

'No,' he said finally, 'I wouldn't, Mother. I think you are more educated than Mister McCarthy even, and he's the most educated one I know.'

'Well,' said Martha, pleased at the doubtful compliment, 'I was only educated up to sixth standard in the convent and then Father O'Riordan took me in hand and educated me.'

'But how, Mother?' Stephen asked.

'He gave me books to read,' Martha replied, 'all kinds of sizes and sorts of books. He made me read books that educated people are not supposed to read, and then he made me read the books of the writers of all the peoples in the world, the English, the Americans, the Germans, the French, the Scandinavians, the Russians, the Arabians, the Chinese, the Japanese. He made me read representative and non-representative writers of each country, as well as histories that nobody ever heard about, geography books, and it wasn't enough that I should read them but that I should assimilate them as well. When I had read one, he would ask me about it, and question me upside-down about it, and if he wasn't satisfied with me he would make me read it again before he would give me the next. He gave me those, and he gave me a dictionary and he said, "There you are, Martha, I present you with education." And I think he was right. I learned a lot that way, Stephen, and I am still learning. I have a lot of those books still and your father has more. They are all here for you, as well as the dictionary, and when you have mastered them I think you can say at the end of ten years that you are more educated than Paddy Rice will ever be, with the priests and teachers beating hell's delight out of him in order to get him into the university. What do you think of that?'

Stephen was silent for a while, and then he looked at her where she was standing in front of the fire about to lift the lid from the potato pot, and he smiled.

'Mother, I think that's it,' he said, and there was an eager note in his voice. 'Because then I wouldn't have to leave here at all. That's what I want – to know things; but, Mother, I hear McCarthy talking about classical education and saying he's the man with one. What does he mean by that, and would I be it after all the reading?'

'Not with the reading alone,' said Martha, testing one of the potatoes with a fork. 'You'll have to learn Latin; but we'll get over that too, because I'm sure that Father O'Hagan up there in the Church would give you so many hours a week when you leave the school.'

'Would he, Mother,' asked Stephen, 'do you think would he?'

'I'm sure he would,' said Martha, 'because he was teaching Latin and Greek in a diocesan college before he was shifted out here, and it would be like old times to him; and besides he's a great butty of Father O'Riordan and he likes me, I think, and I'm sure he would do it.'

She lifted the pot off the crook, and carrying it to the back of the kitchen she drained off the potato water into the tub holding the mashed food for the pigs.

'So there,' she grunted, 'will be your education and I'll bet a penny to a pound that you won't be disappointed with yourself when you grow up and mix with dacent people.' She looked up. 'Your father is coming now, I think.'

Immediately, as if it was a signal, a mask seemed to come over both their faces. That was the effect Martin always had on them. The years had not improved him conversationally. A cloak of silence seemed to have gathered itself more closely around him with the years.

They heard the pony and cart coming into the yard and stopping; and soon the clump of Martin's boots on the cobbles outside the door. He was carrying his short coat on his arm and he threw it on the back of the chair when he came in. The intervening years had left a mark on him. Not so much on his body, which seemed to have become even more heavy and powerful, but a lot of his hair was gone and what remained was streaked like the coat of a badger. His eyes had gone a little further back into his head, and permanent lines around his mouth were the result of tightly closed lips. He was wearing a grey woollen shirt which opened at the neck and disclosed bulging muscles covered with hair coming up almost to his Adam's apple. He gave a kind of a grunt for a greeting, and sat in at the table.

Martha turned out the potatoes on a large plate and brought up the other plates from where they had been resting by the fire, covered with the lids of tin cans to keep the heat in them. It was bacon and cabbage dinner; and a very good dinner too, because in that part of Connemara meat of any kind was the exception rather than the rule. Because the O'Riordans were a little better off than their neighbours they had meat at fairly frequent intervals. Martin speared a big potato on his fork and commenced to peel it with a large hand holding the knife. Not for the first time, Martha noted with a slight tremor the hair that thickly adorned the backs of his fingers. She went to the door and called out:

'Are you coming, Danny?'

A voice from without answered immediately.

'Coming in a minnit now, ma'am, whin I tie up the oul nag.'

Martha laid Danny's plate in front of his chair and then sat down herself.

She was glad Danny sat down to meals with them. He came in presently, an older, more compact edition of what he had been many years ago, when he had come with the trap to Clifden to take herself and Martin home to Killaduff.

'Sit down, Danny,' she said. 'It's all ready.'

'Ah, the blessin's a God on yeh,' said Danny, sitting in to it. 'I have a hunger on me like a stallion. There's nothin' like bein' out on the bog to put an edge on yeh.'

28

'Did you do much today?' she asked.

'Well, we weren't idle,' said Danny, 'but there's a lot to be done yet. It'll be a relief whin me man here is big enough to come out and give 's an oul hand with it.'

'I'll go now after dinner, if you like,' said Stephen.

His father stirred himself.

'No,' he said. 'You'll be time enough.'

His speaking put an end to the conversation, and they all got down to the business of eating. Thank God for Danny anyhow, Martha thought. She had often questioned him as to why he remained with them. She couldn't for the life of her see why a young man like him would be content to stick on a farm in Killaduff, drawing about fifteen shillings a week in wages, instead of going somewhere and making something of himself. Danny always protested that the life suited him, and that the job suited him, that he was without ambition, that he was saving a bit of money and that some day, with the help of God, he would buy a small place for himself and pass away the rest of his life in a little cottage down by the sea. Martha still protested that she couldn't understand him, and Danny asked her if she was content with her lot, if she would like to leave Killaduff, and she, answering, said no, but that it was different for her, she was married and settled down and she liked it. Well, if you like it, said Danny, why shouldn't I like it too? He didn't say why he really remained. He remained because he could never get out of his mind the vision of her as he had first seen her.

He could never forget that. When she had come to work for Martin he had hopes that some day, maybe, she would take a look at him, and see that he wasn't so bad maybe, and that . . . but then she had married Martin O'Riordan. Danny tried to make himself go away then. In his own room he had all his things put together, but then, when she had called him to do something for her, he had gone to her call and looking at her he knew he couldn't leave; that there was something that was going to make him stay and feel pain in him for ever, maybe, instead of being sensible and clearing off to hell like any normal fella would. But he didn't. He

29

remained. And he liked to look at her betimes, when she wouldn't notice him, and think, maybe, that what she was doing now, she was doing for him instead of that black silent bastard that was her husband, who never opened his mouth to her, hardly, from one ind a the day to the other, and never seemed to know that he had a small bit of a son that she had given him. So Danny remained, and Martha, clever and all as she was, never suspected.

Martha was glad Danny was around. He was someone to talk to. He told her things that happened in the village, and what this one and that one was doing, because Martha had never succeeded in getting close to the Connemara people. She didn't know why. They were very nice to her, and would go out of their way to help her, but there was always a barrier between her and themselves which she could never climb. She couldn't understand why. The reason was very simple, and very silly, but that's the way it was. She was unfortunate enough to speak correct English, which the inhabitants called an accent, and considered that she was a wee biteen up on a horse and saddle, where they'd be riding bareback. They just couldn't somehow be 'natural' with her. They couldn't bring themselves to call her Martha, except when they talked behind her back, when she was generally referred to as 'that Martha O'Riordan'.

So Danny was a great help. Then, wherever he got it, he had a fount of wisdom in him, a faculty for hitting the truth on the head first shot, a kind of an understanding of people which was almost incredible in a man who had never been out of Connemara in his life. She was fond of Danny, and now she was afraid of her life that he would leave them, because she knew that marrying Martin had been a mistake.

She had got a glimmering of that when she had been suffering with the birth of Stephen, but she didn't really realize it until she had come home after being operated on in the hospital in Galway. She had returned from there no longer able to be a mother of children, and from then on Martin's interest in her seemed to wane. It was as if the element of the risk or pleasure of being creative being no longer there, the game wasn't worth the candle, so he lost his physical interest in her. As for Martha herself, she realized all too clearly that the animal magnetism which had inclined her to her husband had departed for ever, and that absolutely nothing remained.

She had tried to interest herself in him in other ways. She knew he was very well read. Any money which he didn't spend on drinking he spent on procuring books, all kinds of books, for which Stephen would be later grateful. So she tried to talk to him about those things, but his non-committal grunting defeated her. Then she gradually realized that there was some agony behind his silence. Sometimes on peculiar occasions you would see him, with a book clenched in his hand, with his eyes staring in front of him, his face pale, beads of sweat on his forehead, and his lips pulled back, like the snarl of a sheep-dog, over his teeth. Or she would wake up in the night and find him gone from his place beside her and she would hear him below in the kitchen, walking, walking.

But as husband and wife, she realized that they were poorly matched. So she had her son Stephen. While often resentful, she was nevertheless grateful that Martin took not the slightest interest in him, was uncomfortable when Stephen was looking at him with those calm blue eyes. And she loved Killaduff. She loved the mountains around it, the lakes at their foot, and the sea below at the end of the road, with the most magnificent strand of golden sands in the whole world. It was hard to bear with the silence of her husband. Many nights of restlessness and days of moody thought had driven the white into her temples and lines around her eyes, but she had Stephen, and he was now at the stage where she could begin to mould him, where he would take up her spare time, and she could forget all the rest.

The dinner over, she cleared away the plates and poured out the tea. She noticed that Stephen had eaten a very good dinner. He had a big appetite, but then his body was big too. He would be even a bigger man than his father is now, she thought, and thank God, he had never been really sick.

'I better go an' harness the oul horse,' said Danny, rising, blessing himself, and putting on his cap all in one movement. 'That was a grand cup a tay.' He paused at the door. 'I think the weather'll stay put like this now for a while, thank God,' he said as he left.

Martin had his cup held in his two hands and was staring out the window. He was thinking that he had better call in at the pub on the way down and have a drink before going on. His throat was parched and his thoughts all day had persisted in going back to *that*, no matter what he had done to switch them. Every time he had swung the slean into the soft bog he had seen the face in the bog-hole below him, and he would have to throw a clod into the water to dispel it, but the circling ripples seemed to drag it back together again inevitably and he would have to hand the slean to Danny and go spreading the wet turf for a while until he got a hold on himself again. It was only a drink of something that had power to dim the eyesight of his brain sufficiently to kill the memories and to dispel the faces.

'You were in America, weren't you, father?' asked Stephen suddenly out of the blue, and Martha held her breath, because she knew that whatever was haunting her husband was an American ghost.

The breath whistled through Martin's teeth as he turned to look at his son.

'What's that you said?' he asked in a tense voice.

'I asked you if you were in America, because the teacher was talking today about Niagara Falls and he said to me, "You ask your father all about them when you go home, O'Riordan."'

Martin's face paled as he laid down the cup, and then the most terrifying look of hate and fear came into his eyes.

'You bloody little bastard!' he said.

Martha was on her feet in a second.

'Shut up!' she shouted at him, her face as pale as his own.

'No,' said Martin, on his feet and his arms out from his sides. 'This is you! You tell him things he shouldn't know. Why don't you leave me alone? Why should he say that, if you hadn't put him up to it? What do you want to do to me? Amn't I bad enough that I had the misfortune to marry a convent get!'

'Shut your filthy mouth!' said Martha. 'There's a child here!'

Martin's eyes were staring and his breath coming in short gasps.

'No!' he shouted in his high voice, 'I won't. He's yours, isn't he? He's all yours, isn't he? I never interfered with him, did I? I don't want him, do I? Just keep him quiet, will you, keep him out of my way. I don't want to see him. I hate the sight of him!'

'You're his father,' said Martha.

'How do I know that?' shouted Martin. 'How do I know that I'm his father? You didn't know your father, did you? How do I know that you hadn't the tendencies of a street-walker like your mother?'

'You ghost-ridden swine!' said Martha in a slow, vicious voice, and then she bent double and almost fell as Martin hit her on the left breast with a powerful clenched fist.

'You bitch!' he said. 'You bitch!' and then staggered in his own turn as the little body of his son was flung at his legs like a raging she-cat. With all the power in the immature body of him, Stephen caught hold of his father's trouser-leg with one hand and hit and hit with the other, while all the time his bare feet were kicking ineffectually at his father's shins.

It woke Martin up. What really appalled him was the silence of his son. He had attacked his father without an exclamation of any kind and he was hitting and kicking away now without a word out of him. Just silent and deadly. Martin bent down and lifted him up on a level with his face.

'Don't do that, do you hear!' he shouted. 'Don't do that!'

But Stephen seemed to be in a silent trance of fury, and he lashed out with his small fists at his father's face. Martin raised his free hand and slapped him hard. Then the boy stopped and his father could see the tears squeezing them-selves through his clenched eyelids. Martin laid him down

33

on the ground then, not roughly, gathered his coat from the back of the chair and went quickly out of the house.

Martha had been powerless to stop what had happened because the breath had been knocked out of her. When the pain had departed a little, still bent double, she looked across at the door to where her son was standing facing her. He was looking at her. He was not making any noise at all, but the tears were pouring down his cheeks. She felt around, found the stool behind her, and sat on it. Then she said:

'Come here, Stephen!'

He came over to her slowly, stood between her knees, and then buried his face in her, with his small arms thrown around her. She let him sob away. Gradually his sobs subsided, and his body stopped trembling.

'Listen, Stephen,' she said, speaking very slowly because she found it hard to get the words out, 'your father didn't mean it, do you hear? Stephen, you must believe that! He didn't mean it, I tell you! He has something on his mind, Stephen, and when you spoke about America he couldn't help himself.'

Stephen looked up after a while.

'But he hit you, Mother,' he said.

'Stephen, listen! Your father never raised a hand to me ever in his life and he never will again. Stephen, there are some things in life which we can't understand. Your father is not the man he should be. There is something worrying him, Stephen. He is a kind man, Stephen. Nobody has ever seen your father raise his hand to any animal that ever was. Driving in the trap or the cart, nobody ever saw your father raising a stick to a horse. He isn't cruel, Stephen.'

'But, Mother,' said Stephen, 'he hit you.'

'Stephen, don't judge your father because of today. There is a time in all our lives when things become too much for us and we have to lash out at something, the nearest thing to hand. And it was my fault too, I tell you. I shouldn't have lost my temper. It would never have happened if I hadn't answered back. He was sorry, Stephen. Honest, he feels it more this minute, I tell you, than either of us do. I tell you,

Stephen, he would give anything at this minute if it had never happened!'

Stephen straightened himself.

'Are you hurt bad, Mother?' he asked.

'No, it's nothing at all,' Martha answered, rising to her feet with a great effort which she managed to hide from her son's critical eyes. 'Look, he only knocked the breath out of me, that's all.' She even managed to take her hand away from her breast.

Stephen turned away. Have I convinced him? she wondered.

'Try and forget what happened, Stephen,' she said, a note of entreaty in her voice. 'That will never happen again. Please, Stephen, don't think about it, and don't let it change you towards your father. Do you hear me?'

'Yes, Mother,' said Stephen, 'I hear you, and I'll try to forget it.' He didn't turn to her.

It will remain in his mind, she thought, like a red poker laid across the flesh, because when you are ten you remember more clearly than when you are much older. You live your life in a series of flash-backs that come to your mind all the way, a high-light now and then. Please, God, don't leave him with this to remember. She breathed a sigh of relief when Paddy Rice's perky head was poked in the door.

'Here I am, Stephen,' said he. 'Hello, Mrs O'Riordan.'

'Hello, Paddy,' she answered.

'Can Stephen come out?' he asked.

'I'm sorry, Paddy,' said Stephen before she could answer, 'but I have to stay at home and help my mother.'

'Hah?' said Paddy, and you could have put a sod of turf into his opening wondering mouth. Martha had to laugh at his expression.

'Don't mind him, Paddy,' she said, 'he's going out with you.'

'But, Mother . . .' said Stephen, turning to her.

'That's enough now,' she answered him. 'There's nothing you can do to help me with here. You'd only be in the way. Go on! Off with you now!'

35

'All right so,' he answered reluctantly.

'Where are you going, Paddy?' she asked.

'Oh, I do' know,' Paddy said; 'into Ourish, mebbe.'

'That's right,' she said, 'and you might have a look in there and see how the carrageen is drying.'

'We will for sure,' said Paddy. 'Come on, Stephen!'

'Coming,' said Stephen. 'Goodbye, Mother.'

'Goodbye, Stephen, don't be late for tea.'

They departed. She sat down again for a moment and bent double to relieve the pain. Her face was contorted. She raised herself after a time and went out to the door. She looked down the road that led to the sea.

There they were, quite a distance off. Paddy, as was usual, was hopping and halting and starting, stooping down to pick something up from the road and throw it at a passing seagull, which swerved away indignantly. Stephen was walking along quietly, his hands in his pockets and his head bent. Paddy said something to him and then started running down the road at speed. Stephen looked after him, looked back the road, saw his mother standing in the doorway, waved at her, starting trotting sideways after Paddy, and then turned and took up the chase at full speed. She could hear his shrill shout wafted back on the breeze, 'Hi, wait, Paddy, wait!' Then he was off like a hare and she reflected that, thank God, when the mind was young the load was light, and she turned back into the kitchen to tackle the washing-up.

CHAPTER THREE

Michilin Fagan stood on the height above the lake and, shading his eyes with his hand, looked across the bogs and heather that separated the waters of the lake from the road. Away in the distance he thought he saw the figure of Stephen bowling along the road at a nice pace, so with a grunt of satisfaction he took out his old pipe and cushioned himself into the clump of heather. It was a day in early May and the warmth of the sun was lessened by the heat-haze in the sky and a nice gentle breeze blowing in from the west. So it ought to be a good day for the fishing.

Well, the clock has turned all right, Michilin thought to himself, even though it has taken a very long time for it to do so. The Dublin man who owned the fishing in Killaduff had died on a bed of pain, and for some reason unknown – a sop, maybe, to get him into Heaven – in his dying he had left the Lake of Shandra, in the Parish of Killaduff, to the Parish Priest for the Time Being of Killaduff, and it was to remain the property of the Parish Priests of Killaduff for all time. It was a nice gift enough, Michilin thought, but the oul divil could have left them a bit of the river as well, which was the place where all the good fishing was, although now and again an odd salmon had been known to find its way into Shandra.

'What, in the name of God,' said Father O'Hagan to Michilin, 'am I to do with an oul lake? The only interest I have in fish is to see one of them nicely served up to me on a Friday. But I suppose it'll be a nice draw for the young curates when I get them. It'll while away the time for them, I suppose. Is the oul lake any good, Michilin?'

'Well, now,' said Michilin, 'it isn't too bad at all. There's a very nice class of trout in it and they are big too, mind you. Many's the time I managed to lift a two-pounder out of it when conditions were right.'

'What you mean, you old blackguard,' said the Father, 'is when the bailiffs weren't around. Well, look, Michilin, I'm no good at fishing now, and divil a hair of me wants to know anything about it, so for the love of God will you have a try at it and see what you can do of a Thursday about getting a trout for the Friday dinner out of it? It'll be a nice change for you anyway, to be fishing legitimately.'

'Fair enough, Father,' said Michilin, laughing, 'I'll get the fish for you.'

'And look,' said the Father severely, 'I wasn't born

37

yesterday. I don't want any fishing done in that lake except the right kind. I want none of this otter-board business, or crossline stuff, now, d'you hear me?'

Michilin was outraged.

'Father,' says he, 'will you have a bitta sinse for God's sake! Do you think for a minnit that I'd lay an otter-board out on that lake when it belongs to ourselves? No fear!'

'Hah!' grunted the Father. 'All right so. Go to it now, and I must put that poor man, what's-'is-name, into the Mass for being so kind as to leave it to me.'

'I'll bring Stephen O'Riordan with me, I think,' said Michilin. 'That fella is turnin' into a rale good fisherman.'

'He's a good boy, that Stephen,' said Father O'Hagan. 'I've been at him with the Latin now for three years until he's nearly as good as myself. I'll have to have him sayin' Mass one of these mornings for me if they don't send me a curate quick.' He chortled away at this, his hands sunk into the pockets of his cassock. 'I hope you weren't teaching him any bad habits, Michilin.'

'Not at all, Father,' said Michilin piously. 'I took him out in the oul currach to show him how to pot the oul lobsters and throw a long line. All straight business, snarin' a few oul rabbits here and there and so on.'

'H'm,' said the Father dubiously, 'I see! Well, now you have a lake, so teach him the straight way of doing things. I'll expect results on Friday now, mind!' and off he went down the road, pulling out his breviary, and his white hair flapping in the breeze.

So Michilin was waiting for Stephen to come on the lake, his first legitimate fishing expedition. There had been plenty of the other kind, because Michilin, somehow, had never forgotten the intent young face of the boy who had asked him if he could go fishing with him. When Stephen had bade farewell to old McCarthy, three years ago, he was twelve years of age; Michilin and himself had met somehow, and they had both gone on a few excursions 'during the season'. There was very little now that Stephen didn't know about the correct way to 'lift' a salmon. He could wade with a net as to the manner born, and his eye was quick in the use of the gaff, or the deadly snatch. Also he had the born poacher's knack of concealing himself from the hawk-eyes of the bailiffs. Oh, a grand lad, thought Michilin, and a natural born poacher without any vicious traits in him. Michilin poached for profit. He had a market for his wares which brought him in a nice income every year, but Stephen had a conscience, which he probably got from his mother, God bless her, and he would never take any money; so, whenever he was in Clifden or further afield, Michilin always made it his business to buy him a book of some kind or another, although he had to be careful about his choosing, because, as far as he could see, Stephen had read everything under the sun by this time. The best choice that Michilin had ever made for him was Williamson's *Salar the Salmon*. Stephen had never ceased thanking him for that. Michilin himself had never read a book. He said himself that he knew all he wanted to know. Take *Salar the Salmon* for instance, the wonderful story of the birth, life, and death of a salmon; well, Michilin, if he had been able to write, could have written down nearly everything that was in that himself, from the knowledge he had acquired over a period of years. It was the same way about the essential things, fish in the sea and in the lakes, and animals and boats and birds.

His thoughts were interrupted by a loud hail from Stephen, who was charging across the knee-high heather like an Irish setter. Michilin rose to his feet and waved a hand at him. He's growing up fast, he thought. At fifteen, he was as tall as Michilin himself and very nearly as broad. There was a lot of the immature youth still left in him, the way his large wrists grew out of the sleeves of his bainin jacket; and his long legs, now shoved into boots, were too long for his breidin trousers. He was tanned and healthy-looking, and had a shock of fair hair which was eternally untidy. Michilin smiled at him affectionately. If he had ever married himself (which the good God forbid), he would have liked to have a son like Stephen.

'Ah, this is a change, Michilin,' he said, laughing.

Imagine Michilin Fagan fishing on the legitimate. I nearly died laughing when I heard it.' He threw himself down on the ground.

'Ah,' grinned Michilin, 'it won't be the same at all, so it won't. Imagine hookin' an oul fish an' not givin' a damn if any a the Finnertys is around to see you doin' it.'

'Malachai won't like it, I'm thinking,' said Stephen.

'He can go to hell,' said Michilin.

'I don't think that Malachai likes you, Michilin,' said Stephen.

'He doesn't,' said Michilin, 'because he can never say he found me takin' a salmon, and all the time he knew that I must be doin' it.'

'You'd want to be careful of that fella, I think,' Stephen said. 'He looked like a bad bit of business to me on the few times I saw him.'

'The three of them are bad eggs,' said Michilin, 'and they smell up to the high heavens. They haven't one person in the whole parish that'd say a good word for them. They don't go to church or chapel, and I'm sure mesel' that Father O'Hagan'd have been out after me hammer and tongs over the bitta poachin' if it wasn't that himself, no more than anyone else, can't put up with the Finnertys.'

'Is there only the three of them?' Stephen asked.

'They have a young sister over there living with them too,' said Michilin. 'As nice a little girl as you ever laid two eyes on. She keeps that house a theirs like a new pin, so she does, and little thanks she gets for it, I say.'

'Does she go to Mass and things?' Stephen asked.

'She does indeed,' Michilin answered, 'and she's always about to lend a hand to her neighbours if there is any trouble around.'

'Well, come on,' said Stephen, rising. 'Or are we going to stay gossiping here all day.'

'And who the divil,' asked Michilin indignantly, 'kept me waiting here? Everything is ready. I have the boat below and the two rods fixed up. The wind is right, so if we don't kill them today we'll never kill 'em.'

They went down to the boat. It was a heavy double-oared fishing-boat, painted grey. They got into it and slowly pulled out towards the small tree-grown island in the centre.

'We'll take a drift from the far shore down be the island first,' said Michilin.

'All right,' said Stephen, bending to the oars. They were soon in position and turned the boat lengthwise to the wind.

'They's a grand wave,' said Michilin, and so there was. The water rose in large waves like the rustling of a silk cloth. The top of the waves did not break.

'What have you on?' Stephen asked, picking up a rod.

'On that one,' Michilin answered, 'I have a Connemara Black on the tail, a Butcher on the middle dropper, and a Blue Zulu on the top, and if they don't kill fish then I don't know anythin' about fishin'.'

'Here goes,' said Stephen, loosening the line from the reel and taking a tentative cast at the water. On his second cast, a fish broke water at his tail fly and he struck at him. He missed.

'Well, the divil scald yeh,' said Michilin, 'can't yeh hould on t' yerself, can't yeh? Can't yeh strike 'm quicker, can't yeh? He'd ha' spitted out eight flies be the time y' struck 'm.'

'Don't get excited, Michilin,' said Stephen, laughing. 'This is almost the first time I have ever fished legitimately so you can't blame me for being slow on the uptake.'

'It isn't an oul snatch yer swingin' now,' Michilin said, 'so, for God's sake, whin he rises, hit 'm, an' they's no need to be pullin' up the bottom a the lake.' He was casting himself by this time. 'All yeh have to do is t' give 'm th' oul flick a the wrist.' Just then a fish rose to his own middle dropper. Michilin, whose attention had been divided, made a desperate effort to strike him in time, and missed.

Stephen nearly collapsed in the boat laughing.

'There, now,' said Michilin viciously. 'Yeh see what happens when yeh make me be talkin' to yeh! That was a grand fish, too! Ah, God, he had a tail on 'm as big as the sail 'f a boat. Will yeh watch what yer doin' now, for God's sake, and let me be doin' the same.'

'I never said one word, Michilin,' said Stephen.

41

'All right, all right,' said Michilin, 'that's enough now.'

They commenced fishing in earnest then. As they drifted just off the island, Stephen rose and hooked a fish. A pause, and then the reel screeched as the trout took it in a great run. Stephen felt his heart leaping. Ah, this is the life, he thought, as he tightened on the fish and started to entice him to the back of the boat with the tip of the rod.

'Be careful now! Be careful now!' Michilin shouted. 'That's a two-pounder at least be the way he took yeh.'

So he proved to be, and a great fighter into the bargain. When they finally netted him and gave him the *coup de grace* on the head with the ugly little priest, he lay in the bottom of the boat, a fat, well-fed fish, changing his golden brown to the speckled, many-coloured hues of a landed trout. Stephen felt good looking at him.

'Now amn't I good, Michilin?' he asked.

'Oh, the bee's knees,' Michilin answered. 'I couldn't a done better meself, but it's a pity you couldn't a got that first fella. That was a great fish, so he was.'

Who could live better than this now? Stephen thought, as he cast again and looked around him. It was a perfect day. All the mountains were hidden behind a blue haze from which an outline peeped now and again in case you could forget that this was the land of the mountains. Wouldn't it be terrible if something happened and you had to leave it all behind you, if you had to go somewhere flat, with none of the high mountain air to compress your lungs? Wouldn't it be terrible not to be able to smell the heather charged with the salt breeze that came in from the sea below?

'How is your mother, Stephen?' Michilin asked him.

Stephen came to himself with a start.

'Mother?' he said. 'I don't know, Michilin. I think she looks very tired or something, but she was saying herself that it is the summer; that she always feels washed-out, and has no energy during the summer.'

'She's not looking good, Stephen,' said Michilin. 'I saw her there the day before yesterday and I thought she was looking pale like.'

'She was in bed for a few days last week,' said Stephen. 'I never knew her to do that before. She never had a cold or anything that I remember before, but she says you can't go all your life without something.'

'Maybe she wants a change,' said Michilin. 'She's not a Connemara woman born and bred, and sometimes the mountain air isn't good for anyone that wasn't born in it. Maybe she ought to go away somewheres for a rest or somethin'.'

'That's what I told her, but you might as well be talking to the wall,' said Stephen. And God knows, he thought, she could do with a change, because his father had not improved with the years. The terrible incident of five years ago had never been repeated. Even now when he thought about it, Stephen got a sinking feeling in his stomach and his heart would thump quickly, like it did on that day. There hadn't been much affinity between his father and himself before that incident occurred, but afterwards, they just avoided one another. Martin had become more taciturn than ever, and now that Stephen was older and could understand better, he realized that his father was seldom sober.

He had a certain amount of money in the bank in Clifden. Every Saturday he received a registered letter with the bank's name on the outside of the envelope. Everything they ate, except meat, they got from their farm, but for any extras like clothes or boots his father would go to Clifden and purchase them.

It was only recently that Stephen had noticed his mother was not looking well. She had always been a fine, straight, tall woman, but now that he thought of it, he realized with a shock that all that straightness had departed and that his mother seemed to be constantly bent forward from the waist, just a little, and there did not seem to be as much of her. Her arms were thinner, her hair was whiter, and her face was always the colour of used ivory chessmen.

'There wouldn't be anything wrong with her, would there, Michilin?' he asked out loud.

Michilin looked at him, and, hearing the anxious note in his voice, hastened to reassure him.

'Not at all!' he said. 'What would be wrong with her? It's just that I tell you, that she wasn't born in the mountains and they take a toll of you unless you go away and forget them for a while. If I were you, I'd get after her to hop off to Dublin or somewhere for a change, so I would.'

'I'll do that,' said Stephen determinedly. 'I'll do that the minute I get home.'

Just then Michilin hit another trout and their attention was taken up with him. By the time they had gone back and taken two more drifts, the sun was lower in the sky and they had landed five decent-sized fish, so they stopped at the shore, secured the boat, and proceeded to eat their lunch. In Michilin's case that consisted of a few bottles of stout, which he declared were 'as flat as oul Rice's backside, bad luck to 'm!' and this led them to bring up the subject of Paddy.

He had been away at school for three years now, and every time he returned he presented a more gorgeous appearance. The last time Stephen had hardly recognized him. He was going to collect a cart of turf and he was standing up in the cart bowling along when he saw this elegant young man coming towards him. At first Stephen thought he might be one of the visitors who of late years had begun to infest the Ourish Strand during the summer, and it was some time before he recognized Paddy.

He was wearing a neat blue suit, creased to perfection, with a white collar and a rainbow-coloured tie, and his hair was greased down until it stuck to his skull like a barneach to a rock. Stephen pulled up abruptly.

'Hello, there, O'Riordan,' said this vision, and his face became very red and annoyed when Stephen doubled up with laughter.

'What's so funny, you peasant?' he asked after a while.

'Ah, I'm sorry, Paddy,' Stephen said, after he had recovered, 'but it's an awful shock to see you turned out like that.'

'If it's that funny,' said Paddy, 'come down from the cart and I'll bate the head off yeh, so I will!' forgetting his college accent with the excess of his hurt feelings.

'Right you are,' said Stephen, jumping down, and Paddy realized with a slight shock that Stephen had grown about twice as much as he had in the intervening years. Nevertheless, he took up a fighting stance which his gym instructor in school had taught him, and he prepared for battle. Stephen, looking at him with his 'chin tucked into his shoulder, right arm close to the side, left hand held well forward', had to laugh again, and Paddy, regaining his sense of humour, also laughed, and it ended up with Paddy removing his beautiful coat and going along to help Stephen load the cart of turf.

'Paddy will be home soon again to us,' he said to Michilin with a laugh.

'That's a gas man for you,' said Michilin, 'a rale wild boyo. I'm sure the poor fellas in the college of his must be havin' a terrible time tryin' t' quieten him.'

'According to Paddy,' said Stephen, 'the whole lot of them are eating out of his hand.'

'Ye were always great butties at school, weren't ye?' Michilin asked. 'Yerselves and poor oul Thomasheen.'

'Yes, we were,' said Stephen. 'I don't see as much of Thomasheen now since his father died last year. That was a very sudden thing too, wasn't it, Michilin?'

'Oh, very fleet indeed,' said Michilin. 'The Lord have mercy on 'm. You'd travel many a mile before you'd a found a fella as nice as that Thomas. But the oul eitinn got 'm in the end. It was in his family, you see. I remember a sister 'f his, married over in Crigaun. As fine a stump of a girl as you'd care to lay an eye on. Oh, a grand girl, she was. One day walking around as good as you please, and the next day down with a cold, and dead in three days afterwards from the gallopin' consumption. That's one of the troubles about Connemara, too. It must be the strong air of it or something. It weeds you out. If you can stand up to it you're all right, but sometimes it mows men down like oats in front of a scythe.'

Stephen shook his head.

'I don't think the air has anything to do with it,' he said. 'I think it's the cottages with the thatched roofs and the small windows. I think all those cottages should be pulled down from the roots, Michilin, and good one-storey slated houses put up in their places.'

'Well, God forgive yeh!' said Michilin. 'I could no more sleep with a slate roof over me head than I could fly to the moon. They's nothin' as snug as the oul thatch, I tell yeh. It's nice an' cool in the summer-time and cozy in the winter-time; and it looks nice too, not like thim bloody slated how-are-yees. Give me the oul thatch every time.'

'Well, you're wrong,' said Stephen, 'and if you read what all the doctors in the country are saying about them, they'd put the hair standing on the top of your head. And then if you want the Government loan to build a new house, you'll soon find out that it will have to be a slate one with good wide windows and plenty of air getting into it.'

'I don't give a damn about that,' said Michilin determinedly. 'The country 'd look quare without the oul yellow thatch scattered here and there.'

'Sure it would!' said Stephen, 'and all them fellas that come to paint the beauties of Connemara for the benefit of the people who live in towns would kick up a queer stink if they came one day and found that all their picturesque cottages had disappeared. If I was ever a painter, I'd paint a picture of a Connemara cottage with a skeleton peeping and grinning out of every window of it.'

'Well, the Cross a Christ about's!' ejaculated Michilin, 'but that's a quare thought for a young fella t' be havin'!'

Stephen laughed.

'Ah, I'm sorry, Michilin, those are queer things to be talking about on a grand day like this.'

'Too many bloody books you're readin'!' said Michilin. 'Thim books never did anybody any good. What you won't know won't trouble you, I say, and it's true for me too. Readin' a lot a books oney disturbs a fella's mind.'

'Who's this coming over the shoulder of the hill now?' Stephen suddenly asked.

Michilin turned cautiously, sinking into the heather.

'What the hell am I doing?' he shouted then, raising himself; 'anyone 'd think that it was poachin' we were.'

'It's awful hard to make the old fox change his habits,' said Stephen. 'Can you make him out?'

'Begod,' said Michilin, 'I think it's Malachai Finnerty.'

'It's a good job,' said Stephen, 'that we weren't poaching or we'd have been properly caught out.'

'It'd take more than the Finnertys,' said Michilin, 'to stale up on me if I didn't want them to. Turn around and ignore 'm. I don't like that fella, nor I never will, and if he wasn't too big for me I'd insult him and take a crack at his long black kisser.'

They turned around and looked at the lake. They could hear the rustle of the heather as he came nearer and nearer. They waited for him to pass them by, but he didn't, and although they did not turn around, they knew that he was standing behind them. Eventually they heard his voice.

'A nice day for fishing,' the voice said, and they both turned around to look at him as if they were surprised that they were not alone. His voice was deep and husky, like a voice that had gone rusty from lack of use.

Malachai Finnerty was an ugly-looking man. He was very tall and very broad and he always wore a black jersey and black trousers. Nobody had ever yet seen him clean-shaven. He always wore a week's-old beard, which was jet black, like his hair and all the rest of him. He wore an old greasy cap, which usage had turned almost as black as himself. God, thought Stephen, he is a nasty-looking character, and I'd hate to have to come up against him. I suppose he wears all that black so that he can sneak up on you in the night if you're poaching; and it was true that any man that Finnerty had caught poaching, always appeared before the magistrate as if he had been run over by a steam-roller, because Malachai always believed in the use of force with poachers, and certain it was that anybody he had ever caught had never tried again. Stephen, for some reason which he could not define, felt a slow anger burning in him as he looked up at the face leering down at them. Imagine what he'd have done to poor oul Michilin if he'd ever caught him, although somehow Stephen had the impression that Michilin would be able to look after himself in any contingency.

'Yes,' said Michilin, in a slow drawl, 'it's a grand day for fishing, thank God, and it's we that have a nice bag of them down in the boat.'

'Them must be the first honest fish you ever got in your life, Fagan,' said Malachai, with a sour note in his voice.

'Now what do you mean be that remark?' Michilin asked quietly.

'You ought to know,' Malachai retorted rudely.

'If,' said Michilin calmly, 'you're accusin' me of poaching, you're very much mistaken. And after all, who could know better than yourself, because since you are the bailiff for the grand gentleman that thinks he owns all the fish in Connemara, who should know better than you if I was ever caught taking a fish out of his oul river?'

'Aye,' said Malachai, 'that's it. You were never caught. Because you're too damn cute, like an oul badger. But I know that you took fish out of that river and you've been taking them out of the river for years.'

'I'd advise yeh, Mister Malachai Finnerty, the bailiff,' said Michilin, raising himself a little, 'to be careful of your tongue. I'd remind yeh of the oul Irish proverb which says that it's many a time a fella's gob broke his nose, and also that they's such a thing in this country still as the law a slander, and if I hear yeh repeatin' thim remarks just once more I'll have me solicitor down on top a yeh like a star outa the sky. So repeat them once more in front a me witness here. That's all I ask.'

'Yeh,' said Malachai, 'I see yer rearin' up a whelp teh carry on the good work for yeh.'

Stephen rose to his feet, and realized with some surprise that he must be getting tall himself because Finnerty didn't seem so big to him as he did looking up at him.

'I don't think,' said he coldly, 'that I like being called a whelp.'

Malachai looked him up and down and laughed.

'A bantam cock too, begod,' he said, 'a real fighting bantam cock. You're O'Riordan's son from down below, aren't you?'

'What's it got to do with you?' said Stephen, and was glad his mother couldn't hear him being rude.

'Nothing,' said Malachai, flushing at the neck, 'but I'm telling you that it'll be a sorry day for you if I ever catch you at the game. Maybe I'd teach you a bit a manners that your oul fella should teach you.'

'Go about your business now, Malachai Finnerty,' said Michilin, rising to his feet, 'until we carry on our honest profession, and let me tell yeh something else. This lake is no longer the property of yer master and I don't want to see yourself or any a the brothers a yours hauntin' it like before.'

'You'll have a good excuse now if you're caught with a salmon, won't you?' said Malachai. 'You can always say now that it came out of the lake. But listen, Fagan, the river is still out of boundary for yeh and keep away from it, because it'll be a sorry day for you the day I catch you on it, and catch you I will before you're much older.'

'Come on, Stephen,' said Michilin, turning his back on him and walking down to the boat. Stephen followed after him.

'Remember now what I said,' Malachai shouted after them. 'I'll puncture yeh if I catch yeh, and catch yeh I will!'

'Ah, go to hell!' shouted Michilin back over his shoulder, and then under his breath to Stephen, 'yeh black bastard!'

Stephen had to laugh.

'I wouldn't like that fella to meet us on a dark night, Michilin,' he said.

'Maybe,' said Michilin, 'we could take care of him too. I thought for a minute there that you were goin' teh go for 'm, an' I was sweatin'.'

'Well, he got my back up. There's something about him that seems to make me mad, and I'm not that way generally.'

49

'You're not fit for him yet,' said Michilin. 'A few years more, maybe, when you've filled out, and you might be able to stand up to him. But they're a dangerous family those, Stephen, remember that. If you cut one a them the whole lot a them bleed together. And they prefer to take a stone or a knife in their fist than to stand up and fight fair and square.'

'Ah, forget them,' said Stephen, 'and let's get on with it.'

They went back on the lake and fished indolently. The take seemed to have gone off a bit, so they talked about this and that and enjoyed themselves, and Stephen thought to himself, If ever I become what I feel I want to become, I will remember this day always. Towards evening they heard a voice calling them from the bank.

'That's Danny over there,' said Stephen. 'I wonder what's wrong with him.'

'He wants us, anyhow,' said Michilin, taking up the oars and pulling over to him.

Stephen thought that Danny looked pale, and so he did. He had obviously been running and he was still breathless when they pulled the boat up on the shore.

'What is it, Danny?' he asked, jumping ashore. 'What's wrong with you?'

Danny looked at him.

'It's your mother, Stephen,' he said.

Stephen felt his heart stopping.

'What's wrong with her?' he asked.

'I don't know for sure,' said Danny, 'but the doctor from Clifden was over visiting Father O'Hagan and the priest brought him into the house, and he was looking at your mother and he asked her what was wrong, and then he called in your father and said he was going to examine her, and he did.'

'Well, what happened then?' Stephen asked.

'Well, he said he'd have to take her away immediately in his car and he's going off with her now, and he says he'll have to take her into Galway, so they're putting a few things together for 'er, an' so she told me to hop up here and fetch you down before she wint, so that you would see her before she goes.'

Stephen was beginning to run almost before Danny had finished speaking.

'I'll see you again, Michilin,' he shouted back over his shoulder.

Michilin held on to Danny for a moment.

'Hey, Danny,' he said, 'what's wrong with her?'

'I don't know,' said Danny, impatient to be off, 'he didn't say. They just sent me off for Stephen.'

'The poor woman,' said Michilin. 'I thought she was lookin' very badly for a while.'

Danny took out after Stephen then.

Wasn't it a good thing for me, thought Michilin, looking after the fleeing figures, that I never took a wife, for if yeh were a bit taken to her at all you'd be in a spot like this now. But if I did take a wife, he reflected, tying the bow-chain of the boat to a stake driven into the ground, it would have been someone like Stephen's mother, if she would ever have had me, which I doubt; and that Martin O'Riordan was never good enough for her anyway, a fella that wouldn't bid yeh the time a the day in case he'd have teh use his tongue. And he didn't deserve a son like Stephen O'Riordan either, and I hope t' the Lord God that they's nothin' serious wrong with her, because it'll bust him up; but then agin, min are quare yokes. They'd forget yeh quicker than an oul dog would, but somehow I don't think me brave Stephen is like that.

Stephen's mind was confused as he ran. Of all things it had never struck him that his mother Martha could ever be ill. The fact that she might be seriously ill he put away from him. Even a temporary absence would be queer. He couldn't imagine that house without her. No matter where you were or what you were doing, all you had to do was go home and there she was, and you talked about things and you weren't ashamed, if you saw or heard something which you thought was good, to tell her about it, and she would on her part tell you things; and then there were things they didn't agree

51

about because she seemed to be cynical about people in a humorous sort of a way and he wasn't, because he liked all people nearly and he thought they all had something which you wanted to get out of them, so you asked them questions about what they did and you tried to find out what they were thinking, whereas his mother always wanted to find out what they did, and she judged them on that, and called them funny names accordingly, like Pirates or Piros and Heroes and things. Then they would argue about books, too, and things that happened in history, and it was great to argue about it all, and laugh too.

As he got on to the yellow road he could see the house in front of him, and the motor car drawn up in front of the door brought him to a standstill. Then he sprinted off again, faster than ever.

Don't let anything happen to her, God, said Danny to himself, as he pounded after Stephen. She's the best woman in the whole world and there'll never be another like her, and if anything happens to her I'll pull Connemara to pieces, a mountain from a mountain.

CHAPTER FOUR

When Stephen reached the house he found the doctor and Father O'Hagan talking to his father in the kitchen. They stopped talking when he appeared at the door.

'Where's my mother?' he asked.

The doctor spoke.

'She's up there in your room,' he said. 'Go on up to her and have a chat before we go.'

Stephen went to the door of the room above the fireplace and hesitated a moment before going in. His mother was sitting on his bed. She looked up at him as he came in. He saw then that she was looking very poorly and his heart sank. He went over and sat down beside her. She was wearing the coat which she used going to Mass on a Sunday morning, and she looked pathetic to him, but then a smile lit up her face and she held out a hand.

'Poor Stephen,' said she. 'Were you frightened when Danny went for you?'

'No,' said Stephen, 'I wasn't; I just got a bit of a start. Mother, what is it? What's wrong with you? Why does he have to take you to Galway?'

'I don't think he rightly knows himself, Stephen,' she said, 'but I might have to have some kind of an operation; but it's nothing really, wait'll you see, and in about three weeks or so I will be around and kicking again.'

'Why didn't you say before this that there was something wrong with you?' he asked her.

'Well, I didn't know myself, Stephen. I just felt tired and had no energy, that's all, really, and I didn't think that there was anything wrong with me. Stephen, I was just sitting here thinking, and do you know that when I first came from Dublin to work for your father it was in this room I was sleeping, and I never thought I'd see the day when I'd have a big brute of a son sleeping here.'

'Is it bad, Mother?' Stephen persisted.

'No, Stephen,' she answered. 'Honestly, it's not too bad, and if it was I'd tell you, really I would; but a person can't go through their whole lives and have nothing happening to them, and it will be a rest for me anyhow, Stephen. I have been here now for nearly seventeen years and I have never been out of it for one day even. Not that I really ever wanted to be out of it, but it will be nice to lie back in a bed for a few weeks and have other people waiting on me. I will feel like a queen.'

'Look, Mother,' said Stephen, 'couldn't I go with you?'

'No, no, Stephen!' she said quickly, 'you can't do that! I wouldn't like it, having you with me. No. I'd prefer to think of you out here where you belong. And then you will have to be helping around the place. No, Stephen, please, there's too much to be done here.'

How terrible it would be, she thought, to see him bending

53

over me when I would be helpless. She didn't want her son to see her that way. Their friendship was a healthy one of standing up and sitting down and walking about the country and strong vigorous conversations. It would ruin it all if he were to see her lying down in a hospital ward, helpless. He would feel sorry for her then, and he would pity her, and she would not like that because it would not be possible for them to get back on the same old footing. That was the reason why, for months now, she had suffered alone with the fierce pains tearing at her chest inside, and she would not say anything to anybody about them. Somehow she had felt they were serious.

The first time she had realized that they were very serious, she had sat in the kitchen and cried to herself. It wasn't the pain so much that made her cry as the knowledge that there was something fatal wrong with her. If Martin had been different she might have told him, and it would have been easier to hug the secret to her own breast then, and hide her suffering from the calm worried eyes of her son. She was only weak for that one while and then she became strong again and accepted it. She could have gone to a doctor, but she was afraid that she would have to leave immediately and she wanted a little while longer with Stephen, and she was afraid to die, too. That was the reason those last few months had been so feverish for her. She wanted to pack more reading into the little spare time she had from the housework, and she wanted to talk to Stephen more, and now that it had come to her last talk with him – for ever, maybe (O God, no, not that!) – she couldn't find anything sensible to say except that he mustn't come to see her until she was better.

'While I'm gone, Stephen,' she said, 'you mustn't neglect your reading, and you must keep going to Father O'Hagan for your Latin. Won't you do that?'

'Yes, Mother, I will,' he said. 'But I can't stay here without knowing what is happening to you. Can't I go and see you?'

'Well, you can come and see me,' she said, 'when I send

54

for you. I will want to see you too, Stephen, but not until I'm a bit better. And I'll write to you when that happens, and I'll get the doctors to send you word when the operation is over and everything, and then I'll be looking forward to seeing you and that will make me better all the quicker.'

'I suppose that will have to do,' he said reluctantly.

'But you mustn't be worried about it, Stephen, because there's hardly a woman in the world yet who didn't have to have an operation at some time or another. And then think of all the fun we'll have afterwards, and I can be talking to you about "my operation". We'll never be short of a subject to talk about.'

Nor will there, whatever happens, she thought, be a world without a little of myself left in it. Because Stephen is like me. I'm leaving my eyes after me and some of my features, and if I haven't been wrong I'll leave my nature with him, for good or bad; but still it's a pity if I can't be here when he gets married sometime, so that I can hate whatever girl he picks out for himself.

She rose to her feet.

'We'd better go now,' she said.

He stood up beside her.

There was no danger of either of them breaking down and crying, anyhow. There had never been much of the outward show about them, not since he was very small and she could mawse over him to her heart's content. Connemara was a place that seemed to make human emotions embarrassing to everybody. It made you feel so insignificant that you were ashamed of showing emotions that would be taken for granted in the town.

'You won't forget to write, now, and let us know,' he said.

'Don't worry,' she answered, 'I'll be writing anyhow and asking you to send me on all sorts of things.'

They went down to the kitchen, Martha doing her best not to bend over and alleviate the pain. She was not entirely successful and the effort of getting up from the bed had paled her face even more. The three of them in the kitchen looked at her.

Father O'Hagan thought, My God, the poor woman looks terrible.

The doctor thought, I'd better get her to Galway as quickly as possible and hope to God that it's not too late. These people! he thought. It was the same way all over Connemara. No matter what was wrong with them, they waited until they were almost at death's door before they'd come and let a doctor look at them, and even then they would be very apologetic for troubling him. T.B. could be wiped out of Connemara if the relations of the sufferers didn't go around hiding and covering up. They seemed to think that having T.B. was a disgrace on a family, that it was like being born illegitimate. Indeed they were much more ashamed of their daughter having T.B. than they were of her presenting them with a little bastard. May the divil scald them anyhow, he thought, and then they'd go around saying that Doctor So-and-so must be a bad doctor because he let Nellie die, when nothing under God's Heaven could save Nellie, and Nellie was murdered by her parents as surely as if they had driven a stake through her heart, because they didn't think it worth taking her to a doctor until six months after she had coughed blood on her pillow.

Martin looked at his wife Martha as if he were looking at a stranger. Fifteen years of married life with her had made him so accustomed to her that the only emotion he felt now was a kind of impatience and a dull anger that she should have taken sick at a time like this when there was so much work to be done, with the bog and the hay and everything, and he would probably have to get a girl in to look after the house. That led him away on another tack. If he had to have a girl in to look after the house, he would get a nice young girl, from Dublin maybe, and from the same orphanage as he had got his wife, only this time he wouldn't have to marry her; or maybe it would be better to get one of the local girls, because even with this operation his wife might be out again in six weeks or so, and it would be better not to have to send the girl all the way back to Dublin again when Martha was better. He became quite flushed thinking of this, and wished he could go up and have a drink.

If Martha couldn't read his thoughts, she could hazard a good guess at them. He's thinking now, she thought, the King is dead, long live the King, and it wouldn't surprise her if her husband Martin was to marry six months after her death, which made her more than ever determined not to die. Not that his marrying would move her, but that she wanted to live for Stephen's sake. Because Martin meant less to her now than the dust on the road.

'I think we better be going, Mrs O'Riordan,' said the doctor.

'All right,' said Martha. 'Goodbye, Martin,' she said, 'and I'll write and let you know how things are.'

'Yes, yes,' said Martin. 'Goodbye.'

'I'll see you out to the car, dear,' said Father O'Hagan, taking her arm and leading her out.

Stephen held back the doctor at the door.

'What's wrong with her, doctor?' he asked.

The doctor looked closely at him.

'You'll have to tell me,' said Stephen.

'All right, son,' said the doctor. 'You mother is suffering from cancer of the left breast. She has had it for a long time. She should have been operated on months ago.' He looked reproachfully in Martin's direction. 'Some of you should have come and told me that she wasn't well or that she was complaining.'

'She never said anything to us,' Martin said defensively.

'Do you mean to say,' exploded the doctor, 'that she has been going around suffering the agony of the damned for six months and you never noticed it?'

'She didn't say anything,' said Martin.

'Well, she's a remarkable woman,' said the doctor.

'Is it a serious operation?' Stephen asked.

'I'm afraid it is,' said the doctor. 'Of course I can't be sure without X-ray pictures, but it looks serious to me, and it all depends on how far in it has eaten. But with the help of God she will be all right.' With that he walked out the door.

'Goodbye, now, ma'am,' Danny was saying to Martha. 'We'll keep the place nice and snug until you are back with us again.'

'I know you will, Danny,' said Martha, pressing his hand warmly, and thinking how unobtrusively good Danny had always been to her.

The doctor made her get into the car then, fussing about her like an old hen, grunting, and still thinking with displeasure about the idiosyncrasies of the Connemara people. All of them stood around as the car got under way. Martha turned a little and smiled at Stephen, taking one good look at him. He looked well, but very upset. It gladdened her to see he was tall and well-built and that he would be taller and still better built, because, she reflected, he will want it all in the years to come, if he is to battle his way out of the jungle. Then she turned her eyes away from him and looked straight ahead of her.

'That's a fine bit of a son you have,' said the doctor.

'He is, thank God,' she said.

'Considering all the trouble I had bringing him into the world,' the doctor growled, 'he ought to be.'

Martha laughed.

'You're a very cross old man,' she said, 'and it's a pity you haven't a hard cruel heart to go with all the crossness.' She knew this was true, because he was famous all over Connemara for the growling he did on all occasions; and it seemed to be a good line, because when he came into a house and started grumbling about all the extra work that he had to do, and about people dragging him out in the middle of the night, and the injustice of sick people generally, the patient became a little worried about all the trouble he was causing the good man, and once a patient started worrying about something else except his own illness, he was on the road to recovery. Then it was also well known that if the doctor could collect all the bills that were owing to him, he would be one of the wealthiest men in the world; but nobody had ever received a bill from him, and if you went in to Clifden to pay him, he practically insulted you. That's the kind of a man he was; a real crusty old bachelor, you'd think, until you felt his gentle hands on your wounds and you realized that his manner was a cloak to hide his own distress, because he was a very human old man, and the mass-examination of sick humanity had never succeeded in making him automatic in his dealings with a human being.

'You're not to be worrying about him now, do you hear?' he said to her, as the car turned on to the main road to Clifden. 'He's big and old enough to take care of himself, and you're going to have a hard fight on your hands to save yourself from your own foolishness, because you should have sent for me to come and have a look at you the very first time you felt those pains coming; but no, you had to wait and cause me infinite trouble at the last minute, a poor old man like me, running from pillar to post, without getting a proper chance to cure people, when they won't come to me in time. Nobody ever thinks of me at all. People with anything wrong with them never think of the poor doctor. All they are interested in is their own selfish sufferings; and if I get you out of this a fit woman, I won't get a bit of thanks for it.'

'Indeed you will,' said Martha. 'I'll thank you until the day I die.'

This seemed to annoy him more than ever.

'That's not the point, you silly woman!' he shouted. 'What's the use of thanking me when you are dead? I want somebody living to thank me. I want to see you back there in Killaduff!'

Martha realized that, thank God, the journey would pass swiftly, with nice vigorous conversation like this, because she didn't want to think of doing the journey backwards. She did not want to see it all on the way back, as she had seen it when she was coming the first time with Martin. She would give anything to banish the sight of herself as she had been then, a young, blue-eyed, enthusiastic girl realizing what Connemara was, and feeling it going deep into her blood, or of Martin saying in the train that he always felt safe when he got inside behind the mountains and the rest of the world was shut out. She couldn't see the shoulder of a mountain that she wouldn't think of Stephen standing up on it, silhouetted against the sky, nor could she look at a bog that she couldn't see him swinging the slean. The fields of hay were peopled with him too, the rhythm of his scythe impelled by the power of his widening shoulders, and how he would stand up, leaning the scythe on the ground to watch her struggling up to him with the can of tea in her hand and the egg sandwiches wrapped in a cloth. He would smile at her and wave his hand, and she would feel that it had all been worth while after all, that maybe she had had a purpose in life and that her purpose was to bear a man like Stephen who would grow up and some day do something fine, and she would feel that her existence had been justified; that God hadn't made a mistake when He had left her outside a convent door done up like a Christmas box.

'Look,' she heard the doctor shouting at her again, 'if you start crying, I'm going to stop the bloody car and throw you into a bog-hole. On me solemn oath I will!'

And she had to laugh again and stop looking around her.

'All right so,' she said, 'I'll stop, I promise, and we'll have a long chat about the hypocrisy of the Irish people.'

'Now that,' said the doctor, settling himself into his seat, 'is a subject on which I am a well-known authority. In my experience the Irish people . . .' and he was well and truly started.

Stephen, Danny, and Father O'Hagan watched the car until it had disappeared in a cloud of dust over the hill.

'She'll be all right, with the help of God,' said Father O'Hagan. 'I'll put her into the Mass every morning until she's back again with us. And the Saints better not let me down or there'll be a queer reckoning when I get up there to them. Now, don't be worrying, Stephen. Everything will be all right.'

'I'm sure it will, Father,' said Stephen.

'Don't forget to come around after the devotions, now, Stephen, until we do a bit of Tacitus, and don't forget that you're still a bit weak on the conjugations.'

'All right, Father,' said Stephen. 'I'll be there.'

'God bless you,' said the Father, as he turned to go back to his church, his ragged cassock swinging, and thinking in his heart that it would be a real miracle of the Lord if Stephen's mother was ever the same again.

Danny was moving off down the road, with his hands sunk in his pockets and his head sunk on his chest.

'Where are you off to, Danny?' Stephen called.

'I'm just off down the road a bit,' said Danny, shouting it back over his shoulder.

Stephen watched him for a while and then turned towards the house. His father no longer stood at the door. The whole outside of the house reflected the hand of Martha. When she had come she had known practically nothing about flowers or shrubs, and the garden stretching between the gate and the house had been the playground of all the hens, ducks, and geese and it was liberally besprinkled with their droppings, but she had set to work on it, and had turned it from an untidy wilderness into a garden you could be proud of. She had wired it and segregated the fowls, much to their disgust. At the back and the sides of the house she had planted coniferous darwins and other stunted trees that would stand up to the eternal battering of the storms sweeping in from the Atlantic. When she had succeeded with those, in their shelter she had created a flower garden of exceptional beauty. All the neighbours condemned this garden and said it was a funny thing for a Connemara housewife to be growing flowers, and she must be neglecting something else in order to do it. When they saw the spotless cleanliness of her kitchen and her dairy, and the well-fed animals under her care, they were at a loss to understand how she could do it all, and felt there was a catch in it somewhere.

With the men it was different, because Martha had a way with her that none of them could resist. Most of the Connemara men are sly wits, as many a condescending summer visitor has found out to his cost, and when their sly digs were answered with ones more sly they were delighted, and went home and had a row with their wives because they felt there was something lacking in them. So all the men agreed that Martha O'Riordan had green fingers, because anyone who could make flowers grow in Connemara, in defiance of the spray and winds of the adjacent sea, must have something.

I will have to look after it now while she's gone, Stephen reflected, and there mustn't be a single weed left in it when she comes back, although it will be hard to keep the fowls out of it now that she's away. And he remembered with a smile his mother chasing the hens out if they as much as put a cautious beak past the gate, and for years she made everyone's life miserable with 'Did you shut the gate?' or 'Out with you now and run the chickens, since you hadn't the gumption to shut the gate' until the closing of the gate became a kind of reflex action, and you could no more go out without automatically closing the gate than you could go out without your trousers.

He walked into the house quickly and stopped short inside the kitchen door. His father was sitting in front of the fire reading a book. Stephen was appalled. He had expected anything but this. The kitchen was not the same apart from that. There was something missing in it, and for the first time he noted that they had a clock on the wall above the table and that it had a very loud tick. You would never notice that before, but now the kitchen seemed to be empty, the heart was gone out of it and its place was taken by the tick of a clock. The sight of his mother's apron thrown across the back of the chair made his heart beat fast and made him angry too, because he could not understand how his father could come in from seeing his mother off to the hospital and calmly sit down in front of the fire and read a book.

'Isn't it a peculiar thing for you to do,' he said in a tight voice, 'to come in after seeing Mother off to hospital and sit down and read a book?'

Martin paid no attention to him.

'Do you hear me?' said Stephen, going down and looking at him.

Martin raised his eyes at him.

'Shut up!' he said.

'No,' said Stephen. 'This is too much. I know you did not care for her like you should, but you can't just see her off to hospital and come in and read a book.'

Martin rose to his feet.

'You go back to your fishing,' he said, 'and leave me alone.'

'What kind of a man are you at all?' asked Stephen, and he felt a wave of pale anger sweeping over him. 'Have you no feelings at all? I know you never liked me much, but you must have felt something for my mother. You couldn't be that hard altogether. You couldn't be like one of the animals out there in the field.'

'That's enough!' said Martin. 'That's no way for a young fella to be talking. You don't know what you're saying. Go on out now and leave me alone.'

'I will not leave you alone!' said Stephen. 'And there's something else that's eating into me too. I thought of it the minute the doctor told me about her having cancer of the breast, and I remember the day that you struck her and I'm wondering now if that isn't the reason that she has it.'

'Shut up, you fool!' Martin blared at him, beads of sweat beginning to break on his forehead.

'No, I won't shut up,' said Stephen, 'because if I thought this was true I'd leave this house.'

'Close your mouth!' said Martin desperately.

'It's funny, isn't it,' Stephen went on, 'that she should get it there where she got it, right in the place where you hit her, isn't it? Isn't it a funny thing if she dies that it was your hand that killed her, isn't it? and yet you can come in here and sit down and read a book!'

He fell back as Martin hit him across the mouth with the back of his hand. As Stephen made to retaliate he hit him again with the palm of his hand, and it was the second blow that woke Stephen up from the rage he was in. He saw his father's face through a mist and he saw that his father's face was not suffused with anger as he would have expected it to be, but bloodless with a look of fear in his eyes.

'I'm sorry that happened,' said Martin, 'but don't ever say that again, do you hear! Don't ever say a thing like that again, or as sure as God I'll kill you, so I will!'

Stephen remained unafraid, but he realized that his father meant what he said, and with something of a shock he realized that his father was capable of it. He had the look which was often on him before, like the face of a cornered badger that will sell its life dearly. Martin looked at him for a moment and then strode up to his bedroom and banged the door after him. Stephen stood for a moment looking at the closed door, and then he went slowly out of the house. There was a medley of emotions chasing through his mind that he could not sort out.

Maybe it was a pity, in a way, that he couldn't have seen the book which his father had been reading, because it was named *The Body and its Thousand Ills*.

When he had stood at the door, seeing the car go, the memory of that day five years ago had struck him like the blow he had given Martha, and the combination of the doctor's pronouncement and his memories had sent him hurriedly into the living-room to search for and find the book in which were listed most of the diseases known to mankind, their probable cause and cure. He was reading the chapter on cancer when Stephen had interrupted him. He was reading to see if it was possible, if it was really the blow that had returned to haunt him with the other thing. It would be too much if that blow struck in anger was to be piled on his conscience too.

Outside the door Stephen's anger evaporated and left him feeling very foolish and very young. He realized now what it meant not to have his mother around, because she would have talked to him and explained things. Always before, no matter what had happened, she had a word ready for everything, a simple explanation that set you on the road to your own conclusions. Now he was mixed up and couldn't think properly.

He walked quickly out the gate and almost ran into Thomasheen.

Thomasheen had not changed much. His body had just grown. He was still the same wide-eyed, tactless little boy, with heavy down appearing on his face.

'Jay, Stephen,' he said, 'I oney heard now about your mother going off to Galway and I'm awful sorry, so I am. Nobody 'd ever think that your mother could be taken bad like that. What's up with her?'

'She has cancer, Thomasheen,' said Stephen.

'Oh, jay!' said Thomasheen, and stopped. He was unused to people coming straight out with a thing like that. The general answer would be, 'Ah, she's not well, she has to go for a rest', and the idea of cancer left Thomasheen breathless and embarrassed at the same time. 'If they's anything we can do to help, Stephen, we'd be glad. Me mother could come in an' give ye a hand with the house maybe, until your mother comes back.'

'Thanks, Thomasheen,' said Stephen, 'that'd be grand, because none of us is any good in the house, I'm afraid.'

A silence descended on them then which they found it hard to break.

'I better go back and see Michilin,' said Stephen. 'He'll be wondering what it's all about, I'm sure. I was out fishing the lake with him when Danny came up for me.'

'Yeh,' said Thomasheen, 'I heard about ye on the lake. Did ye do any good?'

'Not bad,' Stephen answered.

'We better go into Ourish, Stephen, and take out some of the carrageen,' said Thomasheen, 'or it'll be gone on 's.'

'We better, I suppose,' said Stephen. 'Are you doing anything on Saturday next?'

'That's a week away yet,' reflected Thomasheen. 'No, we should be nearly finished with the bog then, and we won't want the oul ass, so we can bring him into the island with 's.'

'We'll do that so,' said Stephen. 'I better go now.'

He set off up the road.

Thomasheen looked after him with pity in his eyes. He felt that there were other things he should have said to Stephen that would put his mind at ease, but he realized that he was incapable of saying them, because nobody knew better than Thomasheen his weakness of saying the wrong thing in the wrong place and being sorry then when it was too late. Also he was sorry he couldn't, because he remembered how Stephen had been good to his mother and the family when his father had died, a happening which still left Thomasheen feeling tearful and lost, and made his heart sink when he looked at his mother and five brothers and sisters who now depended on himself, a fifteen-year-old boy. Stephen had made his father's loss appear not so heavy at the time, and had persuaded Thomasheen into the feeling that he, Thomasheen, was after all a great fellow and a giant of a man, and that it would be easily within his powers to look after his mother and her five children.

'Ah, this is a lousy oul life!' said Thomasheen out loud, as he turned towards his home and saw Stephen crossing the bog to the lake, a small figure that looked lonely against the towering might of the Brooding Hen.

CHAPTER FIVE

The sun, breaking through the early morning mist, burst on to the sands of Ourish Strand, lightening the yellow chrome to a golden amber. It was an enormous strand stretching between the island and the ragged mainland, almost as far as the eye could see, to where, on the eye's horizon, the sea glinted. The tide was fully out and the strand lay enormously like a desert, its broad sweep broken in places with clusters of brown rock. To a bird on the wing it would appear like the surprised ejaculation of a bulbous mouth, its upper lip cracked and broken by the many lanes leading to its fringe. At the mouth of the lanes the soft green grass had encroached on and, in places, smothered the sand, and in the pools left by the retreated sea many ducks quacked and paddled, disturbed at intervals by hordes of screaming seagulls who rose, planed gracefully, or sank to the many rocks to beak their feathers.

Stephen shortly reached the strand accompanied by Thomasheen and a diminutive donkey wearing panniers on its back. They paused for a moment at the mouth of the lane and regarded the view before them. This, thought Stephen, must be the most wonderful thing in the world and we don't appreciate it enough at all. Somebody had obviously gone in to the island before them, because the tracks lay in the sands as regular as a laying hen; the tracks of bare feet and beside them the tracks of a donkey like the imprints of a rounded cane.

'We'll be out again before the tide comes back, anyhow,' said Thomasheen.

'Yes, I think we will,' said Stephen. 'Come on, in the name of God.'

They set out after the footprints. I could almost be happy on a day like this, in a place like this, Stephen thought, if it wasn't for my mother lying in a hospital in Galway and one meagre note from her to say she would be operated on during the week and that he was not to worry. It was all right to say that, but a fellow couldn't but worry.

Anyhow, the day was fine and Connemara was grand and he was very fond of poor old Thomasheen. He liked being with Thomasheen. It took you away from your own thoughts, and then it was like having a rest-cure being with him, because he was so fundamental. You never found Thomasheen worrying overmuch about anything except how he was to fill his own belly and fill the various bellies of a voracious family. Let Thomasheen sleep well and eat well, and let God give him fine weather to dry the turf when he wanted it and rain to grow the crops, and everything in the garden was lovely.

'Thank God,' said Thomasheen, 'this spell a fine weather has made a great job a dryin' the turf.'

Stephen laughed out loud.

'Did I say somethin' funny?' Thomasheen asked eagerly.

'No, Thomasheen,' said Stephen, 'I'm afraid you didn't,

but it was just something I was thinking about.'

'Well, you're a funny wan,' said Thomasheen. 'And your mother is just the same. I'd often be talkin' away there to her and she'd break out laffin' for no reason at all.'

His mother was like that. All the time you'd be talking to her you could see she was thinking of something else, even though she would be interested in what you were saying to her, and Stephen had come to think that she would be comparing the speaker with someone else she knew, of a totally opposite temperament, and that the difference seemed humorous. You'd have to laugh at Thomasheen anyway, because he was so intense about the smallest things, and he didn't mean to be intense at all, it was just the impression that the wide-eyed look of his gave you. Thomasheen enjoyed life with a simple pleasure and you didn't have to be talking to him all the time.

They shortly reached the island and mounted into another lane which was soft as carpets with the drifted sand. Whether it was its sandy foundation or not, the island was very green. It looked deserted from the mainland, but when you climbed into it more you could see several whitewashed houses snuggling down between the gently rolling hills as if to avoid the lashing of the Atlantic storms, which burst over it like the furies of hell during the winter. Now it was placid enough. The cattle looked well fed and the sheep were noted for the tastiness of their meat.

They shortly swung away from the road and turned to where the island stretched a very rough forefinger into the sea as if pointing out the road to America. Near them was a rough wall, erected from the rounded stones of the seashore, enclosing the graveyard where the people of Killaduff and the island buried their dead.

'D'ye mind if I hop in an' say a prayer?' Thomasheen asked, as he jumped over the wall.

'No, I'll be with you,' said Stephen, following him and leaving the little donkey to pluck nervously at the coarse grass.

The grave of Thomasheen's father was neglected by his

family but not by nature, because interspersed with the weeds were patches of short green grass plentifully besprinkled with daisies. Thomasheen took off his cap and got down on one knee. Stephen remained standing and watched him. Thomasheen's prayer was fast, but Stephen knew that it was very sincere and that it took an effort on Thomasheen's part to come there at all, because, fundamental as he was, the memory of his father would always stay green with him. Thomasheen rose from his knee, put on his cap, and then, taking up a sharp stone from the ground, he scraped some of the birds' droppings from the headstone of his father, a very simple headstone, crudely lettered, but one that would outlive the ravages of a hundred years or more.

'Thim birds are the divils,' said Thomasheen.

'I don't know,' said Stephen. 'If I have to be buried anywhere, I'd prefer it to be here, and the birds are great company.'

'That's right,' said Thomasheen with a sigh. 'Well, come on an' we'll go.' He hopped out over the wall again and proceeded on his way with his head bent a little and his hands in his pockets. Stephen, having captured the complacent donkey, soon caught up with him.

'It's funny, Stephen, isn't it,' said Thomasheen, 'how a fella can forget too? I thought I'd never see the day that I'd get over me father dyin', and now I find it hard to remember him, except at times when somewan says somethin' that he used to say, or when you do something yerself that he used to do. That makes yeh sad for a while, and then something else happens and you're off agin on yer own hook.'

'That's only natural,' said Stephen. 'If you ask me, it's a good thing that we can forget.'

'Yeh,' said Thomasheen, 'but me mother hasn't forgot. I don't wake up often in the night because I'm a good sleeper, but one or two nights I did, and I heard somebody cryin' quiet like, in the room, an' then I knew that it was me mother. You could hear that she didn't want to wake up the kids, and that she had something in her mouth to stop her from cryin' out loud, and you'd hear a kind 'f a whisper.

'Oh, Tom, Tom!' she'd say, and you couldn't hear nothing else except that. It's so quiet in the night-time. And you'd feel awful quare, Stephen, an' get a lump in your oul throat and feel like chokin', but you couldn't do nothin' because you felt that it was something private like between the two of them. Ah, you know what I mean.'

'Yes,' said Stephen, 'that's hard to hear.' He couldn't say anything himself because you could never measure the depth of another person's sorrow, which was another lesson he had to learn, because he had often thought casually that Thomasheen's mother Bridget wasn't long forgetting her husband. He would never be able to look at Thomasheen's mother again without thinking of this conversation and imagining a woman crying quietly in the night-time.

Just then a frightened rabbit got up in front of them and scampered away, and instinctively with a loud whoop they both gave chase, Thomasheen picking up a large stone to fire it after the disappearing white bobtail. They had no hope of catching him but they ran all the same, and they were breathless when he went to burrow by the side of the surprising lake which was buried in the heart of the island. It was a grand little thing, like a sample from a commercial nature who said, 'Here's a slice of what I can really do, and if you want the real thing, just let me know'. Where they threw themselves on the grass the lake was about ten feet below them and on the far side it shelved to a small beach. They looked at one another.

'How about it?' challenged Stephen.

'Is there anybody lookin'?' asked the modest Thomasheen.

'Divil a one,' said Stephen, firing off his jacket and pulling his shirt over his head. Thomasheen had a careful look around before he followed Stephen's example.

Having thrown off all his clothes, Stephen stood poised for a moment on the bank. His body showed wonderful promise, and he was more than well developed for his age. His arms were thick at wrist and forearm and lithe muscles wriggled on his back. His chest was very deep and his hips

70

narrowed and then swelled out to well-shaped and muscular legs. He dived into the water below and kicked with his feet until he could feel the sandy bottom under his fingers. When he broke surface Thomasheen was standing on the bank, naked and hugging himself.

'Is it cold, tell me?' he asked in an anxious voice.

'Ah, it's freezing, Thomasheen,' said Stephen with a laugh. Thomasheen looked very funny standing up there, modestly hugging his chest. He was nearly as tall as Stephen, but he was not so heavily built, and although he was long and thin he was nevertheless well shaped.

'Jump quick!' shouted Stephen. 'There's somebody coming!' and he had to laugh again as he saw Thomasheen hurl himself precipitately into the water. Thomasheen emerged spluttering.

'Who is it, Stephen? Where are they?' he asked.

'There's nobody there at all,' said Stephen, 'but you should thank me for getting you out of pain so fast.'

'Well, you dirty louser!' shouted Thomasheen, making for him, and the next minute they were engaged in a free-for-all under and over the water, but mainly under.

They stopped eventually when Thomasheen said, 'I'll race you to the beach', getting a good head start because it was his own idea. Thomasheen was an easy winner because he was so narrow, like a fish, as Stephen said. Thomasheen was rather proud of his swimming because it was the only thing he could ever do better than Stephen or Paddy Rice.

They were resting on the bank where they had pulled themselves when a girl's voice addressed them.

'Hello, Thomasheen,' said the voice.

'Holy Mother a God!' ejaculated Thomasheen as he threw himself into the water, and a startled Stephen was a good second.

When their spluttering heads emerged in deep water they looked around them and saw a small, very good-looking girl of about their own age standing on the bank and grinning at them. She had brown curly hair, brown twinkling eyes, and very white teeth.

71

'Well, Nellie McClure,' said Thomasheen indignantly, 'yeh ought to be ashamed a yerself, comin' down peepin' when boys are swimmin'!'

'Well,' said Nellie, sitting down and making herself comfortable, 'ye don't own the lake and a person can come along and look at the lake, can't they, whenever they want?'

'Go on away outa that!' ordered Thomasheen.

'I will not go away,' retorted Nellie. 'I have as much right here as any a ye two.'

'But we want to dress ourselves,' expostulated Thomasheen.

'Well, go on an' dress yeerselves,' said Nellie. 'I'm not stoppin' ye, am I?'

Stephen started laughing.

'This is no laffin' matter,' said Thomasheen indignantly. 'Can't yeh go away outa that, Nellie! How in the name a God can we get outa the water and a girl there lookin' at 's?'

'Well, what harm is there in that? Ye're wearin' bathin' togs, aren't ye?'

'No, we're not!' shouted Thomasheen.

'Thin ye should be,' said Nellie smoothly. 'It isn't right that fellas should go bathin' in a lake without togs. What would the priest say t' ye?'

'Will yeh clear off teh hell outa that, will yeh?' shouted Thomasheen. 'I'm freezin' teh death in here, so I am.'

'Yeh'll have teh ask me nicely, Thomasheen,' said Nellie, 'or divil a foot a me'll stir outa this place until night-time.'

'Ah, look, Nellie, have a heart,' said Thomasheen.

'You'll have to be nicer than that,' said Nellie.

'What d'you want me to do?' Thomasheen asked. 'Stand on me head or what?'

Nellie laughed loudly.

'Oh, Thomasheen, go on and do that will you? Ah, it'd be grand to see you standing on your head in the lake.'

'Nellie!' said Stephen.

'Yes, Mister O'Riordan?' Nellie answered sweetly.

'You know, Nellie,' Stephen said, 'Thomasheen is a very modest fellow, but I'm not, Nellie, and I'm going to give you just two seconds to beat a retreat, and if you're not gone I'm going to come out of the water exactly in the spot where you're standing now, bathing togs or no bathing togs.'

'You wouldn't have the gumption,' said Nellie serenely, but she fled hurriedly when Stephen started to raise himself out of the water.

'I'll wait until ye're dressed over there,' she said, 'and I'll collect the old donkey.'

The convulsions which Thomasheen went through, getting out of the water and hurling himself into his clothes, made Stephen laugh still more.

'Well, you're a real modest character, Thomasheen,' said Stephen. 'Sure, she can't see you now. She'd want to have eyes in the back of her head.'

'I wouldn't put anything past that wan,' said Thomasheen as he pulled his trousers on his thin legs with a sigh of relief.

'You'd have made an awful poor Adam,' said Stephen, laughing again.

'Well, Adam had an oul fig-leaf on 'm, anyhow,' said Thomasheen, 'an' we didn't even have a lump a seaweed.'

When they were dressed they joined Nellie where she was waiting for them. She had her arm around the donkey's neck and she was small-talking him as if he was a ten-months-old baby.

'I love that oul ass,' she remarked as they came up to her. 'He has eyes just like Thomasheen.'

'That's enough now,' commanded Thomasheen. 'Haven't yeh done enough damage in one day, haven't yeh? A nice thing for a young girl to be goin' around lookin' at min swimmin'! Wait'll I see yer mother, me girl, and I'll tell 'er an' she'll warm yer backside for yeh!'

'Sure, I didn't see anythin', honest, Thomasheen, and anyway,' she said, laughing, 'you've nothing to be ashamed of.'

'We won't talk about it now any more,' said Thomasheen. 'That's enough, now!'

'Where are you going, Nellie?' Stephen asked.

'The same place as yeerselves,' said Nellie. 'I was going

back to the carrageen plots to have a look, and if they're all right, we'll be comin' back for them after dinner.'

Stephen had a good look at Nellie and liked what he saw. She was small but very well built, and she would be taller. She was in her bare feet, and they were very shapely feet, supporting a good leg. She was dressed in a sort of pinafore affair, blue, with white dots on it, which was faded considerably by the sun. Nellie was always very clean and neat. They had noticed that always at school, when she used to be chasing everywhere after Thomasheen, and he trying to get rid of her. Stephen remembered now that she eternally proclaimed to one and all that she was going to marry Thomasheen when she grew up, and from the way she would glance at him now from under her long lashes, Stephen felt sure that the years had not changed her mind.

Nellie was a babbler. She would talk and talk about this and that, but there was always an element of humour in her conversation. She had a distinct personality, and indeed the neighbours thought that for a young girl she was a little free with her tongue; but Nellie held that God gave her a tongue to use, and if she didn't use it, what was the good of having one at all. Connemara girls, generally speaking, were very shy with strangers, until you got to know them. Nellie was never shy, and was always willing to talk to anybody about anything, even those things which she knew nothing about. So the people said she was a forward little girl who hadn't much manners, but what could you expect from them people from the island. Thomasheen was fond of her, even when he was trying to dodge her, but that was at school and she was only a nuisance then. Now they were both left school, and the responsibility of his father's death had made him grow up more quickly, and he was surprised at himself, because when he looked at Nellie now, and saw her regarding him with a laugh in her eye, he felt his pulse beating a little more quickly and some sort of a funny feeling running up and down inside his stomach.

'Are you sure, now,' Stephen said, 'that you didn't see us coming into the island?'

'Maybe I did,' said Nellie, 'and maybe I didn't, but if ye never came into the island, I'd have to go back to the carrageen anyhow, and happen that ye did come in, isn't it better to go back there with a bit of company instead of going back there by yourself?'

'That's very logical,' said Stephen.

'Of course it is,' said Nellie, 'and I knew how much Thomasheen would like to have me with ye, when I remember all the times he used to be chasin' me when we were at school.'

'Tryin' to get rid of you, you mean,' said Thomasheen.

'I wonder,' said Stephen, 'how old Bigbum is getting on now?' and that led them to talk about the school and the teacher and to say 'Do you remember the day . . . ?' and the painful memories of their school-days became something to laugh at now, and the journey to the end of the island passed very pleasantly indeed.

At its furthest Atlantic point the island is broken up into huge rugged boulders which are drenched eternally by colossal waves, even on the calmest day, because there is nothing between here and the continent of America excepting thousands of miles of rolling seas. At this point, just out of reach of the ever angry sea, the people have their carrageen plots. Rescued from the sea, the raw carrageen is separated from the other weeds and is spread out on the grass until it is dry and crisp.

Having carefully picked their way through breaches in the land where the sea had eaten its way, the three young people and the patient donkey reached their plots. They tested them with their fingers and found that the carrageen was still damp.

'The best thing we can do,' said Stephen, 'is to give the sun another half-hour to shine on it, and it should be all right then. Let us sit down here, my friends, and we will talk about this and that.'

The three of them threw themselves on the grass, the two boys lying on their backs, and Nellie reclining on her front and chewing a blade of grass. That was one of Nellie's peculiarities, and she was the same at school, Stephen remembered.

'Do you remember, Nellie,' Stephen asked, 'the way you used to be always chewing something at school? Do you remember the day Bigbum caught you chewing the lump of turf?'

'Oh, God, yes,' said Nellie, 'and I thought he was going to murder me.'

'What makes you be doin' things like that anyhow?' Thomasheen asked.

'Oh, I don't know,' said Nellie. 'I don't do it now, but I liked the taste of things in my mouth then.'

The day had become very sultry, so they lapsed into silence. Even the seagulls seemed to have disappeared to rest themselves. The only thing to disturb the silence was the muted roar of the sea coming in between the gap separating the island from the mainland. At this point, the gap was about a hundred yards across and the force of the compressed tide always made a noise like a giant rolling on a gigantic drum.

So they lay and thought, and Thomasheen was pleasantly though lazily conscious of the form of Nellie lying beside him. Although his eyes were closed he could feel the nearness of her and a small drift of wind would waft to his nostrils the faint odour of soap and a pleasant smell that was Nellie.

He felt what he thought was a fly on his nose and he swatted it, but it returned again and again, and opening one eye he was just in time to see Nellie with the blade of grass in her hand.

'Well, the divil scald you!' said Thomasheen. 'Gimme that!'

He tackled her, to take the blade of grass from her hand, and they laughed as they struggled, but suddenly they stopped laughing and looked into each other's eyes for a few moments as if they were petrified. Thomasheen felt his breath coming faster in his throat and his mouth became dry. Nellie's eyes were very serious and concentrated as they looked into his own. The feel of her flesh where his hand was grasping her upper arm made his heart beat faster. Nellie's breast was rising and falling quickly. Thomasheen took one look at the recumbent Stephen and then released her, falling back again to his prone position. Nellie became very quiet too, and it was some time before the blood in Thomasheen's temples stopped pounding.

Stephen had been conscious of something happening, and particularly conscious of the moment's deadly silence. He would have liked to look in order to confirm his thoughts, but thought that it was more politic to keep his eyes closed.

'Come on,' said Thomasheen, rising after a while, 'and get this job done or the tide will be on top of us and we'll have to wade.'

'It's a sin to be working on a day like this,' said Stephen, rising lazily to his feet.

Procuring the two long sacks from the donkeys' panniers, they began to pick the carrageen. Nellie, her babbling silent now, went to help Stephen. She held the mouth of the bag open for him while he threw the carrageen into it. Thomasheen managed on his own, trying to whistle now and again to ease the tension which he felt to be in the air, but it is difficult to whistle when your mouth is dry, so he took to chewing on a piece of carrageen instead. Carrageen is not very tasty. It is dry and brittle when you put it in your mouth, but it soon becomes pliable like gristle, and you have to bite it hard with your teeth in order to digest it.

When the two bags were full, they tied them at their mouths with string, hitched ropes around their middles, and then hung them on the panniers of the donkey. The donkey was a small donkey, and the sacks were very long sacks, so that when they had fixed them the donkey had practically disappeared from view. This caused them some amusement and they laughed, but a silence soon again descended on them as they began to make their way back.

This can't go on, thought Stephen, because it is most embarrassing, as he noticed the way in which Nellie kept close to his side and avoided Thomasheen as if he had a disease. Thomasheen seemed to be closely interested in the flora of the island, because he kept his head down and now and again kicked viciously at a poor innocent daisy.

'I am now going to tell you a story,' said Stephen suddenly, realizing that the only way to ease the tension was to break up this terrible silence. 'I will not vouch for the story, because it was related to me by Michilin, and also it is a fishing story, and everybody knows that there is no such thing as a true fishing story, but anyhow it is very plausible and deserves notice.

'As you know, many people in the past have come to Connemara and have bought the fishing and the shooting rights. One of those big noises who came and bought the fishing rights of a few lakes and the large mansion going with them, which was erroneously referred to as a "lodge", was a certain Oriental. For your benefit, my dear uneducated peasants, I will explain that an Oriental means a person from the Orient. How can I tell the story if you are interrupting me?' He asked this because Nellie had punched him vigorously in the side at the part about the "peasants".

'Will you tell the story, for God's sake,' said Thomasheen, 'and not so much of the law-dee-daw?'

'Isn't that what I'm trying to do?' asked Stephen, delighted that he had got a reaction already. 'But to continue, this certain Oriental was not a nigger, I'll have you understand, but an Indian of sorts, who was but lightly bronzed in complexion, and it is recorded to his benefit that he was a good employer and very decent to the people who worked for him. However, he had one great defect in the eyes of the people, and that was – horrible crime – he could not fish! Imagine that! And he just bought the lakes so that he could ask a few hundred guests down for the weekend and let them hop out on the lakes and fish to their heart's content.

'Now the chief boatman on the lakes, or the gillie, as our despised conquerors would call him, was one Pakey Conneely, who was known far and wide as the best fisherman in Connemara, a man who could tie a fly in four seconds, by plucking a bit here and there from his clothes and fixing them to a hook. In regard to the lakes of this Oriental person, it is related that he knew, personally, the name of every fish in them, what they ate for their breakfast and when they would be willing to take a phoney fly when it was cast to them.

'Now Pakey was an honourable man and he hated to see his employer owning many lakes and not fishing them, so he was frequently dropping hints here and there, saying it was about time that this Prince – did I tell you he was a Prince of some kind? – should learn how to fish. Eventually his hints reached the ears of the illustrious Prince, and, being a humane man, he decided that it was only right of him to accede to the wishes of Pakey, and, to make that worthy happy, he decided that he would go the following day and fish for salmon.

'This was announced to Pakey, who got everything ready, and cleaned up the boat, scrutinized the tackle closely, prayed for a favourable fishing breeze, and told the salmon to be ready to do their stuff. The morning dawned and the Prince arrived, and with much preparation and bowing and felicitations he was tucked snugly into the boat and Pakey placed his own fishing-rod in his hand and rowed out into the lake.

' "What do I do with this thing, Pakey?" the Prince asked.

' "Well, now, Your Worship," said Pakey, "when we start drifting down towards that island there, you will just release a little of the line and you will cast them on the water, Your Honour, and then you will pull the rod towards you, keeping the flies on top. Then, Your Highness, a salmon will rise and take one of the flies, and you will strike him, but not immediately. You will give him plenty of time and then you will strike him by raising the tip of the rod. The fly will stick in his mouth, Your Majesty, and you will play him until he is exhausted and we will then gaff him."

' "That seems to be very simple, Pakey," said the Prince. "I don't know why I haven't become a fisherman long before this."

'So they fished away, Pakey encouraging the Prince, and then suddenly there was a swirl at one of the flies, a grand head-and-tail rise, and the Prince was so surprised that he pulled back his hand with the fright he got, and there was the salmon at the end of the rod.

' "A beauty, Your Majesty!" shouted Pakey. "I have never in all me life seen such a beautiful strike, Your Holiness. Now, for God's sake let him have it, Your Honour, let him take it!" And the reel whirred as the salmon took a run and threw himself out of the water.

' "Hold him, Your Reverence!" shouts Pakey. "For the love of all that's good and holy don't slacken on 'm. Watch him, Your Worship!"

'The Prince was excited somewhat, and when the salmon was back in the water he got his thoughts mixed and he didn't let the reel go with him but heaved a colossal pull on the rod, and the next minute the salmon had broken him and was off down the lake.

' "He appears to have departed, Pakey," said the Prince.

' "Well, you black bastard!" shouted Pakey in a red rage "why, in the name a God, didn't yeh do what I told yeh?" '

They laughed right enough and it did ease the tension a little.

'It could be true as well,' said Thomasheen, 'because I know that Pakey, and I met him in Clifden once, and everyone knows he's a great fisherman.'

'Will ye come over to the house,' Nellie asked, 'and have a cup of tea? The tide isn't far in yet and ye'll have plenty of time to get across.'

Thomasheen was hesitant, but Stephen accepted for both of them. As they were on the rise above the house Stephen stopped to look out at the tide, and away in the distance he thought he could see a tiny figure plodding across the sand. The figure stopped and waved at him. Stephen, wondering who it could be, waved a friendly hand too, and then turned down to the house.

It was obvious that the McClures were very poor. There

were four other children as well as Nellie, and Mrs McClure herself was a worn harassed woman, old long before her time. The house was a small thatched cottage, but it was very neatly kept and the kitchen was as clean as a new pin, and the crowded gear of the farmer-fisherman which it contained was orderly. Mrs McClure had a great welcome for them and asked them all about their people and bemoaned the illness of Stephen's mother. He realized then, with a shock, that it was almost the first time he had thought about her all day, and he was inclined to be ashamed of himself.

Thomasheen talked loudly to Mrs McClure and ignored Nellie, but all the time he felt the remnants of the emotion that had moved him, and he was thinking furiously how he could make an excuse to come in to the island again to see her, or maybe how she might be induced to cross over to the mainland some evening, and anyhow he knew that he would see her after Mass on Sunday, and if her mother wasn't with her, maybe he would be able to walk across a bit of the strand with her.

They were soon sitting at the white-scrubbed table drinking cups of strong well-sweetened tea, and eating potato cake, hot off the griddle, and it swimming in the yellow melted butter. Their day out had given them an appetite and they felt that they had to apologise to Mrs McClure for all they were eating, but it seemed to make her happy that they were enjoying her cake so much and she kept urging them to eat more and more.

'It'll be a long time,' said Stephen, 'before Nellie'll be able to turn out a cake like this.'

'That wan,' said Mrs McClure fondly, 'will be the worst wife that a man ever had.'

'Anyhow,' said Nellie, looking sideways at Thomasheen, 'when I do get a husband, it won't be me potato cakes that'll be worryin' him. I'll keep him amused in other ways and be the time he has got over me I'll be able to tempt his stomach instead of his heart.'

Whereat they laughed some more, and Stephen and Mrs

McClure talked about the miseries which any husband of Nellie would have to endure.

They were in the middle of this when the light was suddenly cut off from the door, and they looked up to see who it was.

It was some time before Stephen made out the form of Danny. His back was to the light and it was difficult to see his face. Nevertheless, Stephen rose to his feet and felt his heart thumping loudly. The last time Danny had come looking for him, he had been a bird of ill omen.

'What is it, Danny?' he asked quietly.

Danny had to make a great effort to speak.

'It's your mother, Stephen,' he said, and the others could hear the tears in his voice. 'We just heard. She's dead.'

Stephen stood as if he was petrified for a moment, and then he went to the door.

As he passed Danny, he could see tears on his weather-beaten face, and to the end of his life that was the thing he always remembered about this day. Then he was free of the house and running towards the strand. Halfway across the strand he stopped to ask himself, 'Why am I running home now?' Then he turned and walked slowly to meet the approaching tide.

CHAPTER SIX

The Hospital, Galway

My dear Stephen,

When you get this letter I will be dead. It is the dramatic nature in me which makes me write a line like that, but I know by the time you get this the first shock will be over, and you will be clearer in your mind about things, and me. You will have to forgive me if this is a very scattered letter and if you find it difficult to follow the writing of the pencil which I am using, but I couldn't manage to work a pen and I am writing this to you at broken intervals.

You see, Stephen, when I got here, they took a lot of X-ray pictures of me, and when they looked at them, they sent the young surgeon to have a look at me. He is a very young man. You would wonder how a boy like him could have the nerve to go around cutting into people, but he is supposed to be a brilliant young man and older than his years. Anyhow, he was very nice to me. He sat on the side of the bed and chatted about this and that, but I knew somehow, from the very, very kindly way he was looking at me, that things were pretty bad, so I asked him. He hummed and hawed a lot at first, but then when he saw I meant business, he told me that the operation would be a desperate business and that I was pretty far gone but that you never knew, etc. etc., from all of which I gathered that my number was up, and I decided to start writing this letter to you. I am not trying to be light-hearted really, just to be nice to you.

It was a frightening thing to know at first that in a few days one would not be any more, but like everything else you get used to it, and then you say to yourself, I'm different. Other people will die, but there's something special watching over me and I'll be all right. If you ever get this letter you'll know that . . . well, that my first intuition was right. I have arranged with the young surgeon that if anything happens to me you will get this letter after you have got over the shock, because I know it will be a shock to you, Stephen, more than to anybody else.

Please don't let it be too shocking. For myself, I don't really mind dying, honest, not after the first fright, anyhow.

My life didn't turn out the way I wanted it to, I'm afraid, and I have nobody but myself to blame for it. When I was growing up, I had a feeling that there were great things in store for me. There was nothing concrete to back the feeling up, but somehow I always thought that, over the horizon, there was a great something waiting for me, and I always felt excited about it. I know it was a silly feeling, but I couldn't help it. No matter what unpleasant thing happened to me, I could say to myself, Well, never mind, Martha, when *it* happens all this will be just a memory which you will be able

83

to laugh at. Maybe it was that that made me enjoy people so much. I was never much interested in people for what they were, but I was always trying to find out what made them go, and to find out what was behind the curtain which everyone presents to the world.

Do you remember the way we used to 'fight' about your saying I was a cynic and that it was impossible for any one person to be going around trying to put other persons in boxes labelled 'Pirates', 'Heroes', and so on? Well, I have watched you with people, and you are unconsciously doing the same thing whether you know it or not, and that gives me a little laugh now, because I know you will be chagrined at the information, my big argumentative son!

Well, that's the way I felt about things, and when I came to Connemara, I still had the feeling of something around the horizon, and I kept waiting for it to happen for years, before the inertia and delightful 'I'll do it tomorrow' of the mountains got into my blood, and then I became content with what I was and ceased to look into the future. Then I had you, you see, and I could transfer that feeling; and now I could say that you were the feeling I had waited for, and that I would just have to sit back and wait around until the mantle of whatever it was I was waiting for descended on your shoulders, and I could have a share of it too.

Then one day in Connemara I found out what I had wanted to do all my life, and decided that I was incapable of doing it.

I'm afraid, in connection with this, Stephen, that I have to apologize to you about it and maybe you will be very angry with me, because just a year ago I went into your bedroom, and you know the wide wooden box under your bed, which you made yourself and put the lock on? well, there it was and it was open . . . and yes, Stephen, I'm afraid I did.

I looked at what you had inside, and I knew you would be angry because it is the only thing in your life, Stephen, that you ever hid from me, and I knew you had a reason; but when I saw all the papers covered with your handwriting, I

84

sat down and read my way through them, and it's a good job that I'm out of your way now or I'm sure you would have told me off properly.

Stephen, when I read those things you had written (when did you write them? – in bed, at night, when the rest of us were asleep?), I realized then that it was what I had always wanted to do, to be able to write things. I realized then that all my scrutinizing of people and their doings meant just that, that I wanted to put them down on paper and laugh or cry about them and make other people do the same thing. But I would never be able to do it, because I haven't got the sacred something that makes a body capable of it. I could talk about them or think about them, but I couldn't write them. Proof? Take a look at this completely mixed-up letter; but I have to get this as clear as I can, because I want to be able to have my last talk with you and to try and say some of the things that I would have said to you in the years to come if I had been left to say them.

Stephen, what you have done is *good*! None of it will ever see the light of day, because it is unformed and I can see the hand of the young mind tracing itself on paper; but, Stephen, my son, it is really wonderful for a boy of fourteen, which you were when I read them (I never saw anything else after that, because you kept the box *locked*, you ungrateful boy!), to be able to turn out things like that; and, Stephen, they have great promise, honest, and this is not a doting mother talking to you now, but a woman who prides herself on being an analyst of things and people; and Stephen, I *know* that you will be good some day, better even than you yourself think now. So will you forgive me for being a Peeping Tom, and believe me when I say that you have what is wanted and that you will be good. But keep on trying and destroying, and please realize that you are a scrutinizer of people like I am . . . was, and that that is what will make a flat sentence look like a snake with wriggling life in it, one that will come up and hit people in the eye.

So please persevere, because you are going to have a much harder fight than anybody else that ever lived almost. The reason? Because, according to most people, you have the misfortune to be born in Connemara, and when people hear the word Connemara, they immediately think of wild animals and pagans and compare most Connemara people to the wild inhabitants of Africa. They say in effect 'Can anything good come out of Connemara?' and if that's blasphemy, I don't mean it to be.

Because look, Stephen! Fortunately for the people of Connemara, they have not yet reached the state of so-called civilization which their fellows in, say, Dublin have. But that makes them more interesting, because you can take it from me that most of the people of Dublin, or the people who emigrate there, are so civilized that they are as flat as pancakes and as interesting as tamed fleas performing in a circus. Because the Connemara people are still *living*. Everything they do is dramatic. When they love, they love unashamedly and tempestuously and in a healthy manner. When they fight, they fight with ferocity and in some cases cunning. Their whole life is a fight against something. They have to fight the sea to drag a reluctant living out of it. They have to fight the crude earth to make it give crops in fields which their ancestors hacked from the cruel mountains with their bare hands. A man with a thirty-acre farm in the Midlands wouldn't take all the land in the parish of Killaduff if you wanted to make him a gift of it.

So you see! What you see about you is something that you could not see in a thousand years in a populated city, because the dramatic things that happen in a city are mean things, and lewd things, and petty things. Isn't it better for a man to kill a fellow man in a straight-up fight, winner take all, than to go when he's unaware and put a pinch of poison in his tea that will make him die in horrible agony? Who ever heard in 'wild' Connemara of grown men violating little children? Isn't it a better thing for a man to go in the middle of the night and steal a load of turf from his neighbour, or a sheep maybe, than to steal into his house and knock him on the head with a blunt instrument in order to steal a diamond necklace?

God forgive me, that's a queer way for a mother to be talking to her child, but I want to point out to you that you have more drama on your own doorstep than you'll ever find in the heart of London or any of the big cities of the world.

But sometime you'll have to leave it, because a person who wants to write things will have to move about among other people and see them and meet them and talk to them *before* he is able to write properly about the people he left behind him. That is a paradox (I think) but you will find out for yourself what I mean. I have written to Father O'Riordan about this, and I'm sure, if you want to, that he would be able to fix up something for you to do there. But this is a matter for yourself and not for anybody else.

So that's that. If it were not for you, my Stephen, I wouldn't mind going wherever I am going, and then I console myself with the thought that it is perhaps for the best that I am being taken from you at this time. Because I was a peculiar mother, wasn't I? I'm not sure that I was a successful one. I never had time for anyone else but you, did I? Maybe that was wrong, Stephen. I would hate to think that I had held you too close to my petticoats and that you might have absorbed too many of my funny ideas. So it will be well for you to be without me for a time so that you can discover yourself and segregate the bits of yourself from the bits of me and find out what you really are and what you are made up of.

There is something else now, Stephen. I know, alas, that you have never forgotten the day long ago when you were ten and your father lost his temper. That day shouldn't mean all to you that it does, Stephen, believe me. It is only natural that you should remember it, because you were so young and so impressionable that it is standing out in your mind like a fester on a finger. Don't let it, Stephen, because it is not that important, honestly. And I know also without being told that you are linking that day with what has happened to me now.

Stephen, that is ridiculous, because what I am suffering from now is an organic disease and what happened that day had no more to do with it than ... well, I can't think of a metaphor or a simile or whatever it is ... but anyhow that day had nothing to do with it. I was doomed before then by this business and it was just nature taking its course, that's all, because you are marked down for those things in a little blue book which the Almighty holds and you can't escape them if you have to have them. So forget that, what you're thinking, I mean, and please, Stephen, try to get closer to your father.

I often think that it may be my fault that you and your father are not the friends you ought to be, but looking back now, when I have nothing to gain by trying to inflate my ego, I think I did everything I could to make you more like father and son, and the reason I have failed is that there is something wrong with your father, Stephen. I don't know what it is. Something that happened to him in America that he can't forget and that's the reason that he is unfriendly, always closed up in himself, and why he is fond of a drink. I have always failed to make him confide in me in order to get the load, whatever it is, off his mind, so now I'm handing that legacy on to you. Try, Stephen, please, for my sake; it's the only burden I leave you, to get close to him. I know that if he would confide in you he would be a different man, altogether. Whatever you do, please don't fight with him now or ever, because he is a phantom-ridden man with a violent temper, and sometimes, watching you, my Stephen, I'm afraid that you have inherited that temper too, and it would be too bad if you were both to clash, because only God knows what would happen then.

So if you fail to get on with him, Stephen, I appeal to you to go and leave Connemara altogether. I know that is sending you out into the waves of the world without any patrimony, and that people would say I am a cruel mother to even suggest it, but when I think of him and the size of him, and his temper, and when I look at you and realize how big you will be, and that you also will have a temper, it is the only thing I can think of; and besides I know that you will be able to make your way, because you have deft hands and sufficient clarity of brain – and after all what more does a person want? So that's something else off my chest.

There's nothing left to me now to do, Stephen, but say 'goodbye'. There are many more things I would like to talk about – to urge you, for example, to keep up your reading and your Latin; but I know that it would be superfluous, because you are caught in the toils of knowledge now, and you can never escape from it, fortunately. There are many other things as well, but I'm afraid that my time is running out and that I am coming to the end of what I have to say.

So this is Farewell, Stephen. I want you to be sorry that I am gone and that you won't see me any more as I was. I'm going to be cruel and say that the next time you see me I might be a corpse, and I'm a funny woman to be talking that way to a son. But, Stephen, however shocked you will be, you must realize that a corpse is not a person, and that looking at it should be no occasion for great sorrow. I will be happy to be one if it does not affect you too much, because I believe in another world somewhere beyond death and I know that when I die it won't be death really. That's assured, Stephen, because if it wasn't, how on earth could we put up with anything at all?

So I know that it will be somewhere else that you and I will meet again, that I will be, God willing, a mute spirit somewhere that can watch over you and see what you are doing, even though I won't be permitted to whisper guidance into your ear, or make some of the remarks about people that always set both of us arguing. But I will be there, Stephen, and I am sure I will be quite jealous when you get married – because some day you will – and when you come to join me at the age of 102, I'm sure I will be quite frigid to your wife, and will try to absorb all your attention. Think of this when you look at me dead in the house and ignore the shell of Martha.

I will be quite happy that my piece of dust will lie over in the Island of Ourish, because nobody could choose a better place for their ashes than that. I loved Connemara and it will be grand to know that I lie under it and that the Atlantic breezes are eternally blowing over me, and I will never be lonely because the seagulls will be always there wheeling and squawking high in the sky.

So goodbye, my son Stephen, and remember me now and again; but don't mourn too much for me, just enough to make my jealous spirit smug, because I will never forget you. You know without my telling you how much I love you, and I know that you have a soft spot for me too and I would be very miserable if you were too sad. So remember me, Stephen, as I was, and I will be just the same when we meet again. Don't remember me as an inanimate something waiting to be coffined. That's not me, Stephen, and you know it. Be careful of yourself, and some day we will meet again and we can have a good laugh about this letter. May God bless you and make you into the kind of person that I can visualize.

Your Mother,

Martha

PS – Remember, Stephen, don't be too hurt now!

PPS – Be just sad enough to satisfy an egotistical mother.

Stephen slowly folded up the bulky letter and put it back in the envelope. He was sitting on a rock at the mouth of the lane leading on to the strand. For some time he remained sitting, his mind a blank as he looked out at the sea.

She is a very clever woman, my mother, he thought. She had seemed to look into the future when she was writing that letter and gauged his emotions exactly. He wondered what kind of an effort it had cost her to write the letter, and then thought that she had meant just what she had said, and that she had faced her death with a smile in her which she had succeeded in getting down on paper. And talking about her corpse like that! She had guessed about that too, and had struck exactly the right note, because the sight of her lying up there in the house was the most shocking thing that he had ever seen. He had been so used to her the other way, that when he had reluctantly forced himself to go into the big room and see her lying on the bed, emotionless, unmoving, he had been deeply shocked and horrified. He had read the letter, and remembering her body now he could imagine that there was a sort of smile upon her face instead of the vacuous rigidity of death.

What a woman! Stephen laughed, and then stopped hurriedly and looked around him to see if anybody heard, because they would never understand a son laughing on the day of his mother's funeral. There was a part of her in him which caused him to hide his emotions under a mask of indifference in case anybody should see him with his defences down. He hoped people wouldn't think that he was hard-hearted, but he just couldn't cry at all. Maybe tomorrow or the day after the full realization of his loss hit him, but how could a fellow turn around and cry when he got a letter like that from a dead mother? Oh, a clever woman!

He looked across the sands where they would be taking her soon. He remembered that Thomasheen's father had gone that way. It was not like a real funeral at all, to see the men with the coffin on their shoulders trudging across the yellow sands, and the people behind them trailing out. No matter how big the crowd was it always looked very small on that enormous stretch of strand. It wasn't like a funeral really. It was more like a kind of adventure. If you were walking with a funeral on a road it would have an air of reality, but not across the sands to Ourish Island.

Then the graves in Ourish were not like the graves anywhere else, because they were sandy graves, with the golden sands on top and the grey silver sands down below. There was none of this business you read about of clods thumping on coffins and tearing the heart out of you. There was just the caressing touch of sea-sand, that's all, and when you were coming away again and leaving the dead, you felt somehow that they had the best part of it, and that you were missing something by not staying there with them.

Wasn't it she that was cute about reading his stuff too, and not letting on? He had never guessed even. Often he had felt like showing it to her, but then he hadn't because he felt he wanted to wait until he had something really worthwhile to show her. Now she would never see it and what was the use of trying to do it any more – but wait a minute! Oh, the cuteness of her again, putting it into his head that she would always be around. She might be up there somewhere beyond the seagulls now, laughing at him. He wouldn't put it past her, he thought fondly. From now on, every time he put a diffident pen to paper he would imagine her somewhere around him, so maybe it would be better in the long run, because he'd have to do things much better now in order to feel that he was satisfying her and that she wouldn't be criticizing too much.

He never felt the approach of Father O'Riordan, who came softly and laid a hand on his shoulder, wondering at the same time what on earth the boy had to be smiling about? Father O'Riordan had aged a lot. His shoulders were bowed now and his long white hair was scanty, but the two eyes of him glittered as brightly as ever they had done.

'You better come back to the house now, my boy,' he said. 'We'll have to start over to the island with her.'

'All right, Father,' said Stephen.

'You got a letter from her, didn't you?' he asked.

'Yes, Father, I did,' Stephen said and waited, but Father O'Riordan had more intelligence than to ask what she had said.

The old priest looked out to sea.

'Your mother was a remarkable woman, you know, Stephen,' he said. 'It's over seventeen years since I saw her last, and yet I could never get her out of my mind. She had a terrible strong personality and a way with her of impressing herself on you. I often wonder if I made a mistake in sending her to Connemara at all. I have often been in me bed at night, lying awake and thinking that I did her a great disservice by putting her out in this wilderness, like planting an orchid in the middle of the Sahara.'

'I don't think it was a mistake,' Stephen said. 'She was very happy here, you know, and for my part, if you hadn't sent her I wouldn't be here.'

'That's true enough,' said the Father, looking closely at him. 'You're very like her, too, you know, not in features altogether, perhaps, but something about you that brings her vividly before me when I look at you.'

'I'm glad to hear that,' Stephen said.

'Yes, a remarkable woman,' said Father O'Riordan, 'and even allowing for the fact that you were to be, I have still the sort of a sneaking feeling that I was wrong to guide her down here. I tried to make her leave it, you know, when they wrote saying they were going to be married. My heart sank then, somehow, not altogether because she was going to marry my brother, but because I felt that there were other things in her, that she would be lost down here as the wife of a Connemara farmer. The first day I saw her in the convent, and she was only a small bit of a thing then, consisting mainly of two gleaming eyes, like an embryonic fish, I was taken by her, and I can tell you now that she had more intelligence at that age than most of the grown-up people that I knew then.'

'I don't think,' said Stephen, 'that she regretted it one bit. Because she was very fond of Connemara and she couldn't have lived anywhere else after that.'

'Maybe so,' said the priest. 'Do you like Connemara, Stephen?'

Stephen paused a while before he answered.

'I do,' he said.

You couldn't really put it into words, the fact that you liked Connemara. Your feelings about it were so vague, just that they were there as firmly set as one of the big mountains. You knew all the disadvantages of life in Connemara. Fortunately for you your father was a man with money, which he received every week from a bank in Clifden, so that it was no worry much if the weather was not favourable, or if this or that happened. But it was much different with the majority. Thomasheen's people, now. They were very poor. They lived on the land and barely managed to exist on it. It was a tragedy for them if a storm of rain beat their small field of oats as flat as a board. It meant that somebody went without some essential clothing, or there would be less bacon for the winter. It was worse with those who depended on the sea for a living, with a small garden as a kind of a desperately needed hobby. You had to work hard for fish, and they were never plentiful because the people around these parts fished from the currachs, which could not venture far into the deep without great danger.

Connemara was a hard mistress and mostly a cruel one, giving rather grudgingly at most times, but sweeping away all the gifts again with the rough hand of a petulant woman. Everybody living there bore the marks of Connemara on their faces or on their bodies, hunger or lines sunken deeply from dangerous occupations, or scars as the result of tempers which flared like lightning. Still, despite all this, most of them liked it, and it was a strange thing that anybody who left it to go to England or America returned eventually to settle down there with the money they had earned. It was cheap to live, and money was the passport to triumph over nature.

'Your mother wrote to me,' said Father O'Riordan, 'and said that maybe you might want to leave it and come to Dublin. I am sure that I would be able to get you something.'

'No, thanks, Father,' said Stephen. 'I don't want to go. It is kind of you, but it isn't time yet to leave.'

'I see,' said the Father. 'Well, if you want to leave in the future, you know my address and write to me there. It better be soon, I'm afraid, because I'm not as young as I was. I'm beginning to feel the age coming on me, and my brain is not as quick.'

If it was, he thought, I would be able to talk better to this young son of Martha's who must be suffering from her loss, but somehow I can't. It is terrible to be getting very old, but it is much more terrible when you feel that your mind is not as fast as it was. When the mind began to throw off something you wanted to press on it, that was the time to beware and make ready for the end. Sometimes now, saying Mass in the morning, God forgive me, I find myself saying the prayers at the end, and realize that I have gone through the whole half-hour without a thought of what I am at. Funerals have no longer become intimate things. Can a man become so callous as to say the prayers and throw in the earth on the coffin and feel nothing at all? Not even when it's Martha? He rose slowly from the rock on which he was sitting, with a sigh.

'Come on, Stephen,' he said. 'We better get back. I will have a chat with you again before I leave. My mind is very sluggish today. Tomorrow maybe it will brighten a little.'

'Yes, Father,' said Stephen, as he looked closely at the priest, trying to see the live, cynical person of his mother's stories. He was no longer there. Just an old man you felt sorrow for, when he was the kind of man, according to Martha, who inspired you with confidence and hope. I don't want to be old, Stephen said to himself. I don't want to be old if it saps you, and I'm glad that my mother will never be old.

'I better help you here,' he said, putting his hand under the priest's elbow to guide him over the rough ground to the road.

A smile twisted the face of the priest. Has it come to this, he thought, that I am an old man, and that young boys feel that they should help me over stiles? For a moment he felt like protesting, but then he didn't. He accepted the assistance, and, worst sign of all, as he said to himself, he felt grateful for it.

So they went towards the house of death, an old priest bowed with his years and a heart that had aged, and a young boy who was becoming a man, with a heart that was very young and very hopeful, but one that would never quite recover from the death of a mother who had poured into him all that she had ever possessed, both good and bad. They walked up to coffin her corpse now, an old priest who had been the beginning of her life, and a young son who had been the end of it.

CHAPTER SEVEN

Down the road, whistling a cheerful and up-to-date ditty, came Paddy Rice. It was a warm summer day. He was just over twenty years of age, home on a holiday, and he was as happy as a lark. He made a brave sight under the sun. He was wearing immaculate grey flannel trousers, a white tennis shirt, open at the neck, and his waist, rather inclined to portliness, was encased in a woven multi-coloured Aran belt. The years had been kind to Paddy. There was nothing in his face excepting a look of blank good humour. He had remained rather small and he was rounding out. It was easy to see that in a few years more he would be like his father, a low-sized fat man who could never lean anything but his stomach on the counter when he was talking to the drinking customers. But Paddy was much nattier than his father. Paddy's father never wore his black hair as beautifully brushed as Paddy did, nor if he had been trying for a thousand years could he have grown the thin black wisp of a moustache that Paddy wore. Life felt good to Paddy on this summer day.

When he reached Stephen's house he turned in at the gate and walked airily towards the open door. He knocked at it, and as he waited for a reply he looked around him and decided that the farm of Martin O'Riordan was going to seed somewhat. The doors badly needed a coat of paint, and the outhouses and stables could have done with some whitewash. It wasn't the same as he had remembered it some five years ago when Stephen's mother was alive. Ah, but then she was an excellent woman, thought Paddy; anyone could see that by the way she made Stephen talk like somebody out of a book. Paddy remembered the way he used to talk himself at the time and shivered delicately at the memory.

'Yes?' said a voice, inquiringly to him.

Paddy turned and then paused a moment before he could

go on. The girl standing in the doorway was the last kind of a girl he had expected. His father had told him that the O'Riordans had got a new girl from Dublin somewhere a few months ago, and Paddy had been picturing, when he thought of the question at all, some sort of a slum slattern. He was shocked, and not disagreeably so, at what he saw.

She was not young, about twenty-five years of age, and she was a very good-looking girl in a rather overdone way. Everything she possessed was on generous lines. Her face was big but well-formed and had plenty of flesh on it. Her lips were just a little thick, and Paddy noticed with pleasure that they were carefully lipsticked. He could see her teeth as she smiled sultrily at him and they were very small and very even. Her eyes were black and her eyelashes long and black, and they formed a suspicious contrast to her fair hair. She was neatly enough dressed, with a gaily-coloured pinafore over a skirt and blouse, and Paddy, who regarded himself as an expert in those matters, decided that her figure had everything plus. In fact she was generously built. Her breasts were large and firm and were pushing their way through her thin silken blouse. She was well-caught-in at the waist, but Paddy couldn't see that that was due to a good corset. Satisfied with the top survey of her, he allowed his eyes to fall lower and decided that she had a nice leg into the bargain, so he smiled sweetly at her.

'I'm looking for Stephen,' he said, and wondered idly why her mouth hardened a little.

'He's down in the end field at the hay,' she said. Her voice was low and husky. This dame, thought Paddy, has practically everything. If I could induce the old man to put her in the bar behind the counter, sales would soar. He couldn't help smiling at the thought. He covered the smile with a pleasant laugh.

'Thank you very much,' he said. 'I will drift down that way and contact him.'

'You're Paddy Rice, aren't you?' she asked. 'The one that's becoming a doctor in Galway?'

'Right first time,' said Paddy. 'That's me. Just home on a

holiday to see the folks. You weren't here last year. I don't remember you.'

'No,' she answered, 'I only came a few months ago.' She looked at him warmly.

'You ought to come in and sit down out of the heat for a while,' she said. 'Mister O'Riordan isn't home either, but he won't be long.'

'No, thanks,' said Paddy. 'I want to see Stephen. But I'll see you around again sometime. I'll be here for a few months.'

'That'll be nice,' she answered.

'So-long,' said Paddy, turning again to go out the gate. He could feel her watching him, until he was hidden by a fold in the road. Nice thing, thought Paddy to himself, a very nice thing indeed, and I bet her name is Denise or Mabel or Clarice or something like that. How in the name of all that's good and holy, he asked himself, did a blossom like that get blown into the heart of Connemara? I'll give her six months, he thought, and then she'll be on the run again to the metropolis; and the look she gave him!

'Well, what do you know!' he said with a whistle, and then sighted the two men working at the hay in the end field. He stood at the wall and watched them for a time. There were two of them. The hay was all saved and they were obviously engaged in building the last cock. One of the men was perched on top of it while the other was pitching. With surprise Paddy saw that the pitcher was Stephen O'Riordan. Surprise, because a single year, when he was last at home, had changed Stephen out of all recognition. He must, Paddy thought, be one of the biggest men in Connemara now. Stephen was wearing a singlet and trousers. His arms were very big. From where he was standing Paddy could see the knotted muscles of his forearms standing out like carvings on an antique chair, which made the simile all the better because Stephen's body was almost burnt black by the sun. His neck was thick but not ugly, his hair was longish and fair, and Paddy could see that his chest was rounded like a barrel.

Paddy let a great shout out of him. Both men turned their heads and then Stephen, having paused for a minute, recognized him, threw down the pitchfork, and came to the wall with long strides.

'Well, Paddy Rice, how are you?' said he, catching his hand and pumping it vigorously.

'Hey, easy on there!' said Paddy, withdrawing his hand and going through the pantomime of massaging it back to life again. 'Don't forget that your big craubs of hands are hardened with toil and that mine are softened by the niceties of civilization.'

'Well, you haven't changed a bit,' said Stephen, laughing; 'but hold on there! Turn about to the light! Yes, no! I'm not quite sure, but, Paddy, did you know that you forgot to wash your upper lip before you came out?'

'I have always suspected,' rejoined Paddy with dignity, 'that you were nothing but an ignorant lout of a peasant, and now I'm glad to see that my prognostications are correct.'

'You don't mean to say,' said Stephen, jumping up to sit astride the wall, 'that that thing is a moustache?' And he laughed loudly.

'Laugh away, you clod,' said Paddy, in quite good humour, 'what can one expect from the native aborigines?'

'Ah, I'm glad to see you, Paddy,' said Stephen, 'even though you're dressed like something off the front page of a magazine. What kind of an outfit is that? The well-dressed haymaker, as visualized by Paddy Rice? Oh, God wait'll Thomasheen sees you like that!'

'How's Thomasheen?' Paddy asked. 'The same as ever?'

'Oh, Thomasheen is a changed man now,' Stephen said. 'He's a serious man. He's doing a great line with Nellie McClure in on Ourish and before we know where we are he'll be married on us.'

'Ah, no!' said Paddy, jumping up on the wall beside Stephen. 'Sure Thomasheen wouldn't know how to coort properly even. I see I'll have to take him aside and give him a tip or two. Where is he now?'

'Well, as a matter of fact, I promised that I'd go down

and give him a hand with his hay when we have this field done. We're at the last cock now. He's down below.'

'I'll give you a hand so,' said Paddy, jumping over the wall, 'and we'll go on down to him.'

'My God,' said Stephen, with simulated horror, 'you're not going to ruffle that beautiful outfit with vulgar hay-making, are you?'

'I have decided,' said Paddy with dignity, 'that since I can no longer beat the head off you, like I used to do long ago, since you have continued to grow up, and I have continued to grow out, that my best plan is to ignore you. Come, lout, lead me to a fork and I'll show you how a Rice can pitch!'

They went over to the cock. The man on top had seated himself down and was contemplatively sucking a rib of hay with a vacant expression.

'What's this?' Paddy asked. 'Atlas holding up the universe? Who is this person?'

'Oh, this is the man we have now,' said Stephen, laughing. 'Seamus Ward he is and he comes from Litirmore. Hey, Seamus, this is Paddy Rice.'

'How'ya?' asked Seamus.

'Hello, my good man,' said Paddy, 'and I hope you are a tireless worker, because you are now facing the best pitcher in the Twenty-six Counties.'

While Stephen sat down on the ground, Paddy set to with a will, forking hay to Seamus, who accepted it stoically and scattered it correctly under his feet. Grinning at Paddy's endeavour, Stephen thought how good it was to see him again, and at the same time, looking at the loutish Seamus, thought what a pity it was that Danny had deserted them. Shortly after his mother's death, Danny had come to Martin O'Riordan and said that he was leaving. None of them could believe it, but Danny was in earnest. He had bought a little cottage down at the strand, which stood in about two acres of fairly good land. The cottage was in a sad state when he went into it, but now it was a model little cottage and a marvel of cleanliness to all the Connemara housewives. Danny lived fairly comfortably on it, and he ran to a currach as well, and supplemented his income by selling fish to the hotels in Clifden. It had always been a mystery to Stephen all the same why, after nearly twenty years with his father, Danny had up and gone on the death of Martha.

Since then they had been cursed with hired men, none of whom had ever approached Danny's standard. They generally didn't last long because they could not put up with Martin's tempers, so they came and went in season, like the swallows.

Paddy's first flush of activity had now ceased, as Stephen noted with a smile. He was sweating profusely and the arm action of the pitchfork had slowed to an alarming extent. After tossing a few more forkfuls, Paddy suddenly threw the fork on the ground.

'Ah, to hell with it!' he ejaculated. 'This kind of work was only invented for slaves. Why should I, anyhow, an honest citizen, and a gentleman of the first water, concern myself with the petty doings of the disgusting countrymen? In other words, go to hell and do it yourself!' He threw himself on the ground panting.

'Ah, you're gone soft, Paddy,' said Stephen, taking up the fork.

'That,' said Paddy, 'is a ridiculous assertion. I am gone sensible. It took me some time to find this out, but I did find it out, and as you hurl hay at the brave Seamus, I will expound to you. The whole world is divided into two kinds of people, viz., the people who work the hands and the people who work the head. The hand-workers lose out every time because the head-workers always gain from their toil. Early in life I discovered this to be a fact, having made a close study of the business of my father. I see him there. What does he do? He invests money in barrels of porter and other alcoholic drinks. He purchases them at a certain price, and then sells them to you mugs of hand-workers at a handsome profit. And why? So that he can keep his one and only son in a state of blissful idleness. It is the same thing with everything else. When, you undistinguished hermit, you go to live in a town of any size you will find that what I say is

101

true, that the people of Ireland fought the good fight in order to get rid of their oppressors, aristocratic landlords, etcetera. Fair enough. But now their places have been taken by a tribe which is much worse than they, because they are louts and ignoramuses. They open shops and become retailers and they get into the racket also as wholesalers, so they make a double profit as middlemen. They buy farms in the surrounding countryside and graze bullocks on them, while small farmers have to emigrate to England. These bastards then die and leave children after them who are as stupid and as parasitical as themselves, and they drink and whore, and go to Mass and Holy Communion on a Sunday as if they were honest citizens. But I don't complain, because my old man is in the racket too, and I have discovered the great fact, that the more idle and useless you are in this country, the greater the respect you will be shown by one and all. It is only the fools and the eejits that stain their hands with toil.'

'That's great talk from a medical student,' said Stephen. 'There, Seamus, you have the last of it now. We'll leave you now to go down to Thomasheen and you'll be able to tie it up yourself. Come on, you lazy devil, Paddy, and take this rake in your hand and we'll go down and give poor ould Thomasheen a hand.'

Paddy rose reluctantly and put the wooden rake across his shoulder, and, accompanied by Stephen, made his way to the wall. They hopped over the wall and got out on the road.

That is something that will puzzle you in Connemara, the absence of gates leading into fields. There are not many gates, because the fields are small, and are divided from one another by stone walls, carelessly thrown together and easy to climb. If you want to get into a field, you step over the wall. If you want to bring a horse and cart into the field, you just knock the wall down and rebuild it afterwards. It would be probably much easier to have gates, if you could get them for nothing, and if you were not as poor as the ordinary Connemara farmer. So, as stones are plentiful, they use them and ignore the gates.

'Did anything of note happen here, since I was around last?' Paddy asked as they swung down the road.

'No, I don't think so,' said Stephen, 'except that the McCartans lost a sow, and somebody's cow was drowned over in a bog-hole beside the lake.'

'Epic,' said Paddy, 'pure epic. Why wasn't I told about this before? Why didn't you send me a telegram about it?'

'Well,' said Stephen, laughing, 'we knew you would be here around now, and we wanted to save a bit of the information for you.'

'Yes, indeed,' said Paddy. 'I was up at the house calling for you and I was greeted at the door by a beauteous maid. Who is she?' He was looking at Stephen as he put the question, and noted that his face hardened a little.

'Oh, she's a maid my father got in Dublin a few months ago. Mavis Mahoney is her name. What's the joke?' he asked as Paddy started to laugh loudly.

'Well, it's not much of a joke really,' said Paddy, 'except I was thinking to myself coming down and I had a bit of a bet that her name would turn out to be something like that.'

'I don't get it,' said Stephen, 'but it's not important anyway.' Because Stephen, definitely, did not like Mavis. He had been prepared to be nice to her, but he soon found out that if he was nice to her he'd have to be prepared to be nicer. He didn't like the way she smiled at him or the way she looked at him, as if she was a judge at a show scrutinizing the finer points of a bull. So he kept out of her way as much as possible, and had as little as possible to do with her, and he had a feeling that she was resentful at his uncivil behaviour.

'Tell me,' said Paddy, 'have you taken to the drink yet?'

'Well,' said Stephen, 'I have. It is a pleasure for me to report that I can now drink a pint with any man in Connemara.'

'Praise the Lord!' ejaculated Paddy. 'There is now some hope for you and I will continue being friendly with you. As soon as we are finished with Thomasheen the three of us must go up, before the tea, and quaff.'

'That'll be nice,' said Stephen.

'How on earth did you start on the downward path?' Paddy asked. 'You were a real prohibitionist the last time I was here.'

'Michilin and the fishing,' said Stephen with a laugh, 'and the fact that a bottle of stout is a real handy way of carrying your lunch around with you.'

'And Thomasheen?' Paddy asked.

'Also a fallen sinner,' said Stephen.

'Allelujah!' said Paddy, throwing his hands in the air.

They soon reached the field where Thomasheen was working with all the members of his family. They were also on the last lap and were raking in the hay preparatory to making the butt of the cock. Thomasheen came running at their shout, and his eyes nearly widened out of his head when he saw the way Paddy was decked out. Thomasheen hadn't changed much in looks. He was still the same wide-eyed, clear-faced boy. He had grown tall.

'Jay, Paddy,' he said, as he wrung his hand, 'you look just like a daisy with a ribbon round the middle of it.'

'That's enough now, my good man,' said Paddy. 'I have already suffered at the mouth of this uncouth peasant.'

'God, you have a moustache too!' yelled Thomasheen.

'Well, there's no need to let them know that over in the Aran Islands,' said Paddy, climbing over the wall. 'Will you conduct yourself like a decent citizen and don't be roaring like a strawberry bull.'

'Ah, I'm glad to see you, Paddy, on me word,' said Thomasheen sincerely.

'Why wouldn't you?' Paddy asked. 'Amn't I the only bit of colour in yeer drab lives? Now lead me to this mound of hay until I disintegrate it.'

They went over towards the hay. Thomasheen had a brother coming after himself, a young lad of about eighteen, and his sister Mary, a good-looking shy girl of seventeen. They knew Paddy well but remained abashed at his bantering and he found it almost impossible to knock a word out of them. There were three other smaller children who were more brave, and approached him after a time to have a good look at him. But Paddy gradually reduced them all to a state of friendliness. Needless to say, after a few flicks with the rake he retired from the fray, and he spent his time lying down and jibing the workers.

Eventually the three small children gave up work also and they were soon tumbling with him on the hay and getting into everybody's way. But Paddy seemed to carry with him an aura of goodwill and good humour, as Stephen thought to himself, and more work was done under his bantering.

When the cock was finally completed he looked at it from every angle and congratulated himself on his day's work, informing all of them that if he hadn't come to give them a hand they would have been working until the moon came up. Then the children were sent off home with the forks and pitchforks, laughing and jingling in their pockets the money which Paddy had slipped surreptitiously to them. Mary and the younger brother were next to depart, Mary blushing furiously at the sallies which Paddy called after her. Finally the three of them were left smoking cigarettes and leaning against the cock of hay.

'Well, you didn't change a bit, Paddy,' said Thomasheen.

'You'd be surprised, Thomasheen,' said Paddy.

'You'll be a doctor soon now, Paddy, won't you?' Stephen asked.

'Another three years,' said Paddy, 'if all goes well and the examinations are easy. Look, what the hell are we sitting down here for? Let us be on our way until we sink our mouths into the froth of a juicy pint, and it's we that have deserved it.'

'I don't know,' said Thomasheen doubtfully. 'I have a lot to do yet and . . .'

'Come on now, Thomasheen, no slipping out of it!' Paddy interjected. 'It isn't every day that Paddy Rice comes home.'

'What's wrong with you today, Thomasheen?' Stephen asked, looking closely at him. 'You're not the good old happy Thomasheen. Is there anything on your mind?'

105

'No, on me oath, fellas, there's nothing wrong,' said Thomasheen, but he kept his eyes on the ground and didn't look at them, which was most unlike him.

'Come on, Thomasheen, out with it now, confess everything,' said Paddy.

'No, on me oath, lads, there's nothing!' protested he.

'That won't do, Thomasheen,' said Stephen. 'I was watching you all the time we were working, and there is something wrong with you,'

'Honest to God there isn't!' said Thomasheen. 'Oh, all right so, lads, come on and I'll go with ye.' And he rose to his feet. Stephen and Paddy looked at one another, and both had a feeling that all was not well with Thomasheen, because for one of his open and tactless temperament it was hard to simulate, and he wore an air about him of something concealed, which normally he would have told to the first one that came down the road. If he wouldn't talk now, it must be serious. They didn't press him any further.

They were soon on the road again, heading back the way they had come, Stephen and Paddy talking inconsequentially about this and that, and pretending to ignore Thomasheen. When they reached the gate of Stephen's house, he paused to throw the pitchfork and rake over the wall and then they continued towards the pub owned by Paddy's father. It lay at the cross-roads and was situated well back from the road. There was nothing to distinguish it from any other Connemara house except the glaring tin advertisement nailed to the wall, saying that alcohol was very good for you particularly if it was this or that brand, which was ridiculous in a way because no man who wanted a drink needed to be told that it was good for him, and since everyone in the district knew where the pub was, there did not seem much point in advertising it. There were also one or two cigarette advertisements, but it was the glint of sunlight on the brown bottles in the window that gave a man a thirst more than anything else.

The inside of the pub was cool and clean, with fresh sawdust strewn on the floor. The seating accommodation was primitive but usual, consisting of up-ended half-barrels and a few rough forms. The pub was empty when the three of them entered, but Paddy, banging loudly on the counter, soon brought his father running.

'Three foaming pints, landlord,' said Paddy.

'Yes, sir,' said his father, tipping a forelock at him, at least what would have been a forelock if he weren't as bald as a lobster-pot.

'The service in this hostelry is becoming very slow,' said Paddy loudly to the others; but his father only grinned because Paddy's father was very fond of his son. He was a very cheerful-looking man with a great beaming countenance and he was very popular with all the inhabitants, even with those who owed him money – and what better testimonial could you give him than that? For a public-house keeper, he was not a gossip, and he was always noted for having the good word for everybody. That was his only failing really, because just when you'd be getting down to pulling somebody to pieces, and sipping your pint, Paddy's father would relate some incident about the castigated one that redounded to his worth, and as a consequence you would look at him with a jaundiced eye; but he would soon again worm his way back into your good books with an inquiry after your wife or your children or a sick calf.

Paddy's father was a grand man, and it was well known that he could have bought a few counties with all the money that people owed him. He would get it eventually, of course, but it was a sort of long-term investment without any profit, and then when you finally got around to paying him off, he would lean close to you and in a kind of asthmatic whisper say, 'Are you sure, now, that you can afford it? I'll wait for a while more if you like.' He was nearly always referred to as 'Paddy's father' ever since he had sent his young son off to school. Before he went to school, Paddy had been a wild lad, and no matter what was done out of the way, the injured one would immediately say, 'It's that Paddy Rice, I betcha! May the divil scald 'm!' or else it would be, 'Go down and tell Paddy's father that his rip of a son did this or that.' So Paddy's father breathed a sigh of relief, mixed with sorrow, when he managed to persuade his offspring to go off to school, and had often thought with pity, and a grin of remembrance, of the hot time the teachers must be having at school with him. Then Paddy always came home on his holidays carrying caustic notes to his father from the head man at the school, pointing out Paddy's lack of discipline and asking plaintively if there was nothing at all his father could do about it. All the same, Paddy managed to pass all his exams, to the amazement of everybody but Stephen, who knew that he had a lot of brains, and who would not be surprised if he turned out to be a very brilliant man some day.

Then Paddy's father was terribly delighted about his son becoming a doctor, and often looked at him wonderingly. He couldn't imagine how he, a country pub-keeper, could rear such a strange and wonderful bird. He was as proud as punch about him, and many a bummer got a free pint after putting in a bit of work lauding Paddy up to the skies.

'Did ye get the field finished, Stephen?' he asked.

'We did,' said Stephen, 'but only thanks to Paddy. He came down there and worked like four men.'

This amused Paddy's father and he rolled all over.

'That's a good wan,' he said. 'If Paddy saw a day's work he'd pass out, so he would.'

'Isn't that a nice way for any man to talk about his son?' Paddy asked. 'That man would be in the poorhouse now, only for the way that I built up his business.'

'It's a great wonder I'm not in the poorhouse,' said his father, 'because of the way yer pullin' me business down.'

'Well, slainte t' ye,' said Thomasheen, sinking his mouth in the pint.

They joined him and there was a pause as they appreciated the draught. Paddy regarded Thomasheen.

'So you're doing a strong line with Nellie McClure, Thomasheen, from all I hear? Come on now, cough it up, and tell us when the wedding is.'

Thomasheen looked at them and there was no joy in his face.

'All right, fellas,' he said. 'I'm getting married next January.'

'What!' ejaculated Paddy. 'Are you serious?'

'Yes, I'm serious all right,' said Thomasheen.

'Well, that's the bee's knees!' said Paddy. 'That's the best bit of news that I've heard for half a century. And let me tell you, boy, that Nellie is a grand girl. Honest, I was delighted when Stephen told me. She was always chasing you at school. It made me jealous. I'd say, How is it that Thomasheen can swim faster than I can, and he has Nellie running after him?'

Stephen, who had been looking closely at Thomasheen, spoke:

'The point is, I think, that Thomasheen is not going to marry Nellie; are you, Thomasheen?'

'No,' said Thomasheen slowly, leaving down his glass. 'I'm not going to marry Nellie.'

Paddy was flabbergasted. He paused and looked at the two of them. He had never seen Thomasheen looking so serious before, never in all his life. His brows seemed to be pulled down over his wide eyes and there was a crease in his forehead.

'It's Bridgie McGinnis, Thomasheen, isn't it?' said Paddy's father kindly, as he leaned his comfortable stomach on the counter.

'Yes,' said Thomasheen. 'It's Bridgie McGinnis.'

Paddy looked at him dumbfounded.

'I heard that,' said Paddy's father, 'but I didn't think that it was true.'

Stephen, with his heart sinking, thought a few moments about Bridgie. She was a girl who lived in Carnmore, who could no longer claim to be a girl because she was forty-five or more if she was a day. When she was young she had emigrated to America. She was an only child, and she had gone to live with an aunt there. Her father died a short time afterwards and Bridgie sent home money which kept her mother from starving. Also the neighbours were very good to her mother Maggie. They sowed her fields for her and they reaped her crops for her, and when she was really badly off they would give her something out of their own meagre stores, because Maggie was a helpless, wispy bit of a woman who was a bit vague about things and a terrible procrastinator. Besides that, however she learned, she became very fond of a drop of spirits, and most of the money that Bridgie sent home went into the reluctant pocket of Paddy's father on account of supplying Maggie with small baby Powers.

Then, five years or so ago, Bridgie returned from America. An employer she was working for had died and left her quite a substantial sum in her will, so Bridgie returned to the land of her forefathers. She was dressed very fashionably when she returned; she wore horn-rimmed spectacles and talked through her nose. She was a formidable-looking woman who had never married, because, the people supposed, she had been too busy making money. Anyhow, back she came. She put the fear of God into her mother when she discovered her failing, and took good care that she would find it hard to get any drink. She issued strict orders to Paddy's father, and to all the pubs in a radius of ten miles, that if they supplied her mother with drink they could do so at their own expense. So Maggie was not at all pleased at the return of her daughter; but there was worse to come. Bridgie decided that the house which had satisfied Maggie and her husband and generations of the McGinnis clan was a pig-sty and an insanitary hole, so she went to a contractor in Clifden, and the next thing the people knew was that Bridgie and her mother had taken up temporary abode in the reclaimed stables, while the old house was pulled down and a two-storey concrete monstrosity with a slated roof gradually took its place.

There is a lot to be said for two-storey concrete houses. They are bright and clean, and sanitary, and they do not harbour the dread germ of the white scourge, but all the same the people liked their thatched cottages, and they look good somehow, snuggling into the rock-strewn soil of Connemara. But up rose Bridgie's new house and it was a marvel. There was one room in it where you just went in and sat

110

down. This seemed the height of luxury to the people, and anyone that was invited in there came out amazed at it, and the seven, or was it eight, lovely kitchen chairs with the soft bottoms on them. The Lord save 's, it was like a Turk's what-you-may-call-ums. There was a wireless set in it too, the very first one in that part of the country, and people would just pass by the house to hear me man with the funny accent talking out of the yoke. Besides that there was a special house built at the back, a lavatory no less, with pipes and yokes, and disinfectants and the divil knows what, and large tanks built up to catch the rain-water and give a permanent supply to the house, and water that was also pumped be a donkey engine, and a big high yoke at the back, too, with a propeller on it and the wind druv it, and it made electricity and stored it in batteries and all you did was press the oul button, and there you were, just like in a town.

Then Bridgie decided that she had endured single blessedness for long enough. Coming home had stimulated her. She no longer had to spare and scrape and worry about getting enough money to get home to Ireland. She felt the need of a man, so she dropped hints that she would refuse no reasonable offer. Immediately all the old bachelors in the neighbourhood called on her, but they were mostly men who had buried several wives and who had not a ha'-penny to bless themselves with, or else old bachelors who, owing to some great criminal defect in themselves, or an unprepossessing appearance, had never found any girl who would be willing to share their bed. Bridgie took one look at them, and having fed them with tea and bread and butter, showed them the road, without even wetting their whistles for them, God forgive her.

Then, one day she had seen Thomasheen, our own nice Thomasheen, thought Stephen, and she had fallen for him. She was her own matchmaker and she had a lot of cards in her hand, because Thomasheen's mother and family were very poor indeed, and the farm they possessed was entirely incapable of supporting them. If Thomasheen married Bridgie, he would be one less mouth to feed in the first place, but there were other advantages. Bridgie made it clear that she would be willing to extend financial aid, to a certain extent, and that she would be willing to have Mary and one of the other children to live with them, because they could work in the house for her anyhow and make themselves generally useful. Also she could give them an extra cow on their own farm. In fact, the fortunes of the family would improve beyond their wildest imaginings.

Thomasheen's mother put it to him, and then, after the first horrified refusal, what could he do? He was a very honest and too-Christian young man, who loved all his brothers and sisters very much indeed. He felt they had been left to him as a sort of legacy from his father, and as well as that, he didn't like the look of some of them – he was afraid that the dread disease that had laid his father low was hitting them, and they had no means of combating that disease, not even the best and simplest weapon of all, a good full stomach. If he did this thing, they would all eat well, and if anything happened, there would be money to get a doctor to look at them before it was too late. So, closing his brain and his heart to the image of Nellie McClure, Thomasheen said 'yes'.

'Look,' said Paddy, 'this is bloody ridiculous! What the hell is wrong with you, Thomasheen? That oul bitch could be your grandmother! No, leave me alone, Father!' Because his father was pulling at his arm. 'I'm going to say this even if Thomasheen never looks at me again. You can't do it, Thomasheen! It's degrading, sordid! You haven't a spark in your heart for her, and you'll regret it to the longest day you live.'

Stephen would have liked to back Paddy up, but what could he do? He knew Thomasheen's family and all about them, and he knew Thomasheen and his liking for his family, and since he, Stephen, had no money to give to Thomasheen (who wouldn't take it anyway), what was the use of fighting something that was as inevitable as the tides?

Thomasheen looked at Paddy.

'Paddy,' he said quietly, 'please don't talk like that. I know the way you feel, and I know the way I feel, and please don't

112

think that I'd do this thing just because I want things to be soft for mesel'. I wint over it in me own mind, and if there had been any way out 'f it, I'd have taken it. So look, Paddy, lave me alone, will y', and don't talk about it any more.'

'No!' shouted Paddy. 'I don't care, Thomasheen! Listen, this is the most awful inhuman thing I have ever heard of. Now listen, Thomasheen . . .'

His words were cut short, because Thomasheen, banging down his glass on the counter, went hurriedly out the door without a word. Paddy followed him and stopped at the door calling 'Thomasheen! Thomasheen!' but Thomasheen didn't look back.

'Why didn't you say something, Stephen?' Paddy asked furiously. 'Why, in the name of God, didn't you stick an oar in?' Stephen could see that there were almost tears in Paddy's eyes. 'I thought you were a friend of his, and yet you sit there and accept it as if it was just something normal when it's the biggest criminal abortion of a marriage that was ever heard of.'

'Will you take it easy, Paddy, and sit down?' said Stephen. 'You're a Connemara man, despite all the foreign schooling, and surely you know, Paddy, that some things are inevitable, and that Thomasheen can no more do otherwise than he is doing than you could lift the mountain out there on the palm of your hand.'

'Here, Paddy,' said his father, 'here's another stout for you, and take it aisy.'

'Paddy,' said Stephen, 'if you were in the position that Thomasheen is in, you would do the very same thing if it was put up to you.'

'No!' said Paddy, banging his fist on the counter, 'I would never sell myself like that! And Thomasheen! If it was anybody else but our nice Thomasheen, that never did anything dirty to anybody else all his life.'

'Paddy,' said Stephen, 'could you take Thomasheen out of it, or could I? Could you take it on yourself to support all his family for the rest of your and their days, in order to save Thomasheen from marrying a woman twice his own age? I feel sorry too, but worse still I feel impotent, because even if either of us were in a position to save Thomasheen now by giving him all the money in the world, do you think he'd take it from us? He would not!'

'Besides,' said Paddy's father charitably, 'she's not such a terrible woman as all that.'

'Oh, for God's sake, Father!' said Paddy, turning his back on them. He stood at the door for a while looking after the retreating figure of Thomasheen merging into the distance.

'Women are bitches!' he said. 'And poverty is a bitch, and I feel sure that this thing would never have happened only for Connemara; and I still think that it is the lousiest thing that I ever heard about and I don't think it will ever leave my mind. If it had been anybody else but Thomasheen!'

'What you want to do,' said Stephen, 'is to change the whole system, so that people can have enough to live on without having to resort to grim things like this. You'll have to change human nature and then find a substitute for poverty.'

'If it had been anyone but Thomasheen!' said Paddy.

Thomasheen went towards the house, fighting back tears which he was ashamed of, because he was a grown man, but it was hard for him to forget Nellie, and to think that he would never touch her again. The day on the island when they heard Stephen's mother was dead had been the start of it. Thomasheen was a shy man to court, and it had taken him nearly five years to get to the stage where he could meet her now at the strand and kiss her and sit beside her, and laugh at her as she chattered away and spent her time pulling his leg about this and that, and looking at him with shrewd eyes that seemed to caress him.

When he reached the house he was able to greet the family with a laugh, even, in fact, able to joke about the wedding when he sat down to his tea and spoke about the grand times they would be having, but it was only his sister Mary who noticed that there seemed to be a furrow coming between the eyes of her brother Thomasheen which had never been there before.

114

CHAPTER EIGHT

The sun was shining, the sea was calm, but there was a very cold nip in the air, and down where the sun was sinking the sky was tinged with bronze clouds that were coming up out of the Atlantic.

Stephen was thankful that they were rowing for home, because, while they had been fishing the long line, the cold had almost frozen his fingers. It had been warmer when they had come out, but all the heat seemed now to have gone out of the sun, and its brightness was unable to heat the haze which was coming between it and the earth. Now and again he could feel the wind on his cheeks as it came in puffs, and the calm sea heaved in places.

'Do you think, Danny,' he asked, 'is there wind behind there?'

Danny continued rowing but looked anxiously back.

'I'm afraid there is, Stephen,' he said, 'but maybe, with the help of God, we'd get home before it breaks on us.'

Stephen turned around for a moment. They were a long way from land, nearly two miles, he thought, and they were the only ones about on the sea. He had noticed some other currachs early on in the day but they had disappeared. Probably they had noticed the sky beginning to look threatening and they had hurried home, because it is not a nice thing to be caught in the Atlantic in a small cockle-shell like a currach when there is a storm ready to come down and beat you into the bosom of the sea.

'If we had turned about when you said to,' said Stephen, 'we'd have been in by now.'

'It's not much good,' said Danny, 'thinking about that now.'

'Greed again,' said Stephen. 'I think it would have been criminal to leave all those cod behind us when we had the luck to run into them.'

'It's better,' said Danny, 'that the cod should be in the sea and we on dry land, than the cod should be in the boat and we in the sea eventually.'

'That's a mixed saying,' said Stephen with a laugh; 'but let us row like the hell now and we'll be home soon. We'll be late for the hooley at Thomasheen's if we don't hurry.'

Thomasheen had been married that morning. Stephen had been at the Mass and had seen him getting married. He had said he couldn't go over to the house for the wedding breakfast, because he had promised Danny that he would go fishing with him. Thomasheen had not been disappointed. He had even seemed relieved, in a way, that Stephen would not be there. He had asked Stephen to be at the hooley that night if he could at all, and Stephen had said yes he would.

Because Bridgie was throwing a great party in the new house and the whole parish nearly was invited, and even those who were not invited would be there, because hooleys are rare things in Connemara; but when they happen everybody is looking forward to them for months, and they dress up in their best bibs and tuckers to go along. Generally it lasts from early on the morning of the wedding until early the following morning. First, the couple are married and then they invite a circle of close friends and relations to the breakfast, which lasts until the afternoon. Then in the afternoon all the older people turn up for a glass of something, a cup of tea, and a piece of cake, and in the night-time all the young people gather to eat and drink and make merry until the small hours of the morning.

Stephen could not put the memory of this morning's marriage out of his head. He could still see Thomasheen inside the altar rails, dressed in a grand new blue suit which had been provided by the bride. He hadn't looked like Thomasheen at all, but like a strange, brooding, silent young man, with a furrowed forehead, whom Stephen felt he was seeing for the first time. The bride had been very well dressed, but after they were married, when she had turned to come down the aisle, hanging on Thomasheen's arm, Stephen had felt shocked. Just as they had passed him, a

116

shaft of sunlight had fallen on them. He could see that she had a lot of paint on her face, and the cruel sunlight had laid it all bare. She wasn't an ugly-looking woman, but her jaws were falling a little at each side and her neck seemed to be very wrinkled. The large spectacles gave her eyes an empty look, and for a horrible moment Stephen was reminded of a grimacing skeleton hanging on the arm of an apple-cheeked child. He almost had to take a grip of the seat to prevent himself from rising up and shouting 'No, no, Christ, this can't go on!' He felt like crying when he looked at Thomasheen, his mouth folded in a straight line and his eyes looking down at the ground. It had been a pleasure after that to come down and launch Danny's currach on the sea and to row hard and fast, and to fish, and to forget.

They had been lucky, too. Their main catch up to late in the day had consisted of hake and whiting, but just when they should have turned for home they ran into the codfish, and nothing would have persuaded Stephen to go home then until they had exhausted the ground. They had been lucky and, all going well, Danny should earn anything up to four pounds on today's outing. If things went well . . . ! Stephen was beginning to doubt it as he looked at the sky, but he knew that once they got into the Priest's Rock, which lay on the lip of the entrance between the Island of Ourish and the mainland, they would be all right.

'I think we ought to make the Priest's Rock all right, Danny,' he said, 'before the main blast hits us.'

'With the help of God we will,' said Danny, 'because I'd like to raise a few of the lobster-pots in there. I promised me man in Clifden that I'd sind 'm in a few be the mail car in the mornin'.'

So they pulled away with even, powerful strokes. It takes knowledge to manage a currach, which looks deceptively light, but it can be as unmanageable as a young untrained filly, or a flighty woman, and it is at a great disadvantage in high seas or waves that break. The weight of fish which they were carrying now did something to make it sit deeper in the water and that would be a help. Danny, who was sitting

117

behind Stephen, couldn't help but admire the width of his shoulders and he could feel the boat jump forward every time the powerful arms tugged at the oars. Oh, a great man in a currach, Danny thought, or a great man at anything. Danny had seen Stephen at work in the fields and on the bog and in boats, and it was the general opinion of the people that he was one of the best men in Connemara. At the sports which were held every year down on Ourish Strand there wasn't a man in it with him throwing the weights around as if they were nothing at all, and he was as fleet on his feet as any light man in the Parish, which was a great thing indeed considering the size of him.

The puffs of wind became more regular now, and more strong, and the advance-guards of the bronze clouds had reached and enveloped the sun, so that the sea lost its bright-green colour and became dark-looking and menacing. The calmness was no more, and the heaving, which had commenced some time ago, became as regular as the wind which was blowing up and carrying an icy sting with it. Behind them Stephen could see where the sea was being whipped white. That was the curse of the sea. One minute it could be so nice and peaceful, and looking into the green waters you thought how nice it would be to be swimming around in it, if it wasn't the month of January and you would freeze to death almost as soon as you put your body into it. All the same, the thought of going into it was not too repellent, but then in a few seconds it could change completely and become a raging monster stretching wide, huge arms to pull you under. Even the men who knew the signs and portents of the sea very well indeed could be fooled.

They were about half-way to the Rock when the storm caught them. First the heaving sea appeared to be flattened into obedience by the wind, and the men sucked in their breaths as the first blast caught them unprepared, and went in and out through them like darting daggers, even though they wore heavy woollen jerseys and bainin coats under their black oilskins. Then the whipped sea, which had been following them like chasing greyhounds, enveloped the boat and for some minutes they were involved in a titanic struggle in order to keep the currach end-on to the waves. They succeeded after a time, and breathed with relief, although the waves were now huge and seemed to be following the boat in order to pour themselves into it.

Stephen was not afraid, but he felt his pulse beat faster, which was a good thing, because generally a man's pulse was sluggish and it did him good to have the blood coursing more freely and more quickly through his veins. He wondered what would happen if the currach was capsized. There would be very little hope of saving their lives because they could not live for very long in the icy water. As it was, the spray which hit their hands now and again seemed to be charged with electric ice which froze the blood. Stephen wondered if he would mind being dead, and at first decided that it wouldn't be too unpleasant, because life at the moment seemed to be so pointless, and everyone around him seemed to be suffering or about to suffer from something, like poor old Thomasheen. Then it would be rather pleasant to have a chat with his mother and a laugh, which he hadn't had for over five years, but then it would be too bad if, despite her belief, there was no such place as another world after all, and if our end was to be like that of a dead dog, just stinking corpses that rotted away into nothingness. He shook away the thought, and decided that after all it would not be so pleasant, because he had a lot to live for. He thought that the things he was writing were steadily improving. They were not world-shaking, if you compared them with the writings of other men, but he thought at the best that they showed promise, and that some day he might be able to write something really good. Then it would be most uncomfortable to die in the very cold water. One would feel better about it if it was the summer-time and you were sucked under the waves into the embrace of nice water with the chill off it at least; and besides there were a lot of people that he wanted to write about, all the people that he had been watching and studying all his life, and he certainly didn't want to die and have the brave Mavis breaking open his box under the bed and sniggering at the things he had written. Stephen laughed aloud as the humour of that reason for not being drowned struck him.

Danny was relieved but slightly shocked to hear him laughing, because he didn't feel a bit like laughing himself. Indeed when they had been caught in the maelstrom a few moments ago he had been offering up frantic prayers to God and all the saints in Heaven to spare him this time, at least until he had a chance to hop around to the Father and make a good confession. But it restored your courage to hear another man laughing at the dangers, and, looking around him now, Danny thought that although the huge waves were enough to turn your blood cold and make your stomach go down to hit your boots, after all he had been out in worse days than this, and nothing had happened. What really restored his courage was the sight he had of all the codfish in the boat, and, suddenly realizing their worth, he thought that it would be criminal to put them back in the sea again, so he took a firmer grip on the oars and put his back into the pulling. Chip, chop, chip, chop went the heavy, narrow-bladed oars in the peculiar circular rhythm of the currach-oaring.

'I don't see anything to laugh about,' he shouted, but the wind whipped the words out of his mouth and carried them into oblivion.

'What's that?' shouted Stephen, having heard something.

'What's so funny?' shouted Danny, leaning forward.

'Nothing,' said Stephen. 'I was just thinking of something else altogether.'

Danny didn't bother replying, because it failed him to understand how in the name a God any man could be out in a bloody sea like this and all the time be thinkin' a somethin' else.

Shortly, assisted by the waves at their tail, which seemed to be fuming that a victim was pulling out from under them every time they got ready to submerge it, they got closer and closer to the Priest's Rock. The waves were not so large near the Rock, because the Island of Ourish was beginning to exert its influence, and was taking a terrible beating on its windward side, but the sea was running much faster because it was running into the channel between the island and the mainland.

So they drove down on the lobster-pots. They could see the heavy cork that anchored them, and, approaching from the windward, they jabbed at the raging water with the oars.

'You keep the oars,' Stephen shouted, 'and I'll lift them.'

'All right,' Danny shouted back, and he manoeuvred for position.

When they reached the first one, Stephen reached over and with one powerful jerk heaved it inboard, but a look showed him that it was empty. If his eyes could have deceived him, his nose couldn't. Lobster-pots are baited with either rotten fish or rotten meat and the more the pieces of bait stink the better your hope of filling the pots, because lobsters are obviously attracted by smell, and the smellier it is the more they are attracted. So they climb into the narrow neck of the pot, gorge themselves on its contents and then discover with dismay, if they have any intelligence, that they can't get out again, unless they retire in reverse position, which they seem to be incapable of doing. The pot that Stephen raised smelled to the high heavens, so he threw it back again and hauled at the second pot, which was attached to the first by a rope. The connections between the pots acted as a sort of an anchor.

The second pot was loaded with one of the dark-green prehistoric-looking animals. For a second Stephen half rose to his feet in order to get it aboard and realized his mistake when it was too late. He was wearing heavy hob-nailed boots, and as he shifted, one of them landed on the head of a leering codfish, a wave came under the bottom of the boat, and almost before Stephen knew it, he was struggling in the raging water.

He didn't hear the frantic shout that Danny let out of him, nor could he see the frantic endeavours which Danny made to bring the boat around and in front of him. Danny was helpless, because the racing ocean had the boat in its grasp and was hurrying it towards the strand.

Stephen managed to raise himself, spluttering. For a few seconds his mind was petrified by the stunning coldness of the water and it was a kind of reflex which made him kick his heavy-shod feet and maintain his head above the waves. He made a grab at the Rock as he was swept past it, and his frantic fingers managed to hold on to a clump of seaweed which was trailing from it. The sea was too strong and swept him onwards, his hand sliding from the slippery weed. Still kicking furiously he turned to face the wind and the waves. Although his head was submerged under the waves several times he managed to struggle out of the oilskin coat, remembering to thank God that he no longer had a mother who would be careful enough to sew on the many steel clips that were missing from it. Then he had a swift look at the shore and saw that it was about thirty yards away, but it was hopeless to try and swim to it because he would have to swim across the big waves. He saw that further along, if he could stay emerged until then, there was a further cluster of rocks about ten yards out from the shore, and that the waves would sweep him more or less into these if he could manage to get a few sideways strokes into them.

Then he realized that he would never make it while he was wearing the heavy boots. They were like the lead-fixings on a diver and were dragging him down, so, taking a good breath and closing his mouth, he attempted to undo them. He was submerged, but the air in his body did not allow him to sink. The sea had not affected the thongs on the boots as yet. The ends were long and when he pulled the lace opened. He came into the fresh air again and breathed some of it, even though he swallowed a large amount of water in the process. Then he kicked off the freed boot with the other one, and, taking another deep breath, went under again and loosened the second lace. He had more trouble kicking that one off with the other sock-covered foot, but at last he breathed a sigh of relief when he parted with it and felt his body more buoyant in the water. It was only then that he understood how cold the water was and he felt his limbs freezing. For a moment he despaired, but then caught hold of himself and saw that he would have to work fast if he hoped to reach the rocks.

His powerful arms, aided by feeble kicks from his legs, managed to pull him a few yards across the waves and then he was swept down upon the rocks. He missed the first one he grabbed at and then saw with fear in his heart that he was being shot between the last two remaining rocks, and he knew that if he failed to catch one of them, his number was up, and he would be meeting his mother sooner than he had expected. A frantic kick and a jump in the water brought him within reach of the inner rock and he wrapped a strong arm around it.

It was only then that he understood the power of the flowing tide which was being driven by a mighty wind. He knew he would never be able to hold on, because the under-current around the rock was sweeping his feet outwards and tugging at the rest of him. He attempted to get his other arm around the rock, and failed. A kind of dimming lassitude was beginning to descend on his brain, and when his eyes were free of the water that was hitting the rock and submerging him, he noticed that there seemed to be a mist over them. The strength seemed to be slowly ebbing away from his body and he hardly felt his arm slipping away from its anchor.

Then something hit him in the face and with a failing gesture of defence he raised his hand to ward it off, and found his numbed fingers grasping what he thought was a heavy rope.

The very feel of it, imaginary or not, brought the strength back into him and he clutched it, and discovered that it was a rope as he felt his body being held against the flow of the tide. He managed to open his eyes then, saw it was a rope, and also saw a dim figure amongst rocks on the mainland. So he brought his other hand to the rope and held it with a grip which he would never relinquish, and to his own amazement felt himself being pulled towards land, but very slowly. He came awake then, and using the rope as a lever, and assisted by a pull from the shore, he hauled himself with desperate strength into the land.

The feel of ground under his feet did much to restore him, although he was unconscious of the pounding which his body was receiving from the waves dashing him against the rocks. Then he felt strong arms hauling him, and soon he was lying out of the clutch of the sea, spread-eagled on the ground with his face gratefully pressed into the small stones that littered the shore.

When he felt less weak, he turned over on his back and looked up at the sky. His body felt numbed and was hot and cold at the same time, if that could be. Then a face floated into his vision, and when he saw it was the face of a girl, he sat up hurriedly and made a mistake at so doing, because all the sea-water which he had swallowed proceeded to come up into his throat and, mumbling an apology, he went as quickly as he could towards the sea and became sick into it. It was a most unpleasant feeling, but he thought weakly that he was giving back to the sea something which the sea had given him, and that there was a kind of poetic justice in that. The spasms of sickness occupied him for quite a time, but he felt much better when the last of it had left him. Then he wiped his mouth with sea-water, an action which caused him more weak amusement, and turned to have a good look at his rescuer.

She was standing, framed against the sky, looking at him. He went closer to her and examined her deliberately. She was a tall girl and a well-built girl. She had very black hair that was curling naturally; strong, black, well-shaped eyebrows above brown eyes, long-lashed; a nose that was inclined to curve as it met her mouth, which was a clean-cut mouth, strong and just the least bit set. Her breasts were high and full, she had a narrow waist, and he could see from the way that the wind shaped the dress to her legs that she was built neatly in proportion.

She was smiling under his scrutiny.

'Do I pass the examination?' she asked, and her voice was deep and melodious.

'First-class honours,' said Stephen. 'I suppose you know that if it hadn't been for you I'd have been waving about the bottom of the ocean now like a dog in a sack?'

'It was lucky I was around here,' she said.

'Yes,' said Stephen, 'it was very lucky, but what I want to know is just how you happened to be around. I have never been a great believer in destiny, but it is a queer thing that you should happen to be just here at this particular spot, with a rope in your hand, at the right time. What I'm after is that it's very funny and inclines one to the belief that an awful lot of things are written down in a book somewhere and that somebody says, "Hello, this is the day to give that O'Riordan fellow a ducking and a fright and to have the young lady along at the right time to fire a rope to him. Get going, boys!" How did you happen to be around?'

'It's easy to answer, so it is,' said the girl. 'You know the McClures in on the island? Well, they're sort of related-like to us, and I went in there today to get back the rope which they borrowed from 's last harvest to tie their hay on the cart taking it home. And I hadn't much to do, so I went in today and got it, and we had some tea and I came out before the tide 'd get me. And then I came up this end of the mainland to see how our sheep were that we have grazing up here and I was watching the currach and wondering who was in it. And I saw the sea catching you, and then I saw you lifting the pots and I waited to see if you'd got anything, and the next minute I saw you falling into the water. I was sure you were finished, and then I saw you coming up again and taking off the coat and vanishing and coming up again; and then I thought I saw you looking at these rocks here and I knew they were the only hope you had, so I came down to them and flung the old rope and you happened to catch it.'

In fact she had been practically frightened to death and the thought that she was about to witness a man drowning had made her weak at the knees. She could have been quicker with the rope if she had not been almost petrified with fright, but then something had come to her aid, woken her from her fear, and caused her to fling the rope at the right time. She was very glad now that she had. She would have been glad, of course, had it been anybody else, but, looking at Stephen, she was very glad it happened to be he, because he was such a fine-looking fellow, better built than her brothers even, and he was very presentable too, and even his standing up there now, in his stocking feet and his clothes clinging wetly to his body, he looked very well, and she was doubly glad that she had been around to fling the rope, and she felt her heart beating a little faster as she saw him looking at her with warm, calm eyes.

'Hadn't you better go home or something,' she said, 'or you'll die from the cold anyhow, and then all the rope-throwing will have been useless?'

Stephen laughed at that.

'How did you manage to get a pull on me?' he asked. 'I'm no lightweight and there was a heavy sea running in.'

'I took a hitch around the rock,' she answered. 'And I think you better get home quick now.'

Stephen approached closely to her.

'Let me shake your hand once,' he said, and he took her hand in his own. His hand was almost numb with cold and wet. Her hand was a large and useful one and he felt it warm in his own. 'By all the rights I should be glad to be rescued from the sea, but should be cursing because it was a girl that did it for me. Because let me tell you that in our Connemara a woman is still regarded more or less as a pack-horse and it is a shameful thing for her to do something useful. But you got me out, and since I think my life is very precious indeed, I will always thank you.'

She pulled her hand away, and felt a little embarrassed.

'You better go home now,' she said.

'What's your name?' Stephen asked. 'I have seen you about all right. I remember you now, but you must be from the other side.'

'I'm from Crigaun,' she said, 'and my name is Kathleen Finnerty.'

'Are you, by any chance,' Stephen asked, 'a sister of Malachai?'

'I am,' she said, 'and if he heard that I pulled Stephen O'Riordan out of the sea, I'm afraid that he would be kind of sorry.'

'Ah, God, that's too bad,' said Stephen, laughing. 'Imagine that now! You know Michilin so, don't you?'

'I do,' said Kathleen. 'I hear all about him morning, noon, and night during the fishing season.'

'Michilin often spoke about you and said what a diff ... well, never mind. I'm glad, Miss Finnerty, that you were about at the right time, and if I can do the same thing for you some other time I will be delighted.'

'Thanks,' she said, laughing, 'but you'll never get the chance to pull me out of the sea. I don't like it.'

'My love for it has waned considerably,' said Stephen. At that moment there was the sound of running feet and, turning, they saw Danny coming towards them. He stopped short at a distance, and Stephen could see that his face was pale. He approached.

'Well, thank God, Stephen,' he said, 'but I never thought I'd see you alive again, so I didn't. I pulled in the oul boat there below and came back to look for your corpse. What happened?'

'Miss Kathleen Finnerty here,' said Stephen, 'happened to be around with a rope and she threw it to me at the right time.'

'The blessin's a God on you, Miss Finnerty,' said Danny, taking her hand and shaking it between his own two. 'I would never have forgiven myself if anythin' happened to 'm.'

'Ah, forget it, will ye?' Kathleen asked. 'And you better go now or he'll die of something anyhow.'

'Come on, Stephen, for God's sake,' said Danny. 'Hadn't you better chase across the land?'

'No,' said Stephen, 'I'll go back with the currach. I don't like running all over the country in my feet. Look, Miss Finnerty, I don't suppose you'll be going over to Thomasheen's hooley tonight, will you?'

'I will,' said Kathleen.

'That's great,' said Stephen. 'I'll see you over there, then, and maybe be able to thank you properly.'

'All right,' she answered, and then the two men hurried away, where below a dip in the land Danny had pulled the currach in and beached it. She didn't move from where she was until she saw the boat out of the water and running in towards the strand with the sea behind it. She saw an arm waving at her. Then she waved back, hoisted the heavily wet rope on her shoulder, and commenced the long trek home to Crigaun.

The two men didn't talk much. Danny was too relieved at what had happened, and afraid to say much in case he would get soft, and Stephen was thinking about the girl.

I suppose, he thought, no matter what girl would save your life, you would look on her as a special sort of person, but he realized that Malachai's sister had affected him in a peculiar heart-warming way, even though he was now shivering with the cold and the discomfort of wet clothes sticking to him was uncomfortably distracting. But something had seemed to click inside him when he had looked into her eyes the first time. Unlike most other young fellows in Connemara, Stephen had never taken to running after the girls. He had been very busy in his spare time with his secret writings, which meant getting to his room as early as possible when all the farm work was done. Then he was always inclined to judge girls according to the person of his mother whom he had set up on a tall pedestal, and they had as much hope of reaching her, by now out of proportion, stature, as they had of flying to the moon.

So he had been a distinct failure at all kinds of dances and parties where the main purpose of the evening seemed to be to pick the lady of your choice, and then, according to Paddy, 'to coort hell out of her in the haggard'. Of course, adolescence had taught him what his main function in life was, and he had his young dream of beautiful women, but the girls in Connemara whom he had met to date had never moved him to any great lustful or romantic feelings. He had liked Thomasheen's Nellie – poor Nellie, and poorer Thomasheen. He wouldn't have minded, perhaps, kissing her and holding her hand under a harvest moon on Ourish Strand, but then he felt more friendly towards her than anything else, and if he had to proceed to coort her it would have been something more in the nature of a performance that one did – the accepted custom – than the real McCoy.

But Kathleen Finnerty had moved him, somehow, in a vague way which caused stirrings deep down in him, and made his breath come a little faster, and although he thought it might be the fact that she had saved his life, he had a feeling that it was more than that, and he thought that attending Thomasheen's wake, as he called it in his own mind, would be less of a hateful duty now, and more of an enjoyment.

They were in the shelter of the mainland and the island both, and the sea was just a pocket edition of what it was outside, but Stephen was becoming aware of the terrible cold, and also, as the numbness wore off, he felt that he was very sore and stiff in places where he had been presumably pounded by the sea against the rocks.

Their journey was soon over and they pulled the currach up on the sands at the lane leading up to the main road.

'Will you go home now, Stephen, for God's sake,' said Danny, 'and dry yourself out and get into some dry clothes, or you'll go down with pneumonia or somethin'?'

'All right, Danny,' said Stephen. 'I'll be off. Will you be going over to Thomasheen's tonight?'

'I will, with the help of God,' said Danny.

'I'll see you there so,' said Stephen, and turned off, running up the road; but he had to stop running after a time and set down to a slow jog-trot, because he was aching all over as if a giant had been pounding him on the body with a telegraph pole.

CHAPTER NINE

That evening, Mavis had been making a cake when Martin had come home. He had quite a lot of drink taken. His face was more flushed than was usual, and this, combined with the cold wind, made his nose look like the Shakespeare song. He was no longer the tall strong man that had gone to Galway to meet Martha so many years ago. His head was falling in a little on his shoulders, his hair was sparse, his body leaner. Nevertheless he still looked immensely strong, like a pucaun, no longer newly built, still capable of breasting the roughest seas. He removed his overcoat and looked over at the girl.

She was kneading the dough and there was flour up to her elbows, which were neatly rounded and nicely fleshed. Martin had had many girls from round about and from Galway and Clifden since Martha had died, but all of them had been unsatisfactory. He still, when his thoughts became too much for him, lost his temper to an alarming degree, and most of the girls had been unable to put up with this constant threat of the Master breaking into a nerve-shattering fury. Also, if they had been any way presentable, he could never resist attempting to seduce them, and he always woke the morning after the attempt to find that he had to start the search again for a new maid.

He soon found it impossible to get any girl to come near the house of Martin O'Riordan in Killaduff. He didn't know it, but the word had spread that he was no man to trust your daughter with, so he had to go much further afield. He had found Mavis in Dublin, where he had gone to attend the funeral of his brother, the Father O'Riordan who had been such a friend of Martha's. He had gone into an employment agency there and had succeeded in getting Mavis. He had never stopped to think why a girl like her, with all the accomplishments of a successful barmaid, should have been willing to bury herself in a farmer's house in the heart of Connemara. Actually she had just done a term in prison for petty theft from her last employer. She had been once let off under the Probation Act, so she had been finding it very hard to get work as a maid in Dublin. She had thought that it would be a grand way to spend the winter to go to a farmer's house, even in Connemara.

Martin had found it hard to understand her. She had a hard streak in her which made him diffident of attempting to approach her on intimate terms. She was not like any woman he had met before, and this streak of hardness which he had noticed, and her obvious contempt for himself, made him interested in her. He tried to get her to talk to him, but the results were negligible. She always answered him in monosyllables like 'Yeh', 'Um', 'Do say', 'Funny', 'Now', and so on, and she seemed to have a perpetual Woodbine hanging from the side of her mouth. She was not a good maid by any means. Her work was sloppy, and if he said anything to her about this, things seemed to become more sloppy and the house more untidy, and more things were left for himself and Stephen to do. So he had learned to take things as they were.

In one of the few conversations which he had with his son, Stephen had asked him why he didn't get rid of her, and he had muttered about it being impossible to get girls now, they were all going to England where the wages and terms were becoming very attractive. Actually he kept her because he found that he was interested in her. It was so unusual for him to find anyone who remained completely unmoved by his anger or his animal appeal, which he had been relying on unconsciously all his life. He wanted to find out what made Mavis Mahoney move and have her being, and trying to make her react to him kept his mind off other things which he didn't want to think about.

Stephen, all these years, remained in ignorance of the reputation which his father had acquired; but this was natural, because whereas his father was one of the most actively disliked men in the parish on account of his

131

taciturnity and rudeness to his neighbours, Stephen was very popular, and was always being compared to his mother, the Lord have mercy on her, and how fortunate it was for him that he took after her instead of that quiet oul divil of a father of his that wouldn't bid you the time of the day. So the people never mentioned Martin in the presence of his son. Stephen remained as friendly with Martin as that man would allow him, and he respected him, not as his father, but as the husband of his dead mother, and it would never strike him in a million years that his father, having had the honour to live with his mother, could look at another woman.

Apart from a casual glance which she threw at him when he entered, Mavis continued with her cake-making. The drink he had taken made Martin more brave, so he went over towards her now, saying:

'It's a very cold night, isn't it?'

She grunted in reply.

She always wore very thin clothes in the house, and whenever she bent or stooped her figure was always outlined. Going closer to her now, Martin reached forward and put his two hands on her thighs. Where another woman would have screeched or pulled away, Mavis just continued with her cake as if a fly had landed which she couldn't be bothered brushing off. This annoyed him, so he caught her by the shoulder, turned her around and pulled her close to him.

'What kind of a girl are you at all?' he asked her, with a touch of hoarseness in his high voice.

'Listen, mister,' she said, 'I didn't come here for any business like that. I'm here, and I'm getting underpaid enough for the work I do without that thrown in, so would you let me go now until I get back to my cake?'

'I suppose you've been saying that all your life,' he sneered, 'whenever a man put his hands on you?'

'No man,' she answered, 'is going to get away with anything with me until I have a marriage certificate locked away in the old oak chest.'

'Is that so?' he said, pulling her closer.

'That's enough now,' she said. 'It isn't a little Connemara

girl you have in it now. My name is Mavis Mahoney, remember. I'm from Dublin, and I'm well able to look after myself.'

'Is that what you were after coming to Connemara?' he asked. 'Did you think that all you had to do was to come here and that you'd be ending up in a church wedding with me?'

'I don't think that I would like to be married to you, Mister O'Riordan,' she said bitingly.

'What's wrong with me?' he asked. 'Tell me that? What's wrong with me?'

The latch of the door lifting made him release her as if she was a hot poker out of the fire, and then they saw Stephen standing in the doorway, his clothes sodden and crinkled. Stephen didn't notice anything out of the ordinary. He was too cold and stiff. He came in quickly and closed the door behind him.

'What happened you?' his father asked.

'We had an accident,' said Stephen, 'and I fell into the sea. Would you get me the big basin, and a kettle of hot water, Mavis? I want to dry myself out and change my clothes.' He went over and pulled a chair in front of the fire. He removed his dripping socks and held his feet out to the blaze of the turf fire.

'That's a funny thing to happen,' said Martin.

'It wasn't funny for me,' said Stephen, discarding his bainin coat and pulling his shirt over his head.

'Hurry up with the tea when you're ready,' said Martin to Mavis. 'Is there a fire in my room?'

'Yes,' said Mavis, 'there is.' She looked after him sardonically as he went up to his own room banging the door after him.

'Here's the basin,' she said, leaving it on the floor in front of the fire. 'I'll get you the towel.'

'Thanks,' said Stephen, standing only in his trousers. He went to his own room beside the fire, and quickly gathering together a clean shirt, socks, and his new navy-blue suit, came down to the kitchen again and left them within reach.

Then he poured the kettle of water into the large basin of cold water, testing it with his hand until it was sufficiently hot.

'Would you mind turning your back now?' he said to Mavis, who was handing him the towel.

'Don't mind me,' said Mavis, going back to her cake.

Stephen stepped out of his trousers and into the basin and proceeded to rub himself briskly with soap and the hot water. That and the great heat coming from the open fire soon reduced him from a state of shivering numbness, until a warm glow began to steal over his body. He thought that it was almost worth being thrown into the sea to be able to feel himself getting warm again. Looking down at his body he could see places on it which were as black as a sod of turf and sore to the touch. Then there were other places where the rocks had peeled the skin away from his flesh until he looked like a badly plucked fowl, and the carbolic soap touching him literally on the raw made him draw in his breath.

It was this that made Mavis turn and look at him. His back was towards her, and she regarded his enormous body with admiration tinged with dislike, because she had tried hard to make Stephen see in her a girl who would be glad to do business with him, and he had always treated her either with coldness or else simply ignored her. Like now. He just carelessly says to her, would you mind turning your back, and then stripped himself naked before her as if she was a domestic animal that didn't matter. When Mavis had come first she had liked the look of Stephen and she had decided that it would be a nice thing to marry him, maybe, and settle down until the old man died. He obviously had money, and if she could marry Stephen, they could sell out the place and beat it to Dublin. She had always understood that country boys were easy to get, because they had not the sophistication of their brothers of the town, who would recognize Mavis, and class her immediately. So Stephen should have been easy.

Mavis was wrong, because nothing which she could do, none of the charms which she possessed and which she had used to advantage many times on the sons of her employers, seemed to work with Stephen. She had the oul fella eating out of her hand already, but he would be a poor reward in place of his son, whose flesh was as firm as anything and with those bulging muscles he'd be a marvellous man to have for a lover and a husband into the bargain if the old man would snuff it in a few years and leave some of the dough behind him. At the rate he was going now, there couldn't be much left when he departed the earth, and besides he was nearly as strong as his son yet, although he must be well over fifty, and then he didn't seem to like the son much, and maybe when he died he'd leave the whole thing to a cousin that nobody had ever heard of. God, before she'd let that happen she'd almost marry the oul fella herself, so she would, and then, she thought, me brave Stephen'd hate like hell having me for a stepmother. That'd teach the bloody hayseed a thing or two, I'll tell you, and I'd make life very uncomfortable for 'm, you bet your sweet life I would.

Stephen was soon washed, rubbed down and dried, dressed in a clean shirt and the trousers of his blue suit, his Sunday suit. The Sunday suit in Connemara, and indeed in all country places, is a necessity. You may go around all the rest of the week dressed like a tramp or a slave, but you must have your Sunday suit ready for Mass and all outings which require respectability, and men who do not possess a Sunday suit owing to poverty or other reasons are scarcely ever seen abroad on Sunday, not even at Mass. Nobody can say why, but the colour of the suit must be navy blue, and the choice of a shirt is left to the good sense of the wearer. It is generally a white shirt with blue perpendicular stripes and a collar is scarcely ever worn. You just put a brass stud in the front, and there you are, any girl's fancy. The only change Stephen made in his attire was that he did not wear the brass stud, and he left the neckband of his shirt open.

He went up to his room then, and carefully shaved himself. When he came down the tea was on the table, and the three of them sat down to eat it in silence.

* * *

Meanwhile, in a house three miles away in Crigaun, Kathleen Finnerty was in her bedroom washing herself. The Finnerty house lay on the side of a green hill overlooking the sea. There was a beautiful bay below, formed by the mainland and the high island of Ottermore which lay like a small Ireland two miles out in the sea. Below, the village of Crigaun nestled in against low cliffs, and it was a much more populated place than the village of Killaduff. There was a large quay there, where many pucauns and gleoidhteoigs were stretching short stumpy masts above the wall. A good business was carried on with the Island of Ottermore, which was heavily populated. Why it should be heavily populated nobody seemed to know, because it was not a very fruitful island, apart from the fish, and even the people of the mainland with their thin scratches of earth were at a loss to understand how in the name a God the islanders managed to live at all.

The Finnerty house was a three-roomed cottage which was carefully kept. It was better kept, as most of the people said, than the three brutes that inhabited it, because none of the people liked the Finnertys. There is something in the Irish nature anyhow that dislikes bailiffs. This is probably accounted for by the fact that bailiffs had always played a sinister part in the history of the people. Bailiffs were not always men, like now, who kept a constant patrol in the fishing season to see that none of the people managed to sneak an oul salmon or sea-trout out of the preserves of the wealthy. The bailiff had always been the iron hand inside the velvet glove. He had been the mouthpiece and strong right arm of the absentee landlord. His had been the hand which had set the torch to the thatch, the hand to the furniture, the halter on the seized cow, the whip to the hide, or the gun to the breast. It may seem unbelievable why any landlord should have been interested in throwing Connemara people off their bare patches of earth. What earthly use, you might say, could he make of that barren soil? Not much, perhaps, but he wanted to rear sheep on it, and it was cheaper to rear sheep than to rear people, particularly the type of people who inhabited this god-forsaken wilderness, nasty peasant types, who would split a bailiff's skull as soon as they'd look at him, or plaster a peeler with stones from behind a wall.

So the name bailiff, now not even a shadow of its former greatness, remained a sinister one in the minds of the people. Apart from that, a good Connemara man just naturally hates anything that smacks of compulsion. Then the three Finnerty men, Malachai, Tim, and Jack, were very black-looking, very lowering-looking, and also very big-built men, and their appearance did nothing to make them appeal to either the mind or the eye. They were heartily hated and cordially disliked, and they would have been damned utterly by one and all only for their sister Kathleen. The people were very fond of Kathleen, because she took after her mother, the Lord have mercy on her, and it was a relief when she was called to her account, having that black bastard for a husband and three whelps for sons that'd gut yeh as soon as they'd look at yeh, God save 's. Kathleen's mother died before the old man passed on, and everyone was glad she had got that relief; and when the oul fella died, they cursed the seven daylights out of him but turned up to his funeral in strength, as if they were all unanimously glad to see the end of him and as if they had been looking forward to his funeral for years. Michilin, who had particular cause to dislike him, expressed the opinion at his funeral that he was bound to be roasting down in hell and that the divil better look to his battalions or he'd find himself oney second in command. And one and all shushed Michilin and said he ought to be ashamed of himself, and reminded him that mebbe even Judas was in Heaven, and to speak well of the dead and all that pishtush, and all the time they were chuckling inside themselves and saying aside in a whisper, On me oath it's true for 'm, so it is.

Kathleen had her room very neat and clean. The furnishings were severe, consisting of an iron bedstead, a press for her clothes, a few chairs, and a small table. But there were nice coloured curtains draping the window, and the

137

prints of the Blessed Virgin and Our Lord hanging on the walls were not too outrageously cheap-looking. Before her father had died some years ago, Kathleen had been working as a servant in England, so she had lost a lot of the country ways, and also a lot of the flat way of speaking. She had returned from England when her father had died, and the men had persuaded her to stay and help them. In their own dark way they were fond of her, as if amazed that anything so presentable could have been forged from the loins of their father. Besides, she liked Connemara, as long as she knew she could get out of it again when she wished.

She had a basin on the small table and she was washing her face vigorously with soap and water. The slip she was wearing was eloquent proof of her sojourn in England, because it was a very good one, and very pretty, like all the hidden clothes which women wear. Keeping her eyes shut to keep out the soap, she fumbled for the door of the room, opened it, and shouted down to the kitchen:

'Hey, Nora, will you fire me up the towel, please? I forgot it.'

Nora was a girl from the other side of the mountains who had had the good fortune or misfortune, whichever way you look at it, of having met and married the brother of Kathleen who was called Tim. She soon appeared carrying the towel. She was a small, fat, sloppy-looking girl. Her clothes were too tight for her and her dress gaped under her arms where it needed stitching. Her face was blotched in places, and she was pregnant. She was wearing the big heavy man's boots which housewives in Connemara don when they have dirty jobs to do like going out to the pig-sty, or into the stables to milk the cows. She wore an air of discontent.

'Here y'are,' she said. 'Isn't it well for you to be going off to the hooley?'

'Why don't you come along too?' said Kathleen through the towel.

'Such a thing to say,' said Nora, 'and me this way! I'd look nice at a hooley now, wouldn't I?'

'Sure nobody'd mind that,' said Kathleen, thinking that

Nora was so insignificant that nobody would notice whether she was there or not.

'Wouldn't all the wans,' said Nora, 'be puttin' their eyes through me like six-inch nails, an' countin' up the time since the day I was married to see if thin's were wrong or right? Oh, I know them!'

'That's only silly talk,' said Kathleen, drying her arms.

'And then, I've nothing to wear, either,' said Nora in a sort of a fat whine. 'It's all right for you, so it is; you have all the clothes that you brought back from England with you, but I was never in England, so I wasn't. Did that cost much now, tell me?' she asked, fingering the slip.

'Ah, I forget now, so I do,' said Kathleen, trying to be patient, because Nora went on this way all the time, about you having this and that, and sly digs about we all can't have that because we weren't in England, so we weren't. Nora never seemed to be able to catch up with her work, and it always devolved on Kathleen to finish everything for her. Now that she was expecting a baby, what with getting sick and everything, she seemed to reach today's jobs some time next week.

'Did you milk the cows?' Kathleen asked, just so that she could have something to say.

'I did,' said Nora, sitting on a chair, with Kathleen wishing that she'd get to hell out of it, so that she could dress properly and think about Stephen O'Riordan. 'And it's freezing out now, too, and I nearly slipped comin' in, and me heart was jumpin'. I don't feel too well at all, so I don't, and I think it's terrible the thin's women have teh put up with, so I do.'

'You're bound to feel bad for a while longer,' said Kathleen.

'Ah, you don't know what it's like at all because you're single,' said Nora. I'll know all about it before long, thought Kathleen, because there's very little that you try to hide from me. Then she chided herself for being so impatient with Nora, but in order to save herself more revolting revelations which she knew were coming, she said:

'Nora, would you ever pass me up my stockings? They're down drying in front of the fire.'

'All right,' said Nora, rising, 'although I can't see what any girl wants to be wearing silk stockings in Connemara for, so I don't.' She went down to the kitchen.

Kathleen pulled a plain white silk blouse over her head and then pulled on the skirt of her costume. It was dark green and fitted her figure very neatly indeed. She took the stockings from Nora at the door, saying that she would be down in a minute. Sitting down, she pulled on the stockings very carefully, because to ladder silk stockings in Connemara is a tragedy. You can't run across the street to buy a new pair, even if you had the money, and when you had the money it meant a journey all the way to Clifden on the bicycle to get them. When she had them on, she held them out in front of her to admire her legs, and thought it a very nice-shaped leg even if I say it myself, and she remembered with a reminiscent smile the way the lads at the corner used to whistle after her legs in England, the time she was working in London, and walking down Ealing Broadway.

Then she put her feet into her best shoes which were shaped like a court shoe, but had a medium heel that suited her build. She spent a long time in front of the mirror doing her long, long hair, although its natural curl didn't appear to need much doing. Next she powdered her face and carefully applied the Connemara-despised lipstick.

This was a major source of quarrel between herself and her brothers, and indeed any of the young girls in Connemara who dared to use lipstick in front of their parents were in for a hot time of it. Nobody seemed to know why everybody else disliked it so much. It was probably a relic of the days when the people believed that the parish priest had the power to turn them into ducks and drakes if he so willed, and that all the notorious whores of the Bible were quoted as be-painted Jezebels. However it was, the prejudice against it was very strong, but the frequent comings and goings of the young girls to work in England and the Irish cities were doing much to kill the antipathy. The colleen of the romantic novel, with her naturally blooming cheeks and her ripe, red apple-blossomed lips, was always a figment of the imagination of authors, and had no foundation in fact, because everybody in the world now appears to have something wrong with their stomachs, and everybody knows that the condition of your stomach governs the colour of your lips; and anybody who saw a Connemara girl neatly lipsticked and powdered standing beside a companion with pale lips and freckles, realized that nature had a lot to learn about a face. So the young girls argued, and who can say that their argument was a vain one, and why on earth should a streak of red, expertly applied, break up a friendship?

When Kathleen reached the kitchen, her three brothers were seated around the table, and looked at her when she came in. They were very big men all right and seemed to fill the kitchen. It was to Malachai that you would first look, because his was the dominating personality of the trio, apart from his being the eldest. The Finnertys were not too badly off, because as well as the farm which they ran, and which was a sizeable one, between them they were drawing nearly sixty pounds a year out of bailiffing the fishing in summer and the shooting in winter. They ate well and the table was piled with thickly cut slices of home-made cake, deeply buttered with the yellow and freshly churned butter. Also they each had enormous plates in front of them loaded with eggs and fried salt bacon. A dribble of grease was flowing down Jack's chin.

Of them all Kathleen was least fond of Jack. He was the shortest of the three and he never spoke much. He was very taciturn and anything he wanted to say, said it with a beck of the head or a grunt, and when he was put to it, he would only speak in monosyllables. Tim was fatter-faced and more good-humoured-looking; whether this was caused by his being married or not, it was hard to say, because he rarely spoke to his wife Nora, unless it was time to go to bed.

'Y've got that stuff on your face agin,' said Malachai accusingly.

'So what?' Kathleen asked pertly.

141

'So nothing,' answered Malachai, 'except that it makes you look rale cheap, that's all.'

'Aye,' said Tim, grinning, 'like a street woman, so it does.'

'That's my business,' said Kathleen, pulling into the table and sitting down.

'It's a funny thing you're sitting down to eat,' said Tim, 'when you're going out to a hooley. Wouldn't you think they'd be something to eat there? That old haybag has plenty a money.'

'I wonder,' said Nora, who had been filling the teapot with hot water and coming back to leave it on the table, 'if poor Thomasheen'll get much of it.'

'Divil a fear 'f 'm,' said Tim. 'That oul wan has it tied up in a stockin' an' she'll make 'm work hard for every pinny she gives 'm.'

'Well, that's his business,' said Kathleen, biting into a piece of bread.

'Wasn't he a quare fella,' said Nora, sitting into the table, 'to let poor Nellie McClure down like that, and he goin' with her for five years nearly?'

'He wasn't the first man,' said Tim, 'to dump a girl for the wan with the money.'

'He couldn't help it,' said Kathleen.

'You didn't say,' said Jack suddenly, 'you pulled that O'Riordan out of the sea.'

All of them looked up at this.

'What do you mean?' Malachai asked.

Jack nodded his head to Kathleen, who was trying hard not to blush and cursing him under her breath. He was leering at her angry stare.

'When did this happen?' Malachai asked her.

'Oh, today,' said Kathleen, 'when I was coming home from McClures' with the cart rope. They were lifting the lobster-pots and the sea caught him and he fell in. I threw him a rope, that's all.'

'It'd be a bloody good job if he was drowned,' said Malachai viciously.

'You better not be gettin' soft with that fella,' said Tim,

142

'because we don't like him at all, an' we wouldn't like our sister gettin' soft with him, so we wouldn't.'

'Ah, shut your dirty mouth,' said Kathleen furiously, rising from the table. 'Would I be expected to let a man drown just because ye don't like him on account of him takin' a few oul fish outa me man's lake?'

'They's no need to get so floostered about it,' said Tim.

'What I do is me own business,' said Kathleen; 'and wasn't it quick you got the wind a the word, anyhow?' she said, glaring at Jack.

'I have a way a picking things up,' he grunted.

'Yes,' said Kathleen, 'and a way of tryin' to make trouble too. I'm goin' now.' And she pulled on the jacket of her costume. 'What's it like outside now, Nora? Would I need a coat, do you think?'

'It won't rain, anyhow,' said Nora. 'I think it's freezing, and I better light the lamp, too, it's getting dark.' She rose to her feet, sighing audibly as if to point out all she had to do, while Kathleen there could go gadding off to hooleys.

'Don't be coming in here too late now,' said Malachai.

'I'm not a child, am I?' asked Kathleen. 'I'll come in whenever I like. It's seldom enough we have anything to go to.'

She went out the door then, before any more admonitions could come her way. She was angry that Jack had found out about what had happened, and as she walked down the road into the gathering dusk, she hoped that many more people hadn't heard about it, because they might start codding Stephen, and he might think the less of her then, and not have any time for her.

CHAPTER TEN

It was a very cold night, with a piercing wind coming from the north, and a misty, cold-looking moon riding high in the sky. Most of the lads of the village were gathered at the gable-end of a house opposite the new dwelling of Bridgie McGinnis, now, since the early hours of the morning, bearing the honourable title of Mrs Thomasheen Flannery.

Gable-ending is a favourite occupation of the Irish country people at any time. Many a reputation has been shattered for ever, and many a young girl has been coorted furiously and successfully at a gable-end. It is the poor man's Dail, the village hall, and recreation ground rolled into one. A convenient gable-end abutting on a public road could tell more tales, if it had the power of speech, than the best seanachie that ever lived or will ever live in the future.

Tonight it sheltered the lads from the cold blast as they waited for the old people to leave the house of celebration and give them their chance of fun, and food, and dancing until the early hours of the morning. The door of the house was open and a bright rectangle of yellow light was illuminating the night. Within could be seen the figures of the old people as they gurgled their mugs of porter and talked about this and that in the slow ponderous way of the aged.

Michilin had been the first to arrive at the gable-end. By all the rights of seniority he should have been inside with the old people and then retired at a respectable hour to make way for the youth, but all the people knew that Michilin was great gas, and that no do would be complete without him, because he kept a party going when it was in danger of petering out. He always got a great welcome at wakes, and he could talk for long hours about the good points of the dead man, the Lord have mercy on him, and how he did such a thing in 1914, and another thing five years later, until the relatives of the dead felt that they were sheltering the corpse of a mighty man and that they didn't half appreciate him when he was alive and they really ought to be ashamed of themselves. So, in order more or less to placate the dead, they would ply Michilin with porter until it almost came out through his eyes. But Michilin was a great porter drinker. That was recognized on all sides and nobody would ever dispute it.

First on the field, he was shortly joined by some of the

young men. They were dressed in their blue suits and they shone with cleanliness, so that you could see the moon reflected on the sides of their faces where they had shaved themselves into the bone, almost. They were excited and ready for anything, and they were all looking forward very much to the night. There is very little in Connemara to amuse the people, which perhaps is why most of the young are deserting the farms of their fathers like migrating birds. The moralists tell them that they should be happy with their lot, that the moving pictures wouldn't be good for their minds anyhow, and they say, stick around the farm, my boy, and grow vegetables and food for the love of Ireland and the profit of the great city middleman. Why, in the name of God, they say, does a country boy need amusement? Wouldn't the pictures and the theatre and going to those town dances only ruin his primitive mind? What, in the name of God, does he want anything else for? If he did an honest day's work in the fields, he'd be too tired at the end of it to feel that he should have some kind of amusement.

Fair enough, but then why should this same class of gentleman go on a rampage when he hears that the number of illegitimate children in the country districts is appalling, and when he sees the court-room filled with people from the country who have maimed sheep, or stolen turf, or attacked another man from behind a wall and beaten him into unconsciousness with a pointed rock? The answer is, say the intelligent countrymen, that you must give the young man something else to amuse himself with after dark than playing around with girls, or nursing grudges about this and that, and if you give him a look at a few good looking acting women on the pictures even a few times a week, or give him a hall where he can go and play or dance, he will not be inclined to do all the other things. Which may be right too.

Anyhow, all the boys were looking forward to Bridgie's hooley because everybody knew that she was rotten with money and that she should put up a good show, so they gathered and watched the house for the exit of the old people and chafed like young stallions under the delay.

'Why don't they go home to hell outa that?' asked one.

'At home sayin' the Rosary they should be, be this time,' said another.

'Well, God blast ye!' said Michilin. 'Haven't the poor oul divils as much right to a night out as ye have yeerselves?'

'Well, they've been there all the day,' said the other, 'and you'd think be this time that they'd have enough porter drank, so you would.'

'Aren't you the young goshlin' now,' said Michilin, 'to be hankerin' after the porter. It was oney last year yeh were drinkin' mother's milk.'

This caused a laugh at the expense of the impatient young man, so they settled down to wait more patiently, watching the road for the figure of a favourite girl.

Stephen had been sitting on the wall at the cross-roads since after his tea wondering if Kathleen Finnerty would come this way to the hooley, or if she would take the other road round to the house. He was pleasurably excited, and although the cold wind was making his bruises ache, he was not inclined to go in case he missed her. He had been waiting there some time when he saw a girl coming up his own road. He watched her for a long time to see who she could be, and at last, when she came much closer to him, he jumped down from the wall and approached her. It was Nellie McClure.

'Hello, Stephen,' said she, 'I called at the house on the way up, thinking that you would be there, but they told me you had gone.'

'You're not going to the hooley, are you, Nellie?' Stephen asked, dismayed.

'Why wouldn't I go?' Nellie asked, wide-eyed. 'Wasn't I invited?'

He could see her chin was set and her eyes were bleak. Going to the hooley was a grand gesture to show how little it meant to her, but he knew that she would suffer every minute of it, and he hated to think of Thomasheen's face when she walked in. But what could you do?

'I don't think you'll enjoy it,' said Stephen.

146

'Why wouldn't I?' Nellie asked. 'Amn't I young, amn't I, and I can dance, can't I? And I'm not an oul hag, an' I'll get a fella all right, and Thomasheen Flannery isn't the oney fish in the sea.'

'Nellie,' said Stephen, catching her hand, 'that's only a lot of talk and you know it better than I do. Going to that hooley is not going to do you any good and it's not going to do Thomasheen any good. I know well that you want to go to show them all that you don't care a damn about them and that you're not hurt a bit, but, God, is it worth it, Nellie? What the hell is the use of hurting yourself and of hurting Thomasheen?'

Nellie turned away from him and didn't answer.

'Look, Nellie,' Stephen went on, 'if you won't go, I won't go. We'll go for a walk or something, and sit down and talk or something. Come on, will we do that? Let's go over to Crigaun and we'll go into the pub there and you can drink a port wine and I'll drink porter and we'll talk.'

'No,' said Nellie, with a tight face, 'I'm going to the hooley.'

'So be it,' said Stephen.

'Are you coming?' she asked.

'Well,' said Stephen, 'I'm waiting for a relation of yours.'

'Who?' Nellie asked, showing a slight interest.

'Kathleen Finnerty,' Stephen answered.

'Where'd you meet her?' Nellie asked.

'She was coming back from your house today,' said Stephen. 'I fell into the sea like a child that never saw a sea before, and she happened to be there with a rope and she threw it to me. I owe that girl quite a bit. She said she was going to this thing, and I thought I'd wait until she passed by, but maybe she will be going over by the other road.'

'No,' said Nellie, 'she always comes this way. Can I go with ye?'

'Sure,' said Stephen, 'I'm going to keep you under my wing tonight,' and knew he had made a mistake when he saw her face tightening again.

'There's no need for anybody to keep me under their

wing,' she said, turning off to go up the road.

Stephen ran after her and caught her.

'Ah, look, Nellie,' he said, 'don't be like that. There's no need to pick up everything I say. I didn't mean it like that. What the hell is wrong with you anyhow? You were always able to face up to Bigbum in school and everything else. Can't you see that this is something the same that you have to face up to in the same way, and beat it too?'

'All I know,' said Nellie, 'is that I was very fond of Thomasheen, and I was that way all my life, and I can't see why he should do this thing. I always thought that Thomasheen was strong under all that innocence of his. I'll never be able to find out why he should have done it.'

'I know it's no use telling you now, Nellie,' said Stephen, 'but what Thomasheen has done required more courage than you or I or anyone else will ever have. Thomasheen is of the stuff that heroes are made of, because he had sufficient ideals to put his family before himself and do something that would give them economic security.'

'Thomasheen was a coward,' said Nellie. 'He was afraid to try and make a living for his family with his own hands and his own brains and he took the easy way out, and that's why it was such a bad thing.'

'Would you have Thomasheen and his family starving and scraping all their lives on a two-by-four bit of land that wouldn't feed a chicken? Do you think that Thomasheen would ever ask you to marry him under those conditions?'

'What's wrong with being poor?' Nellie demanded. 'Haven't we been poor all our lives, haven't we, but we still had enough to live on? Wasn't Thomasheen's father poor, wasn't he? But he was happy and he didn't mind fighting and slaving hard for his happiness. But Thomasheen was different. Thomasheen took the easy way out. He probably looks on himself as a martyr now, and is saying to himself what a marvellous fellow he was, selling himself to put food in the mouth of his family. Well, he's wrong, I tell you, and he'll find out that he's wrong and instead of just making a haimes of his own life, he's done it to a lot of other people

148

as well, including the oul bitch he married, and I don't call that being noble and good. I call that being selfish and mean and small and cowardly.'

'Maybe you're right,' said Stephen. 'But wait for a few minutes anyhow, can't you, and let me go with you.'

'Hello,' said the voice of Kathleen behind them.

When she had recognized the big frame of Stephen O'Riordan, Kathleen had felt her heart jumping, but it had fallen to an alarming degree when she had seen that there was another girl with him and that he appeared to be holding her arm in an affectionate manner. She told herself that it was ridiculous to be feeling jealous when she had only met him for a few minutes that evening, but somehow in the intervening period she could not get the image of him out of her brain, and she sighed with relief when she saw that the girl was Nellie. That made her mind go off at a tangent, because, when she had been talking to Nellie early in the day, Nellie had no intention of going over to the hooley, and in fact she would allow neither Kathleen nor her own mother to mention the matter that they were all thinking about. What was she doing on the road now, all decked out in her best dress and coat, if she was not going?

'Are you going over, Nellie?' she asked.

'Yes, I am!' said Nellie defiantly.

'That's great so,' said Kathleen. 'The lot of us can be over together.'

'That's just what I was saying to her,' said Stephen, taking a place between them as they turned up the road. Although his mind was filled with the tragedy of Nellie and visions of Thomasheen's face when he saw her coming in the door, he was nevertheless conscious of Kathleen walking beside him and he could see in the light of the moon that she was very neatly turned out. He turned his head to look at her, and found that she was looking at him. Their eyes held each other for quite a time and Stephen felt his pulse beating quickly, and his mouth dried up. That was bad, because it reminded him of the day long ago when he and Thomasheen had gone swimming in the lake at Ourish and Nellie had

149

come down and sat on the shore and joked at them, and he remembered the air of tension at the carrageen beds afterwards when Thomasheen and Nellie had suddenly found out that they were no longer a little girl and boy going to school, but that they had grown up and that they felt things for one another that they didn't properly understand.

What a different Nellie she was that day to the sullen girl now trudging along beside him without a word out of her! He tried to think of something to say but found that he couldn't think of anything that would be suitable, so he held his peace and thought wonderingly about the start he had got when he had looked into the eyes of Kathleen.

Michilin and a few of the lads were at the gable-end when they arrived, even though by this time most of the old people had departed and the young people had taken over. There could be heard from the house the strains of the fiddler playing a set-dance and the light from the open door was blotted out at intervals by the passing forms of the dancers.

Michilin and the lads were probably telling a dirty story just before the three arrived because they were all laughing with that kind of laughter that only a dirty story can arouse. They stopped abruptly when they saw the girl beside Stephen was Nellie McClure, and you could feel the air heavy with things unsaid, which would be said as soon as Nellie was not there to hear them.

'It's yourself that's there, is it, Michilin?' Stephen asked, peering a bit.

'Begod, it's me all right, Stephen,' said Michilin, 'and I thought that you'd never turn up, so I did. Who's the piece you have there with you?' he asked, coming forward to scrutinize Kathleen. 'Well, damn me soul to hell if it isn't Kathleen Finnerty! How are you, Kathleen, and I'm told be people that ought to know that you caught a whale today when you were down near the sea.'

'Well, God bless you anyhow, you little thing,' said Stephen, 'but wasn't it quick now that you got the wind of the word!'

'I never thought I'd see the day,' said Michilin to nobody

in particular, 'when the great big Stephen O'Riordan could be hauled outa the sea like a mackerel on the end oo a line be a slip of a girl. Oh, shame, shame, shame!'

This extracted a lot of facetious remarks from the assembled company, none of them at all flattering to Stephen, but they were the type of bantering remarks which had an undercurrent of affection.

'All right, Michilin,' said Stephen. 'You can laugh away now, so you can, but some day you'll regret it.' He was glad that the talk had turned on himself, because he had been afraid that some of the more tactless of the youths would have said something to Nellie about Thomasheen and that would not have been so good.

'What on earth are we waiting here for,' said Kathleen, 'when they're dancing inside? Can't we go in?'

'As straight as a die,' said Michilin. 'Come on, Nellie McClure, and yourself and meself'll show them how to do the step a tar-ah-ra.' He caught Nellie by the arm and hustled her towards the house. As he turned to follow him Stephen felt grateful. Michilin could always be relied upon to sum up a situation and to take it in hand, and if anybody could tide the lot of them over the awkwardness of Nellie at the hooley, it would be Michilin. As he was walking, his hand brushed against Kathleen's hand. Both of them seemed to make a convulsive movement, and then he found her hand in his own, and she almost winced at the sudden pressure which he applied to it. They looked at one another then again, and smiled, and their bodies came a little closer. Stephen was sorry when they reached the door of the house and he had reluctantly to break the contact.

The hooley was taking place in the kitchen. The house still smelt of new concrete and lime, and the as yet unpainted walls were glaring whitely under the light of the naked electric bulb hanging from the ceiling. There was no open fire to be seen, but a wide glistening turf-range. Outside, in an outhouse, the lady of the house had even put a special boiler for cooking the animals' food, so that, however much the people might sneer at these innovations, they were forced

151

to agree that it was snug and there was not much labour remaining to a harassed housewife.

From wall to wall the kitchen was packed closely with the sweating people. A range is primarily designed to throw out the heat, whereas an open fire loses much of its heat up a chimney, but it is more comfortable for a hooley. Now the fumes of the range, and sweat, and stale porter, and cigarette smoke rose in a cloud and made you hold your breath until you got used to and accepted it. Everybody was talking loudly to everybody else, which was just as well because very few of them noticed the entrance of Nellie. Girls giggled as muscular fingers pinched their rumps, and there were loud laughs and cries, and now and again the sharp impact of the palm of a hand applied vigorously to the leathern cheek of the owner of wandering fingers. Whereat all close enough to the victim would break into uncontrollable laughter, which was induced by the heady porter and the general loosening of restraint which it engendered.

It was some time before Stephen's searching eyes could contact Thomasheen and then he saw him standing out from the range, and Bridgie standing by his side. Thomasheen had just seen Nellie and his eyes were glued to her. She was looking at him too. For just a moment Stephen could see the pain in the eyes of Thomasheen and the frightening look of dark longing in them. Then, sighting Stephen, and pulling himself together, he made his way towards them with Bridgie bringing up a close rear.

'You're welcome, Stephen,' said Thomasheen, taking his hand and pressing it. Stephen felt very sorry for him but brought a smile to his lips and then took Bridgie's hand in his own. He noticed that her hand was cold despite the heat, and that the flesh of it seemed to be loose and coarse, like, he thought, shaking hands with a fish that has been out of the water for a few hours.

'This is a great night you're giving,' he said to her.

'Hope you'll enjoy it,' she answered, and he could not see her eyes because at that moment the big lenses of the horn-rimmed spectacles had caught the light and just reflected blankness. Her voice was like herself, efficient and masked, giving nothing away. Years of servitude had made her that way, had made her understand 'her place', and she would never be able to rid herself of the discipline over feeling which is possessed by the best and most servile servants, because it is well known that employers of servants have no desire to probe the inner feelings of their attendants and prefer to regard them as emotional eunuchs.

'Do you know Kathleen Finnerty?' Stephen asked, bringing her forward and shouting to make himself heard above the noise.

'How-dee-do?' Bridgie asked, shaking her hand perfunctorily. 'Isn't that Nellie McClure with you?'

'Yes, this is Nellie,' said Stephen. 'Do you know Bridgie, Nellie?' he asked her as she closed on them, framed by Michilin.

'Glad to have you,' said Bridgie, but didn't hold out her hand. Again the glasses hid her eyes but Stephen could almost feel how she tightened even more, if that were possible, while Nellie looked at her with open loathing as if she was being introduced to a dragon with a stinking breath.

The fiddler striking up a tune made Stephen sigh with relief.

'Come on, Nellie,' said Michilin, 'and we'll bate the flure.'

'No,' said Bridgie. 'The first table is set back in the room now and I'd like you all to come back before the evening starts. You are all old friends of Thomasheen, and we can have a chat before the place gets too crowded.'

They should have protested. Stephen could imagine what it would feel like 'back in the room'. Nobody said anything, however, because to protest or to accept too quickly would talk about hidden emotions more plainly than open speaking. So they allowed themselves to be herded unprotestingly to the room. It was Bridgie's new parlour, and the door, closing behind them, shut out much of the noise but left them wordless.

It was quite a large room with an oval table in the centre laid with cups and saucers, plates and cutlery, and almost

153

groaning with the weight of roast chickens and ducks, geese, hams and beef, with sauces and condiments, and behind on a sideboard were shaped jellies and blancmanges that trembled as the stamping feet and hurrooing in the kitchen shook the floor. Bridgie's mother was there, with a white apron on her, and Thomasheen's sisters going around pouring out tea, and feeling very important and looking very clean and neatly clad for the first time in their lives. Bridgie's mother had a bright gleam in her eye, and her voice as she welcomed them was slurred, and her closeness to them as she held their hands wafted the fine smell of whiskey on her breath.

So they sat around the table on the chairs with the soft bottoms, and they found it very hard to say anything, because anything they could say would be so much better left unsaid, but Bridgie soon took command of the situation.

'Let you eat well now,' she said, 'because I was holding the first table until you came. You are Thomasheen's friends and we would like you to enjoy yourselves. You can pour out the tea now, Mother,' she said, and they could all notice that she seemed to frown as she addressed her mother. It was plain to see that she had noticed the old lady was a bit squiffy and she didn't like it at all.

'Did ye hear,' said Michilin, forgetting himself and leaning forward to pull the leg off a chicken, 'what happened me brave Stephen?'

The sight of Michilin pulling the leg off the chicken seemed very funny somehow to Kathleen and she laughed loudly, nor could Stephen refrain from laughing despite the atmosphere. The others looked at them blankly.

'It's no laughing matter at all,' said Michilin severely. 'How any grown man could fall into the sea and let a slip oo a girl pull 'm out agin like a wet codfish is beyond me, so it is.'

'Did that happen today?' Thomasheen asked.

'Yes, it did,' said Michilin, 'and instead a bein' ashamed oo 'msel', there he is laughin' away fit t' bust, an' any ordinary man'd be goin' around hidin' 'msel' under the bed in case the neighbours 'd hear anythin' about it, so he would.'

'Ah, I am ashamed too,' said Stephen. 'Can you imagine that, Thomasheen, me, Stephen O'Riordan, falling into the sea, and I'd be a dead mackerel now if it hadn't happened that Miss Finnerty here came along at the right time and threw me a rope. It was a near thing, so it was.'

'It was a bad catch for her, the poor girl,' said Michilin, stripping the leg bone with his still-white teeth. 'She'd a been better off t've caught an oul dogfish even, than that yoke oo a thing there.'

'Maybe I can sell him sometime,' said Kathleen. 'He's worth more than a little piece of a thing like you, anyhow.'

'That's the family spite, now, for you,' said Michilin. 'Just because her oul brother has a down on me.'

The general appetite of the company seemed to be poor on the whole. Stephen almost felt ashamed of himself. He thought that, owing to how things were, it was wrong of him to be eating so much, but he was a big man and had always possessed a hearty appetite, and for the life of him he could not ignore all the grand things that lay under his eyes, so he walloped into them and noticed, with a comfortable feeling, that Kathleen was keeping him company and eating strongly. Michilin was also eating vigorously and pausing now and again to throw a few quips at the company from a full mouth. Of the rest, Nellie kept her eyes on her plate and just toyed with the food, while Bridgie watched her surreptitiously from behind her glasses like a great blind Buddha. Apart from stretching food to them at intervals, and grunting now and again, Thomasheen was silent, and looked everywhere but at Nellie. It was a gathering on which ominous and pregnant silence descended, which even conquered the good spirits of Michilin, and he was reduced in the end to silently chewing the cud like a munching mumchance.

It was Bridgie's mother who broke up the last silence.

'Would ye like a drop a somethin', now?' she asked, wetting her lips, and ignoring the frowns of Bridgie. She had the bit between her teeth, and a sufficient supply of alcohol in her stomach to be careless of the frowns of her dictatorial daughter.

'I wouldn't say no to a drop a somethin' mesel',' said Michilin.

'Right you are,' she said, hurriedly opening the sideboard door and withdrawing a bottle of whiskey and sherry from its bulging interior. 'You'll have a dreas too, won't you, Stephen?' she asked.

'I will indeed,' said Stephen, thinking that it would ease his thoughts a little anyhow.

'How about you, love?' said Bridgie's mother to Nellie. She was of course completely ignorant of the relationship that had existed between her son-in-law and Nellie.

'I'd like some whiskey,' said Nellie, with a defiant note in her voice. There was another silence.

'Now you're talkin',' said Bridgie's mother, unconsciously covering up. 'There's nothin' like a dropeen to get a party goin', so there isn't, and seein' the day that's in it I'll have a little drop with ye, altho' I don't generally touch it at all, you know.'

She filled out four generous glasses and added an extra drop to her own. 'Here ye are,' she said, giving Michilin, Stephen, and Nellie a glass. 'And how about yourself, Thomasheen, and you, Miss What-do-I-call-yeh?' to Kathleen.

'I'll have one,' said Thomasheen.

'A drop of sherry for me,' said Kathleen.

'Here we are so,' said Bridgie's mother, pouring them out. 'Bridgie there never touches a drop at all, so she doesn't. A good girl she was since the day she was born, and a help and a guidance to her poor oul mother in her declinin' years.' And she handed the glasses to Thomasheen and Kathleen.

'Well,' said Michilin, rising to his feet, 'hey's long life an' happiness to the pair a ye, money teh burn, food teh throw t' the dogs, an' a quiver as full a childer as a horse-creel a turf. Slainte agus saol agaibh. Seo slainte na lanamhain oga agus sliocht sleachta ar shliocht a sleachta. (Health and life

156

to you. Here's health to the young people, and may their children's children have children.)'

The rest of them half-rose and silently drank the toast. Then Thomasheen hurriedly downed his drink.

'Will yeh come outside with me a while, Stephen?' he asked, 'because I want to talk to you. You don't mind, do you?' This last to his wife.

'No,' said she, 'I'm sure that ye have a lot to talk about. The rest of us will go down and dance and make room for the next people to come and have a bite.'

They pushed their way out through the door, Thomasheen keeping as far away as he could from Nellie. They were once again encompassed in smoke and noise and the great heat. Dancers were taking up the centre of the floor and the rest of the young people were huddled and squashed against the furniture that was pulled back to the walls. Over in the corner there was much squeezing and shouting as men got their mugs filled with porter from the half-barrel that was on tap and was being issued by one of Bridgie's rejected suitors, an old, old man in a bowler hat, whose countenance consisted of a large splayed moustache, a fiery red nose, and crimson cheeks.

'I won't be long,' said Stephen to Kathleen, as he pushed his way to the door after Thomasheen. 'Don't go away.'

'It'd be hard for me,' said Kathleen, laughing.

While Bridgie went around gathering the people for the second round back in the room, Stephen noticed that Nellie, her cheeks flushed, was laughing at Paddy Hernon, who was bending down over her. He frowned as he made his way out because everybody knew that Paddy Hernon was a very bad egg indeed and had a bad reputation with the girls. He was a tall, well-dressed fellow, with a square face and sidelocks coming down to the lobes of his ears. He had been in England working for a few years, and he was now home on a holiday, and his conversation mainly consisted of all the silly little good-looking Irish skivvies he had led astray after dancing with them in the Hammersmith Palais or the Shamrock clubs.

It was great to get into the cold night air again, and he drew large draughts of it into his lungs.

'Have a fag,' said Thomasheen, offering him the packet. Stephen took one, and as he lighted it from the cupped match in Thomasheen's palms, he reflected again how much Thomasheen had changed and he noted with a sinking of his heart the deep cleft between his eyes, from which the laughing wrinkles seemed to have departed for ever. They walked down the road, now brightly lit by a cold-looking moon.

'Why did Nellie come, Stephen?' Thomasheen asked suddenly.

'I don't know,' said Stephen. 'I suppose she came just to show the people that she didn't care and you getting married to another woman didn't mean a thing to her at all.'

'I'm sorry she came,' said Thomasheen, 'very sorry I am, because I was getting along all right until I saw her again and it would have been a straight run only for her showing up like that, because I had almost put her out of my head, but now it is worse than ever. Look, Stephen, how can I go to bed with Bridgie now, seeing Nellie and seeing the difference and what I have done? If I had the morning over again, I wouldn't do it, not if the whole of my family were laid out at me feet as corpses.'

Stephen didn't seem to be able to find the words, and he realized that, after all, he was very young himself, and that even Thomasheen now was older than himself in experience, the last few weeks seeming to have aged him.

'Thomasheen,' he said finally, 'you made up your mind to this thing long ago, and you worked it all out and in your own mind you decided that it was all for the best and that it was the right thing to do. Now you have done it, and you can't look back, so you can't. You can only go on.'

'That,' said Thomasheen bitterly, 'is very small comfort. Bridgie is an old woman, Stephen. Any woman almost, if she is young enough, can strike a spark out oo a fella for long enough to be able to make him love her like some of the animals, just enough urge and he can do it. But she has nothing to make me love her like that, and that is all she

158

wants, to go to bed with a man whenever she wants, and let her look after the place and try and make all her dollars go further than they are going now. She oney bought me, Stephen, because I was to be bought, just so that she could have me around the place like you would have a young bull that would be good for the cows. You see, she was too busy all her life gettin' money to be bothered about her body. Now she has the money but her body is too old, so the oney way she can satisfy her body is to go out with her money and get a nice fat young fella that will meet her needs. But I can't, Stephen! Holy Jesus, can't you try to imagine it yourself? I had mesel' worked up to it all right until Nellie walked in the door, and then I thought, and I looked at her, and I looked at my wife, and I felt everything leavin' me body.

'I'm sorry for talkin' like this, Stephen, but I'll have t' get rid oo it, and you won't never hear it any more; but what's makin' me afraid is that when I was in there and the two of them at the table, a great feelin' came over me and I looked at her neck with the wrinkles in it below the hair that she puts colour in, and I thought that the best thing to do was for me to put me two hands around her neck and to choke the life out 'f 'er. To put me hands on 'er neck and squeeze and squeeze and squeeze.'

He stretched his two hands before him and his whole body was shaking.

'Stop that, Thomasheen!' said Stephen, catching him by the shoulder. Thomasheen turned his head away and Stephen wasn't sure whether he was shaking with anger or shaking with sobs. He left him to himself. Thomasheen turned back after a time.

'I'm sorry,' he said, wiping his forehead (or was it his eyes?). 'I drunk too much all the day, and that last whiskey almost finished me. Come on, Stephen, and we'll go back to the house.'

Stephen stood and let his large hands drop by his sides and never felt more impotent or powerless or helpless or useless than he did at that moment. You bastard, he said to

159

himself, you no-good hopeless son of a bitch! Why can't you do something, say something, you who boast that you have read all the good books that were ever written, books filled with the philosophy of men of genius, who starved and suffered and died to impart their modicum of knowledge to you, and here you stand like an ignorant lout, a tongue-tied virgin? And the very worst part of it, he thought, is that I find myself storing this moment up in my memory, and that some day I'm going to use it, and I'm looking at Thomasheen now, completely detached from him, studying his reactions, so that some day I will write about him, put his sufferings under a pen like a bug-hunter pinning a butterfly to a board.

'Yes,' he said, turning, 'let us go back to the house.'

He walked beside Thomasheen and knew that he had failed him and knew that Thomasheen knew. Also he felt that their relationship would never be the same again, because Thomasheen would like to forget all that he had said, particularly since there had been no return to it, no reaction. It was like hitting a hard rubber ball against an alley and instead of bouncing back the ball had burst and fallen deflated.

As soon as they entered the house, Stephen sought Kathleen with his eyes, found her, and made his way to her. And they danced the night out when there was room on the floor, and Stephen drank porter every time it was offered him, because then he could only see Thomasheen as through a mist darkly, and he would not be so concerned about Nellie who was sitting in a corner with the arm of the Hernon snake around her shoulders, and his greasy head bent close over her, and she drinking sherry maybe, and even a glass of stout sometimes, with her face flushed, and a synthetic gleam of joy in her eyes – a girl who had come to show how little she cared but was only succeeding in making it more patently obvious than if she had stayed away altogether.

So Stephen clung on to Kathleen, and shouted to her over the eternal din, while the moon cut its way through cold flitting clouds in its futile chase after the sun.

CHAPTER ELEVEN

The frozen fingers of the dawn were stretching lazily across the sky, silhouetting the mountains blackly, when Stephen and Kathleen turned up the road. The hooley at Bridgie's had finally come to an end. They were almost the last to leave, and they were delighted to get into the air. The house behind them resembled a large litter-basket built into the shape of a dwelling. All that could be drunk was drunk. Nothing remained except the empty barrels of porter sucked as dry of their contents as a sod of turf which is saved by sun, and the bottles which had once held whiskey and port and sherry lay in forlorn piles everywhere. Of food there was nothing left except great ham-bones as clean as whistles, and the once plump carcases of chickens, ducks, and geese were now only a memory and nothing remained of them except their bones and the pope's noses, which would provide hearty eating for the local dogs. Not everybody had reached home as yet. Before them and behind them they could see the figures of little men, some drunk and staggering home supported by a neighbour. Others were just now getting down to the serious business of coortin', and each gate which they passed, and every gable-end, held a pair of lovers clasped in an embrace.

'Well, thank God that's over,' said Stephen as they stepped out.

'I'm sorry,' said Kathleen, 'that it's over, because only God knows when we will have another one, and certainly it will be a long time before we have one which will have as much money spent on it as that.'

'I suppose so,' said Stephen, 'but it is a terrible thing to be friendly with Thomasheen and all this business about Nellie and himself, and everything. That's why I drank too much porter altogether and why I don't feel too well at all now.'

His tongue was thick, his head muzzy, and the soles of his feet felt as if they were on fire, or as if somebody had run a very sharp knife here and there across them. Then he thought ruefully that he no longer felt the tingling in his veins which he had felt when he had met Kathleen first in the night. Then it would have been no bother to have taken her hand in his, and maybe they would have gone into one another's arms and kissed maybe, and the dormant thrill that came to him now made him realize that it was only the weariness of his mind that kept him from doing it this very minute. But he couldn't, somehow, and he felt that it put a strain between them. But then all the Thomasheen business and Nellie and the porter and wondering and worrying and thinking about them had knocked all the good out of him.

'Have you never been away from Connemara at all?' Kathleen asked suddenly.

'No,' said Stephen, surprised. 'Why do you ask that?'

'Oh, no-why,' said Kathleen, 'but I think that you should. Do you want to stay in Connemara all your life?'

'I'm not sure,' said Stephen, 'but I think I do. Why?'

'It seems to be funny for a man like you, with a bit of brains and something, not to want to clear out of it.'

'Why do you say that?' he asked.

'Well,' said Kathleen, 'you see them all going every day. Any fella who has anything at all leaves it sooner or later, whether he comes back or not. No man seems to be left in Connemara but the slaves, the men that are willing to make themselves old before their time and to be always fighting against everything like the sea and the storms and things. And they are always poor, except the shopkeepers, maybe, and I was just wondering why someone like you should want to stay here and not stir out of it at all.'

'It's funny you should ask that,' said Stephen, 'and I'm not sure if my head is clear enough to answer you. But you see, apart from the fact that Connemara has something which I like very much, and which I don't think any other place has at all, some day what I'm going to do concerns Connemara, and everything about it, and to do with it, and

I don't see any sense in leaving it when that's the way I feel about it.'

'I think that you're very silly,' said Kathleen, 'because, after all, it is just a place, and how do you know that there are not a lot of other places much nicer and better than it? You don't know and you can't tell because you have never seen them, and you have nothing to compare it with. How can you say that one place is better than another if you have never seen the other place?'

Stephen laughed.

'That sounds like common sense,' he said.

'It's no laughing matter,' said Kathleen seriously. It wasn't to her, because this night that she had spent out with him had made her feel towards him as if she was his mother or something. She felt as if she had known him for a long, long time, and just before the party broke up she had been sitting down looking at him dancing with some girl on the floor, and then coming back to take up his mug of stout, and she had felt her heart sinking. She looked at him, with his great build and his clear eyes that were always watching, watching, watching, and seeing what people were doing; and she listened to him asking people questions, and always his questions didn't seem to be practical at all, but questions about themselves and what they were feeling and why; and suddenly she realized that this Stephen had something which none of the others had at all, and she asked herself, What is he doing here with all those ordinary Connemara boys, drinking porter and setting, and avoiding the eyes of Thomasheen, and frowning every time he looked at Paddy Hernon and Nellie? Suddenly then, she had thought that it would be a terrible thing altogether if this man was to spend the rest of his days here, and if he was to get old among those nice unambitious people, and then if he was to die, just ordinary like, and be buried in Ourish and nothing be left of him but a name rudely carved on a granite headstone. And although she was not a very imaginative girl, as she said to herself, the thought of this seemed to weigh on her, and she told herself that she must talk to him about it and that she must find

163

out why, and although it had been an effort, she had brought it out.

Stephen, whose head was clearing rapidly under the cold air, looked at her and saw that there was a frown on her face, which was still very good-looking in the morning air, even after a night of dancing. He felt his interest in her rising, and felt again as he did when he had seen her properly after being pulled out of the water. Something had made him very interested in her then, apart from the fact that she had probably saved his life. Now he was sure that she was not just any Connemara girl because none of them he knew would have asked him questions like this in the cold light of an early morning.

'What, in the name of God, put things like that into your head?' he asked.

'I don't know,' she answered, 'just things.'

'You went away, didn't you,' he said, 'and what good did it do you? You came back again like a wild duck.'

'I did, maybe,' she said, 'but there were other reasons for that, and, like a wild duck again, I'll be spreadin' me wings one of these days.'

'Back to London?' he asked.

'Yes,' she said. 'Because I like England, and it's very different from here. I like a lot of people around and you meet all kinds of people, and no two of them are the same. But here you can nearly always tell beforehand what people are going to do and what they are going to say.'

'That's not a bad thing,' said he.

'I can't explain it right,' she said, 'but it is a good thing for a person to leave their own place and see other places, because then you really find out what your own place is like; and you say you want to be here, and whatever you are going to do is about the things here, and the people here, and I say that you will never see the people here or the things, not properly, unless you get away from them altogether, and then when you look back at them they all become clearer somehow. Oh, I don't put it right, but it's something like that, so it is.'

164

'Well, you're a funny one,' said Stephen, catching hold of her arm.

'Don't be laughing at me,' she said, 'because I'm serious, even though I can't tell it right.'

'I'm not laughing at you, on me oath,' said Stephen, sliding down his big hand and taking hers into it. 'I think what you're saying is very sensible and I'm very glad you said it, because, listen, Kathleen, there is a great lot in what you say, and I never thought of it like that before; but you've put it clear to me, and now that I see what you say, I see that it is time for me to pull up stakes and depart from Connemara.'

'Do you mean that?' she asked, turning to him.

'Cross me heart, I do,' he said. And suddenly he saw that she was right, and that that was what was wrong with what he was writing now. There was no comparison in what he was doing. It was like being in the middle of a fire and trying to explain how it was burning hell out of you, whereas if you were outside it and looking at somebody else burning, or read about somebody burning, you could give a better picture of it altogether.

'When are you going to go?' he asked her, and he was surprised that he should feel hurt at the very thought of her going anywhere.

'When I can get rid of the spell that this oul place puts on me,' she answered. 'I'm helpin' at home, of course, but that's only an excuse for stayin'. But you see, when you go away, all this, the mountains and the sea and all that, come into your mind again, and when you're in London or some place and you never see a mountain and you can only have a glance at the sea at so much a peep, all this Connemara acquires a great kind of magic and you're burstin' to get home to it. And then you come home and it is grand, for a while. And then you start thinkin' again, and you see all the people and how they have to work so hard for such a very poor return, and how cruel they can be when they like, because they have nothing else, and then you start thinkin' of the things in London, small things like proper lavatories and pictures and dancing and libraries and things, and then you get the itch again to get out of here, and it all looks very shoddy to you and ... oh, well, you know ...'

'Yes, I think I do,' said Stephen. 'And what you mean is that the oul spell is going again and you feel it was time you were off. Is that it?'

'That's it,' said Kathleen.

'Well, I'm glad,' said Stephen, 'that it didn't hit you before this morning, anyhow, or I'd be in a queer way, so I would. Will it be long before you are off?'

'Oh, a time yet,' she answered, saying to herself that she was not sure if she wanted to go now that she had met him.

They walked a little up the road and they were silent, and from the way his hand held hers slackly she knew that he was thinking about something.

'Did you have many boys in England, Kathleen?' he asked suddenly.

'That's a queer question to put to a girl,' she said.

'I know it is, maybe,' he said, 'but I just thought I'd ask.'

'Well, every girl, nearly, has a lot of boys once she grows up,' said Kathleen, 'and I suppose I had as many of them as any other girl.'

'And did you like one of them more than another?' he persisted.

'I don't know, really,' said Kathleen, 'it's so long ago.'

'You see,' said Stephen, 'I have never had a girl before.'

'You have one now,' said Kathleen, and then she stopped, appalled, because the words had slipped out of her without her noticing.

Stephen stopped too, and turned her towards him.

'Do you mean that?' he asked, putting his hands on her arms.

'I do,' said Kathleen, after a pause.

Then he kissed her. Considering he had never had any practice at all, it was a very good kiss indeed, but it didn't strike him that way, because it seemed such a natural thing to do. He felt her lips soft under his own and he could feel her high breasts pressing into his chest, and he was breathless.

As soon as she felt his mouth on her own, Kathleen knew that she had never felt like this before, and let herself sink in against him.

Eventually they parted, and he looked down at her. She was looking at him through half-closed eyes.

'That was very nice,' said he tritely.

'Very tasty,' Kathleen agreed, and they both laughed as if they had been very witty, and then they turned and walked slowly up the road, his big arm about her waist and their thighs touching. They did not talk because it seemed so much more comfortable just to walk and think how very nice it was to be walking on a Connemara road in the early dawn, after such a great discovery, and just to be thinking.

They were not far from Kathleen's house now, so they stopped.

'You better not come any further,' she said, 'because I'm afraid Malachai doesn't like you, and he's often out and about this time of the morning.'

'I'm not afraid of anyone,' said Stephen, looking at her.

'That's what I'm afraid of,' said Kathleen, 'and I don't want me brother, and ... well, and somebody I like, not to be friends.'

'I'll kiss him,' said Stephen fervently, 'the next time I see him.'

She laughed at that.

'I don't see how I am going to get you friendly with Malachai,' said Kathleen, 'if you keep on at the poaching with Michilin.'

'Malachai,' said Stephen, 'would be sorry if we stopped, because then he would never have the chance of catching us, and it wouldn't be fair to deprive him of the pleasure he will get out of that when it does happen.'

'We better go,' said Kathleen, 'and we will talk about it again. Good night, Stephen.'

'Good morning you mean,' he said, and he took her in his arms again.

167

They were so taken up that they didn't notice the door of the Finnerty cottage opening, nor the appearance of the tall black figure of Malachai coming out. He was carrying a double-barrelled gun under his arm. He closed the door. There was a stream running across the front of the house, a very pretty stream running from the lake to the sea at Crigaun. He crossed this stream by the footbridge, and it was when he was across the other side and preparing to go off towards Crigaun that he saw the figures of a man and a girl he saw to be his sister, clasped in an embrace. He paused, and then deliberately he walked towards them.

It was his foot striking against a stone that hit on the poacher's ear of Stephen, and he raised his head. Even when he saw it was Malachai he did not release Kathleen too quickly. She knew from the tenseness of his body that something was wrong, so she looked up and saw her brother.

Malachai stopped a few paces from them and looked at Stephen. Stephen realized then that there was very little hope of himself and Malachai ever agreeing or being friendly, because, as had happened on the few other occasions on which they had met, he felt a great antagonism in him to this man with the black countenance who seemed to wear a continual sneer. Always when he had met him a primitive urge had surged up in him, and he felt it would be a great thing to start a row with him so that he could sink his fist in his black face.

'Get into the house,' said Malachai, addressing Kathleen.

'She'll go when she's ready,' said Stephen, answering for her in a tight voice.

'Do you hear me talkin' t' yeh?' said Malachai roughly, ignoring him.

'I hear you,' said Kathleen, rebelling, but not wishing to start any bad feeling between them.

'Well, get in so,' said Malachai, 'and don't be makin' a show a yersel' on the public road.'

'You mind your own business,' said Kathleen, annoyed.

'It's my business,' said Malachai, 'to see that me sister

doesn't make a show 'f 'rsel' with every trickey that comes the road.'

'I'd advise you to watch your tongue, Mister Finnerty,' said Stephen in a quiet voice through which the suppressed anger mounted.

'Don't pay any attention to him,' said Kathleen. 'G'bye, I'm goin'.'

'Hold on a minute,' said Stephen, stopping her with a strong hand on her arm. 'You're a big girl now, and I don't see why me man should be dictating to you.'

'Let me go, Stephen,' she said.

'That's right,' said Malachai, sneering, 'you can't handle girls as easy as you can handle a stolen salmon.'

'Maybe I can handle them better than the bailiff that's supposed to mind them,' said Stephen.

When Kathleen saw Malachai's fingers tightening on the gun, she broke loose from Stephen and faced Malachai.

'You go on your way, Malachai,' she said. 'I'm goin' now.'

'I'm goin',' said Malachai, and there was a shake in his voice. 'But I'd advise you, O'Riordan, to get outa this district and to stay out; and somethin' else – you can go after the salmon and the grouse an' the pheasants until yer caught, and maybe no harm'll come t' yeh, but I'm advisin' yeh now to keep away from my family. Do you hear that?'

'I hear it all right,' said Stephen, 'but I don't think it worries me much. What your sister does is her own business, and what I do is my business. You may have a right to protect the salmon and the game, but what human beings do is their own business. I'll come here as often as I like, and I'll see your sister as often as she'll allow me to, and if you want to stop me you'll have to be a better man than I am.'

Having issued the challenge, Stephen thought for a minute that Malachai was going to take it up, and he found himself exulting savagely.

Malachai's eyes narrowed and his breath came faster. Kathleen stood petrified, because she knew that both of them had forgotten her. Then Malachai turned on his heel and flung up the road, saying back over his shoulder:

'Remember I warned yeh!'

They watched him for a while. Stephen was disappointed, and unclenched his fist and let the pent-up air out of his body.

'You shouldn't have goaded him,' said Kathleen.

'What's that?' Stephen asked, still looking after Malachai.

'You should not have minded him at all,' said Kathleen. 'He's always that way in the morning, like a bear with a sore head. A great hope there is now of your ever being friendly with him, I don't think.'

'I'm sorry, Kathleen,' said Stephen, turning to her. 'I shouldn't have said anything, I suppose, but there's a little of the primitive in the best of us, and it would be hard to keep silent.'

'If you weren't in Connemara, you'd be able to keep silent all right,' said Kathleen. 'That's what makes me so sick of Connemara. Everybody is ready to fight just on account of words or things that don't mean anything.'

'I'm sorry,' said Stephen. 'I'll go now, and let you get to bed. Will I see you again soon, I wonder?'

'Not for a while, anyhow,' said Kathleen, 'because I'll have to do a bit of work to make up for the time lost at the hooley, and I'm sure Nora, my brother's wife, will have left a lot undone, because she is going to have a baby and she's a bit helpless. How about Sunday night?'

'That'll suit me,' said Stephen. 'Where?'

'You know the Dead Lake?' she asked.

'Between Carnmore and Crigaun? Sure I do,' said Stephen.

'Well, I'll see you there,' said Kathleen. 'We have sheep over that way and I have to pay them a visit on Sundays.'

'That's grand,' said Stephen. 'So-long so.'

'Good morning,' she said, and having looked at one another for a while, she turned to cross the footbridge, and Stephen turned homewards.

Stephen felt very alive and stimulated. It isn't every day, he thought, that you fall in love with a girl, and the same day feel like beating her brother into pulp. For a moment the thought of Malachai drove the thought of Kathleen from his mind. Malachai was dangerous and everybody knew it. Nobody knew what went on in his mind, but everybody suspected that it was nothing good, and his two brothers were as bad as he was himself. There was that business of the sheep. The Finnertys had a neighbour, a nice inoffensive man who never troubled anybody. One of his fields adjoined a pasture of the Finnertys', and they sent him a complaint that part of his fencing was down and that his sheep were inclined to wander into their pasture and they requested him to mend his fences.

For some reason he neglected to do so. One morning he went into his field and found one of his sheep with its throat cut, and the head almost severed from its body. So he took the hint, built up his fences, held his peace, and avoided the Finnertys, and so did everybody else. Michilin Fagan had been the only man in the whole of the Three Parishes who had the guts to buck them, but then Michilin was afraid of no man and it was rumoured that Michilin himself would be a very handy man in a fight, and that if put to it he could use a knife almost as well as them black bastards out in Africa that you heard tell about that'd have the guts cut out of you as soon as you'd be looking around.

To hell with him, thought Stephen. I'll avoid him as much as I can, but I hope I don't bump into him too often, because he gets the hair up on the back of my neck like a mongrel. I'll put him out of me mind and I'll concentrate on Kathleen; and the thought of Kathleen brought him home, and followed him to his bedroom and lasted him until he fell into a tired sleep. She followed him there too, because his body was paining him from the bruises he had got, and the morning's experience pervaded his dreams and in his visions Kathleen was a peculiar kind of a mermaid who, when he was drowned at the bottom of the sea, came and wrapped long black hair about him.

At about the same time, Nellie McClure was lying in the field near to her house and she was thinking of Thomasheen and the tears were very near to her eyes. She did not protest when Hernon's hands fumbled at her blouse, but then, because she was unused to the drink she had taken, she had to be sick, and Paddy had to go home unassuaged, just when he thought the game was in his hands; but anyhow, he thought, as he walked home along the strand, I can always say that she did, and who is there that'll believe her, and thank God I'll be goin' back to England agin soon where the game is plentiful and they don't know yeh, and the'r' not so gaddamn suspicious as they are here.

It was high morning.

CHAPTER TWELVE

Another month had passed over the heads of the people of the Three Parishes and the winter was drawing to a close, somewhat to the regret of everybody except the old people, whose aching bones longed for the hot sun of the summer. To the young people the winter meant a kind of enforced holiday, because that was the time when the earth refused to grow anything, and a farmer's chores consisted of looking after the animals, to feed them in their stalls and walk them to scanty pastures on the fine days. Apart from that, there was not much to be done, except sit in front of roaring turf fires in your own or a neighbour's house. The next best thing was to adjourn to one of the few snug pubs and pass the night sipping slowly at big pints and enjoying the foolish talk of men with loosened tongues.

After unsuccessfully stalking pheasants, Michilin and Stephen, finding themselves in a wooded slope just above Crigaun, decided to pack in and go down to the pub. From where they were, they could see the pub below near the quay and the yellow light shining from its unblinded windows. Everyone knows that public-houses in Ireland are supposed to close at a certain time and that there are heavy penalties, fines, and endorsements if they do not do so. This law, in theory, applies to the country districts as well, but is seldom respected, particularly, as was the case in Crigaun, when the nearest Garda station was about twenty miles away, and if a Guard would go to the trouble of travelling twenty miles on a cold frosty night to catch out a poor man that was doing a charity to his neighbours, he'd have a very poor reception, I can tell you.

The public-house in the winter-time was the poor man's club. Like the rich man, the poor farmer also desired on occasions to get away from his wife and his cares, and since the pub was the only place to which he could go, he went. He could stay there all night if he liked, sipping at a single pint, and he could chat with his neighbours or he could play a few games of Twenty-five for a duck or a goose or a pair of chickens, and if he did win one now and again, it was very pleasant to bring them home to the wife and stop her tongue nagging about going over there, night after night, and your child there needin' a pair a boots terrible bad.

'We better cut around and get down to the road and approach from there,' said Stephen, 'so that nobody will be any the wiser.'

'Fair enough,' said Michilin. 'Anyhow, I'm afraid that I'm gettin' old. I'm afraid I'll have teh give it up altogether, so I am.'

'Go on ou'r that!' said Stephen. 'You wouldn't be able to rest in your bed if you thought there was a spare pheasant or a woodcock or a grouse that could be taken and the neck of it wrung so that it wouldn't squawk. The day you give up following the birds on a winter's night'll be the biggest miracle since the loaves and fishes.' And he laughed.

'Ah, it's all right for you,' said Michilin, 'but I'm not as young as I was all the same, and it's time that I turned respectable, so it is.'

'You're not as young as you were all right,' said Stephen, 'not half you aren't.' He was addressing Michilin's back which had vanished somewhere into the black night. If Michilin wasn't young any longer, he was able to travel in the dark at about twice Stephen's speed, and he could still beat Stephen going down a hillside on a dark night as now. He seemed to have eyes like a cat and made his way about dangerous mountains as if the sun was shining in the sky. Often, indeed, he came back for Stephen to see what was delaying him, even though Michilin always, on excursions like this, wore on his person the neatly-broken double-barrelled gun which was no light weight. I wish to God I was as young as he, said Stephen to himself, as his foot caught in a rabbit-hole and he just saved himself from falling.

Eventually he reached the road at the place where the bridge was that spanned the Scarlet Thread where it flowed towards the sea, not the delicate stream now that flowed outside the door of the Finnertys, but a wide rushing torrent swelled by the rains of the winter which it drained from the surrounding hills.

'Watch your step,' cautioned the voice of Michilin, just in time, or Stephen would have fallen over him where he was putting the parts of the gun away in the crotch of a convenient tree. 'We better lave this here until we're comin' back. I never like drinkin' a pint whin I cun feel the barrel a the oul gun agin me leg. S-s-s-h! Hould it! Hear anythin'?' he said in a sudden whisper, his hand grasping Stephen's arm.

Both of them froze where they were and listened tensely. Stephen was not certain, but he thought he heard a rustle which was like the end of some movement which had been made just as Michilin was talking. No, nothing now, just the thunder of the river running to the sea, and the dry rustling and cracking of the leafless trees on a calm frosty night.

'Wait here,' he heard Michilin whisper in his ear, and then he was gone. Stephen crouched low to the ground and waited, his muscles tense. Strain his ears as he would, he could not hear even a suspicion of Michilin. What could it be, he wondered, and, of course, thought immediately of Malachai. They had had a few narrow shaves in the past few weeks, because, good as Michilin was, Malachai was almost as good, and it was just because Michilin had that

174

extra little something that they had not ended up either in the court or in hospital with unsympathetic nurses pulling lead pellets out of them.

One night, after the grouse, they had almost been caught. It was Michilin's quick ear and a dive into a bog-hole that had saved them. Crouching there, with water up to their waists, they had seen a dark form, with a gun held well forward and a hand around the trigger guard, sliding slowly and noiselessly in the direction they had been going a minute before. Michilin wasn't sure if it was Malachai, but Stephen was certain, because as soon as that dark figure approached he felt that awful feeling of primitive dislike rising up in him and he knew it must be Malachai.

He knew that Malachai was hunting them as he had never hunted them before. That was on account of Kathleen. He also knew that Malachai would never stop to ask questions if he caught up with them. He would just shoot at the taller figure of the two first and ask questions afterwards. He would get away with a killing like that, because much as the law would frown now on killing a poacher, still Malachai would have the law on his side, and a statement that he shot in self-defence would have to be believed, particularly when they themselves were carrying a gun.

It was some little time before he felt Michilin beside him again.

'It's all right,' said Michilin. 'It must have been only a bird or something.'

'That's a relief,' said Stephen, letting his breath go.

'I'll finish hiding the gun,' said Michilin, 'and then we'll hop down to J. J.'s. I can do with a pint.'

They were soon out on the road and heading towards Crigaun.

When they were well gone, a dark figure detached itself from the limb of a tree near which they had been and, sliding to the ground, made its way to the tree where they had hidden the gun. It did not take him long to find it. He did not remove it, however, but going back a little from it, pulled his coat closer around him, shifted the gun to a handy position across his knees, and settled down for a long vigil.

The pub was crowded when they reached it, and as they closed the door behind them they were encompassed by the warm fumes of tobacco and porter and men, and all the other fumes which go to make up the atmosphere of a pub on a dark cold night.

J. J. himself was behind the bar. Actually the man's name was Aloysius Moloney, but nobody ever called him that. He was called J. J. because he had a habit, when excited and wanting to emphasize a point, of slamming the counter with his hand and yelling, 'But Jumpin' Jaysus, I tell yeh . . .' So they called him J. J., and how if you shouted Aloysius at him it was doubtful if he would hear you. He was a big fat man. Why public-house owners should be big and fat is a mystery which nobody seems capable of solving, but J. J. was indubitably big and fat. He was unmarried and was well off. There was a large grocery and ironmongery attached to his place as well. He was also the local post-office. In fact there was nothing you couldn't get in J. J.'s, from a baby's napkin to a pine coffin with brass handles. His face was big and red and rosy like a child's bottom. Stephen had never really had a good look at a child's bottom but he was sure that if he ever did J. J.'s face would be just like it. His beard, which he carefully shaved every morning, was a very scanty one. His nose was pug, and very little hair remained on the top of his head. He was a picture of good humour and benevolence, like a Friar Tuck who had missed his vocation somewhere down the centuries.

There was a great shout of welcome for the two when they entered and J. J., who was talking earnestly to Liam the Postman, beamed at them without breaking his conversation, and automatically started to fill two pints.

Stephen loved J. J.'s pub. The ceiling was low and raftered, and the windows were small and square, and two oil lamps swung from the rafters and swayed gently as the currents of air from the opened doors caught them. It was like being in a ship at anchor in the bay to be in the room. If you looked out of one window you saw the placid water and the yellow light of that same window reflected on it. If you looked out of the other window you saw the hill on the other side of the bay towering blackly into the sky and bearing on its topmost part a light that flashed at regular intervals to warn the ships at sea that they were bearing down on what was probably the most dangerous coast in Europe.

The Great War with its submarines and torpedoes had provided them with unlooked-for things, and many a man's wealth had been founded on the things like wine and bales of goods and rum and umpteen other things which had been washed from the bellies of the blasted ships. Then there had been mines as well, and many lives had been lost because the people had not known what they were.

The seating accommodation was primitive, but in character. You leaned against the counter or you sat on the tops of half-barrels, and afterwards remembered instinctively to wipe off your backside on account of the red paint that was on the tops of them. There were one or two forms, but at the moment these were occupied by the Twenty-five players, about eight of them, who appeared to be more than somewhat excited. With the pint in his hand Stephen went over and stood behind them. He gathered that the fate of a goose was at stake.

There is a ritual about playing the game of Twenty-five in the country which no other card game possesses anywhere. How the elegant bridge-players, or the stoical poker-players would snort and jeer and shudder if they were to see this! No man hides his excitement. Each man plays his card in his own time. Everybody watches him. He slowly pulls it from the fan in his hand, raises it above his head and then brings his hand down slowly to display it. It is not laid down gently. Oh no. It is brought down faster and faster and banged triumphantly down on the table. Some use different methods, but the favourite way is to hit the bottom of your clenched fist on the table as you lay down the card. If it is a good card, it is delivered with all the force or verve of a steam-hammer. If it is a minor card, it is hit even harder to show the disdain of the player for it. A bad card is accompanied by a wallop and a kind of disgusted snort of hatred and dismay. This of course may be pure bluff in order to get the others to imagine that your hand is a lousy one, and to come back at you with their best, when you will be able to annihilate them with a leering smile of triumph. So if you close your eyes, as Stephen was doing now, you can distinguish a game of Twenty-five from any other game on earth. You hear thump, thump, grunt, thump, thump, grunt, and an 'Ah, ha!' now and again to break the monotony.

Stephen smiled and wandered back again to the counter.

Liam the Postman was talking in that slow, emphatic, and blasphemous way of his. He was a character, was Liam. He knew the secrets of everybody in the parish. He read your telegrams, he read your postcards, and some said that he was not above steaming open the envelopes to read your letters. He'd say, handing you a letter, 'I see Johnny is writing to you at last from Ealing, London, or from Yorkshire, or from Dublin or Galway or Miami, Florida. It's about time, too. Should have written long ago, he should. Sent you three pounds, too, he did; got the docket for it here in my pocket. I don't know that he should marry that young wan he's goin' with now. Flighty,' and so on, but he had a good heart and was incorrigible and was always willing to help if there was anything that he could do.

Everybody liked him because he was a pagan. He never attended church or chapel, although every priest and nun and minister that had come the road had tried to show him the error of his ways. He just didn't believe in anything, and the novelty of having someone in their midst who didn't go to Mass on a Sunday, and who always had fried steak and onions on a Friday for his dinner, put him apart in the eyes of the people. It would make your mouth water to pass by his house on a Friday at dinner-time and get the beautiful smell of fried meat being wafted to your nose. Some said he should be prohibited by law from doing this because he was only grigging his neighbours, and it was a hard thing to pass by his house, smell this, and then go home with an easy mind and try and tear at an oul salted herring. Then his morals were not of the best. He was given to doing an odd spot of love here and there with any woman that was willing.

You wouldn't mind, as everybody said, but look at him! How any woman could sleep with him was beyond the powers of imagination. Stephen, thinking of all these things now, looked at him, and smiled as he started in on his second pint. Liam was very small and had the bandiest legs in Connemara, and that was saying something. He never seemed to be properly shaved. He always wore the blue breeches of the Post Office with the red stripe down the side. On top of this he wore an old blue jersey and a coat that was so patched as to have lost its original cloth altogether. A hat completed the picture. As long as Stephen could remember, Liam had been dressed like this, and he had a funny feeling that if you walked in on Liam when he was asleep you would find him dressed in just the same way. Whether this freedom of action was the cause or not, Liam was a confessed Communist. His brand of Communism was very broad, because any of its tenets that didn't agree with his own form of living he castigated heartily and blasphemously, but he was for ever holding up the Russian people as the acme of perfection, and comparing them with the Irish people with much scorn and not a little spitting.

'The Irish people,' he was saying now, 'are a nation a spineless bastards that has no more brains or intelligence than an oul ram, bless the mark. Backbone is it? There'd be more backbone in an oul dogfish than is in them. They go out and throw the English out in the nineteen-twenties an' thin what do they do? Tell me that! What do they do?'

'All right,' said J. J., spluttering, 'you tell us what they do since you're such a bloody genius.'

Liam remained unperturbed.

'They sell themselves,' he said, 'to a gang a lousy politicians. They sit back on the oul backside and they say, We freed the oul yoke 'f a country now. We'll take it aisy an' let the boys carry on, so we will.'

'And what did you want off them?' J. J. asked.

'They freed the country so,' said Liam, hammering his glass on the counter to point whatever moral he was after, but never catching up with, 'an' thin they turn around and let me brave Cumann na nGael boys an' me brave Fianna Fail boys take over an' feather their nests. Have a look at the bastards now! Whin they wint in, they were like ragmin that was outa work for seven years, but have a look at thum now! Fur coats for the wife a every wan a thum an' moty cars with bonnets on them as long as clamps a turf. An' thin go inta an oul factory an' ye'll see little children sweatin' their guts out in places yeh wouldn't let a pig ate his dinner, while me min are up in Dublin lickin' cream offa their fingers an' hobnobbin' with the gangs a industrial bastards that's makin' money hand over fist, an' shovin' a bitta backhand to the boys in office. An' that's what the Irish people did. Sold their freedom, which they won be their blood, an' handed it over lock, stock, an' barrel to a gang a swindlers an' thieves that's worse than the English ever was at exploitin' them.'

'I didn't notice,' said Michilin, lighting his pipe, 'that the brave Liam the Postman was doin' much in 1920 teh save his country an' win 'is freedom.'

'Now yer talkin',' said J. J. 'Where was me brave Liam in 1920? Down below he was, hidin' in a mail-bag, with His Majesty's Mail wrote on it in big black letters.'

'Wasn't I a wise man?' Liam asked indignantly, deeply wounded. 'Wasn't I a wise man? What has me brave Michilin there or thousands like 'm that wint out an' fought, although the Holy Romans told him from the altar that he was committin' a sin an' a shame an' that his sowl'd burn in the bottom pit a Hell for all eternity because he was takin' up arms agin the English heathens – what did they get out 'f it, I ask ye? Bugger all they got out 'f it, with all the other feckers that got inta the Government makin' Joe Soaps outa them, the very fellas that they put inta power at the tips a their forty-fives an' their home-made bombs. They turn t' them an' say, Flog off now, little boys; ye did yeer bit an' we're thankful to ye, but go 'way now, because we want to put in our cousins an' our aunts an' our uncles an' our brothers an' sisters an' all our relations to the seventy-eight degree inta nice cushy jobs that we threw the English fellas outa. Wouldn't I look sweet goin' out teh fight for a pack a bastards like them?'

Michilin was getting hot under the collar at this, because he was a great supporter of the Government, and he was also drawing a nice little monthly pension for having done his bit.

J. J. was being left almost speechless, because as it happened he was a relative, not close, to one of the reigning Ministers and it was recognized in the Three Parishes that if you wanted a little favour done over the heads of some department or other J. J. could 'fix' it for you.

'Jumpin' Jaysus!' spluttered J. J., his neck as red as a turkey cock.

'Y'oul eejit, sure enough,' said Michilin. 'It's damn aisy for you to talk, but there was never divil a fear a yeh takin' an oul gun an' goin' out an' doin' anythin'. Yeh could a gone out in good faith, couldn't yeh? and hoped for the best, couldn't yeh? No bloody fear a me brave Liam goin' out! No fear! Whin he had a nice cushy spot, snuggled up in some oul wan's bed, an' listenin' teh the bullets flyin' teh the min that was freein' his country for 'm.'

'Ye can't,' said Liam calmly, 'shake me beliefs be tauntin' me with this an' that an' callin' me names. I still sez that the Irish people is a nation without a whole set a guts among the lot a thum, an' yeh can take it or lave it.'

'I think,' said Stephen, intervening before the argument became too serious, 'that you're overlooking a lot of things, Liam. Give us another pint, J. J., and the same for Michilin.' It was a good move to make J. J. fill out a few pints. It took his mind off his indignation.

'You look around you in Connemara, Liam,' continued Stephen, 'and you'll be surprised at what this nepotism-ridden Government despised by you has done. Take the houses even. What's happened to the thatched cottage? It's on the way out, isn't it?'

181

'Isn't that another a me pints?' asked Liam. 'They won't even let the common man stay in a house a his own choosin'.'

'It's a damn good job for you that they wouldn't,' said Stephen, 'or you'd be a dead duck long ago. And a dead T.B. duck at that. If the Government did nothing else but get rid of the disease-infested thatched cottage, as far as I am concerned they could do whatever else they liked and they would have been justified.'

'What's wrong with the thatched cottage?' demanded Liam.

'Ah, for God's sake,' said Stephen, 'you're the one that's always telling us about what Joe Stalin is doing for the people in Russia, how he's putting them all into great big blocks of flats and the farmers into grand, clean, neat houses with water laid on, and electric light and tractors and the devil knows what else to save them slaving, and all the rest of it. Well, aren't our own Government doing the same? Aren't they taking you out of the flea-infested, germ-infested cottage and putting you into a decent house with a slated roof and big windows to let in the air?'

'Now you're talkin'!' said Michilin.

'Can't you see,' said Stephen, feeling himself getting a bit hot under the collar, 'you poor blind eejit, that a new house with a slate roof is the sign of freedom and that a Connemara man that doesn't have to live in one and who can go out of a Sunday in a suit of factory-made cloth which he can afford to buy, instead of his bainin and ceanneasna trousers, can't you see that that man is really gaining his freedom? You can polish off a pound of steak on a Friday and more power to you. There isn't a house in Connemara hardly that can't have a piece of meat a few times a week if they like. These are not small things. These are the results of Michilin and the boys going out with their guns, while you were lolling with your doxy, if that's what you were doing. Because twenty years ago a Connemara man could not afford to eat meat at all. He could eat it once or twice a year if he was lucky. These are small things, Liam, but they are all the important things and you are overlooking them, and spoutin' a lot of claptrap which you have only quarter-digested from some book that you don't understand.'

'What you got to say to that?' J. J. asked triumphantly.

'I say,' said Liam, thinking furiously, 'that yeer goin' away from me pint altogether, so ye are. I maintain that the Irish nation have no guts an' ye can't prove that they have. Ye talk about goin' out with yeer guns. Well, how many a ye wint out? A few thousand at the most out oo a population a millions. D'ye call that havin' guts?'

'What's me brave Michilin there?' asked J. J. 'Isn't he a brave man? Would you be willin' teh go out night after night on expeditions like he does, an' Stephen there, an' take a chance with thim bloody Finnertys, an' mebbe never knowin' whin yer goin' teh get a charge a shot in yer back?'

'Any oul eejit could do that,' said Liam.

'Is that so?' Michilin asked, bridling.

'Sure it is,' said Liam. 'All you have teh have is good eyes in the night-time, an' wringin' an oul bird's neck before it clacks is no great thing. Now what I'd call courage is me man that wint down to the Lobster Pool there last year and whipped a few dozen lobsters out 'f it and the weather just as cold as it is now.'

'He got six months in jail for it, didn't he?' Stephen asked. 'You can't call that being a success.'

'No, but it takes courage,' said Liam, 'an' that's the pint that I'm tryin' teh make. Now if ye took a turn at the oul Lobster Pool instead of goin' out spearin' an oul yoke oo a salmon, that's me pint.'

They were all feeling muzzy about this time because they had had quite a lot to drink. The argument had stimulated them. Michilin looked at Stephen significantly. Stephen regarded him for a moment, and then his eyes lighted up and he nodded his head a little.

'So you think,' said Michilin, 'that we wouldn't have the courage teh go down an' whip a few oul lobsters out 'f a pool?'

'That's me pint,' said Liam, draining his other one.

'Oh-ho!' said Michilin.

J. J. looked at him anxiously.

'Hey, now, hould on, Michilin!' he said. 'This is oney a problematical argumint that we're havin'. They's no need to be doin' mad things.'

'What's on your mind, J. J.?' Michilin asked innocently.

'Ye wouldn't be thinkin' a goin' down to the Pool, would ye,' he asked, 'just because this oul eejit dared ye teh?'

'You're crazy, J. J.,' said Stephen, 'if you think that we'd let a poor old man like Liam put anything so silly into our heads.'

'I'd look nice,' said Michilin, 'hoppin' out in me pelt on a winter's night just to satisfy me brave Liam there. Well, we'll be shovin' off, so we will. We have a few things teh do. Good night to ye.'

'Good night, lads,' said Stephen.

'Now, look here,' said J. J., still doubtful.

'Arrah, don't be worryin', J. J.,' said Michilin, 'd'ye think that I'm a born eejit altogether?'

'Good night, lads,' said Stephen to the card-players, who, refusing to be distracted, waved a card-packed hand in the air and grunted. One that was winning actually raised his eyes and wished them good night.

They had to pause when they got outside the door in order to get their eyes accustomed to the darkness, and also because the cold night air made Stephen's head whirl. He had never been a very heavy drinker. Not even his long association with Michilin had taught him to carry a load of porter without feeling its effects.

'Well,' said Michilin, 'how about it, hah?'

'I'm on,' said Stephen.

'If it was oney,' said Michilin viciously, 'to make that bandy-legged blower turn on the other side of his face, I'd do it.'

'Probably when he hears about it,' said Stephen, 'he'll think of some other argument that'll nullify it, but what matter? How is it, Michilin, that we didn't think of this before? We've done nearly everything else.'

'I'm damned if I know,' said Michilin, 'but I wish teh God

we had thought of it when the weather was warmer.'

'Are you getting cold feet already?' Stephen jeered.

'Well, may the divil scald yeh!' ejaculated Michilin. Stephen laughed.

'Ah, come on,' he said. 'I was only joking.'

'Fair enough,' said Michilin, and they went down the road, leaving behind them the cheerful yellow that illuminated the pub windows.

The figure crouched behind the tree at the bridge heard them coming, and then, standing up, got behind a tree which he had selected, where he could cover anyone trying to recover the hidden gun. His fingers felt the triggers of his own gun to make sure that they were cocked. He was assured. It would have been too late to have cocked them then, because he knew that Michilin had ears of extraordinary acuteness, and if he had heard the slight click he would have guessed immediately what it was, and would have been able to tell you the make of the gun and whether it was loaded or not. He pulled back further into the shadows, letting his feet down carefully so that they would not land on rotten twigs, which would sound like cannon-shots in the quiet of the night.

Michilin and Stephen stopped just outside the wall.

'I'll get the gun,' said Stephen, laying a hand on the wall and preparing to leap over it.

'No,' said Michilin, arresting him.

'Why?' Stephen asked.

'What's the use,' said Michilin, "f takin' the gun with 's? Won't it be oney an extra load to carry? Can't we do what we're goin' teh do and we can fetch the oul yoke oo a gun on our way back?'

'All right,' said Stephen, and strode after Michilin.

When they had gone a few paces, Malachai Finnerty came out from behind the tree.

He raised the gun to his shoulder and got his eye in the sights.

He paused then, and lowered the gun, and a sibilant curse broke from him. He saw it would be of little use to fire after

185

them because they had already disappeared into the darkness. Besides he'd have a lot of explaining to do if a body was found on the public road. It would be different if they were recovering the gun, because then they would have no defence at all, but who was to swear but himself that the gun belonged to them and that he had seen them hiding it under the tree? If one of them survived the shot he could say that the gun hadn't belonged to him at all, and then Malachai would be down for murder instead of just homicide in the execution of his duties.

He wondered where they could be going. They would be coming back for the gun again, but it was likely that they would change their minds and leave it there until the following night. He thought for a few seconds, and then, making up his mind, he glided over the wall and ran swiftly along the grass verge bordering the road. When he had come sufficiently close to hear them talking, he slowed down, and, making sure of each step, he kept within sound of them and remained, a black figure, merged with the darkness of the night.

CHAPTER THIRTEEN

Had Liam the Postman only thought of using it, the Lobster Pool at Carnmore was the best argument he could put forward to prove how spineless was the Irish nation. The Lobster Pool had been built now for about five years. A foreign merchant who supplied the Continent with lobsters had come to Carnmore one day and looked about him. Then he had seen this spot where he had put his pool. At this place the sea entered a gap between two low hills to form a small natural bay, which was about ten feet deep at high tide. He had simply damned the mouth where the tide entered, and built sluice-gates, so that even when the tide retreated he had a grand pool where he could keep his lobsters alive until the ship called to transport them to the Continent. He paid a good price to the local fishermen, and what had been formerly a haphazard occupation became a lucrative one for all the local lobstermen. Of course, when it was too late, they all realized that they should have seen the advantages of this pool before and built it themselves, because it only cost the merchant about £20. However, they were saved the trouble and expense of marketing the lobsters, so they were quite content.

The pool lay almost at the end of Carnmore and it was approached by a very poor road which branched off the main circular road that joined Carnmore proper with Crigaun.

When they reached this point Stephen and Michilin came to a halt.

'Do you still feel like going on with it?' Michilin asked.

'What do you think?' said Stephen.

'I don't mind whippin' a few oul salmon and things from the fellas that owns what doesn't belong to them,' said Michilin, 'but it seems to be a mean thing to be stealin' lobsters from a man that paid good money to the boys for them.'

'Sure it's not stealin' at all,' said Stephen. 'We'll only take a half-dozen and leave them outside Liam's door on the way home, just to show him, and then the next time Danny is lobster-fishing I'll get him to throw in half a dozen for nothing. Isn't that fair enough?'

'Fair enough,' said Michilin. 'That'll take care a my conscience all right, so it will. Be careful now. We better cut in across the fields and dodge the bailiff's house. He has an oul yoke oo a dog there with a nose like an elephant, an' if he as much as gets the wind 'f 's, he'll raise a racket that ye'd hear out in China. So we'll have teh approach with great care an' caution, although me man Mullins'll be in bed, I'm certain.'

'Isn't he the old fellow,' Stephen asked, 'that married a young girl from Ourish last year?'

'That's what I mane,' said Michilin. 'The divil 'msel' wouldn't get 'm outa bed at this hour. Whin he gets up in the mornin' all he's thinkin' about the whole day is goin' to bed agin at night with 'r.'

Stephen laughed.

'For God's sake, go aisy, will yeh?' admonished Michilin. 'We'll have teh do this job as if we thought that me brave Malachai was on our heels.'

They set off across the fields. Whatever breeze was in it was coming from the south-west so there was a good hope that the dog wouldn't get the scent of them. They moved very cautiously, and when they came to the hill overlooking the house they lay down and surveyed it.

The house was in complete darkness and only the brilliant whitewashed walls disclosed its position.

Well, we're the silly eejits, Stephen thought, as they waited. To be taking up a dare from a bit of a thing like Liam the Postman, when they should be at home and sleeping. All the same he supposed that he himself, anyway, was cut out for this sort of thing. It had never yet failed to thrill him. To be out, ready to snaffle a salmon or to blind a pheasant on his perch, and all the time to know that there was a certain element of risk, that unless you remained all the time conscious of this risk you might be jumped on by one of the Finnertys, made your blood course faster through your veins and made your heart thump heavily, so that when you did reach home you sank into a heavy exhausted sleep immediately, and woke in the morning wondering what the hell you wanted to be doing things like that for. You were grown-up now, you'd tell yourself, and you had found Kathleen, and your scribbling was improving, so why on God's earth couldn't you confine yourself to doing things that were sensible?

Indeed the coming of Kathleen had cut down his adventures quite a lot. Michilin would say, Well, I'll see you tomorrow night, and Stephen would answer, No, I'm sorry, I have to see Kathleen. And then Michilin would start cursing and would want to know what was the world coming to when a fine fella like Stephen was being ruled be a red petticoat, and hadn't he more sinse than that, and didn't he know that it was a dangerous thing teh be caught up with a girl, and before he'd know where he was he'd be married

188

maybe, and instead a bein' out in the hills of a night breathin' in God's good air, 'ye'd be at home in front a the fire, with wan child roarin' in yer arms like a bull, an' another wan roarin' in the cradle like a lion, an' you rockin' it with yer foot, an' yer freedom, an' the birthright a yeh, sold for a bitta skirt.' Then Stephen would laugh and say that maybe it wouldn't be such a bad idea, which would make Michilin stump off in high dudgeon.

What would Kathleen say if she knew where they were now, and what their intentions were? he wondered. He could imagine how mad she would be, because she could never understand why grown men should be going around poaching, and besides she was worried in case Stephen and her brother should clash. Then, every night when Malachai was going out to patrol his territories, he would click the triggers of his gun and would look at her significantly, break the gun, load it with cartridges, look along the barrel and pull the gun slowly around as if he was aiming at something, before he pulled on the safety-catch and strode purposefully out of the house.

Nights like these, as she told Stephen, she could never settle down until Malachai had returned to the house, and she could see from his black looks that the hunt had been unsuccessful. So the only time she felt safe was when she was with Stephen and they were talking about things that interested them, or else when she was close in his arms, and they were lost in an embrace and one or the other would have to pull away before it became too dangerous.

Thinking of her now, Stephen felt his heart miss a beat and for a moment he thought he could feel her black silky hair touching his face.

'All right now,' said Michilin, pulling himself to his feet, and gliding down the hill like an old fox running in on a hen-house.

Despite their caution, just as they were outside the front door of the Mullins's house the dog barked. They sank down in the shelter of the wall and waited tensely. It must have been something else that disturbed him, because the barking stopped after a time and they proceeded on their way.

They reached the pool without any further disturbance.

'Now for it,' said Michilin. 'One 'f 's 'll have teh strip off. Look, Stephen, maybe we better lave this oul silly racket an' go home to hell, hah?'

'Don't be an idiot,' said Stephen. 'We came this far, and I'm not going home now without doing what we have t' do.' He started to take off his coat.

'Whist!' said Michilin suddenly, a hand on his arm.

They listened tensely. They could hear Mullins's dog barking again in the distance. It did not last long.

'The curse a God on that oul mongrel,' said Michilin. 'He has the life frightened outa me.'

'Here we go,' said Stephen, stripping himself quickly and ignoring the cold. It was a trick he had learned long ago, when he would have to go into the lake or a river after the body of a bird which had flopped there, and because Michilin never believed in using a dog on his expeditions. You never know with a dog, he'd say. So Stephen became a retriever, even on the coldest nights.

He soon stood shivering.

'Here,' he said, handing his clothes to Michilin. 'You take those in case of an emergency.'

'Right,' said Michilin, 'an' be quick now, or you'll pass out with the cold.'

Even in the darkness he could see the amazingly well-developed body of his companion, and where the big muscles knotted themselves there were deeper shadows.

Stephen let himself down to the water from the bank, which was almost perpendicular and raised about five feet. The only fear he had was that he would step on one of the large discarded crawfish which generally littered the sides of the pool, but he soon forgot them in the icy caress of the water. He plunged in and swam strongly towards the centre. He knew exactly what he would do. He would swim to the large floating box, pull himself up on it, open the trap and insert a cautious hand. Fortunately the incarceration in the box, even though it was water-filled, would have knocked most of the activity out of the lobsters and they would not be so fast about waving and snapping their clippers.

He was almost at the box when he thought he heard some shouting from the bank he had just left. He stopped and treaded water. He thought that he could see moving figures on the bank, and then he heard a voice crying 'Here! Here!' and he recognized the voice of Michilin, and realized that they must have been caught. Mullins must not have been abed as they had imagined. He turned and swam strongly, and as silently as he could, in the direction of the figures. In the midst of the danger and the freezing cold, he had to grin when he thought of Michilin shouting 'Here!' Any other man would have shouted 'Stephen!' but not Michilin with the quick mind of the poacher and the instinct not to give anything away.

He was hauling himself up the bank when suddenly there was a bright flash and a loud bang.

Stephen saw a lot of things while the light of the flash lasted. It came from a shot-gun which was more or less pointed into the air, and he saw the black suffused face of Malachai Finnerty towering above Michilin who was keeping a tight grip on the barrel of the gun and forcing it into the air. At the tail-end of the flash he saw Malachai letting the gun go, drawing back his arm and hitting out with his closed fist. He heard the blow landing with a kind of dull splash, and then Michilin, gun, and flash had vanished out of sight.

Stephen came over the bank like a streak of lightning. He had gauged exactly where Malachai had been standing and found that he had guessed correctly when his two hands, stretching out, wrapped themselves around the body of the bailiff. The sight of Michilin taking that terrible blow had lighted a flame of rage in his heart, and when he felt his arms encircling the body of Malachai, the instinctive antipathy which had always been aroused in him by Finnerty's nearness surged up in him and he rejoiced that the time had come to get to grips with a man who was his enemy.

191

There was a gasp of surprise from Malachai and a grunt as the enormous arms of Stephen started to squeeze in his ribs. At first he relaxed, and then he applied pressure on his own behalf, but knew he was defeated when his stretching arms slipped and failed to get a hold on the wet naked skin of his antagonist. He drew back his arm then and brought it around with all his strength to crash his fist into the side of Stephen's face. The only result of this was that the pressure on his ribs was increased, and the determined silence of Stephen frightened him. He tried to catch Stephen's head and push it back with his hands, but it was like trying to shift a concrete column. Even when he caught his hair and tried to pull his head back with that, the silence and pressure just increased. Malachai could feel his eyes being squeezed out of his head and was afraid that, if he did not do something quickly, he would hear his ribs cracking like rotten twigs. Then he remembered the naked body.

He raised his right foot which was covered with the heavy boot, steel-tipped and hob-nailed, and brought it down with all his strength where he judged Stephen's foot would be.

Stephen felt the heavy boot tearing into his shin, which deflected it but did not save his foot. The boot landed on his big toe.

The pain forced him to release his hold, and then he felt Malachai's other boot crashing into his stomach. Fortunately he had been bent a little and the boot first landed in his chest before sinking in. Also the pain of his foot had caused him to tense his stomach muscles, or the fight would have been over. As it was he could not help himself from falling to the ground and writhing.

He had forgotten Malachai, and Michilin, and everything else until he felt Malachai's heavy weight descending on him, and knew dimly that Malachai was after his eyes when he felt the big calloused hands coming down on his face. With a great effort, he raised his hands from his stomach and caught the two hairy wrists before they settled into the gouging position. He had the advantage because his elbows were on the ground, but then he felt Malachai's heated breath on his cheek and knew that the mouth was open and that the teeth were coming down to catch some part of his face, so with all the strength left to him, he pulled his chin into his neck and brought up his forehead sharply. It landed on Malachai's nose and he could imagine the way his eyes watered. But Malachai was not finished and Stephen knew that there was extraordinary strength in the writhing body. He was sure of it when he felt Malachai pulling himself to his knees. With amazing clarity he knew that Malachai meant to rise a little and bring the force of one knee down into Stephen's naked crotch.

Stephen had recovered a little from the kick in the stomach, and Malachai had sold his advantage by moving his position, because as he was rising Stephen suddenly twitched the wrists he held, and with a great heave of his body found himself on top. He didn't waste time. He hit Malachai between the eyes with his fist. The blow did not land properly because Malachai reacted strongly and soon both of them were on their feet, swinging fists and bodies at each other. Stephen's naked body was easy to see in the darkness and he knew if the fight lasted much longer that he would not come out of it safely, so he reached out, caught Malachai's coat with his left hand, and drove his fist again and again into the other's face. He felt the blood on his hand after one or two blows, and then out of the corner of his eye he saw the boot coming at his stomach again. This time he was ready for it, and he caught the heel in his hand and was about to heave when Malachai's long arm came around his neck and a blow from the other fist landed on his thigh, just missing his middle.

Stephen was consumed with a great rage and it made him move twice as quickly. He dropped the leg, stood Malachai before him, and rained blows on every part of his body with fists that had hatred and anger behind them. Malachai fell back and Stephen followed him. He hit him again with all his strength and then stretching out, he caught his coat with his left hand, his crotch with the other hand, bent at the knees, and then lifted the big man into the air. The dull glint of the water showed him his position. He took two or three steps, bent and heaved, and Malachai, a dark mass of waving arms and legs, flew up and out and landed with a great splash in the water.

Stephen stood on the bank, his chest heaving.

'Come on and run, for Christ's sake,' said the voice of Michilin in his ear. 'That's enough for one night. Here, you bastard,' he said then, and his arm swung and Stephen could see the gun heading for the water, 'take that with you and may it never be of any use again.'

They turned then and trotted off. Stephen felt himself stumbling on the rough ground, and every time his toe hit anything, agonizing pains emanated from it.

'Here, Michilin,' he said, 'I'll have to put on some clothes.'

'Holy God,' said Michilin, 'that shot will have wakened the whole parish and me man Mullins'll probably be waitin' with another gun at the top a the road.'

'To hell with him!' said Stephen. 'Hand over!' And he sat down on the ground.

'Well, hurry, for God's sake,' said Michilin, throwing the clothes down beside him. Stephen pulled his sock and boot as delicately as he could over his wounded foot and, quickly lacing the other boot, he pulled on his shirt and trousers, and started trotting off with his coat on his arm.

'He didn't hurt you, Michilin, did he?' he asked.

'Arrah, not he,' said Michilin. 'All I got was a puck in the kisser, but he has an awful big fist that fella, and I couldn't do anythin' t' help yeh until it was all over. Holy God, I thought he was goin' teh do for yeh!'

'Look,' said Stephen, 'there's a light in Mullins's house.'

'To hell with 'm!' said Michilin. 'We'll just take a good run past. He won't know who the divil it is in the dark, an' if he does take it inta his head t' go down t' the Pool, I hope t' God he puts a loaded cartridge, a number one, inta the dirty pelt a that black bastard!'

They ran swiftly, and as silently as they could. Just as they were passing the house, the door opened and they saw

Mullins standing in the doorway, a storm lantern in his hand, and he wearin' nothing but his shirt.

'Ah, God, look at that,' said Stephen, laughing despite himself.

'Hey, y'oul eejit!' suddenly shouted Michilin out of the darkness. 'Go down quick to the Pool. They's a fella there whippin' lobsters out 'f it be the ass-cart. G'wan, an' run after 'm!'

The only result of this was that the figure of Mullins went in the door more quickly than he had come out, and they could hear the bolt being shot home. But Michilin's shout had disclosed their position to the dog and they saw the streak of him coming after them.

Michilin dealt with the dog. He ran on and the dog followed, and then, judging his position and timing nicely, he turned, met the dog full tilt, and kicked him with his heavy boot. The dog gave a bark of pain, then turned and scuttled back to the house.

Stephen and Michilin ran on.

They slowed their pace when they came out on the road leading to Crigaun.

'How'r' you feelin', Stephen?' Michilin asked.

'Not so good,' replied Stephen. 'My foot is sore, my shin is sore, my stomach is sore as well as a few other places, but apart from that I'm all right. But I'm warm, anyway. There's nothing like a good fight on a cold night for warmin' a fella up.'

'Ah,' said Michilin. 'It was great while it lasted.'

'That fella is a dangerous man, Michilin,' said Stephen, 'and he's stronger than I thought he was. I'd like to meet him in the daytime when I have my clothes on.'

'I'll say he's dangerous,' said Michilin. 'It was the grace a God put the sound 'f 'm inta me ear, and whin I saw him risin' 'msel' up from the ground with that bloody gun in's hand, I knew he meant business, so I just ran for 'm and shouted.'

'It was a damn good thing you did,' said Stephen, 'but I can't understand how he managed to catch us out there and why he didn't call Mullins instead of tryin' to handle 's himself.'

'That's easy,' said Michilin. 'D'you remember that time at the bridge when we were hidin' the gun? You remember that I thought I heard somethin'?'

'Yes,' said Stephen.

'Well, that was me man,' said Michilin, 'and I should be executed for havin' been put off so easy. He was waitin' there, an' I'd say that he was there when we passed back from the pub. I'll bet the dirty divil was all set to give 's a charge a shot whin we wint back for the gun, an' 'twas the luck a God that made 's turn on the road an' go off to the Pool.'

'So you think he'd have taken a shot at 's, do you?' Stephen asked.

'Can a duck swim?' asked Michilin.

'Yes,' said Stephen thoughtfully, 'I'm afraid that he's a bad enemy.'

'Who'r' yeh tellin'?' said Michilin. 'But there's a special saint somewhere that watches over the poachers and he brought 's safe. Not only that, but me brave Malachai must a left our gun exactly where we put it, an' if we hurry now we'll be able to get it before he chases up the road after 's.'

'He wouldn't be drowned by any chance, would he?' Stephen asked.

'Haven't we had enough luck for one night,' Michilin asked, 'without the good God bein' too kind to 's altogether? You don't expect miracles twice in the same night, do yeh?'

'No, I suppose not,' said Stephen. 'Do you know, Michilin, I have a feeling now about Finnerty, that this place is getting too small to hold both of us.'

'It's a grand mess to be in,' said Michilin. 'One man gunnin' for yer blood, and you coortin' the same man's sister.'

'Yes,' said Stephen.

'There'll be holy rooteach,' said Michilin, 'whin she hears about this.'

'If she hears about it,' remarked Stephen. 'I can't see Malachai talking about it, and oul Mullins will pretend that it was all a dream.'

'Yes,' said Michilin, 'but wimmin is quare eels. They have ways a knowing thin's and findin' out thin's that an honest man can't understand. Whin are yeh seein' her agin?'

'Tomorrow night,' said Stephen.

'You better have yer story ready so, me boy,' said Michilin.

When they reached the bridge they found that the gun was in the place where they had left it, showing how sure Malachai was or he'd have shifted its position and they would never have found it in the darkness.

They took it with them.

Coming through the village of Crigaun they saw that the pub was closed and in darkness, or they could have gone in and got something to take the cold out of their bones, and Michilin said he'd knock up J. J. now only he didn't want him looking too closely at the cut of them, and a blind ram could have seen that they were in the wars, which would have given rise to a lot of questions and answers which they would find it difficult to make, maybe.

Stephen left Michilin at his house, which lay on the fringe of the village. He refused Michilin's offer to come in an' rest 'msel' an' have a sup a hot tay, because he wanted to get home and examine his bruises.

Outside the Finnertys' house he stopped. He knew Malachai couldn't be home yet, and he thought of giving Kathleen the whistle which they had arranged between them. He knew she would come out, but on second thoughts he realized that he would have to explain things, and then Malachai would come home and find her out, and there would be trouble in store for her. So he passed on.

It was very late when he reached home.

All the house was in darkness, but he could feel the heat in the kitchen although the fire had been raked for the night. He pulled out a few of the red coals and boiled some milk for himself. He sat before the ash-covered fire in the lamplight, drank the milk, and ate a thick slice of home-made bread thickly coated with butter. He reflected that how-ever sloppy Mavis might be about other things, she could certainly bake a cake, wherever she had learned to do so. In fact, she had learned to bake in the girls' reformatory where she had been when she was young. She wouldn't have learned to do that well either if the nun in charge of the kitchens hadn't applied a birch cane to her backside many a time and oft.

Groaning, Stephen pulled himself from the chair, lighted a candle, doused the lamp, and went up to his own room. It was a warm little room because it was backed on to the fire-place. The box in which he used to keep his scribblings under the bed was a thing of the past, because just beside his bed he had built a small neat cupboard in which he could keep his manuscripts locked up. The other end of his wall was completely covered with bookshelves which he had made himself, buying the timber out of his illicit earnings. Now and again also, to his amazement, he would find a ten-shilling note or a pound on the table in his room, left there, he supposed, by his father when he was good and tight, and reflecting that if he hadn't Stephen to work for him he would have to pay a man at least fifteen shillings a week, so it was good business to drop a few shillings at him now and again, in case he should become too discontented.

Stephen undressed and looked himself over.

His toe was in a bad way. As well as being cut, it was badly bruised and was as black as the outside of a pot, but to his relief he found that it was not broken. There was a nasty cut all down his shin where the steel tip of the boot had found him. He opened his press, and extracting a bottle of iodine, flinchingly applied it to his cuts. There was a greenish bruise on his stomach, and the tip of his chest-bone was very sore, but he decided that they would do. The knuckles of his right hand were skinned, but he got some satisfaction out of that, because he knew that Malachai's face must be feeling tight and sore at this very minute.

He got into his shirt again preparatory to getting to bed.

Very few people in Connemara rise to the luxury of pyjamas, because they think it is a silly notion anyway dressing yourself up to go to bed, and the time it wastes. You go to bed in your shirt, and you get up in the morning and pull on your trousers and you are halfway dressed. If you put on thim other yokes, you have to strip yourself naked and stand shivering in yer pelt while yeh pull on a cold shirt over your head. Besides it's very nice to go to bed in your shirt and feel the sheets, or the blankets, nice and warm against your legs.

Stephen looked into the cupboard and smiled ruefully. He was almost twenty years of age now, and all that the cupboard contained was one manuscript of twenty pages, carefully pinned together. This was no wonder, because a month ago he had gone through the whole lot of them and they had so disgusted him that he had gone down in the middle of the night, pulled out the fire, and burned all of them, lock, stock, and barrel. Shortly after the hooley, and the first night he had kissed Kathleen, he had come home and, sitting down, he had put Thomasheen's travail on paper and he had called it 'Love's Young Dream'. He flicked through it now again, and his interest was aroused. He sat down on the edge of the bed and read it through.

He sat on for a little while after that, and said to himself, That's good, that is, if I say so myself. It is the only thing that has ever come near to pleasing me. I have it all right. I have something all right and the time has come to get down to serious business and begin trying to make a living out of it.

But how, he thought, pulling aside the bedclothes and getting into bed, and then Kathleen's philosophy came into his head, and he said to himself, You'll have to leave, my boy, you'll have to leave Connemara and get to Dublin. That's the place to get in touch. He knew he would get a job of some kind in Dublin, because he had the optimism of all the big men with strong lungs and healthy bodies. The examples of other men were before him, men who didn't need to have a degree from a University tacked on to the tail-ends of their names in order to make something of themselves. There was Sean O'Casey, to name but one, who had pulled

199

himself from the poverty and vileness and the, for him, beautiful inspiration of the filthiest slums in Dublin, to build a monument for himself in literature. Stephen's eyes caressed the plays of O'Casey on his bookshelves, *The Shadow of the Gunman*, *Juno and the Paycock*, *The Plough and the Stars*, *The Silver Tassie*. Aye, and there were others, too, who had woven tales and plays and stories and classics from their humble beginnings. Great men. It was an insult to couple your own name even with theirs, but you could, in your mind, hold them up as an example of men who started from nothing, who had no person on earth to give them a little shove from behind, and yet they had clawed their way to the top, often hungry, often ill, but the fire for ever burning in their eyes. They had something to say and they decided that they would say it, come hell or high water. And be Christ, said Stephen, blowing out the candle, I have something to say too, and I'll say it before I die or I'll know the reason why; and then he lay back with his arms under his head and thought what a great story it would make to put down about Malachai and himself fighting on the edge of a lobster pool and the anger and hatred that was burning in their breasts.

The sound of a heavy body making the springs groan in the bed in the other room brought him from his thoughts. He wondered why Mavis was sticking it out so long in Connemara, and wondered why she disliked him so much and why he couldn't bring himself to like her at all.

Then he thought of Kathleen, and he went to sleep, smiling.

CHAPTER FOURTEEN

The headland on which rests the village of Carnmore stretches like a cancerous finger into the sea, which has chewed its way into it at many points. At the base of this finger between Killaduff and Carnmore there is a small lake. It is a very peculiar lake that the people call Dead. Now there are many lakes in Connemara. It is very doubtful if any man ever tried counting them. Maps of the area will show at least a thousand, but there are indubitably many more which have been seen only by the eyes of those brave people who for ever live in bleak loneliness in cabins clinging to the gigantic sides of almost inaccessible mountains. The thing about all these lakes is that all of them have fish in them. If not salmon or sea-trout lakes, there are brown-trout lakes where the fish, for lack of the proper feeding, are scarcely as big as sardines, but beautifully shaped and coloured as delightfully as their big brothers. So that there is scarcely a lake in the hundreds of square miles that you could be uncertain of a fish from it.

Now the funny thing about the Dead Lake is that there were fish in it all right but no man had ever been known to catch a fish in it by fair means or foul, and that made it very mysterious indeed. It is not a big lake. It lies a short distance from the sea, and on its seaward side there is a very tall granite bank about ten feet above the water. On the opposite side, as is the way with all the lakes in Connemara, it slopes off into a little yellow-sanded beach, like a miniature strand. How do they know there *are* fish in it? I'll tell you. They know because many times during the year if you stroll down that way you will quite possibly find a dead fish stranded on that little beach. He will be a nice fish, but as you will see he will be very old, and even though you are not an expert you will see at once the reason the fish died. He died of old age. It's the most amazing thing. Every fisherman in the Three Villages had a shot at trying to take a fish out of this lake, and the much-vaunted 'gintlemin' fishermen that fished the neighbourhood during the season tried to take a fish from it. Despite all the equipment they carried, despite their split-cane rods, and greenhearts, and steel casting rods, despite their baits and lures, despite their books and books of flies, their Connemara Blacks, and Blue and Black Zulus, and Scarlet Devils, and Fenians and Fancies and Cowdungs and

Blue bottles, to assuage their own defeated egos, they ignored the evidence of the found fish and departed, cursing quite frequently, but stoutly declaring that there couldn't be a fish in the so-and-so, such-and-such cursed goddamn hole in the ground, because if there had been, by-damn, sir, the old Zulu would have pulled him out of it like the shot out of a gun, or the old Fiery Brown or one of a million others. A great fly in early July, the Zulu, dammit. Killed thirty-seven sea trout and four salmon on Inagh and the Derryclare butt last season, curse it. Fish there? Go boil an egg!

So they departed.

Now the people could have told them before they started that they were only wasting their time, but then they knew that all these yokes that go around with fly-books and castin's hanging out of them like Christmas trees, are mad anyhow and do nothing else all their lives but waste their own time and the time of the poor man who has to pull them around a lake all day.

The people could have told them it was fruitless because Michilin had been known to try everything in the book to get a fish out of it and failed. He started with the rod and the flies and flogged it for weeks in all kinds of favourable fishing conditions. Next he tried the earthworms on it. No use. Then he bought meat and left it until it was rotten and stinking to the high heavens, and when the little white maggots in the meat had grown fat and fulsome, he fished with those, and everybody knows that if there is a trout within fifty miles of one a the white maggots, he'll come to it like a suckin' calf to your fingers. He might as well been at home fishin' in the basin for all the notice they took of 'm.

Michilin tried some more dodges. He flung an oul otterboard in it, and he netted it and did other things which it wouldn't be good for respectable honest fishermen to know, but all failed. Then, thoroughly exasperated, he came down one evening just as the sun was setting and he flung enough dynamite into it to blow up half the village, but all he got was a great drenching for all his pains, so Michilin, cursing the oul yoke 'f a lake sulphureously, departed, never to return and try again.

And the Dead Lake returned to its original placidity and remained undisturbed.

Another peculiar thing about it was that the birds always avoided the Dead Lake. Now birds are very friendly little things that everybody loves, except when the bastards are goin' after yer oats, and it was no doubt a funny thing that you'd never see one of them hovering around. Even the oul saygulls or thim horrible yokes a dirty oul cormorants avoided it as if it had some kind of bird-plague. So there you had a very peculiar lake. Wasn't it only natural, then, that the stories should start springing up about it, and that some sinister reason should be found for its peculiarities?

The reasons were found.

About a few hundred yards from the Lake there are to be seen the ruins of a house lying, moss-grown and terribly silent, in the centre of a flat, very green and verdant field. It is obviously the ruins, not of a thatched cabin, but of what was once a tall two-storey house, which must have been very large and very commodious, and probably carries more grandeur in its decay than it ever did when it was alive. The house is fact number one.

Behind the house is the sea. At this point it has eaten its way very forcibly into the land. There are not-very-high cliffs there which have resisted, sturdily enough, the pounding of the waves. At one point, however, the sea found a soft spot and battered its way through. It is a peculiar but not unusual sight. The top part of the cliff resisted the sea and remains towering in a great arch over the chasm below where the sea for ever thunders. Even when the tide is low the sea still beats at the bottom of this narrow gorge. This arch over the chasm is fact number two.

Now the people said to themselves, Somethin' terrible musta happened here long ago or we'd be able t' get a few oul trout outa that yoke oo a lake, and then they would turn to their old Momos, drooling in the corner and nodding their old lives away, and they'd say, Hey, Momo, what happened down beyant at the Dead Lake when me man What's-his-name had the big house there? And the old Momos, resentfully awakened from their puerile dreams, would cup a hand to the ear and say, Is it oul Martin's place y' mane? Ah, the poor man with the broken heart, the Lord have mercy on 'm, even tho the bastard was a black Protestant, so he was, God between 's an' harm; and the Momos would go on talking, but nobody paid any attention to them any more, and the legend of oul Martin and his broken heart grew up and was suitably embroidered.

The story now ran thus. One bleak November evening, whin the rain was comin' down in torrents an' the lightnin' runnin' acrost the sky like me man What-you-may-call-'m with the wings on 's heels, poor oul Martin comin' home after a hard day's work in the fields, goes inta the house there an' what does he see but me brave wife a his, the one with the beautiful hair like the tops a the oats when it's ready for the cuttin', an' there she was, if y' don't mind, up in the bed with the satin sheets on it an' she larkin' away with the tall good-lookin' fella that was supposed t' be lookin' after the farm for poor oul Martin. The poor man couldn't believe his eyes, so he couldn't, but whin the sight came back to them he jumps on me man with a roar a rage, an' before yeh could say 'Iosa' he has the life throttled out oo 'm, an' melassie there still in the bed an' her clothes all disordered and she watchin' brave Martin chokin' the gits out me man until the two eyes pops out oo 's head. Hah, you bitch, says he to her then, and catchin' her, fires her over his shoulder an' off with 'm down to the Lake an' she screamin' the head off 'rsel'. An' fair an' square he dumps her inta the Lake, and she comes up three times t' beg for mercy, but every time she does he fires a lump of granite into 'r kisser until she gives up the ghost.

Me brave Martin isn't finished yet. No fear! Back with 'm to the house, an' snatchin' hot turfs from the hearth he goes around an' sets fire to the whole place, lock, stock, and barrel, an' then he goes out an' dances on the lawn while the flames consume the mortal remains a the man that cuckoo'd 'm.

He's not finished yet. No fear! Off with 'm down to the cliffs, an' with a yell a fear an' desperation an' the last cry oo 's broken heart he lepps under the arch an' down inta the ragin' sea, an' it batin' on the rocks to pound 'm inta nothin'; so that's why the Dead Lake beyant'll never give up a fish, and why the birds will not come next or near it, and why often if you're down near the arch there you'll hear a despairin' cry over the beat a the sea, an' some nights if yer passin' the oul ruin you'll see a man in funny clothes dancin' on the green grass.

So nobody ever came near the Dead Lake or the ruined house or the arch of the sea if they could avoid it at all.

That was why Stephen and Kathleen always met there when the weather was fine, because they knew that they would be undisturbed.

The raised bank above the Lake was split at one point, and many ferns and soft green grass grew there. It was about four feet deep and it provided great shelter from the cold and the wind.

Kathleen sat there now and waited for Stephen. Although it was late spring, the winter had remained very late, and this night now was a cold one and the frost still hardened the ground. Kathleen was sitting in the cleft, but she was wrapped warmly in the black shawl which she had borrowed from her sister-in-law. It was not quite dark, but it was very still, and she could hear the sea flogging the cliffs behind her with green and white whips. Her thoughts were not pleasant because she was disturbed by the row she had had with her brother Malachai.

That morning he had been late in bed, which was not usual with him. The breakfast had been eaten, the cows milked, and the hens fed before he had put in an appearance. When she had arrived in the kitchen in the morning she had seen the clothes which he had been wearing last night hanging on a chair in front of the fire and they were sopping wet. Tim, when he had come down from Nora's bed, had fingered them and asked Jack what had happened to Malachai. Presumably Jack knew, since himself and Malachai slept in the same bed, but he just pulled on a blacker face than usual and said, 'How the hell do I know? For God's sake give 's the breakfast.'

They had left it at that. The two men had gone to examine the sluices, and Nora had arrived, big and complaining, from her bed, before she had heard Malachai stirring at all.

When Malachai did appear he was dressed in his Sunday clothes. One of his eyes was black, he had a cut on the bridge of his nose, and one of his front teeth was missing. Kathleen stood looking at him in amazement, and when he saw the look, he had almost snarled at her.

'What the hell are yeh lookin' at?' he said. 'Wouldn't you be better employed makin' a sup a tay?'

'There's no need to bite the nose off me,' said Kathleen. 'Is it any wonder I'd be lookin' at you? What happened to you?'

'Mind your own bloody business,' he shouted, 'and get the tay!' And he pulled a chair to the table and sat down noisily. Kathleen proceeded with her work, but she was thinking.

She had seen too many men after they had been fighting not to know that Malachai had been beaten, and she wondered what he had done to his antagonist. That made her catch her breath and she wondered if it had been Stephen. She didn't know why she had thought of Stephen, except perhaps that she was always afraid that they would come to blows some day, and then she hadn't seen Stephen last night. She knew he had been with Michilin, and wondered if by any chance Malachai had at last caught up with them. Then the thought of Malachai's gun came into her mind.

'What did you do with your gun?' she asked suddenly and anxiously.

'Did I tell yeh t' get the tay?' shouted her brother, turning on her, and the glare in his bloodshot eyes made her hold her peace.

Malachai couldn't very well tell her that his grand gun was at the bottom of the Lobster Pool, and that somehow or other he'd have to go back to oul Mullins and try and persuade him to empty the pool until he could get it; and a nice mess it would be in when he did get it, after being immersed in sea-water for so long.

Malachai had not come home to his dinner at all, but had taken bread and butter with him in his pocket when he was going out. He arrived home for his tea, and he was carrying the gun. After his tea, he had cleared the table and, taking the gun to pieces, had started to clean it. Nora was sitting in front of the fire, resting her big stomach on her knees, when Kathleen was preparing to go out and see Stephen. Tim and Jack had gone over to J. J.'s pub in Crigaun for a drink.

'I'll take the loan of your shawl, Nora,' said Kathleen.

'All right,' said Nora. 'It's little use I have for shawls now anyhow, and the condition I'm in.'

'Where are you goin'?' Malachai asked, looking up from his work.

'Mind your own business!' said Kathleen tartly.

'I hope you're not goin' out to meet that O'Riordan fella,' said Malachai.

'If I am atself,' said Kathleen, 'that's nothing to do with you.'

He rose to his feet.

'I'll make it somethin' to do with me,' he said. 'I warned you before, and I'm warnin' you again now to have nothin' t' do with him or you'll be sorry for it, so you will.'

'Look,' said Kathleen, getting angry, 'I came home from England to help ye, so I did, and the only reason I'm not gone back long ago is because Nora here is so helpless expectin'; but you just keep your nose out of my affairs or I'll pack up tomorrow mornin' and go, as sure as God made me, so I will!'

That stopped Malachai for the moment, because even he could imagine what the house would be like if a pregnant slattern like Nora was left to look after it on her own.

'I'm warnin' you,' he said. 'That fella is no good. No honest fella would be breakin' the law like he does. He's dodged me for long enough. Isn't it enough that they are laughin' at the way himself an' Fagan are goin' on, besides havin' them laughin' at me about 'm goin' round with me sister? I'm tellin' yeh now, so I am, that I'm goin' to catch up with that bastard, an' when I do that there'll be very little of 'm, so if you want 'm to stay whole, keep away from him, because I'm goin' t' settle for 'm.'

'Maybe,' said Kathleen, looking significantly at Malachai's face, 'that he's well able to look after himself.'

'You . . . !' said Malachai, his face suffused with red rage, and he came over to her with his hand raised. His demeanour did not frighten her, but she was sure that he was going to hit her.

'I wouldn't do it, Malachai,' she said. 'Because if you do, I'll hit you back with something, so I will, and I swear on my solemn oath that I'll leave this house.'

That stopped him, but it was some time before he could recover himself. Then through his teeth he said 'Get out!' and went back to his gun-cleaning. Kathleen left then and made her way to the Dead Lake.

She threw a stone at the dark water. It entered with a plop, and left large lazy circles when it sank. Funny, she thought, that I'm not the least afraid sitting by the Dead Lake when the dark is falling, and she remembered when she was a child being terrified in case she would have to pass by it even though one or other of her brothers or a companion would be with her. Now, the thought that she might see some of the phantoms that were supposed to walk hereabouts did not disturb her at all. The only part of the story that affected her was the part about the young wife drowning here in this very lake at her feet, and the husband, mad, pelting her with stones to make her stay down, just like she had seen Malachai do long ago when they were children and their mother had sent them out to drown six unwanted kittens in the near-by lake.

She remembered being surprised that day. She had always

thought that cats could not swim, and before the deed she thought she would remain quite unmoved. Then Malachai deliberately threw the furry balls into the water one by one. The water made the fur cling to the little bodies so that they became very tiny and helpless-looking, and they started to mew as they swam around trying to get back to the bank. When they reached it, they would scratch with their little paws at the clay and look up with barely-seeing eyes at the two children above them. Then Malachai bent down and picked up some heavy stones and began to fire them at the kittens. The second stone he threw landed sickeningly on one of the little skulls, and she heard it crack before she turned away crying bitterly, and ran out to the road. Malachai just turned his head after her and then continued with his occupation before following her home slowly. Her dislike of her brother dated from that day, and she could never feel towards him as she knew other girls felt towards their brothers. She had never quite succeeded in blotting that memory out of her mind.

The thought of the poor golden-haired wife dying like one of those kittens made her shiver and look at the dark water, so silent and secret-keeping. She rose hurriedly to her feet and looked over the bank.

She forgot her fears as she saw the big body of Stephen coming towards her across the field that divided the lake from the road. She waved a hand at him. He saw the wave and started to run towards her. Reaching the cut, he jumped down into it.

'Hello,' he said.

'Hello,' she said.

'It's a nice night,' said Stephen.

'What are you trying to hide?' she asked.

'Nothing,' said Stephen, laughing.

'Every time,' said she, 'that you start talking about the weather it means that you don't want me to talk about something else.'

'What a brain!' said Stephen.

'Where were you last night?' she asked.

'Let me see,' mused Stephen, looking up at the darkening sky. 'I met Michilin, and we decided that it was too dark to do any "work", so we went into J. J.'s and we leaned on the counter there and we had a couple of nice frothy pints, and we walked home, and went to bed like respectable citizens. Now, does that satisfy you?'

'No,' said Kathleen, 'it doesn't.'

'I'll have to make up a story for you so,' said Stephen. 'Look, Kathleen, suppose I had the utter misfortune to be married to you, would you be questioning me to an inch of me life every night about what I did and where I was and all the rest of it?'

'You bet I would,' said Kathleen.

They both laughed, but then Kathleen sobered.

'Stephen,' she said, looking down and pulling a daisy to pieces with her finger.

'Yes?' said Stephen interrogatively.

'When Malachai got up this morning,' she said, 'he had a black eye, a split nose, one of his teeth was missing, and his clothes were wet.'

'Goodness,' said Stephen, 'he must have tripped over a match-box.'

'I was thinking,' said Kathleen, 'that he stumbled over you.'

'It could be,' said Stephen, after a pause.

Kathleen lifted her head then.

'Let me look at your face,' she said.

He turned his face towards her and she put a hand on his cheek, and bending forward she looked closely at him. So he kissed her.

'No, Stephen,' she said, pulling away, 'this is serious.'

'So am I,' said Stephen, kissing her again, but she hardened herself to him and held him off with her hand.

'Please, Stephen,' she said, 'will you tell me what happened?'

'I will,' said Stephen. 'We went down to the Lobster Pool, because we had a few drinks taken and we were silly enough to listen to that oul bladder, Liam the Postman, who dared us to pinch a few lobsters out of the Pool. I was swimming in the Pool when the brave Malachai comes up and tackles Michilin. Michilin shouted and I came out, and Malachai and myself had a few rounds and Malachai ended up in the water. That's all.'

There was a silence for a moment.

'But you are not marked at all,' she said, puzzled, 'and Malachai is a very big man, nearly as big as yourself. Did he do nothing at all to you?'

'My dear Kathleen,' said Stephen, 'the injuries which I suffered are in places which I couldn't possibly show you unless we were married, and even then I wouldn't strip off on a cold night like this to show them.'

'They are not too bad, are they?' she asked anxiously.

'I'll get over them,' said Stephen.

'I'm sorry this happened, Stephen,' she said. 'If it was any other two men, I would say that it was the best thing that could happen, but not with you and Malachai, because neither of you are the kind that can fight and forget, and I'm afraid that Malachai will be only worse after this. Besides this only makes it harder for me. It was bad enough before to have them talking at home about you, but after this it will get worse and worse. It makes me afraid, Stephen, so it does.'

'All right,' said Stephen. 'Here, Kathleen, give us a bit of the shawl, it's cold, and I'll tell you about thoughts I was thinking when I was lying awake this morning. Come on.'

She put a bend of the shawl around him and he put his big arm around her waist and they rested against the bank, with her head on his shoulder. Her black hair was rubbing against his cheek. He was silent for a time, thinking how grand it was to be just this way, and remembering Michilin's taunt that before he knew it he'd be married and mindin' kids. He reflected that, with Kathleen, he wouldn't mind at all.

'What were the great thoughts, Stephen?' Kathleen asked.

'Well,' said Stephen, putting his other arm across below

211

her breasts, 'it's this. Even last night with Malachai, I knew that this Connemara was too small to hold both of us, and since there is little chance of Malachai packing his bags, that it better be me. That was number one. I decided to go. Then you remember the night you were giving me down the banks for sticking in Connemara when I should be up and off and getting new slants on life? That decided me as well. But there was a more important reason yet, which I only fully realized then, and that was that I love you very much indeed, and that the primary aim of my life must be to marry you.'

'Oh, Stephen,' said Kathleen, turning her face up to him.

Stephen kissed her, and the kiss lasted a long time. This time it was he who pulled himself away.

'None of that, now,' he said, 'if you want me to tell you all my thoughts. Where was I? Yes, I had decided to marry you. I said to myself, How the hell am I going to do that? Then I reviewed the position, and I must admit that it looked very black indeed. I have a father who has a farm, an amount of money which I know nothing about, and who is not particularly attached to me. Ignoring that, he is a very strong man with a sound body and will probably live to be a hundred and ten, so there is little hope there of being able to marry on the farm. That's the debit side. What have we on the credit side? We have me – the animal. A good strong animal, sound in wind and limb, who should be a good worker and who should be able with the strength of his body to keep a wife, and at least to keep the life in her body. So, the solution is that I will leave the Connemara of my fathers and probably seek work in Dublin, because in Dublin alone, I'm afraid, can I find the fulfilment of my ambitions, the beginning of them, anyhow. In Dublin I will work for some time until I have earned a little capital, and then you will join me there. We will be respectably married, and with you to be there, to have to work for, I will become what I want to be after many years of endeavour. What do you think of that?'

'It's sensible enough, up to a point,' said Kathleen, 'but why must I be left here alone while you're up in Dublin?

Why can't I go along with you, and why can't I work too, so that we can have more money?'

'Because,' said Stephen, 'there's some prehistoric feeling moving in me, a real old-fashioned feeling that refuses to let my wife work for my living, and I refuse to keep a wife if I can't feed her.'

'But, Stephen,' said Kathleen, 'I don't want to be just married to you. Can't we leave the marriage business until later when we have money? Why can't we just go off together and then become respectable when we can afford it?'

'That's a nice way,' said Stephen, 'for a young Catholic girl to be talkin'! Is that all the meas you have on the catechism?'

'The only real meas I have, Stephen,' said Kathleen, 'is on you, and whatever you want to do, I'll do it.'

'Stop temptin' me, will y'?' said Stephen. 'No, Kathleen, I worked this all out last night. It's a long-term plan, but I know that it will work, because I have the feeling inside me for it, and the inclination too. Let's have it my way.'

'All right,' said Kathleen, 'but when are you going?'

'I'm going,' said Stephen, 'as soon as the ray-grass is green in the hay-meadows. I don't want to walk out on the old man until then, because he finds it so hard to get hired men. But as soon as the hay is neatly cocked in the field, I'll take up my bag and depart.'

'That'll be about two months so,' said Kathleen.

'Yes,' said Stephen.

'How long will it be, d'ye think,' asked Kathleen, 'before you send for me?'

'I can promise you,' said Stephen, 'that it won't be long, because I want to have you around more than you could like having me.'

'But how long?' Kathleen persisted.

'Say a month,' said Stephen.

'That's not too long,' said Kathleen. 'Nora's baby will have been born then so that I can leave them with an easy conscience.'

'Won't it be nice?' said Stephen.

'I wish it was now,' said Kathleen, and then they lapsed into a thoughtful silence. The thought of being married to Kathleen made Stephen feel very good. He had a vision of her head on a pillow and her face framed by her black hair, that would look kind of blue in the light of the morning.

'Wasn't it terrible, Stephen,' said Kathleen, 'what me man did to his wife when he drowned her in the lake there?'

'What man?' asked Stephen.

'Oul Martin,' said Kathleen. 'I get a kind 'f a shiver when I look at the water there. I'd hate to have to be drowning in it.'

'Don't be silly,' said Stephen. 'That never happened at all.'

'How do you know?' Kathleen asked.

'Because I do,' said Stephen. 'It's a grand story, but it's too good to be true. Martin was a man that came here from Dublin and built the house for some reason or other. Then he just packed up one day and departed. Probably Connemara got him down. So he went away, and all the inhabitants started helping themselves to his house. If a fella wanted a few slates, he just went down and took them off the roof of Martin's house. They started with the roof and then worked their way through the floors and the stairs and all the rest of it. And when all the timber had gone they helped themselves to the stones to build their miserable cottages. It was a good job the poor man never came back to look at his property or he'd think the ants had been at it.'

'I don't believe that,' said Kathleen.

'That's because you're romantic,' said Stephen, 'and you like to think of the poor, yellow-haired, unfaithful-to-her-husband lassie being drowned in the lake and the poor simpleton dancing on the lawn with the flames roaring to the skies. It's a grand story but it's pure seanachie stuff, and it was invented solely to supply salve to the guilty conscience of the house-breakers.'

'You're an awful man,' said Kathleen, laughing, 'for ruining a lovely superstition like that, and I'm sure you'll get no one to believe you, so you won't.'

'Nobody,' said Stephen, 'wants to believe in the mundane.'

'Would you do that to me, Stephen,' Kathleen asked, 'if you found me shenannagin with the hired hand?'

'You bet,' said Stephen, laughing, 'and much worse than that. I'd think up a much more sticky end for you than that.'

'You won't ever have the need to,' said Kathleen, looking up at him again.

'Won't I?' asked Stephen, bending down to her.

'No,' said Kathleen, 'you won't, because I will always want you.'

As Stephen bent to kiss her, his closing eyes noticed where her blouse loosed from her neck. He could see her chest where it whitened below the sun-tanned place exposed to the weather, and he saw the upper part of her full breasts, gently rounding.

His breath caught in his throat as he kissed her and his encircling arm pulled her towards him until he could feel his chest against hers. Their bodies sank further down the bank. The night triumphed over the dusk and the stars took brilliant possession of the skies.

CHAPTER FIFTEEN

It was late evening during the first week in July, and Stephen was eating his supper in Danny's cottage.

It was a very tasty supper. All that day they had been mackerel-fishing with great success. They had returned when the boat was almost filled with mackerel. They had put the currach away, cleaned the gear, packed the fish-boxes and dispatched them to Clifden where they would be whisked by lorry to the Dublin agent. So now they were eating fresh mackerel and potatoes, to be followed by tea and home-made cake, as well as the butter which had been churned from the milk of Danny's cow.

Mackerel is not a nice dish unless it is fresh, but when you have a mackerel that has just died and when you cook it in the pan, it curls up at the edges just like a trout, and it tastes very well indeed.

As he ate, Stephen marvelled again at Danny.

His cottage was very small but it was a model for any housewife in Connemara. The table at which they were eating was white from eternal scrubbing, and you could almost imagine that the top of it was a clean tablecloth. Then the dresser over there with all its delf and they shining and reflecting the lamplight from the polishing which they received. The cottage consisted of just two rooms, the kitchen and a bedroom above. The bedroom was severe in its simplicity, just a bed and a chair and a home-built cupboard for clothes. There was a little table too, with books on it, mostly magazines that told you about fishing and farming and the ailments of domestic animals and how to cure them. Apart from that, Danny did not seem to read much. He wouldn't have much time for reading anyhow, if he was to look after his little piece of land and the cow, and fish as well.

But it was the cake that took Stephen for a walk.

He remarked on it as he sunk his strong teeth into a large hunk of it which was thickly coated in freshly-churned butter.

'How in the name of God, Danny,' he asked, 'do you make a cake like this? Honest to God, there isn't a house in the whole place I know that can make one as good as it.'

Danny smiled, and each side of his face creased into a million wrinkles.

'Oh, I just picked it up,' he said.

'Well,' said Stephen, 'with cake like that, and the way you can make butter just right, and keep the house so that you could eat all your meals on the floor if you wanted to, if only you were a woman, Danny, I'd marry you in the morning meself, so I would.'

As he said that, he wondered why Danny had never married. There was nobody in the Three Parishes who didn't have the good word for him. He was known as a very steady and good man, who took a few pints during the week but who was never known to have been seen drunk and disorderly. Then he was always willing, in his limited spare time, to help a neighbour, and you could be sure that if he did help you, he would do so with the minimum of blather and the maximum of efficiency.

'Why did you never get married, Danny?' asked Stephen, buttering another piece of bread.

Danny was silent for a time.

'Maybe I never wanted to,' said he then.

'That's something I don't believe,' said Stephen. 'Speaking from my own limited experience, I know damn well that we are all put into the world with strong masculine desires, and whether you are good or bad there always comes a time in your life when you want to settle down with some woman and have kids. There must have been a time in your life when you wanted to marry someone.'

'There was,' said Danny, lifting his head, which was grey-streaked like a badger's fur.

'Why didn't you?' asked Stephen.

'I never got around to asking her,' said Danny.

'And when you did get around to it,' said Stephen, 'I suppose some other fella had beaten you to it.'

'It happened something like that,' said Danny.

'But,' said Stephen, filling himself another cup of tea from the brown enamel teapot, 'you're not going to tell me that, just because you were too slow with the first one, you didn't ask any other woman after that.'

'No,' said Danny, carefully, 'I didn't.'

'But why?' Stephen asked. 'I know there are such things as a man wanting to marry one woman, and if he doesn't get her he is lonely and sorry and all that, but surely you can't go on like that all your life.'

'This woman,' said Danny, 'was a very special sort oo a woman.'

The laughing wrinkles had gone from his eyes, and there was something in his voice that made Stephen look at him closely.

Funny, he thought, if even Danny should have a story. You would never think somehow that Danny, with his careful, clean method of living and his quiet efficiency, had ever had anything happen to him in his smooth, even life that would make him feel deeply. Stephen knew Danny well, and of all the people he knew, he thought that Danny was an open book. He would be one of those people his mother would have called a Hero, and left him at that.

'What happened to her?' he asked, almost cursing that something in him which never allowed him to leave things as they were, that forced him to be always asking questions and probing away at things that were no concern of his, just to find out, and then that other sly part of him that was for ever arranging details of things which he heard in their proper order, fixing them up, adding and subtracting from them, romanticizing them, and putting them away to be brought out and dusted off when they would be required to fit into a pattern.

'Nothing happened to her,' said Danny, 'except that she married somewan else. That's all.'

'Do I know her? Is she someone from about here?' Stephen persisted.

'She's not around here any longer,' said Danny, leaving the first part of the question unanswered. He rose from the table, pulled the wooden chair around to the fire, and sitting in it, took a well-worn pipe out of his waistcoat pocket, shoved it into his mouth, extracted a plug of tobacco from his pocket and commenced to cut into it with a penknife. 'But I met nobody since,' he went on, to Stephen's surprise, 'who was even a patch on her. In fact, I learned my cake-making, that you seem t' like so much, from watching her.'

'Well,' said Stephen, 'if she was the one that taught you how to make cakes like this, I don't blame you for staying faithful to her memory.'

'She could make a cake all right,' said Danny, rubbing the tobacco into his palm.

'Did you ever ask her to marry you?' asked Stephen.

'No,' said Danny, 'I didn't.'

218

'Then how the hell,' said Stephen, stretching for more bread, 'could you expect her not to marry some other fella?'

'I couldn't,' said Danny, 'but she was too good for me altogether, I'm afraid, and besides, that time I was working for your father, I had only fifteen bob a week, an' you could hardly expect a woman to share that with you.'

'How do you know that she would or not,' Stephen asked, 'if you never asked her?'

'Oh, I knew all right,' said Danny, filling the bowl of the pipe from his palm. 'She wasn't cut out for me. She was a woman with great education and a mind. She couldn't have lived long with me, because you know the kind I am. I can't talk about things much, except the little things that matter to a fella's life. I could never be talkin' about books an' things, and the fellas that wrote them. But she was a great wan for that, so she was, always gettin' new books, an' she could talk about anythin' under the sun. The oney thing was that you'd feel then, that she would never be plazed to set up house with yourself, when you could be talkin' about nothin' all the year except cows an' manure an' hay an' all thim other things.'

'Maybe she would have been quite happy to listen to them,' said Stephen.

'No, she wouldn't,' said Danny, shaking his head.

'Was the fella she married well up like that so?' Stephen asked.

'Well,' said Danny, 'he was a great one to read, and he had travelled about and all that and he was a clever man.'

'Was she happy with him?' asked Stephen.

Danny paused for a long time before he answered.

'No,' said he at last, 'I don't think she was happy with him.'

And then suddenly something clicked in Stephen's brain. He held the cup he was about to drink from clenched between his hands. Whether it was the early reference to his mother or not, all the little pieces from his childhood memories started to fall into place, and he remembered a lot of things. He remembered Danny's face when he came to the Lake with the message to hurry home, that his mother was going off with the doctor. He remembered Danny's face after she had gone, and he wandering off the road by himself. He remembered Danny when they had got word that she was dead. He remembered noticing that Danny never spoke much to his father and that he had often seen him looking at his father with actual hostility. Would that be it? Of course it was! It couldn't be anything else. All the guarded references to the books and much too good for me.

Stephen set down his cup, and taking his chair he brought it down beside Danny at the fire. Then he sat and lighted a cigarette with a hot coal from the fire, and leaned back in the chair.

'Danny,' said he, 'was it my mother?'

Danny was holding a coal to the tobacco with a tongs when Stephen put the question. He stopped pulling at the air, and then slowly left the tongs beside the hob. Stephen noticed that even now he was careful to leave the tongs in its correct position. Then he rested his elbows on his knees, and started to twist the bowl of the pipe between his fingers.

'Yes, Stephen,' said he. 'It was your mother.'

Stephen was silent, because he could not think of anything to say. His mother had been dead five years now, was it? Five years seemed a long time to him, but if Danny had a feeling for his mother he must have had it since she came to Connemara, which would be more than twenty years ago. Twenty years! My God, a whole lifetime. Stephen felt that he just could not assimilate it, and again he thought how foolish it was for a fellow like himself, who thought impudently that he knew a lot, to go around appraising people when he didn't really know the first thing about them. Imagine a calm, ordinary-appearing man like Danny, having a thing like that inside him for such a long time.

'I wouldn't mind having you for a father anyhow, Danny,' he said.

'There was little hope of that,' said Danny, with a laugh.

They were silent then, and Stephen felt that the happy care-free life of fishing which they had known was over, because they would never again feel the same with this shared knowledge between them. Memories of his mother came flooding back to him as he sat there, the way she smiled and the way she talked and the most unorthodox way she had reared him. For some time the air seemed to be full of her. He had not thought of her often in the intervening years. After the blow of her death had softened, he had put her away in a cranny of his brain and sealed it. On a few occasions he had taken her letter to him out of his cupboard and had read it and suffered some more, but not a lot, because as time passed she seemed to him to have been some kind of a fairy spirit who had lived for a short time on earth in an assumed form and had again departed to other climes.

The thought now, that Danny had loved her, and still did, and had remained in a lonely cottage on the lip of the strand, aye, and from where he could see the headstones in the island forming against the horizon, backed by Atlantic clouds, all this seemed to give her body again, and bring her before his mind as she had been. He remembered the feeling he had of being alone when she had died. The same feeling of helplessness descended on him now and he felt that all his little plans, all his confidence in himself, were misplaced. He rose to his feet.

'I better be going, Danny,' he said.

'If that's the way you feel,' said Danny.

'No, Danny,' said Stephen. 'Don't be thinking now that I feel insulted that you should have had a feeling for my mother. I can say sincerely that it would have been better for all of us if she had taken you. It's difficult to talk about things like this, but I feel good that you could have felt that way about her, and from what I remember of her, I think it is a great pity that you did not tell her how you felt at the first and things might have been much different.'

'Maybe so,' said Danny, rising too. 'But that's the way things are. Will you be able to come out tomorrow?'

'I don't think so,' said Stephen. 'That meadow above will be ripe for tramping tomorrow, and I want to get it finished. It's the last field.'

'You're goin' then, aren't you?' Danny asked.

'Yes,' said Stephen, 'I'm going then.'

'I'll probably come up and give you a hand with it so,' said Danny.

'That's the stuff,' said Stephen, standing at the door and regarding the brilliant summer night. 'I'll see you then. It's going to be fine tomorrow too.'

'There's a good set on the weather now,' said Danny.

'Well, so-long,' said Stephen, stepping into the darkness.

'Good night,' said Danny, and watched him until he had gone out of sight. He stood at the door for a while, and looked over at the graveyard at Ourish. Then he went in and tackled the dishes.

Walking up towards his house Stephen seemed to be hearing the voice of Martha all about him. He remembered that often as they had walked this road to the strand of a dark night she had talked to him about the Connemara fairies, trying to frighten him, because reading and hearing about the good people in the daytime is entertaining, but when you are on a country road at night they assume sinister proportions. At least that's what his mother tried to instil into him, but Stephen could never be afraid. She thought he had some lack in him on account of this, but it was really the fault of her own early training, when she would set out to demolish in his mind the bogies that haunt the thoughts of the living. Then he had always been big of body with a questioning mind, and he had never been really afraid of anything.

He could almost feel her walking beside him now, the jerky way she had at times, her eyes dancing in her head and her hands moving to explain something, and the clear ringing laugh of hers, that made something loosen inside despite yourself and you would feel happy and cheerful and think what a great thing it was to have Martha for a mother.

But Danny! Stephen thought it was a great pity that she hadn't noticed Danny enough and married him, even though it meant that he would never have been born, or if he was born he would have been a different hybrid altogether. But

222

Danny would have suited her. He was so quiet and peaceful and he would have been so good to her. He would never quite understand her, but then she could have mothered him, and maybe she would have tried vainly to educate him, and he would be willing to be a guinea-pig just to please her. Danny was an eye-opener.

He was an eye-opener, because up to this Stephen had had fixed ideas about the love-life of the Connemara people. According to him, many years of illiteracy and hard living had made them completely unconscious of the finer emotions. He had regarded them as animals really as far as living in their minds was concerned. He had seen them when he was young. According to all the books he had read, the civilized world, as the writers knew it, was plagued and pestered and poxed with this problem of sex for the young. Between psychologists and doctors and eminent wives and playwrights, the whole thing was wrapped up as confusingly as a fly caught in a large ball of cotton-wool. It was simple in Connemara. The children were used to sex almost since the day they were born. Crowded living had made them familiar with the bodies of each other, and seeing the animals in action had simplified the whole thing for them. So it all developed into a question of whether you should or you shouldn't. The Church looked after the shouldn't part of it and it was not unsuccessful, but Mother Nature took care of the other part, and many answered the call. To Stephen it had developed into a question of mind over body. He had read quite a bit of Saint Augustine and other thinkers when he was young, who claimed that abstinence and continence were good for the intellect. Then he was so taken up with his own egotism and his pettifogging little thoughts that he never much felt the call of the wild, or the call of the jungle, as he remembered his mother calling it.

He had been disgusted at intervals to hear about this girl and that girl having a baby, and every year that there was a Confirmation, the Bishop had always given down the banks and braes to the inhabitants an account of their careless way of living, but then he realized that all those girls who had had

223

babies without the benefit of a marriage licence, were soon after married to the men who had been careless with them, so everything had turned out for the best, and everybody seemed to be happy for ever afterwards, and it was such a usual thing to occur that nobody remembered afterwards to cast aspersions on the first offspring, except in heated moments you might say, 'Hah, you little bastard!' but then you called everybody that in heated moments.

All this was unimportant excepting for the effect it had on the mind of Stephen. He had come to regard all these things as being natural, and regarded the Connemara men as having no finer feelings than to cohabit with the first girl that came along and be quite willing to marry her afterwards if things turned out for the worst. He couldn't see where love and the finer emotions entered into it at all. It was just a matter of convenience, and any girl at all might be regarded as the vehicle for carrying any man's excess energy.

Thomasheen, of course, had been his first set-back, because none knew better than he that Thomasheen really was in love with Nellie McClure, and because he went and married another woman for the economic security and well-being of his people, was no reason, despite romantic authors, to assume that his love for her wasn't greater than if he had turned around and married her. Stephen felt that his argument was weak there somewhere, but at least Thomasheen had shown him that he had a mind that had finer feelings.

Danny, of course, was another. And then there was Kathleen and himself. Stephen felt that he was not a very nice character himself, and as he walked the road now, he realized that he had gone about all those years regarding himself, unconsciously if you like, as being quite a cut above all the other Connemara people of his acquaintance. He was an eejit. How any man living in Connemara could feel that way was beyond him, he now thought. All you had to do was to look at a towering mountain, and compare yourself with the size of it. If they buried you on the side of the mountain, your grave would be like a pin-hole in the Atlantic Ocean, so what size would your body be and your tiny little egotistical brain-box that made you out a much better man than your fellows? To hell with it, said Stephen, and laughed. He felt excited as if somebody had presented him with a great gift. Was it the talk of his mother that had set him thinking like that? Did she think he was getting a bit above himself, and so she had decided to come back from wherever she was in order to dish out a rebuke? He turned on the road and looked about him. 'Thanks very much, Mother!' he shouted to the surrounding night, and waited to hear her laugh.

There was no laugh, so he turned on his heel and swung into the gate of his house, smiling. He was a very great amadaun, but still he felt elevated with a new discovery and decided he must go back to Danny, first thing in the morning, and tell him that it was a great pity his mother didn't marry him. He would be nice to Danny, and he would get him to talk about Martha in order to see her through Danny's eyes.

There was a light in the kitchen window.

He lifted the latch of the door and quickly entered.

He walked into what was the main turning-point in his life.

He just got a quick flash of the picture, his father and Mavis standing over near the fireplace. The startled look in both their faces as they saw him standing there, then the curtain coming down over the eyes of Mavis and her quick unhurried fingers buttoning up the front of her blouse.

He could have left it like that and pretended that he had seen nothing. He could have if the thoughts of his mother had not been uppermost in his mind just before he came in. Then he looked at Mavis, and he saw her in comparison with his mother, a cheap, tawdry wretch without an ounce of real intelligence. Immediately he guessed what she was after. She had summed up his father accurately, decided what kind he was, and made up her mind that she might as well settle down on a farm in Connemara until he died and she could sell out and depart.

'You bloody bitch!' he said, through clenched teeth, and his face was white.

Mavis looked at him with hatred, but at the same time she thought quickly that it might be all for the best. She had decided to marry Martin O'Riordan. She had noticed that even though he was still big and strong, the drink was taking its toll of him. There was a hunch to his shoulders and his face was becoming greyer with every month that passed. In her mind Mavis gave him five years at the most, and she decided that in five years she could go back to Dublin without fear, and be nice and cosy.

It was pure instinct that made Stephen raise his forearm and take the blow of the pot-stick that was aimed at his head. He had forgotten his father in those few seconds. Martin, his face suffused and his body expressing the rage of disappointment and loathing and self-reproach that was boiling in him, stretched his hand to the table beside him and, taking the first thing that came into his hand, went for his son.

Stephen's arm went numb for a few seconds, but he brought over his other hand and, wrenching the stick from his father, he threw it into the corner. Then his father hit him in the face and there was great strength behind the blow.

Stephen lost count of time, because a veil seemed to come down over his mind. All the years that his father had not bothered his head about him, the blow, so poignantly remembered, which he had struck Martha, the distaste which he felt at the scene into which he had walked, exploded in him, and he turned and attacked his father.

It was the cries of Mavis, and her urgent pulling on his arm, that brought him to his senses.

He loosened his hands from around his father's throat.

His father was lying on the floor beneath him, and Stephen was straddling him. Stephen couldn't remember what had happened. All he remembered was the blow in the face and the blow on the arm. Now he saw that his father's face was heavily injured. He felt blood trickling into his own mouth from one of his nostrils, and he knew that his eye was puffed and almost closed.

He took his hands from his father's throat, expecting him

226

to rise, but he didn't. He remained lying where he was without movement.

Stephen thought his own heart would stop then.

He bent forward and shook his father's shoulder.

'Father! Father!' he cried.

There was no answer from his father.

'Holy Jesus, you've killed him!' said Mavis, crossing herself.

'Shut your mouth!' said Stephen, 'and get some water.'

He had rested his hand on Martin's heart and found that it was beating.

He took the jug of cold water from her, brought a handkerchief from his pocket and dabbed the cold water on his father's face.

Soon his eyes fluttered and opened.

Stephen noticed how bloodshot those eyes were.

He let him lie there for a short time and then he raised him and put him sitting in a chair, holding him in case he would topple over. Shortly Martin became stronger and shook off Stephen's arms. Then he leaned forward with his head in his hands.

It was only then really that Stephen realized that his father was an old man. He was no longer the tall giant bogy of his imaginations, the big unfriendly figure that would never salute him except with a growl, who would never come back from town like other fathers with a small bag of bull's-eyes in his pocket, so that his son could stretch in a grimy hand and pull them out with squeals of delight. In Stephen's mind he was always a man to be avoided, whose presence put an end to conversations, whose absence lifted your heart.

Now he was old and seemed to have shrunk into himself. The big beefy arms no longer filled the shirt-sleeves tightly and the once thick column of a neck was pitted with hollows. The grey hair and the round bald patch on the back of his head made Stephen realize, with a sick feeling at the pit of his stomach, that he had used his young strength to batter an old man into insensibility.

He turned quickly and went up to his room.

He threw off the clothes he was wearing and dressed himself in his clean shirt and his good navy-blue suit. He stripped the pillow of its slip, and opening the cupboard he took his things out of it: his few manuscripts, the letter from his mother, a few things which he had gathered during the years, as well as the six pounds eighteen shillings and elevenpence which were the fruits of a lifetime of hard work and scraping, and of poaching with Michilin. He had meant before he had gone to ask his father for some money, when he would have told him that he was probably leaving for good.

He packed his old clothes into the pillow-slip as well, and then going over he looked longingly at his bookcase. He couldn't take that with him. His eyes skimmed the books and remembered them in the setting in which they had been read – most of them in this room by the light of the candle or by lamplight; others out under the clear sun on the strand, or on the side of the Brooding Hen, or by the lake, or else he stretched in a boat in the lake, when the sun was shining glassily and the fish had retired to the depths to avoid the stifling heat. Shakespeare, Marlowe, Sheridan, Ostrovski and the Russians, Yeats, Synge, O'Casey, Carroll, Coward, Anderson, and many others occupying the shelves for the plays; the histories and biographies from the *Decline and Fall* to Belloc and Churchill; all the great cheek by jowl with the not-so-great; and a quota of murders and mysteries, disdaining in their own turn the blood-and-death stories of his boyhood.

He quickly took a few of his favourites from the shelves and stuffed them into the slip.

He had one further look around the room and then, blowing out the candle, he came down again to the kitchen.

Mavis was sitting by the fire. The look in her eyes was uncertain. She had never thought that things would have exploded like that. True, it looked as if she was getting rid of Stephen, but these Connemara men were so unpredictable that you never knew where you were with them.

'Where is he?' Stephen asked harshly.

She nodded her head towards his father's bedroom, her eyes hardening.

Stephen swung the pillow-case over his shoulder and turned the handle of the sitting-room door.

He went through it quickly to the bedroom door beyond. The sitting-room had been the pride of his mother. She it was who had installed the leather-covered suite, had papered the rough walls with cheerful coloured paper, had hung bright chintzes on the windows, and cheap prints of good pictures on the walls. Since her death it had been little used, and a fire seldom burned in it. It smelled musty. Stephen thought it still smelled of the day when her corpse was lying in the bedroom and the people were sitting around here and in the kitchen, drinking and snuffing and smoking tobacco. It still smelled of snuff, he thought.

He did not knock at his father's door, but opened it and walked in.

The lamp was lighted and his father was lying on the bed, with his eyes staring unseeingly at the ceiling. When he heard the door opening he turned his face to the wall.

Stephen had not been in this room since his mother's death, and after one look at it, he concentrated on looking at his father, because it was not the same room as he had known it when She was alive. It was a careless room now, untidy and smelling of bodies and closed windows.

'I'm going,' said Stephen to his father.

He waited, but his father did not turn his face towards him.

'I meant to go very soon anyhow,' said Stephen, 'and I was going to tell you then. Well, I'm going now, and I don't think I will ever be back. I'll send for my books sometime when I can afford to have them sent to me.'

He paused, but his father remained numb.

'I'm sorry what happened happened, and it wouldn't if I hadn't lost my head. I want to tell you that. Also I'm sorry that we never seemed to get on like other people, and maybe that was my fault too as well as yours. Anyhow I'm sorry, and goodbye.'

He waited another few moments, but when he saw there would be no response, he left, closing the door quietly after him.

He waited a few moments in the sitting-room, fingering one or two of the knitting-books belonging to his mother which still remained there, and were just lifted and replaced when the room was having a careless dusting.

He smiled then, because his mother got those books, and there wasn't a worse knitter in the whole of Ireland. She would knit and rip-out, knit and rip-out, with a few soft curses to help her exasperation. She could never learn how to knit properly, and when even the holy nuns, as Stephen often said, couldn't teach her, he failed to see why she kept on trying. But she did, and never as far as he remembered had she ever succeeded in knitting one single garment of any description. She always gave up the socks when she came to the heels. He sighed, and going out, he closed the door after him.

He stopped at the kitchen door, his hand on the latch, and looked at Mavis. She glared back at him defiantly.

'You better make up your mind,' said Stephen to her. 'If you marry him you better watch out, and you better be careful, because you are too stupid to realize that there are things abroad that you don't understand and they might catch up with you. If I were you I'd pack a few things in a case and get back to your own environment before you regret it.'

'You mind your own bloody business, will yous!' she spat back at him.

Stephen pulled the door open then, and walked out into the darkness.

CHAPTER SIXTEEN

He paused outside the door to think.

His sudden decision to depart had been inspired by things which he had not reckoned on, and he had not even stopped to consider their implications. If he was to go now there was six miles between himself and Clifden, and what was he going to do after that. Whatever he did he would first have to go and see Kathleen somehow. Having decided that, he set out towards Crigaun.

He was very mixed up in his mind, and the only coherent thought that remained with him was that he was leaving Connemara. That thought did not depress him very much because he had meant to leave soon, whatever happened. In fact, now that he had made the break, he felt a lifting of his spirit and his heart beat a little faster. As he walked on, he started to settle things in his own mind and his plan was roughly shaped when he stopped outside Kathleen's door.

There was a light in the kitchen, and he could see forms moving around in the lighted interior. He would have to wait until they were all in bed. He didn't feel like meeting Malachai just now. For Kathleen's sake, and because he shrank from the wave of hatred that encompassed him every time he saw the black visage of his enemy, Stephen had avoided Malachai since the fight at the Lobster Pool. His nocturnal wanderings with Michilin had been made very circumspectly, and he had been more often with Kathleen than with his friend.

He decided that he would go back the road to Michilin's house, borrow his bicycle if he could, and then return and trust to luck that Malachai and himself would not meet.

Michilin was surprised to see him at the door, and still more surprised to see the packed pillow-slip on his shoulder.

'Where the hell are y' off teh, in the name a God?' he said. 'I wasn't expectin' t' see yeh t'night, an' I don't think it's any good goin' after the salmon because the water is very low.'

'Don't worry,' said Stephen. 'I have no intention of going after salmon.'

Michilin closed the door after him, and followed him down to the fire.

'What's in the white yoke?' he asked, and then looking at his face, 'Is it fightin' with that Malachai agin you were?'

'No,' said Stephen, sitting into a chair, 'I wish it was Malachai. No, it was my father left those marks on me.'

'Your father!' said Michilin, surprised.

'Yes,' said Stephen, 'we had a bit of a set-to, so I decided to clear out.'

'Holy God,' said Michilin, 'that's bad business so it is. And where would you be off to now, might I ask?'

'Provisionally Galway,' said Stephen, 'and then I'll go to Dublin.'

'You have it all fixed, haven't you,' said Michilin.

'I have,' said Stephen, 'only I'm going sooner than I thought I would. I expected to have more money to get me to Dublin properly, and a bit over to keep me until I got a job. Now I'll go to Galway and get a job and work until I have enough money to get to Dublin.'

'Well, I must say!' ejaculated Michilin, sitting down in the other chair. Michilin's cottage was poorly and roughly furnished. Most of his possessions he had made himself, and the table and two chairs, as well as the roughly made dresser, lacked the touch of the skilled carpenter. Then things were not as carefully bestowed as they were in Danny's, but he kept the place clean enough, and excused any untidiness by remarking that it was he himself that had to live in it, and if the visitor didn't like it he could lump it.

'I don't like this so much, Stephen,' he said, after cogitating for a time. 'About your father, I mane. It's a bad business to be gettin' t' grips with yer oul fella. I hope y' didn't hit him back, did yeh?'

'I'm afraid I did,' said Stephen uncomfortably.

'Ah, God, that's bad!' said Michilin. 'No fella should

232

ever raise a hand to his oul fella, no matter what the prevarication. If a fella'd hit his oul fella, he'd hit anythin', so he would, an' it's a bad start, so it is.'

'Ah, dammit,' said Stephen, 'I couldn't help it. He came for me first and before I knew where I was it was all over.'

'Lookit, Stephen,' said Michilin seriously, 'you'll have t' try an' get a better control over yer timper, so you will. You see, it's all right for a small fella t' get inta a timper, because divil the much damage he can do, but a big fella like you, with the timper y' have, an' y' have one, me boy, an' one a the bad quiet wans too, you'll have t' stop yersel' or before you know where y' are you'll end up be killin' somwan an' it'll be too late thin to be sorry, so it will, whin all the damage is done.'

'It's not like you, Michilin,' said Stephen, 'to be sermonizing.'

'I know it isn't,' said Michilin, 'but that's been in me mind an' I had t' say it.'

'I know, Michilin,' said Stephen, rising and pacing the floor. 'You are right too. I know mesel' I have a bad one, and I thought I always had it well under, but when certain things happen, that're too much for you, you just can't stop and think.'

'You'll have t' stop an' think,' said Michilin. 'But look, forget it. Why don't you doss down here for the night, and then beat it for Clifden the first thing in the morning?'

'No,' said Stephen, 'I'm going to go into Clifden tonight, so I am. I've made up my mind and I want to go. I'll be able to dig somewhere in there for the night and then the bus goes at nine in the morning. No, Michilin, I'm going tonight.'

'Fair enough,' said Michilin, 'if your mind is med up to 't.'

'I'll want the loan of your old bicycle, Michilin,' said Stephen, 'and I'll get your man to take it out in the mail-car in the morning.'

'You can have it,' said Michilin. 'But it's a terrible oul crock.'

'It'll take me the six miles, won't it?' said Stephen.

'It will,' said Michilin, 'if the dirty oul yoke doesn't fall to pieces on the way. There's ne'er a light or a brake or a thing on it, and it's a bad oul dirty road, until y' come out on to the Clifden highway.'

'If you get it,' said Stephen, 'I think I'll be on me way.'

'Fair enough,' said Michilin, rising. 'But look, you can't be luggin' that white yoke all the way t' Dublin with yeh.'

'Why can't I?' asked Stephen.

'Is it disgracin' 's you want to be?' asked Michilin indignantly. 'I have an oul bobby-bag up here in the room, that I'll give yeh. Yeh'll be easier able to tie it on to the bicycle. Hould on a minnit.'

He went up to his bedroom and soon returned blowing and wiping the dust from a large square black patent-leather bag with all sorts of straps hanging out of it.

Stephen took the bag, emptied his own stuff out of the pillow-case, and found that it fitted neatly into the other.

'Here,' he said, handing the pillow-case to Michilin, 'you keep this thing.'

'Thanks,' said Michilin, 'I will. I always wanted t' know what it was like t' lay yer head on wan a thim yokes.'

They got the bicycle out of the shed and, bringing it to the window outside the house, succeeded in tying the bag on to it.

It was as Michilin said, a terrible oul crock.

All that remained of it were the wheels and the frame. The frame was rusted so that at least it was uniformly coloured. There was a large saddle, split and holding on to the broken springs by the grace of God and some twine. No brakes, mudguards, nor any of the perquisites of a civilized bicycle graced it. When the bag was firmly tied to it, Stephen stood back and laughed.

'I don't blame you,' said Michilin. 'That oul yoke has been with me, man an' boy, since it was a wheelbarra.'

'It's just like yourself, Michilin, so it is,' said Stephen, 'battered and broken and weatherbeaten, but still goin' strong.'

They paused then.

People who live in primitive places find it very hard to say goodbye. If you are in a town and you are departing you just turn and say, Tooty-fruit, see you in Elysium; or, Goodbye, dear, I'm so sorry I have to go; or, Don't forget to write, darling; or, I do hate those train farewells, don't you? Emotions are not so easily disguised in the country, and farewells are awkward and embarrassing.

So Stephen stood holding the bicycle with one of his feet on the pedals.

'Well, I better be going, Michilin,' he said.

'You better,' said Michilin.

'Would you see Danny for me,' said Stephen, 'and explain that I left in a hurry or I'd have gone back to see him?'

'I will,' said Michilin.

'Well, I better go so,' said Stephen.

'You better,' said Michilin.

'Be careful with the Finnertys now, Michilin,' said Stephen.

'They haven't cotched me yet,' said Michilin, 'an' whin they have long white whiskers down to their knees they won't catch me either. They'd want teh get up very early in the mornin' t' catch me.'

'Maybe they might get up early some morning,' said Stephen.

'There's a fear a th'm,' said Michilin.

'Well, so-long,' said Stephen, pushing on a bit.

'Will yeh ever be back agin, d'ye think?' Michilin asked, following him up.

'Some day,' said Stephen, 'I will be back.'

'Aye,' said Michilin. 'Don't forget to let me know how you're gettin' on now.'

'I won't,' said Stephen. 'And listen; see Kathleen now and again, will you, Michilin? When I'm more or less fixed somewhere permanently, I'm going to bring her wherever I am. But keep an eye on her, will yeh, until then?'

'I will,' said Michilin.

'Well, goodbye, y'oul poacher,' said Stephen, holding out his hand.

'Goodbye,' said Michilin, taking it, squeezing it lightly, and dropping it again, because he was afraid that if he held on to it too long Stephen would find out how he was feeling. The years he had been with Stephen had made him realize fully the loneliness of his own existence. He had looked forward always to having him with him, and watching him grow, and he had often chided himself about the sinful things he was teaching him. He watched him until the darkness had swallowed up himself and the bicycle that was rattling like an ass-cart full of tin cans.

Stephen was surprised at the loneliness he felt at parting with Michilin. It came as a surprise to him, because when he had made up his mind to leave Connemara, it had never struck him that he would be sorry to leave anyone behind him. Now the memories of the times he had had with Michilin came flooding over him – the days on the lakes and the sea, the evenings on the rivers, the nights on the sides of the mountains after the birds. It came to him now that by going away he was leaving all that, and it was very unlikely he would ever get near them again unless he became rich and could afford to go after them in a legitimate manner. Certainly from what he knew of Dublin, while the fishing was poor enough, it was as tied-up and preserved as a mediaeval grass-widow in a chastity belt. You wouldn't mind that in a way, if you had a Michilin Fagan beside you to teach you the ropes and to take chances on the poaching. But he was leaving Michilin behind him for ever, and unless he came back sooner than he imagined with his ambitions unfulfilled, there was a poor hope of his ever seeing Michilin again, because he must be a fairly old man now, and even he, with his tough old strength, could not outlive time.

I better stop thinking in this manner, Stephen said to himself, or before I know where I am I'll be bursting into tears, and it's a nice thing to be getting homesick before you even leave a place at all, so it is. It was a good thing that it was night-time, he reflected, or if he could see the Brooding Hen and the Scarlet Thread, and the lakes shining in the sun, and currachs tossing on the sea, he would have to change his mind, say To hell with ambitions and schemes and hopes, and wouldn't I be better off settled down in a cottage in Connemara with Kathleen, where the world is as you like it, instead of gallivanting off into unknown regions to meet unknown people, and God knows how you'll turn out in the end, when your mind is as unformed as it is, with all sorts of embryonic ideas muddling around in your head?

When he drew near Kathleen's house, he dismounted from the bicycle and left it resting against the wall, because you could hear the old thing rattling a mile away. There were no lights in the house.

Stephen offered a silent wish that the dog would be tied up or in the kitchen, and that Malachai would have gone to bed for a change, instead of being out trying to get an opportunity to riddle himself or Michilin with lead pellets, and walked as silently as he could towards the house. He knew where Kathleen slept – the room behind the window on the left-hand side of the door. In the room at the back of that Tim slept with his lazy Nora, and Malachai and Jack were in the room on the other side of the house.

He succeeded in getting close to the house without rousing the dog. Then he listened for a while and, assured that everything was as it should be, he raised his hand and scratched at the window-pane. He stopped and listened, but there was no sound from within. Then he scratched at the glass more strongly. After a time, there was an answering scratch from within and, hearing this, Stephen retired as silently as he had approached and took up a position around a bend in the road, where he had left the bicycle. Just near it was a disused gravel-pit, which was hidden in deep shadows. He waited here for Kathleen.

As he waited, he reflected that leaving Kathleen was not going to be as easy as he had imagined either. The months that he had known her had strengthened instead of weakening his attachment to her. Kathleen had all he imagined he would ever desire in a woman. She wasn't beautiful but she possessed regular features and her body was regular too. She had a mind that was shrewder and more kind than his own,

237

and she had the knack of judging people not by how they appeared to her sight, but how she imagined them within. She was better even than his mother there, because she didn't put people in a little closet with a label on the outside. Then she was firm-minded, and if she made up her mind to do a thing she would do it, unless she was diverted on the way to help somebody who needed something done. She should have been in England long ago amongst people she liked, doing things she liked to do, but instead she waited at home, working like a slave because her brother's wife had got around her, on a plea of her helplessness. So she waited and worked, which was just as well for him or he might never have met her.

He went to meet her as he saw the shadow of her approaching him. She had pulled on a skirt and shoes and an overcoat, and her hair was loose and fell in black waves almost to her waist.

'What is it, Stephen?' she asked breathlessly. 'What happened?'

He told her what had happened.

She was silent for some time and he could almost feel her thinking about the whole thing, weighing it all up in her mind, and whatever she felt was the rights of it she would say. So he waited for her to speak, and he was smiling a little.

'It's for the best, Stephen,' she said. 'I think it is and I hope so too, so I do. But look, you didn't hurt him much, did you?'

'No, Kathleen,' said Stephen, 'I don't think so. He'll get over that, but it won't be so easy for me to get over it.'

'Maybe,' said Kathleen, 'it would have been better if you waited until the morning. Maybe things would have been all right between you then after it.'

'I don't think so,' said Stephen, 'because the things that are between us go too deep to be wiped off the slate like that in a few hours. You see, we have never really spoken to one another about any of the things that matter, and it would be almost impossible to start in now as if we had been chatting together all our lives.'

'But, Stephen,' said Kathleen, 'it's awful sudden havin' you goin' away like out of the blue.'

'Well, I was going to go next week anyhow, wasn't I, and it's only a biteen early,' said Stephen.

'Yes,' said Kathleen, 'that's right, I suppose, but I had made up my mind to saying goodbye to you next week and I find it hard now to fix it all properly in my mind.'

'Don't be that way about it,' said Stephen, winding a thick strand of her hair about his wrist. 'Sure the sooner I go the sooner you'll be able to come. Isn't that the way to look at it?'

'That's right,' said Kathleen. 'The very minute Nora has her baby, and that should be in two weeks or so now, I'll pack up my bags and depart to you, so I will, even if you haven't a job or anythin' and you're livin' somewhere in a garret. Not directly she has the baby but a week or so after it, because she might kill the poor thing not knowing how to handle it, and then when she is properly better I'll go.'

'That's the stuff,' said Stephen. 'That'll be about a month, and I'll be in Dublin then, I hope, and we'll burn the oul Liffey together, so we will.'

'What'll you do in Galway?' she asked. 'Where will you live or how will you get some place or what?'

'I don't know,' said Stephen, 'but I will. Paddy Rice is there all the time anyhow, and I have a letter he wrote me with his address on it. He will be able to fix me up with a cheap digs, I'm sure, until I can get going myself.'

'Will you write to me?' she asked.

Stephen laughed.

'How many times,' he said, 'have I read that line in books and it always seemed a silly remark? Now it's not silly and maybe I realize what it means. Don't you know well I'll write to you, me brave Kathleen? That'll be the only relaxation that I'll allow myself. You'll have to take a half-day off every day to read all that I'll write to you, until you become tired of me and my writing to you, and then years and years from now, when we are in our big mansion somewhere and we are having very big shots in having tea with us, I'll be trotting out the same reminiscences and you'll have to pretend that they are new to you too, and you'll have to be laughing in the right places, and lookin' at me with your eyes wide in admiration, and they saying, Isn't he wonderful? and under your breath you'll be sayin', Well, the oul eejit, that's eight hundred and ninety-four times that I have to listen to that same oul piece of blather, so it is.'

'Ah, I will not!' said Kathleen.

'I hope not,' said Stephen, 'but I'll always suspect you.'

'Stephen,' said Kathleen, 'aren't we dreaming too much, don't you think? How do we know that it isn't something else altogether that's laid out for us, like the people you remember in that book you gave me by that American, that Steinbeck, about all the way the fellas in it had everything planned down to the last detail and then everything happened to upset it? Haven't we very little to go on, you with a few pounds and your dreams, and me with nothing at all but in love with you? Aren't we right down at the bottom of the cup?'

'We are,' said Stephen, 'but there's something inside of me that's always talkin' to me. I suppose it's inside every other person in the world too. It says, You do this, me boy, and you do that, but do it, and you'll be all right. I tell you I know that we will do what we set out to do. There's a fire of it burning inside of me, Kathleen, and it'll take fifty years to burn out, so it will, and then after fifty years I'll admit that I was wrong and the feeling was only a lump of Celtic twilight that put the *mire meithimh* on me.'

'Yes,' said Kathleen, 'I know that you'll do what you want, Stephen, and maybe it's just because this happened at night, and we're talking at night now, and I don't feel as hopeful as I do in the daytime, but I have a different feeling now. I have a great fear, Stephen, and something that's telling me that you should not go at all, that we should hold on to what we have here and make the most of it.'

'Isn't that a nice thing for you to be sayin'!' said Stephen. 'You the one that was eternally after me to get up and out.'

'I know,' said Kathleen. 'I'm sorry, Stephen. Ah, we'll

forget it, but all this seems unreal, so it does, just as if I was in bed now, and I just dreamt it all, about you scratching on the window and me coming out and you telling me that you're going. I'll wake up in the morning, I'm sure, and I'll have to go down to Michilin to make sure that it's not a nightmare I had.'

'This is no nightmare,' said Stephen, taking her in his arms and kissing her.

She kissed him fiercely, and he could feel both their hearts throbbing together. It was Kathleen who pulled away first.

'You better go, Stephen,' she said. 'It must be very late now altogether and they'll never give you a bed in the hotel at Clifden if you don't go.'

'All right,' said Stephen.

They talked again of what he was going to do and how he would write and she was to see Michilin on occasions, which she was only too willing to do, so that she could talk about himself, although he didn't know that, and she wished for a minute that Stephen was like other men, that she could be talking about him at home to her own brothers, or that she could hop down to his house and talk about him to his father, but imagine the look that would come over Malachai if she started to talk soft about Stephen. She arranged that he would send her letters in an envelope to Michilin, and she could go down there and collect them.

They kissed goodbye several times more before Stephen was ready to get up on the bicycle. Then he allowed Kathleen to go in, and when she had done so, he carried the bicycle past the house, in case any of them should have heard her entrance and would associate the two.

Then he headed into the darkness for Clifden.

Kathleen tried not to, but when she was in bed again, a feeling of foreboding and helplessness and loneliness came over her and she cried bitterly. It was almost the first time in her life that she had given way to the luxury of tears.

Stephen did not feel so good as he rattled off on the bicycle. He couldn't help feeling that there was a hint of desperation in Kathleen's voice, and the happenings of the night were so crowded that they appeared like the figments of a mixed-up and rather terrible dream.

He could not, however, devote much attention to his thoughts because the bicycle was erratic, the night was dark, and the road was very bad. The bicycle swerved violently as the black form of a cow loomed up on the road ahead of him and he just saved himself from tumbling into a ditch by getting one of his feet on the ground and falling.

He pulled himself and his bicycle to an upright position, and standing on the road he cursed the cow fluently and violently, and got rid of some of his pent-up feelings. Then as he imagined the stupid look on the cow's face, which he could not see, he stopped and laughed and felt better. Since it was a road in Connemara, there were many hills to be surmounted.

Climbing the hills was no great hardship, but flying down one of them at speed, when he was ignorant of what lay at the bottom, was an ordeal, the danger of which was not lessened by the lack of brakes on the bicycle. All he could do was to apply the country cosg, and hope for the best. The country cosg is to a bicycle what a sheet anchor is to a boat. Lacking brakes, you stretch out your right foot and clamp your boot down on the front wheel. This slows the wheel, destroys the rubber of the tyre, but assists mightily in the reduction of excessive locomotion. One would think that the simplest thing would be to dismount from the crock and walk to the end of the hill, but this is obviously regarded unfavourably by all country cyclists as being a waste of time, so it is best to place your foot on the wheel, your trust in God, and hope for the best.

He finally broke out on to the main road to Clifden, and he sighed with relief when he felt the even tarred road under his wheels. From here the road climbed upwards practically all the three miles to the capital of Connemara. It must have been nearly one o'clock in the morning, but people were still up in their houses. He saw the yellow lamplight in some of the houses by the roadside, and away up on the sides of invisible mountains he could see squares of light like will-o'-

242

the-wisps halfway between heaven and earth. The smells of the night were different too, because the land he was passing through was more fertile and less boggy than the land of the Three Villages. The smell of the cut hay was heavier and was mingled more with the odour of decaying weeds and flowers, and large fields of ripening oats gleamed yellowly on either side of him.

He knew that he was coming into Clifden when he saw the tall spire of the church outlined darkly against the sky, and the tang of the sea and its weed came up to meet him from the valley. Then he was under the light of the first E.S.B. standard and he cycled along beside the footpath which was the forerunner of civilization.

He left the bicycle a little way from the hotel before he went and pressed the bell on the door.

It was opened by the small butty boots who had welcomed his mother for a cup of tea over twenty years ago. He had been with the hotel, as some of the commercial travellers said, since he was an old man. Nobody knew his age. His body was very young-looking, and if it wasn't for the fierce Guardsman moustache he hid behind, you would have taken him for a boy.

He stared curiously at the enormous figure almost filling the huge doorway.

'Yes?' he said interrogatively.

'I want to sleep here for the night,' said Stephen.

'Oh,' said the maneen. He paused for a time after that, and then opened the door wide. 'Come on in,' he said. 'I thought for a minute you were the Guards from the size of yeh.'

'I have a bicycle out here too,' said Stephen.

'Don't bother,' said the other, 'I'll look after that for you.'

'Thanks,' said Stephen, stepping into the hall.

'Have you a bag?' asked the little chap.

'Here it is,' said Stephen, showing it held in his large fist.

The maneen closed the door and went over to a small door which led to the office.

243

'I'll get the key,' he said as he disappeared.

Stephen looked around him.

Just opposite him there was a large lounge, the door of which opened at this moment and a large man with a red face and a huge belly shoved his head out and shouted, 'Hey, Andy, the same agin!' Then he retired and left the door open after him. Stephen looked into the room.

He saw seven or eight men in various stages of intoxication looking out curiously at him. They were all sorts and sizes; one or two young men well dressed, with ties awry, one man with big boots and a large pint covering his face. Stephen could see where the trousers came away from his boots that he was wearing thick socks of a dark-grey colour with white tops, and above this a bit of what was obviously red flannel underwear. He turned away because he felt awkward under their gaze, and became conscious of his size, and his big hands and feet.

Andy came out of the office then, jingling a key, went to the lounge door, shouted in 'Just a minnit now, Mister Hegarty,' turned to Stephen, said 'Come on,' and set off up the carpeted stairs.

He stopped at a room on the third storey. The door was painted white. He opened it and, leaning in, switched on the light.

'Here you are now,' he said, stepping back.

'Thanks,' said Stephen, entering.

'What's the name?' asked Andy.

'Hah?' said Stephen.

'What's the name?' reiterated Andy. 'Have to call you something to get you up in the mornin'. What time?'

'Oh,' said Stephen. 'The name is O'Riordan and I want to catch the nine bus to Galway.'

'O'Riordan. Nine,' repeated Andy. He looked at Stephen, summed him up quickly, decided that it was useless to shenanig around looking for a tip. 'Night,' he said then, and departed as quickly as he had come, wondering to himself what could have brought a big, fine, young, good-lookin' fella like that to a hotel in Clifden at two a'clock in the mornin'. The longer y' live the more y' see. A boy from the country obviously, but why two a'clock?

'Coming, Mister Hegarty, comin',' he answered the bellowing floating up the stairs, and ran down quickly.

Stephen, closing his door, looked around him curiously. It was the first night that he had ever slept in a hotel. In fact, apart from a night now and again when he had slept at Michilin's when it was too bad to go home, he had never been out of his own bedroom. The hotel bedroom struck him as being coldly and cleanly efficient. It was a small room with a cream-blinded window, and lace curtains, spotlessly white and stiff with starch. There was a chest of drawers with a mirror on top of it, a dark wardrobe in the corner, a neat-looking bed with a pink eiderdown quilt and cover, the first one Stephen had ever seen outside the advertisements in magazines. He sat on the bed and he felt the springs sagging gently under him. There was a fireplace, shiningly black-leaded, with a fan of newspaper taking the place of a fire.

He undressed himself quickly, left his clothes neatly on the chair beside the bed, and got between the sheets. They felt delightfully cool to his hot body. He found that there was another switch beside his bed to turn off the light, and he marvelled at the delights of civilization. Then he had to get up to raise the blind and open the window wide.

He got into bed again and switched off the light.

This, he thought, is a little different from Killaduff and Michilin and the rest of the boys, but he wasn't sure if he liked it. Then he thought, if I start thinking like this it won't get me anywhere at all. He thought of Kathleen, lying awake, he was sure, in her room in the Finnerty's in Crigaun, and then he said, You better stop that too, me lad, or you might change your mind in the morning and hop back to her again.

So he turned on his side, and emptied his mind, and because he was young and very healthy, he was fast asleep in a short time.

CHAPTER SEVENTEEN

At a few minutes after nine the same morning, Stephen was safely ensconced in a lightly filled bus which was bowling along to Galway. He had been duly called at eight o'clock, and it had taken him quite a time to awaken properly, and a still further period of time to adjust his mind to his strange surroundings. Then his heart had fallen a little as he looked around him, and he felt as if he was wakening up after an anaesthetic. He was the same and yet not the same, because some vital part of him seemed to have altered. Leaning back in the bed with his head cupped in his hands, he wondered what kind of an eejit he was at all to be doing a thing like this, with hardly anything at all to back him, excepting an overweening self-confidence which was sadly watered this morning. Then he threw off the clothes and without giving himself much time for further thought, he jumped out of bed, dressed himself, and washed his face and head in the cold water from the jug on the washstand. Then he opened his bag and, getting his equipment, shaved himself carefully.

He left his bedroom without any regret and went down the three flights of stairs. Most of the hotel seemed to be still asleep. Passing one door he heard the sound of water being splashed around and some man singing in a broken baritone 'Bonny Mary of Argyle', which song seemed to consist solely of bits about Bonny Mary, whoever she was, and then a lot of bumb-bumb-dee-dee-dumps, hoarsely emphasized, and enunciated with vigour.

When he had reached the hall-way he stood wondering which door to open to find his breakfast. Just then a very neat little cailin, with a grand, small, white starched apron over a black silk dress, came out of one door carrying a tray, and seeing him, paused at another door. He smiled hesitantly at her.

'Hello,' she said, and he felt easier when he heard the

Connemara tones of her voice. 'Is it lookin' for your breakfast you are?'

'I could do with it,' said Stephen.

'Come on in here so,' she smiled at him. 'You're the first down, so you are.'

She held the door open and he found himself in the dining-room. She put him at a table set for four people, and chatted amiably with him as she placed further cutlery and jugs of milk and bowls of sugar on the table.

'Where are you from?' she asked.

'Oh, from way behind,' said Stephen.

'I never saw you in here before,' she said.

'You didn't,' said Stephen, 'because this is the first time I have ever been in here.'

'You don't talk like you should,' she said to him.

'How do you mean?' Stephen inquired.

'Well,' she said, 'you haven't as much of a brogue as you should have from the way you look. You are a Connemara boy, aren't you?'

'I am,' said Stephen.

'There!' she said triumphantly. 'See what I mane?'

'Do you want me to be talking with a sod of turf in my mouth,' Stephen asked, 'just because I am from Connemara?'

'You'd look quare that way,' she said, and laughed, and he noticed that her teeth were small and white. 'I suppose you want your breakfast.'

'I could do with it,' said Stephen. She went then with the tray, and he thought how nice it was to meet somebody in a strange place on a strange morning who would smile at you and be friendly.

She had just laid his breakfast before him, one to which he was not used, consisting of fried bacon and eggs and three sausages, when the door opened and the man he had noticed last night, with his red underwear showing, came into the room and paused on the threshold.

'Isn't this a mornin',' he declaimed, 'that'd put the cockles leppin' in yer heart! Katie, me own true love, how

247

are yeh?' and he proceeded to put his large tweed-clad arms about the diminutive Katie and hug her.

'Oh, for God's sake, Mister McLoughlin,' she said to him, giggling, and pulling away from him. 'Isn't this a bit early in the mornin' t' be feelin' that way? You were properly plastered last night too, so you were, and I don't know how it is that you can be so jizzy.'

'I was not plastered last night,' said he, taking a chair opposite Stephen. 'I am a man a temperate habits like a Franciscan in an asbestos gown. I drink with me friends if they're male, and squeeze 'm if they're female, and more power t' me too for it. Amn't I right, son?' This last was addressed to Stephen.

'Well,' said Stephen, 'it depends on the company, doesn't it? I can't blame you doing that to ... eh ... Katie,' and he looked at her to see if she'd mind his using her name.

Katie was, of course, delighted.

'G'wan,' she said. 'All min is the same. They all know what they're after.'

'Sure they do,' said the man, 'and hey's a fella now that's after bacon an' eggs, an' if he doesn't get them he'll start in on the table. Retire, Katie, retire,' he said, and pinched her neat bottom.

'Oh, Mister McLoughlin!' she said, and duly retired laughing.

'Are you goin' to Galway?' Mister McLoughlin asked Stephen.

'I am,' said Stephen.

'That's good,' he answered. 'I'm goin' there too, and I was always a man that liked a bitta company. You can call me Mac, so you can, and what do you answer to?'

'Stephen,' said Stephen.

'Stephen what?' asked the other, thickly buttering a slice of bread and shoving it into his mouth.

'O'Riordan,' said Stephen.

'You wouldn't be anything to Martin O'Riordan of Killaduff now, would you?'

'I might,' said Stephen, 'be a son of his.'

'Is that so?' said Mac. 'I was around that way a couple a times, and ran into him. Ah, well, it's a small world, so it is. Don't mind me. I'm a terrible man for askin' people all about their business and never givin' anything away mesel'. I'm a cattle-jobber, so I am, but don't ask me what me margin a profit is, because I won't tell y', so I won't,' and he laughed uproariously at this. He was a big hearty man who seemed to be always talking loudly and laughing loudly. Even when other diners came into the room he abated his conversation not one jot.

Their breakfast finished, Stephen had paid ten shillings and sixpence out of his meagre store and had given two shillings to Katie, who had smiled at him in a very loving manner, and hoped he'd be back with them again soon. Stephen said he hoped so too, and that she would be here when he returned. He gave another shilling to the porter and arranged with him to put Michilin's bicycle on the mail-car, although the porter was looking at the same bicycle with loathing and abhorrence, and wondering how in the hell he could get it to the car without anyone seeing him in the act.

Mac and Stephen mounted the bus and got a seat in the middle of it, because Mac assured him that when you were travelling by bus it was as well to take the middle so that you would not feel the jog of the wheels and you could see what was happening in front and behind.

There were very few travellers on the bus. In the front seat one of the fishing fraternity sat stiffly with his wife. It had taken him some time to stow all his fishing gear, consisting of about ten rods neatly cased and all sorts of bags and what-nots. Then they sat in the front seat, erect and at attention, threw an odd word at one another, and sometimes looked back with loathing and disdain at the rude fellow in the centre of the bus who was talking loudly and learnedly about cows, heifers, bulls, and dung, and their habits and customs and peculiarities. Stephen was laughing, sometimes at Mac's stories about times he had bought a two-year-old down in Leenane, but mostly at the effect they were having on the couple in front.

249

Eventually the driver pulled himself into the cabin in front, the conductor pressed the bell, and they were away.

Mac conducted a loud conversation with the conductor about the conductor's wife, and said that he had heard she had had the last one very hard indeed, and was she all right now again? The conductor said she was, except that she'd have to have something done to her inside, and Mac said babies was the divil, and that seein' the conductor had seven 'f them now it was about time he pressed the bell wance t' stop an' put a halter on himself. And then the conductor laughed, and Mac roared, and slapped his knee, and Stephen thought he noticed the neck of the fisherman turning a deep puce colour, so he had to laugh too.

Things calmed down a little after that. The conductor collected the fares from the frigid couple, and Stephen looked out of the windows at the country, which was very beautiful but not as beautiful as it would be when they came into Recess and had the Twelve Pins on their left.

'Do you know this country at all?' Mac asked Stephen.

'Not well,' said Stephen, who didn't like to admit that this was the first time he had ever travelled over it outside his mind, when he was looking at the maps in *The Angler's Guide to the Irish Free State*. 'But that's Ballinahinch Lake we're coming up on now, isn't it?'

'Aye, it is,' said Mac, 'and one 'f the best salmon lakes in the whole country, so it is. Did y'ever hear about the time me man from India or Africa or somewhere had the castle there?'

'I heard something about it,' said Stephen.

'Ah, thim was the days,' said Mac, and launched into a spate of rumours and anecdotes, which the coming of a Rajah with full suite and personnel, ladies of the court and what-not, had evoked. Stephen only gave it half his attention because his eyes were caught with the breathless beauty which a Connemara lake evokes, with its tree-clustered islands and the shimmering water and a purple-clad mountain rising steeply behind it. The road ran just beside the edge of the lake. On one side you had the lake and on the

250

other the bogland leading away to the mountains, broken in places by the rough roads climbing to houses far, far away, and broken again by other roads turning off to the bogs where the people cut their turf. You could see neat stacks of turf, standing out against the purple and yellow of the heather, and sometimes tiny figures trundling the heavy turf-barrows, or bending over the foots, or diminutive donkeys waggling along, panniered with the cisaun.

The bus stopped at what used to be the old railway station of Recess, which lies just beside the lake of Glendalough.

'Wasn't it a great crime for them,' said Mac, 'to go and destroy that railway from Galway to Clifden?'

'That's just what I was thinking myself,' said Stephen. 'I remember my mother talking about how when she came to Connemara first, she came in the train. Why did they have to scrap it altogether? Couldn't they have even pulled up the sleepers, left the bridges, and made a grand road out of it?'

'Did you ever,' asked Mac, 'see the bloody Irishry do anything that was reasonable? That was the finest scenic railway in the whole a Ireland, and they tore it up, like an oul dog at a corpse, because a couple a fat oul bastards in Dublin weren't gettin' enough dividends.'

There was no engine now to cover up Mac's loud remarks, so the fisherman in front turned deliberately and glared at them. He did not speak, but his expression was enough. Mac waved a hand at him and beamed.

'Isn't it true for me, General?' he asked.

Stephen was sure that the General, if he was one, was on the point of bursting into little pieces, but he nobly held himself in and, turning, made some remark to his wife about natives. At this moment the bus appeared to be invaded by more fishermen. Actually there were only two, but they were carrying so much equipment and were talking so loudly that it seemed to be an invasion. You could hear very few of the words which they spoke. They seemed to be talking high up in their heads, and then a word here and there would

251

explode from them, like 'old boy', or, rather, 'frightful old chap', or 'fine', say, and one or two others.

'More bloody fishermen,' said Mac loudly. 'That's what's ruinin' this country, so it is. The finest fishin' lakes in Ireland an' no man can get a crack at thum if he hasn't an income a four thousand a year, an' a certificate t' show that his father was born inside the Pale, an' that his mother's blood was as blue as your nose on a cold night.'

'You don't,' Stephen asked, 'know a fella called Michilin Fagan by any chance, do you?'

'Do I hell?' said Mac. 'Wasn't I out fightin' with 'im in 1920 in thim very hills up there, whin we were makin' the country free for the people, so that me min that grabbed all the fishin' could have it nice an' cushy, an' spind their holidays in Connemara? D'ye see up there now?'

The bus had got into motion again and the two new fishermen had settled down in the other front seat opposite the irate General, and were conducting a loud conversation, about the Good season, what? and D'you remember that eighteen-pounder up on the Derryclare butt?

Stephen looked out to the left where Mac was pointing. At this point there was a low hill behind the road that hid the view beyond, but you could see four of the Twelve Pins rising mightily into the sky.

'Up there it was,' said Mac.

'Isn't it funny?' said Stephen. 'I thought you would be sure to know Michilin when I heard you talking about the fishing.' And he laughed because Michilin's virulent comments flashed into his mind.

'Oh, begod I was,' said Mac. 'And Michilin Fagan was the best man that ever walked a hill, so he was. The rest 'f 's'd have been dead mutton oney for 'm, with the grey crow pluckin' the eyes out oo our heads. We blew a bridge below back there, whin a lorry a the Tans was goin' over it, an' then we took to the hills up there with all the bluebottles swarmin' on our heels with their oul carbines. The first lake up there is the Derryclare, and after that is Lough Inagh. Ah, God, they's a sight for your eyes, so it is! Lough Inagh

252

drains three 'f the Twelve Pins, so it does, an' whin the Bucks was after 's, up we go on the far side, and we were stuck in a sweepin' valley up there that knew nothin' but the hoofs a the sheep, an' an odd oul pony trottin' over them, with his mane layin' out on the breeze. Well, if it wasn't for Michilin we'd 'v' been dead ducks, so we would, because the further in the valley we wint, the further down we wint in the bogs, an' thim bloody R.I.C.ers closin' in on 's an' lettin' an odd shot fly across our bows. But me brave Michilin took 's through, so he did, while the oul coppers was flounderin' behind goin' up to their water-marks in grand juicy bog, and we got out 'f it all right, and where does he take 's thin but up the side 'f a bloody mountain that y'd think a bird couldn't get up, an' came the night an' we were perched up there like eagles, so we were, an' we lookin' down at me min tryin' t' extricate thimselves from the morassey, an' to get around be the other side. Thin some fella says, "Jay, I'm hungry, so I am," an' thin we all find out we are too, so Michilin ups an' slips away like a shadda. "I'll be back soon, lads," he says, an' he is gone. We were quiet for a while, an' thin somebody else says, "We'll never see that bastard agin," he says, "unless we go to hell, because he's done a bunk now back to a nice cushy bed while we're up here, ticklin' our fannies on the wet rocks." "You shut up," I said then. "Michilin'll come back all right; Michilin'll be back with somethin' t' ate too, so he will." "He will in me tail," says me man, so I ups then to give 'm a puck in the kisser, but the lads stops us, and says, "Holy Christ, are we supposed t' be fightin' the English, or are we startin' a civil war?" So we sit down an' wait an' it's bloody cold, so it is, because it was late November.

'What happens then? I'll tell yeh. Back comes me brave Michilin an' a salmon under 's arm that's nearly as big as 'msel'. On me oath! "Ah," says he, "the blessin's a God on oul Lord What's-'is-name. I rang 'm up on the telephone," he says, "an' asked 'm if he'd mind if we took an oul salmon to keep the heart up in 's. An' back he comes an' tells me t' take five a thim if I wanted, as long as I had paid me

253

two-pound salmon licence." He lighted a fire too, so he did, that wouldn't reflect inta the skies, an' we cooked that oul salmon there, the divil knows how, with wet newspaper an' all sorts a rackets, an' let me tell you that nobody ever tasted a bit a fish that was as sweet as that wan. I've et salmon since, so I have, but it oney tasted like a bit 'f an ould dogfish compared to that.'

'You got away from there so, I suppose,' said Stephen.

'Some 'f us did,' said Mac, 'an' some 'f 's didn't. When we woke up the next mornin', the mountain was swarmin' with police like ants round a jam-jar. We hadn't enough ammunition or nothin', so we inded up firin' rocks at thum. Michilin an' a few a th' boys went further up the mountain, where even an oul goat couldn't go.'

'It's funny,' said Stephen, 'that I never heard Michilin talking much about that at all.'

'You'll never,' said Mac, 'hear Michilin talkin' about any a the good things he did. Imagine you knowin' Michilin Fagan! Well, well. An' how is he? Still poachin' away, I suppose?'

'I'm afraid he is,' said Stephen, with a reminiscent smile.

'More power to 'm,' said Mac, 'and long may he live to be at it. I'm always manin' to go round that way to look 'm up, but I've oney seen 'm once or twice since thin.'

At this point the bus stopped again to take on three passengers who were waiting by the side of the road. One of them was an old Connemara woman, her head wrapped in a white shawl, her body in a black shawl and a red petticoat with a checked apron. Her face was wrinkled like a strand after the ebbing tide. There was a young girl with her and a tall lanky man, with a short blue coat, a cap, brass-studded shirt, and ceanneasna trousers.

Mac hailed them when they got aboard and the bus was under way. He called the man Tom, the old woman Ma'am, and the girl Nora, and started to shout intimate questions at them, about How was oul Patsy? and What happened the strawberry bull?

Stephen turned his eyes to the scenery again.

As soon as one picture-postcard lake was passed, another one shimmered in the distance, to be caught, travelled by, and passed in its turn. This would be on the right-hand side of the road, while on the other side the mountains all the time held sway. Such a succession of lakes: Glendalough, then the Recess river to the right, then the lakes of Cappahoosh, Dereen, Oorid, and Shindilla.

Shortly the bus pulled up beside the hotel at Maam Cross.

Mac looked around from his conversation, and rubbed a hand on his moustache.

'The time has now come,' he said, 'to be contemplating a large pint, with a top on it like an angel's wing. Will yeh have wan?'

'I don't mind if I do,' said Stephen.

'Then let us dismount in the name of God,' said Mac, rising and barring the way to the fishermen who were bent on the same mission. If they were expecting Mac to get out of the way and let them pass like the gentlemen they were, they were sadly mistaken. He kept his big behind planted in the passage-way while he talked a little further to Tom. No matter how much the gentlemin coughed or tut-tutted, or said 'I say, old boy', Mac ignored them until he was good and ready and then, turning to Stephen, said, 'Well, come on, son, what's delaying you?'

They left the bus and went into the public-house.

Mac seemed to know everybody in the public-house as well, the drivers of the mail-cars and the man in the shop and everybody round about. All of them had a special beam for him and he would ask them intimate questions about their families or their animals or their personal ailments, as well as offering advice about liniments and lotions and potions for cows and humans. The two fishermen had joined up with the General by this time, and they were talking loudly about flies and the 'day I got stuck in that big white trout, remember, George,' and ignoring the natives about them, and commenting audibly on the atrocious whiskey one got in country pubs, drinking it nevertheless, and saying how grand it would be to be back in civilization in Dublin again. 'One got rather fed-up with the country, you know, the fishing, yes, grand, old boy, but dead, Lord, and then the incompetent gillies. Remember that day, Perce, when I was stuck in that fourteen-pounder? Damn sure he was a fourteen-pounder, a tail on him like a shark. Anyhow I do a neat, very neat, bit of striking on him, play the blighter for almost three-quarters of an hour, haul him near the boat. And then what happens? Off he goes! Honest, you wouldn't believe it, I tell you. That gillie's fault. Shoved the gaff out too soon, he did, and then has the nerve to say I should have looked to the tying of my fly better. I ask you. There was a little rust on the gut at that point, but it had nothing to do with it. Imagine the nerve though. Oh, they're getting above themselves all right.'

'You could say that again. Lost a beauty myself the same way. Think after all those years they'd be able to handle a boat. No. Lets the damn thing come back on the fish so he goes under the boat and breaks me. Yes. A fact! Then claimed I gave too much slack. Incredible. The gall, you know. I told him off, I can tell you. Wouldn't mind, but what they cost.'

'Yes, that's a snorter. Five shillings a day. It's outrageous. Nothing to do but sit in a boat all day and dab at the water. And get free porter as well as their lunch. Must say it's getting a bit steep. They are asking for the three half-crowns a day now too if you don't mind. Don't know what the world's coming to. Those English blokes have them spoiled, take it from me. Well, here's how.'

Stephen drank his pint with appreciation and listened to the talk around him. Mac was outside talking to his friends. Then the conductor puts his head in the door and says, 'We're going now, gentlemen,' and the General says, 'Hold on, conductor, until we have just one more.' 'Sorry, sir,' says the conductor, 'have to keep to a timetable,' and he goes, and one of the gentlemen says, 'Sauce, that's what I call it. That's what the Trouble got for us now.'

Soon the bus was under way again. Stephen, looking behind him, could see the last of the mountains, where they swept down steeply to form the magnificent Maam Valley. From this on he could see that the mountains were giving way to foothills, and, although he didn't know that, he felt, as his father had expressed himself to Martha years ago when they were on the train to Clifden, that when you left the mountains behind you you felt insecure and missed them compassing you. That's the difference between a plainsman and the mountainy man. You get so used to towering heights that you have a feeling that all the land without them is a plague spot and a breeder of discords and diseases.

Mac was talking to him again.

'Tell me,' he said, 'is it to England you're goin'?'

'No,' said Stephen, 'I'm going to Galway first, and then I'm going to Dublin. Why in the name of God should I go to England?'

'Because,' said Mac, 'it is the usual question you ask if you see a Connemara fella with a bag all packed, a new suit, and he on his way to Galway. They talk about the flight of the Earls, me boy, but the people are flyin' outa Ireland now like locusts on the move, so they are. That's why I thought you might be going to England.'

'Not me,' said Stephen. 'I want to find out all about my own country first. It's a poor country if it can't give me a job. When I go to England I just want to go and see it on a holiday or travelling or something, the same way I'd like to see the other countries in Europe as well.'

'Well, Holy God,' said Mac, 'it's a great thing to meet a fella that doesn't want t' go t' England. For God's sake don't let anyone hear y' sayin' it, or they'll probably catch yeh and lock yeh up in a cage in the Zoo, and charge a tanner a time to show you off as a great curiosity, like King Kong.'

Stephen laughed.

'Are you wantin' to stay in Galway?' Mac asked.

'Yes, for a while, anyhow,' said Stephen.

'You'll be looking for digs so,' said Mac.

'I will,' said Stephen.

'Well, look,' said Mac, 'I'll be able to fix you up in a little place where I stay mesel' when I'm there. It's a nice clean spot and very good food, and very decent people, and they oney charge a pound a week. How about that, hah?'

'That would just about suit me,' said Stephen.

'Fair enough, I'll do that when we get in,' said Mac. 'I'm not waitin' in Galway this trip: I'm shootin' off on the train to Ballinasloe. Ah, God, that's the place for the bullocks, that is! It does yer heart good t' take a look at them. They make the Connemara cattle look like abortions outa skeletons, so they do. How yeh, Charlie?' he suddenly roared, leaning out the window beside Stephen and waving furiously at a figure standing by the roadside.

Everyone in the bus jumped at the suddenness of it.

Mac leaned back again in his seat. The others were looking at him curiously.

'That was Charlie,' said he to Stephen.

'I gathered that much,' said Stephen.

'He lives there at the foot a Boffin Lake,' said Mac. 'That long one we're just passin' now. Charlie was one a the boys too in 1920, so he was, and a terrible savage man whin he was in a timper. He could use a knife like a butcher, so he could. Ah, they's the Oughterard reservoir now. We won't feel until we're in Galway, so we won't.'

The road here ran beside the Oughterard river which drained the Boffin Lake. It was shallow and very rocky, this river, and flowed turbulently beside tall trees. A grand spot it was, just before you came to the bridge that turned over it. Passing this narrow bridge and looking back, Stephen was reminded of a story he had read by Padraic O Conaire called 'The Trout in the Big River'. The river wasn't big, but the spot could have been the same. Then the bus pulled into the little town of Oughterard. There was a five-minute stop there. Stephen refused Mac's invitation to come in for another pint, and instead, got out to stretch his legs, and wandered a bit about the main street.

Actually, as he soon saw, Oughterard consisted of only one street, and every second house seemed to be a large hotel catering for fishermen. He knew that it was the principal resort for the anglers who fished the huge Lough Corrib.

He decided that he didn't like Oughterard. It was a town of glaring contrasts which were all the more perceptible because it was so small. One minute you would have a grand hotel with its clean curtains and a sight through the windows of many tables with snow-white linen on them and glittering cutlery, and then you would see a small thatched cottage, set several feet below the level of the roadway, dark, gloomy, and, he was sure, insanitary. The contrast of luxury and poverty was too obvious to be overlooked. You saw it in the wandering anglers, carelessly but expensively dressed, and then the women with ragged shawls, or the men wearing clothes that had been new maybe twelve or fourteen years ago, patched and greasy and colourless, or the little children running around in their bare feet (which was not unusual) wearing gansies much the worse for wear, thin and riddled with holes, and the backsides out of their britches (which, alas, was not unusual either). But a hell of a lot of good it was, he thought, to be noticing things like that – it would get you nowhere; and he got back into the bus again feeling depressed, and realizing that he was seeing a foretaste of what towns were bound to be, and the bigger the town the more glaring the contrast, but the harder it was to see, because it was so big. Then he thought it was no bloody wonder that the boys and girls were flying to England like swallows. They'd give a quare look at you if you told them they ought to settle down in their own country. For what? To live in one of those cottages that was probably a breeding-house of the T.B. germ? A fat chance you'd have of getting them to stay. He reflected that poverty in Connemara had been at least a kind of a clean poverty, and if Oughterard was a foretaste of what he was going to see in Galway and Dublin, he'd have to try and close his eyes, because in the jungle it was every man for himself and God help us all.

He was relieved to get out of Oughterard. More passengers had entered and Mac was taken up going from one to the other talking about this and that.

Some miles from Oughterard they came on the Corrib,

259

and even the small-lake-man, Connemara-loving Stephen had to admit that it had something. The day was very fine, but the atmosphere was clear, and you could see the big lake stretching away into the distance like an inland sea. It was speckled with islands in all directions, and the islands seemed to be very verdant, and were massively coated with thick trees and shrubs. Now and again on the glassy water you would see the fishing-boat and its two or three occupants like a black silhouette painted on to it. Stephen promised himself that some day he would go fishing on the Corrib. Its bigness made it a slow lake, but the fish, he had heard, were very large, twelve- and ten-pound trout being quite common, and an odd eighteen-pounder not unusual. If you never got a thing, he thought, it would be worth while just getting on it on a fine day.

Their next stop was the little village of Moycullen, and after that he could sense that the town of Galway was coming closer and closer.

You began to see more cars flashing by, and heavy turf lorries converging on the town; more horses and carts with farmers or their wives sitting relaxed up in them, the men freshly shaved and dressed in their best short-coats, and the women cradling huge baskets in their laps, and looking curiously at the bus as it passed, to see if they knew anybody in it.

Stephen saw where the lake faded into the river, and was surprised at the foresight of some engineer, or whoever was responsible, who had replaced the stone walls at the side of the road nearest the lake, with iron stanchions and wire netting, so that people passing could get a view of the Corrib country as it stretched magnificently away.

Civilization, as usual, he thought, was approached by a footpath and the electric standards, and he wondered if that's the way one would go into Heaven too, a long hard road, and then a footpath and electric light.

Soon the people became more numerous on the roads, and houses began to flash by, nice houses enough, he thought, with slated or tiled roofs, and gardens front and back, then private houses converted into shops to cater for the outlying population, a large white building on the left, with two crossed arms with nail-holes in their palms which, he thought, but was not sure, was the coat of arms of the Franciscans.

After that his mind became confused, there were so many things to look at on each side of the road. What he noted with some wonder was the way everybody looked curiously at the passing bus. You would meet the eyes of men and women and girls who would stare blankly at you. He wondered if everybody all over the world looked at a bus like that as they sped by.

The bus made its way over what he thought was a canal and then what he knew must be a bridge over the river Corrib, up through streets that wound narrowly, more tall buildings, and then it came to a halt in the public square.

'All out now, please,' intoned the conductor.

CHAPTER EIGHTEEN

Stephen alighted from the bus with the bag thrown over his shoulder and waited until Mac had extricated himself from the bus and his friends.

'Right we are now,' said Mac. 'Up this way.'

Stephen saw that the square was a rather big one. In the centre was a railing-enclosed park, high on the side nearest to the bus, with an old re-erected historical entrance of some kind. All around this railed park were tall houses, with small houses resting grotesquely against them. The whole thing seemed to be thoroughly disorderly, like a town-planner's nightmare. If one of these buildings wasn't a hotel, then you could almost bet it was a pub, with, here and there, a clean-cut bank building, disdaining its more vulgar neighbours.

He followed Mac, who made his way hurriedly up and away from the centre of the town. There seemed to be a terrible lot of people about. At least it seemed so to Stephen, who was used to seeing a road stretching miles into the distant horizon, with maybe a small figure at the end of it. He was glad to be free of the bus, because he had found it hard to think in it. Your mind seemed to have been replaced by the engine which took over when the driver switched on the ignition. Your body was your own, but it felt top-heavy and sluggish. Now he could think, and he was interested in all that he saw around him, and wished Mac wasn't rushing so much, but then he thought that he would have plenty of time to see things on his own. But first impressions were things that it would be hard to recapture, and he couldn't very well say to Mac, Here, hold on, I have never been in a town before in my life and I want to walk slowly and have a good look at it.

They topped a hill, and Stephen saw that the shops had given place to lines of houses on each side of this long road. They were very peculiar houses. They were mostly one-storey or two-storey, small, compact, and completely ugly, but what amazed Stephen most, was that each of them seemed to be constantly vomiting children. There were children of all sizes, running and shouting and singing and hurrooing, and dodging the wheels of cars, and death by inches, and sticking out red tongues at scared and blaspheming drivers who stopped a car or a lorry to lean out of the window to curse them fluently for a pack of snotty-nosed little bastards whose mothers were unmarried female dogs. The farther they proceeded along the road the more children there seemed to be. Some of them were very clean, some of them very dirty, some of them eating bread and jam, and some of them eating bits of turf or stick, and larger sisters or brothers walloping them heartily for so doing.

Then tall lean women would lean out of half-doors and shout at Tomeen or Mareen to come into hell ou'r that or what would their father do to them when he came home from work, and others would be rushing to house doors crying synthetically and rubbing their eyes to make them red and shouting, 'Mammy, mammy, he hot me, so he did,

262

Padneen Murphy hot me on the kisser and I wasn't doin' nothin', so I wasn't,' and the tall, poor exasperated woman would come out of her door and shout across at a house on the other side of the street, 'You keep that little bastard away from my Tomeen, you so-and-so, or I'll cure him for you. A quare place indeed when people won't look after their bloody children, lettin' them run wild all over the country, but thanks bitta Christ they'll ind up at the ind of a rope, so they will.' Sometimes there would be no reply but more often there would be, and another hot-looking, exasperated face would appear out of the other door and a fitting reply would be made about Renmore whores setting themselves up to live in a house with decent neighbours, soilin' the very air with their putridity, and why was the same oul what-you-may-call-her to be worryin' about her illegitimate children when all the town knew that the same children were rotten with the T.B. or the pox or some disease that was as infectious as the porter that the mother'd be drinkin' on a Saturday night an' her poor offspring at home scratchin' their fleas like a cuddy. To which suitable reply would be made, and then the whole thing would fizzle out just like it commenced, and a blind cat could see that the two children who had caused all the disturbance were playing away in the gutter and completely ignoring what shameful reference was being made to their birth, parentage, and bodily ailments.

Stephen was delighted and couldn't help smiling.

'Is it always like this up here?' he asked Mac, who was walking away and seemed to have noticed nothing.

'Oh, that,' said Mac. 'You won't find decenter people on the face a the earth, so y' won't, than the people up here. They'd give yeh the last bite in the house, so they would. Why the hell can't they have a bit oo an argument whin they like? If you had to keep a house an' a family goin' on a few bob a week, y'd bite the nose offa yer grey-haired mother.'

'I don't mind at all,' said Stephen, 'and they seem very decent to me, and it'll make life interesting, so it will.'

He patted the head of a child who was crawling between

263

h:s legs. The child looked up at him. Its face was dirty, its nose in a state of unseemliness, but there were bright fair curls topping the lot.

'Hello,' said Stephen.

'Goom-morra, Jack,' said the urchin, and then giggled loudly and ran away along the path. Stephen was puzzled at the jargon they were speaking. All the children were using words which he had never heard before; but then Stephen had yet to see a Hollywood film, and when the time came for him to see one, he would remember the children and also the source of their vocabulary. There were of course a lot of words he could recognize, mostly biblical, and strictly blasphemous, and to hear the most frightful swear-words dripping innocently from the bud-mouths of soft-eyed children was a most upsetting experience.

'Here we are now,' said Mac, stopping at a neat two-storey house. Stephen guessed from the curtains, which were very neat, and the window-panes, which were blue with cleanliness, that the owner of the house would be something like what she turned out to be. Mac had told him about Mrs Mulreaney. She was a widow whose husband had been killed in the Great War, and she assisted an ungenerous pension from the British Government by taking lodgers.

She was a small woman, whose hair was very grey, but she reminded him of a sparrow just after a bath, her hair was so closely pulled back in a bun, and the apron was so close around her body. She held a hand out to him and said she was glad indeed to put up a friend of Mac's and she was sorry Mac himself couldn't stay this time. Her hand was almost lost in his own, but he felt drawn to her immediately, and thought that it was all wrong for a neat little lady like her to have hands that were hardened with toil.

She offered him a chair, and he was glad to sit down, because standing, his head seemed to be touching the ceiling, and it made Mrs M. look like a doll. The kitchen was small, and the furniture seemed to be small too. Even the dresser which held the delf seemed to be just a miniature of the huge dressers which grace the whitewashed walls of country kitchens. There was a bright coal fire burning in the range, the steel parts of which shone as if they had newly come from the foundry. The brass pipes leading away from the range were polished until you could see yourself in them.

Mac did not delay long.

'Sure I have to be catchin' the train, Mrs M.,' said he, 'and divil a hair a me'll get near it if I don't hop off now, and they's nothin' I'd like better than to sit down an' have a cuppa tay, because God knows that nobody on God's earth makes a cuppa tay like yeh, and wasn't I oney sayin' that to them in the hotel the other night. The wringin's a the dish-cloth is all it is, I said, in comparison to what Mrs M. of Galway turns out. I couldn't have come at all if I hadn't wanted t' say how were yeh, an' to leave me young friend here in your keepin' because he's a nice young fella and I want 'm t' be well looked after.'

'I'll look after him,' said she seriously, 'don't you worry.'

'Isn't that why I brought him?' said Mac. 'Goodbye now, and I'll see you again, Mister Stephen O'Riordan, whin I'm back in town. You'll be here for a few weeks anyhow, I'm sure, and I'll be around this way for the July fair, so I will, with the help of God.'

Mac finally got away, and Stephen really hoped that he would see him again.

'Would you come up and I'll show you your room now, Mister O'Riordan?' she asked.

'Don't call me mister, ma'am,' said Stephen. 'I'd prefer it if you called me Stephen.'

'Well, then, I will indeed,' she said, 'because it is easier that way, and I have a great devotion to Saint Stephen, ever since I read about the way they killed him, and when I look out on the street there and see the way some a those children are flinging rocks at one another I say a prayer to him that murder won't be done on one of them.'

'That's as good a reason as any,' said Stephen, laughing.

'You are a Catholic?' she asked anxiously.

'Indeed I am,' said Stephen.

'Thank God for that,' she said, 'and I ought to have

known from the cut of you; but God forgive me, I had one or two of the others stayin' here with me and it used to hurt me to the quick to be givin' them steaks of a Friday, and I'd hop down to the chapel after dinner and light a candle to the Blessed Virgin, to forgive me, because I had to keep them, and what could I do? If they wanted meat, they'd have to have it, and unless I turned them out of the house, which I couldn't afford to do, they would have to get it.'

'I'm sure God won't be hard on you for that,' said Stephen, following her up the narrow stairs. There was linoleum on the stairs and the walls were distempered in a light green. His room was microscopic, but he liked it the minute she ushered him into it. It was so compact, and so brightly painted, and so cheerfully curtained, that he couldn't imagine himself feeling lonely in it.

'I hope it will be big enough for you,' she said, looking anxiously at the immensity of him in comparison to the small room.

'Of course it will,' he assured her, laughing. 'The one I had at home was hardly half the size of it.'

'That's good so,' she said. 'When you have washed yourself I will have the dinner on the table for you.'

'Thanks, ma'am,' said Stephen. 'I'm hungry too.'

This seemed to please her very much, and she left him to himself.

He proceeded to empty his bag of its scanty possessions: his shaving tackle, his brush and comb, his old clothes which he hid away in the small wardrobe, his shirts and socks and his books, which he left on the table beside the bed. Then, when he was about to throw the bag into the wardrobe, he thought he saw paper at the bottom of it. He put in his hand and to his amazement he pulled out three rather dirty pound notes. He remembered then Michilin coming out of the bedroom with the bag and slapping the dust off it, and he was sure of the origin of the money.

It made him feel soft for a few moments and he muttered, 'The bandy little so-and-so!' He saw Michilin then clearly, with the weather-beaten face and the twinkling eyes and a heart in his body as big as the biggest salmon he ever landed. From Michilin he went to Kathleen and then decided hurriedly that he better wash himself, so pouring cold water from the ewer into the basin he flung off his coat and lathered his face with soap and water; but he couldn't shut off the warmness he felt at that gesture of Michilin's, shoving in what was probably the only few pounds he had, and saying to himself, Sure, I'll be easy able to make it up agin, with a good night's fishing.

When he went down to the kitchen, the table was laid. He sat down and Mrs M., expressing the delight she felt that he was hungry, laid one of the most loaded plates he had ever seen in front of him. It held an enormous thick steak, with boiled turnips and potatoes almost swimming in the gravy.

He tackled it vigorously, to her appreciation. She stood over him like a hen over a chicken, and every time he'd have a potato eaten or some of the turnips, she would replace them with more, until at last, fully replete, he had to beg her to desist. Then she made him eat a great helping of jelly and custard, and followed that up with large cups of tea and sweet cakes.

All the time she was sitting down beside the fire, watching him and asking him questions. It was hard for him to parry questions he did not want to answer, because all her questions were put in the most kindly way. She almost wept over the death of his mother and she was quite worried when she heard he had come to Galway looking for a job, and she promised to go straight down to the chapel after dinner and start a Blue Rosary to Our Lady that he would get a good job quickly. She asked him what he was going to do after dinner, and he said he was going to go and look up a chap he knew from his own place called Paddy Rice, and he pulled out the last letter Paddy had given him to get the address. He was afraid she would maybe ask to see the address for herself. She didn't, which was lucky, because he would have to refuse to show it to her, since the opening lines of the letter under the address contained a few very naughty words.

Paddy had never been able to write a letter without expressing himself very strongly.

She told him how he would get to 'Mayville', St Pedro's Avenue. He was to go out of her house, walk down to the square where he had got off the bus, and then if he wanted he would get a bus that would leave him right at the door of the house. If he didn't want a bus, all he had to do was to start walking and follow the bus signs until he came near the sea at Salthill, and anyone would tell him then where the place was, and he was to be back at six for his tea, because she would have a very nice tea ready for him, and since at the moment she had no other lodgers staying with her it gave her great pleasure to have someone in the house to do something for.

Before he left, Stephen paid her three weeks' lodging money. She was indignant about this, and didn't want it. She had faith in him and knew he would get a good job and there was no point in his giving her money when he would want all he had to be going around looking for work. In the end he had to give it to her forcibly, and went out of the house reflecting that if all the Galway people were like Mrs M. it would be very hard to leave it, and he did not feel as lonely as he had been feeling, and thought how fortunate he was in having met Mac in the first place.

The street was quiet enough when he got out there. Either outraged grown-ups had committed mass child-murder, or all the little devils were in having their dinners. However it was, the street wore an aspect of sublime calm and uneasy armistice. Reaching the square he plunged into the main opening of the town, which was a narrow street flanked by tall buildings, mostly shops with the usual number of *pro rata* public-houses.

The shops amazed and delighted Stephen. He had never in his life seen such a profusion of everything. Looking at the drapers' windows with their wax dummies clothed like gentlemen in magazines, he felt that his own navy-blue suit was awkwardly cut and very shoddy. For the first time he looked into the lady-outfitters' windows and peeped at the mysteries of girls' underwear. He couldn't believe that girls could possibly wear all those filmy businesses under beautiful frocks and he had to laugh when he thought what some of the old Connemara women would look like, decked out in them pink silk yokes with cream lace on the end of them, instead of the bleached and converted flour-bags that served their purpose, or how Bigbum's wife would look if her enormous bosom was stuffed into the delicate what-u-may-call-it with thin straps and things and a shape on the front of them. It was a haughty-looking face regarding him amazedly from inside the shop that made him realize he was laughing out loud. Despite himself he blushed, and moved on.

Every shop he passed held him. The jewellers' gave him an idea of what luxury articles were like, which up to this he had only known as pictures in a book. The grocers', with all the cold meats and sausages and jams and jars, and pots of this and that, and pictures and advertisements of other things, would have made him feel very hungry if he hadn't had such a terrific dinner. Shoe shops, cake shops, sweet shops were like new worlds to him which he was discovering for the first time. He saw an enormous building towering up, white-faced and not beautiful with its ugly neon-tubing looking naked in the light of day. Outside it were pictures of handsome, sissyish-looking men with thin moustaches and side-whiskers, clasping in their arms luscious women with even teeth and coloured faces, and he presumed this must be a cinema where they showed the pictures, and he must go the first chance he got and see what they were like.

He went into a pub and called for a pint to see what the pubs were like. They weren't much different from the ones which he had known. The only things he missed there were the personal proprietors like Paddy's father and J. J. Here the assistants that gave you your drink were hurriedly polite, and too busy pulling, and measuring for other customers, to give you more than a casual look and decide that since you were new they didn't have to pause and chat you for a few minutes to keep you sweet.

But the customers were the same as he had always known them. One or two men, at the incoherent stage, shaking hands with one another over and over again, and rejoicing with tears that they had met. Others in the corner, talking quietly and drinking efficiently with the air of the hurried toper. Young fellows taking their drink for the first time, smoking a cigarette casually and holding the glass as if they had been doing it all their lives.

Stephen finished his pint and continued his journey.

When the shops had ceased to attract him so much he looked at the people who were passing, and the town.

The people were a mixture of all sorts. Haughty dames in very neat clothes, with dogs on leads maybe, or tiddly husbands, avoiding the passing contact of shawled women with lined faces, who shuffled by with their purchases under the shawl and the yellow powder of snuff clinging to the hairs on their upper lips. Fat, comfortable-looking men, alighting from cars, with creases in their trousers under heavy stomachs, carrying attaché cases or packages, and bustling importantly into banks or shops. Tall, small, long, or short, hungry-looking men, dressed in old clothes, some of them with shirts, some of them without shirts, holding up the corners of buildings turning into side-streets, sucking the butts of Woodbines, or reading the racing results or sliding hurriedly into bookies' shops.

The girls he saw were very nice girls. Most of them appeared to be good-looking and well lipsticked. Some of them were very dowdy. All of them seemed to be in couples, a good-looking girl passing by and talking confidentially to a not-so-good-looking girl. Then there were the obvious country people, leading or driving ass-and-carts or horse-and-carts, or nice-looking pony-and-carts, or just walking on the road with purpose in their faces and short ash-plants or whips in their hands. The men wore the bright ceanneasna trousers and the frock-cut braidin coat. Some of them wore the stiff shirt-front collars with inadequate ties, some of them just wore their clean striped shirts with the brass stud shining in the front. Women with heavy beige shawls, red petticoats covered with check aprons, and heftying large baskets which they unconcernedly used to lever a way through the crowds.

Then you would see the green-clad soldiers talking away in Irish to girls who answered them back in Irish, and from the amount he heard Stephen thought that soldiers were the same the whole world over. The big-built military police in pairs would pass by, walking carefully and eyeing every group of soldiers they passed. Then the blue-clad Civic Guards, all huge men, with leather-encased batons at their waist, walked by in the stately traditional manner associated with policemen everywhere. Now and again one of them would pause to warn a country man about holding up traffic in the narrow streets with his horse and bag-laden cart.

He thought the town was a peculiar town. The streets were very narrow and the buildings tall. There seemed to be no end to all the side-streets, which were also narrow. He went down one or two of them and discovered that the poor people mostly lived down there. Some of them were never touched by the sun, and they seemed to be crawling with children, and because they were so narrow, held the eternal smell of children who were completely uninhibited and answered the minor calls of nature with unabashed precocity. It was funny to see how some of the well-dressed ladies passing by so patently ignored the odd child here and there wetting a wall.

Of course, he thought, Galway had been a walled town, and this accounted for the narrow streets. It had a peculiar air of being mediaeval which it flaunted vigorously despite all the efforts of modern methods of commerce and trading to bedeck it with black pseudo-marble, chromium fittings, and the ugly neon. It would not require much imagination to see the figures of dark foreign sailors, dressed in doublet and hose, and swinging large cutlasses at their sides, jostling to one side this spineless civilization-ridden populace, that was their descendants. Even the churches, although some of them were obviously modern, added to the air of antiquity.

Stephen decided, as he hurried his footsteps toward

271

Salthill, that Galway was a mongrel city indeed, but not unattractive in its complete ugliness.

He kept his eyes open as he followed the bus signs. He soon reached the long bridge spanning the river Corrib. The water was shallow and rushed furiously over many rocks. He reflected, as he looked down at the water, that it was a pity it was such a shallow river. If it had been much deeper, then Galway would have been a much bigger town, and its commerce much greater. He turned and followed the course of the river with his eyes. It flowed under another bridge farther down, but where it joined the sea there was a long pier built out, cutting off the sight of the meeting, and providing safe anchorage for many small pucauns and gleoidhteoigs, the tops of whose masts he could see raising themselves above the piers.

There was a marble plate set into the bridge and he stopped to look at it. It read:

> WILLIAM O'BRIEN BRIDGE
> By Resolution Passed
> By the Town Commissioners
> During his Imprisonment
> in Galway Jail, A.D. 1889

He wondered who this William O'Brien might be whose memory was preserved in granite. There were a number of boys and not a few men seated on the wall which was the continuation of the bridge, and since they were near he walked towards them. They were three young fellows, who looked at him curiously.

'Who was William O'Brien?' he asked.

They looked at one another in puzzlement.

'Who d' y' say?' one of them asked, screwing up his face questioningly.

'This William O'Brien the bridge is named after,' said Stephen.

'Never heard of him,' said the questioner. 'Did you, Jack?'

'No,' said Jack. 'If he wasn't out in 1916. . . . Was he out in 1916?' he asked curiously, turning to the third.

'Nah,' said the boy; 'a bloody MP or some'in'.'

'Thanks anyhow,' said Stephen, moving on.

How low are the mighty fallen, he thought. Way back in 1889 there was probably all sorts of confusion and disturbance about this William O'Brien being confined to a dungeon in Galway Jail, and now out of a population of twenty thousand you would be lucky to find ten who knew why a bridge was named after him, and fewer still who had read the inscription on the bridge. Only casual tourists passing through the town who read the notice would give a passing thought to William O'Brien, whoever he was, and wonder why on earth he had been incarcerated in the jail.

He followed the bus signs down another long narrow street of shops and the inevitable pubs, and crossed a bridge at the end of it that flowed over what must be a branch of the Corrib, diverted to give power to mills or something, because the flowing water carried sawdust and all sorts of things upon its bosom. Above, he could see the high gates of a lock which must be a canal connecting the river with the sea.

From here he noticed that the town seemed to take on a new aspect. The old town had the grace to be old through its tawdry decorations, but here all was new, all was garish, and breathed nothing but ugliness and haphazard building, and the streets still remained crooked and narrow. Probably, he thought, even when the need for the wall around the town had gone, the people couldn't get out of the crooked street building, and he smiled as he thought how a modern engineer must be tearing his hair trying to work out plans to meet the advent of the mechanically propelled vehicles, and what sleepless nights this town must be giving him.

Beyond another church, with a narrow steeple pointing into the sky, the road became broad and tree-lined, and was flanked by obviously better-class dwelling-houses. It swung broadly around a corner and from here all the houses bore

the name-plates of doctors. The houses stood well back
from the road and had long gardens in front of them. They
looked as if there was money behind the neat curtains, and
the trim maids who appeared from one of them now and
again to shake a mat at the air, gazed curiously at the passer-
by below the gate, and then retired haughtily to the house.

There was a cross-roads here and he was undecided which
one to take, but a bus conveniently arrived, stopped at a
sign, disgorged a few passengers, and chugged off. He
followed it past a small garish cinema which told about the
synthetic beauty of some gorgeous female whose name he
could not pronounce in a thousand years, and then he got a
clear view of the sea away in the distance and hurried his
steps. He had not realized how much he had missed the sea.
From here the place deteriorated rapidly into small boarding
houses, and large boarding-houses, broken at intervals with
shops, and even a thatched cottage with a few larger buildings. The farther out he went the more depressing became
the view. Houses and hotels seemed to have been built just
anywhere, as if they had been dropped from the sky higgledy-
piggledy by passing storks making sport, and most of the
small houses had signs in the windows reading APARTMENTS,
and sometimes the signs were stained and old. You got a
view of white, linen-covered tables, laid out for a meal, and
sometimes an old man reading a newspaper or a young girl
leaning on the window-sill with her head in her hands gazing
into nothing and looking very bored, as if she was fed-up
with living and was getting rather tired of waiting for a rich
man to come along and tuck her into a Rolls-Royce.

But everything was saved by the noble sea which beat at
the rocks along the long promenade. The good old sea,
thought Stephen, banging away and completely unperturbed
by the tall buildings and the small buildings, by the cars or
the carts, by the well-fed people who wandered by with golf
bags, or the poor harassed-looking woman pushing a pram
and surrounded by what appeared to be legions of children
smathering themselves with ice-cream cones. The sea was
indifferent to where it beat as long as it had its coast. Why

should the sea worry about the big horrible-looking tin building, which must be a dance-hall, lying sprawling like a colossal tawdry whore in the midst of beauty, because it was surrounded by a well-kept park in which thousands of flowers blossomed and opened their hearts to the sun?

Stephen stopped a young man coming toward him with togs and towel flung carelessly around his neck, and his hair still wet from a dip in the sea. He asked him if he knew where St Pedro's Avenue was.

'Sorry,' he answered, 'I'm a stranger here myself.' And he hurried on to where he would probably get a much-needed lunch or dinner or whatever they called the main meal in Salthill.

He was more successful with his second inquiry. This was an old man with bowed shoulders, leaning on a walking-stick, who had obviously been out for a constitutional.

'You have passed it, young man,' he said, 'but if you will deign to walk with me I will direct your footsteps to the place.'

'Thank you, sir,' said Stephen, turning and matching his pace to the old man's.

'You are not a native of Galway, I presume?' inquired the old man.

'No, sir,' said Stephen.

'It's just as well,' said the old man.

'Do you like what you have seen of it?' he asked.

Stephen hesitated.

'Ah-ha!' ejaculated the old one.

'No, it's not that I dislike it,' said Stephen, 'but it's the kind of a place that would have to grow on you. Then I have lived in Connemara all my life and it is hard to adjust your eyes to buildings. Your mind is confused.'

'Understandable,' said the old man. 'Galway will give you a very bad first impression, but it grows on you, my boy, it grows on you. I'm not speaking about its abominable architecture, but the kindness and personality of its people. I came here on a visit, it must be forty years ago, and I remained. Then of course this Salthill was not as it is now. It was a small adjunct and not unlovely. When I pass through it now, I close my eyes and pretend that it is the tidy little place that it was forty years ago. I know one must sacrifice to progress, and that one must have the big hotels and the dance-halls and petrol stations and God knows what else; but there you are, I am old-fashioned, I suppose, and hate to see the tawdry enclosing on the green fields and the wild shore. The only concession I make to civilization is the modern ocean liner.'

He turned and pointed out the bay with his stick. It was a grand bay, Stephen thought, enclosed on this side by the city and on the other by the low-lying Clare hills, and away out to its mouth you could just see the Aran Islands rising out of the heat.

'There, near the lighthouse, out there,' said the old man, 'the liners pull in, and it is a very beautiful thing to see one of those huge boats riding at anchor out there at night-time and it lighted up like a minor firmament.'

'That must be a nice sight,' said Stephen.

'It is,' said the old man, 'it is a noble sight. Anything that has to do with the sea is noble, excepting modern holiday resort towns on its lip, like a cancerous growth on your mouth.'

Stephen tried to imagine what Ourish Strand would be like if somebody came and built a lot of dance-halls and garages and hotels on it, and he didn't like the thought at all. Of course it would be good for the people, and it would lift most of them out of their grinding poverty – that was the principal advantage and one that must be taken into account before you judged – but still, he thought, but still . . .

'There is the avenue you are looking for now,' said the old man. 'Straight up there, and I think the house you are looking for is the one at the very end.'

'Thank you,' said Stephen. 'I am very grateful to you.'

'It is a pleasure, my boy,' said the old man. 'Goodbye.' He went on his way with his bowed walk.

Stephen paused before the last house, and then he knocked determinedly on the door.

CHAPTER NINETEEN

The door was opened by a very large woman with fat rosy cheeks and a great big smile that was in no way destroyed by a mouthful of grand, even, small false teeth. She was a very fat woman and a very comfortable-looking one. She wore a large, enveloping, coloured house-coat, and seemed to be eternally raising a small plump hand to brush back a stray wisp of hair that was determined to fall down on her forehead. Paddy had often mentioned Mrs Hartnet in the infrequent letters which he wrote, and Stephen was glad to see that she was almost exactly as he had pictured her from Paddy's letters.

'Good afternoon,' she said brightly, 'and what can I do for you?'

Stephen noticed that her voice was a refined one, with clear enunciation.

'I'm looking for Paddy Rice,' he answered her.

'Oh, that Paddy Rice!' she said, and laughed, shaking all over. 'Come in, come in. I think he's somewhere about and I will get him for you.'

She held the door open for him, shut it after him, and showed him into a room looking out on the street. It was a kind of living-room. The furniture was good and modern-looking, a three-piece suite covered in green leather, several easy-chairs, and a table over against the farther wall that was littered with books and tomes and note-books of all descriptions. While he waited for her to get Paddy, after she had exhorted him to make himself comfortable, he turned over the pages of the books – Gray's *Anatomy*; *Physiology*; *Gynaecology* – and the pictures in them would turn the stomach of any honest citizen, particularly the one of casual rubber-gloved hands piercing the head of a small infant with a forceps with a screw on the top of it. Stephen closed the book hurriedly and deposited his large bulk in one of the chairs.

He heard the door opening and turned toward it. Paddy's face was framed there with a puzzled look on it, which changed to one of amazement and disbelief when he saw who his visitor was. Then he came over quickly and grabbed Stephen by the arm.

'Well, for God's sake,' said Paddy. 'Stephen O'Riordan as sure as I'm alive! What the hell are you doing here? And how did you get here, and why in the name of Michilin's seven blind b's didn't you tell me you were coming?'

He was the same Paddy, grown a little older. He had always had a passion for clothes and he was very well dressed now, albeit a trifle loudly as was his wont. Stephen thought he had got fat since the last time he had seen him, and could discover his father taking shape in him.

'Ah, it's a long story,' said Stephen.

'Well, for God's sake,' said Paddy, 'sit down and give us a synopsis. I'm going back home myself in a fortnight and I was looking forward to having you there. What in the name of all that's good and holy brought you out from the fastnesses of Connemara?'

Stephen told him briefly the reason for his coming, but he didn't say anything about Kathleen.

Paddy rose and walked about. Stephen reflected that he had never lost this nervous kind of tension. He found it almost impossible to stay quiet for more than a few minutes at a time, and that was probably the reason he found it so hard to read books, apart from his medical tomes, which he was forced to read.

'Well, blow me down!' said Paddy. Then he turned on Stephen. 'It was bound to happen sooner or later, mark you, Stephen, because yourself and your old man are temperamentally unsuited, and it's a great wonder the clash didn't come before this. Anyhow, it's about time that you stirred out of your burrow and decided to see the great big world turning. Lookit, how about digs? Will you stay here with me?'

'Thanks, Paddy,' said Stephen, 'but I'm already fixed up,

and I'd never have been able to afford what you pay for your digs.'

'And what about that?' said Paddy angrily. 'Amn't I supposed to be a friend of yours? Wouldn't I have stuck you the bloody oul digs for a few weeks until you cleared off to Dublin or wherever you are going?'

'I know you would, Paddy,' said Stephen, 'but what I want to do is to do things on my own. After all, damn it, I'm over twenty-one, and big and strong enough to look after myself. Besides, I'm going to do what I have to do without sponging on anyone, so I am.'

'Like hell you will!' said Paddy. 'All right, all right, have it your own way. The trouble about you is that you've read too many oul books about fellas goin' out and doin' for themselves. You take it from me that that's all hooey. The only way you'll get on in this world is to have somebody behind you or in front of you opening a few doors here and there. And I suppose you are all fixed up for a job too? You don't have to ask about that, I suppose?'

'Well,' said Stephen, laughing, 'if you could even show me the knob of a door like that, I wouldn't mind.'

'No fear you wouldn't. Well, as it happens I think I can get you something all right. At least I know the very man that can put you in the way of something. He's a peculiar sort of a guy, but if he likes you he'll fix you up all right.'

'Lead me to him,' said Stephen, rising to his feet.

'Not now,' said Paddy. 'We'll dig him up tonight when he's half-cocked in some pub or other. He's always like a bear with a sore head when he's sober. What are you doing now?'

'Holidaying at Salthill,' said Stephen. 'I came to recuperate by the sea.'

'I'll tell you what,' said Paddy. 'I have to go up to the hospital. I have a job or two to do up there. Come on up with me, and then we'll go somewhere and have tea, and then we'll meet someone else, and maybe I'd be surprising you for a change. Is that all right with you?'

'I'm in your hands,' said Stephen.

'Fair enough,' said Paddy, and then shoving his head out of the door he shouted, 'Hey, Mrs Hartnet!' Then he turned back and looked at Stephen again. 'Imagine you being here!' he said.

Mrs Hartnet appeared at the door.

'This is a friend of mine from Connemara, Stephen O'Riordan,' he said.

'How do you do?' said she, coming across to shake hands with Stephen. 'There must be great feeding in Connemara to turn out a big fellow like you.'

'They don't feed them out in Connemara,' said Paddy, 'they turn fellas like him out in pasture during the summer.'

'You're not doing Paddy too badly yourself,' said Stephen, 'judging by the way he's filling his clothes.'

Mrs Hartnet laughed heartily.

'There, Paddy,' she said, 'didn't I tell you you were getting fat?'

'We'll leave my figure out of this now,' said Paddy.

'Is your friend going to stay with us?' Mrs Hartnet asked.

'He is not,' said Paddy. 'He is not in a position to afford the outrageous prices that you charge for digs.'

This seemed to amuse her mightily.

'And anyhow,' said Paddy, 'you wouldn't have a bed in the house big enough to fit him.'

'Well, he'll have a cup of tea anyhow,' she said, when she had stopped laughing.

'How about it?' Paddy asked him.

'No, thanks,' said Stephen. 'I just polished off a colossal meal before I came searching for you.'

'What I wanted to tell you,' said Paddy, 'is that I probably won't be back for tea. We'll have it somewhere in town. And don't wait up for me tonight, because we'll be with the right hon. Mister Bishop, Esquire, and it's harder to lever that fella out of a pub than it is to pass the second medical, and God knows that's hard enough.'

'All right so,' she said. 'I'll expect you when I see you.'

'That's the ticket,' said Paddy; 'and don't forget to leave the Andrews' beside the bed, because I know now, in my sober senses, that I'm going to have a head tomorrow morning like a prize pumpkin, and a mouth like a head of cauliflower.'

'I'll attend to it,' she said.

'Come on, Stephen,' said Paddy.

'Goodbye, Mrs Hartnet,' said Stephen.

'Don't say goodbye, Mister O'Riordan,' she said. 'I hope you will come back and see us again.'

'It's the same the whole world over,' said Paddy bitterly. 'Give them a big body, a brown face, and white teeth, and they fall over like ninepins, so they do.'

'He was always jealous of me, ma'am,' said Stephen in explanation.

'Enough of this banter,' said Paddy. 'Come, Colossus.'

So they left the house, Stephen having promised to return again at frequent intervals.

'She's a nice woman,' said Stephen.

'Grand,' said Paddy. 'I was chased out of about twenty digs until I hit on her, and I never looked back since. Tell me all about Connemara and the lads.'

So as they walked back the way Stephen had come, Stephen related to Paddy all that had happened since he had last been in Connemara. Also he told him how Nellie McClure had packed up her bags and left for parts unknown, and this led them to talk about Thomasheen and his marriage, and Stephen was surprised that after such a length of time Paddy should be still so virulent about it.

They got on to a bus at Salthill. Stephen would have preferred to walk, but Paddy refused, and claimed that God had other reasons for giving men legs than making them use them in silly steps. So they mounted the bus.

They were talking then about their school days and started a hare of 'Do you remember?', and they laughed loudly, and people turned to look at them and to wonder who was the fellow with that wild Paddy Rice, and hoped the poor young man would not be corrupted by the wilful habits of his associate.

They finished their journey to the hospital on foot.

The hospital was a big scattered kind of a building, and almost before you came to it at all you could get a smell of the disinfectants that pervaded the air.

'Will I wait here for you?' Stephen asked, pausing in the gatehouse.

'No,' said Paddy, 'come on up. I won't be long. You can wander around for a while. It will do your soul good.'

Stephen followed him in reluctantly, thinking that it was here his mother had died, and then chided himself for being ridiculous.

A long corridor seemed to stretch away to eye level. The air in the corridor was warm and smelled strongly of all sorts of things. You could see nurses dressed in white hurrying here and there, carrying things, and girls pushing trolleys, and nuns bustling around wearing check aprons over their habits, and rattling keys. It had a dream-like quality because the floors were covered in rubber matting and you could see what you could not hear. Now and again you could hear somebody laughing cheerfully and you would be startled. They went down another corridor that cut across the main one. There was a grating here in the wall and a loud humming noise.

He saw the legs of people coming down as if from heaven, and then a lift stopped buzzing, the gates clashed open, and an attendant and a nurse came out of the lift pushing a stretcher on wheels. There was a woman lying on it, covered with a blanket. Her face was very pale and her eyes were closed. Stephen felt his mouth going dry.

Before going off with the stretcher, they greeted Paddy loudly and cheerfully, and he asked them if they had seen Curly.

'There she is behind you, just coming off duty, the lucky cow,' said the nurse, departing with her burden.

'Who's taking my name in vain?' said a voice behind them, and they turned to see a small neat girl wearing a blue dress, caught in tightly at the waist, and covered with a white apron. Her sleeves were rolled and were caught back with white armlets. Brown curls were popping out from under her white cap.

'Ah, Curly,' said Paddy, going up and putting his arms around her and lifting her off her feet. 'Me oul darlin', how is every bit of you?'

'For God's sake,' said Curly, releasing herself quickly, 'will you be careful that the Matron doesn't see you.'

'Me and the Matron,' said Paddy, 'are practically bosom friends, and I have her express permission to cuddle any or all of the probationers with whom it is my pleasure to do so.'

'Who's the big boy friend?' asked Curly, regarding Stephen with interest.

'There it goes again!' said Paddy. 'What kind of yokes are women at all? The very minute they see anything over six foot and wearing trousers the light comes into their eyes. He's not for sale, kid. Look, did ye never hear about Napoleon? Napoleon was a small kind too like me, and all the women were crazy about him.'

'You're no Napoleon, sugar,' said Curly, patting his cheek, 'and the House Surgeon will tell you that, and a lot more when he sees you. Don't you know that you were supposed to be on duty with him yesterday and today? Baby, when he sees you, it will be just too bad.'

'That's what I came about now. I want to go and see him. Look, what are you doing now?'

'I'm going off duty, and what I do after that is private and confidential, and is none of your business,' said Curly.

'Look, Curly,' said Paddy, 'while I'm up with me man for an hour or so, would you take Stephen here under your wing? I have an important date with him, and I don't want to lose him.'

'It'll be a pleasure,' said Curly, coming over and slipping a hand through Stephen's arm. Then she looked up at him. 'God,' she ejaculated, 'he must be bigger than Finn McCool!'

'No,' said Stephen, 'I believe he was nine-foot-eleven.'

'What did you say your name was?' Curly asked.

'Stephen O'Riordan,' said Stephen.

283

'You'd be a real handy height for lifting me over the wall when I'm coming in late,' said Curly.

Stephen laughed.

'It'd be a great pleasure,' he said.

'Look, I'm off now,' said Paddy. 'I'll finish up with this fella as quick as I can, and I'll be back.'

'Don't hurry,' said Curly, smiling at Stephen. 'Why didn't you turn up anyhow?'

'I was attending me mother's funeral,' said Paddy.

'Aren't you mixing dates?' said Curly. 'I thought your mother died and left you a lonely orphan at the tender age of three. At least that's the opening gambit in all your conquests.'

'My grandmother so,' said Paddy.

'I don't believe,' said Curly, 'that you ever had a grandmother.'

'He did,' said Stephen, 'I'll go bail on that, but I couldn't say when she died anyhow.'

'That'll do, that'll do,' said Paddy. 'It's a good lie and I'm sticking to it. Look, I'm off now. The trouble about that doctor fella is that he's too sincere altogether. You'd think that it was himself that infected everybody in the hospital with this and that, and if he didn't cure them quick that he'd be hanged be the neck until he was dead. Don't go away now, Stephen. I won't be long.'

Paddy hurried away and disappeared down another corridor.

'What do you want to see?' Curly asked.

'I don't think,' said Stephen carefully, 'that I want to see anything. I'm afraid I'm not much good at looking at sickness and things.'

'We'll just wander around, anyhow,' said Curly, 'and it will be good for your education. Are you from the same place as Paddy?'

'I am,' said Stephen. 'We went to school together too.'

'What do you do for a living?' she asked him, turning and walking to the end of this corridor which seemed to give on to a garden.

'I am a simple farmer-fisherman,' said Stephen, stepping by her side, 'who has come to the big city looking for a job.'

'I haven't seen you in Galway before,' she said.

'That,' said Stephen, 'is because I have never been in Galway before.'

'You mean to say,' she asked him, 'that you have never been out of that place, what-you-may-call-it, where you were born?'

'No,' said Stephen, 'I haven't.'

'But,' she said, 'you don't talk like that.'

'I wonder,' said Stephen, 'why everyone says that. I don't talk like that, because I had a mother who insisted on me talking like she did herself, and because she made me read books and things.'

'Oh,' said Curly, interested, 'she must be a strong kind of woman.'

'She was,' said Stephen. 'She died somewhere in this hospital five years or so ago.'

'Oh!' said Curly. 'I wouldn't have known her anyhow. That was long before I came. Here, we'll go out in the garden and I may be able to sneak a smoke without anyone being the wiser.'

She opened the steel, glass-panelled door, and he followed her into the garden. They emerged on to the drive that led to the main gate. Facing them was a tall-storeyed building of modern design.

'That's where we live,' said Curly, waving her hand at it.

They were walking down towards the end of the garden when a door at the back of the building opened and two men appeared carrying a stretcher. There was a figure on the stretcher covered with a sheet. The head was covered too.

Stephen's blood ran cold when he saw that it was a corpse. You could tell because the body was so motionless under the sheet. The two men carrying it were out of step and as they walked the corpse jogged up and down. He could hear them talking. It was a casual conversation. The first one was saying how he had gone up and there was Joe holding a glass in his hand and singing the 'Rose of Mooncoyne' and he had nothin' on oney his shirt and trousers. 'Laugh?' he said, 'I thought I'd split my sides.' The man behind laughed then, and said, 'Jay, that's was gass I bet, so it was; I saw 'm the same way last Galway races. Sozzled? Boy, was he that way! Laugh? Oh, a proper howl he was when he'd start in on that.' And they moved off towards a small house at the end of the garden, talking cheerfully, while the shrouded corpse moved grotesquely to their irregular footsteps.

Stephen had stopped to stare at them. He couldn't help it.

'What is it?' Curly asked, looking at him curiously.

'That was a body, wasn't it?' Stephen asked.

'Yes,' said Curly, 'they're taking it down to the morgue. Are you shocked?'

'Kind of,' said Stephen. 'Country boys, you know, are not as hard-bitten as ye people that are always knocking about a hospital.'

'Yes, I suppose so,' said Curly. 'We're always inclined to forget that. But you get very used to people dying, and when you see how some of them suffer you are quite glad, for their own sakes, when they die.'

'I don't think,' said Stephen, 'that I'd ever get used to it.'

'You'd be surprised,' said Curly. 'I was terrified first when I had to handle a corpse, particularly when I had to wash them and I was left alone down there in the morgue with them. But you get used to it.'

'I'm looking at it from a personal angle,' said Stephen. 'That one that's just gone past now. Can't you imagine the suffering he's causing a lot of people somewhere? He's somebody to them, so he is. They are waiting now maybe somewhere to hear about him, and soon they'll get a message to say he's dead, and it will throw them into sorrow and confusion and expense, and they will mourn for him and a lot of other people will mourn for him, and somewhere there will be somebody that will never forget him. He's precious to them. And here we've seen him being carted about as if he was a sack of potatoes. He's just another corpse here,

286

when really he's a very precious thing to real people some-where.'

'That's nonsense,' said Curly, 'although I see what you mean. But can you imagine how everyone would be worn out, if you had to start crying and feeling sorry for every-body that dies, even though they mean nothing to you? If a surgeon was to feel personally like that about everyone he operated on, he'd never be able to do an operation at all, and in the same way if we were to feel each death personally like that we'd never be able to stick it.'

'I know all that,' said Stephen. 'But I'll never marry a nurse all the same.'

Curly laughed loudly at that.

'There's no hope for me so,' she said.

'I'm sure,' said Stephen, 'that a good-looking girl like you is not without plenty of prospects.'

'And then,' said Curly, to the sky, 'they tell you that these nice quiet boys from the country are shy and awkward and here's one that's a subtle Connemara complimenter. Come on, and to get you out of the morbids I'll show you the marvels of modern medicine. There's a marvellous X-ray machine in here. It's a wonderful business. There's no part of you that it can't look at and take pictures of, in the twinkling of an eye.'

So she brought him into the X-ray room and showed him around and he was deeply interested in it. At least it took his mind off the corpse.

From the X-ray room they seemed to have wandered by accident into the main corridors of the hospital, and Curly would open a door here and there, if it wasn't already opened.

What Stephen saw made him long for the green fields, the tall mountains, and the sea that beat eternally on a Conne-mara shore.

Every long ward was a repetition of the last. A row of beds down one side and another row of beds down the other. In some of the beds men or boys or children would be sitting up, their backs propped with pillows. All of them wore the

287

look of the sick, and the suffering they had endured or were enduring. Their skin was tightly drawn across their cheek-bones and it seemed to be as fine as paper, and was the colour of old ivory. Their eyes would be sunken back deeply in their heads, and blue shadows under them seemed to give them an extraordinary brilliant look.

Then others would be walking carefully and slowly towards the end of the ward, wearing dressing-gowns. Every effort they made seemed to bring sweat to their brows, yet there was a flame of triumph in their eyes as if they were discovering that this short walk they were doing now was the greatest achievement of their lives, and they were savouring it, because they would never make such an effort as this again, since by their own indomitable will and the help of skilful doctoring and nursing they had succeeded in pulling themselves back from the lip of the grave.

Others would be lying back in bed with their eyes closed, their very faint breathing hardly disturbing the blankets that covered them. Others still would be asleep and moaning as if somebody was torturing them. Around some of the beds screens were drawn, and your eyes would peer frantically, trying to pierce the cover to see the agonies of the dying.

Stephen had only seen two or three wards when he gave up.

'Would you mind if we went now?' he said to Curly.

'So you can't take it,' said Curly. 'All right. Come on.'

Stephen followed her and wiped the sweat off his brow.

He didn't speak until they were out in the garden again.

'I think that's terrible,' he said.

'You're right,' said Curly, 'it is. And I always believe in bringing rude healthy people like you into a hospital so that it will make you think. It will make you appreciate your own health more anyhow.'

'It certainly does,' said Stephen.

'You see,' said Curly, 'when you saw that corpse going out you were saying to yourself that weren't we a crowd of heartless so-and-so's up here, that we paid no more attention to a body than if it was the carcase of a cat. Well, you saw

288

all those people in the wards up there. Practically every disease that scourges the body is up there, my big, well-fed, muscular Connemara man. And it is the quick we have to be sympathetic about, not the dead. Isn't it better to be glad when you have helped to save somebody suffering from consumption, or cancer, or pneumonia, or pleurisy; or people who have been cut up so many times for so many things that it's only their faces that are left untouched to them; or the people in that other building over there, who are dying and fighting and living despite the infectious fever diseases: isn't it better to be glad when one of those lives, than it is to be wasting your sorrow on somebody who is better dead anyhow; than to be watching him suffering agonies which you have never known, and which you better pray you never will know?'

'All right,' said Stephen, 'I understand, and I am duly humbled and apologetic, but I still say I wouldn't marry a nurse.'

'You might be damn glad to marry one, some day,' said Curly.

'Not unless she's something like you,' said Stephen with a smile.

'Ah,' said Curly, 'that's a very nice remark and takes the sting out of your rudeness, but I wouldn't marry a big strong man like you if you had a million a year. And do you know why? Because I have found out that big men are the divil when they have anything wrong with them. Give them a cut on the big toe, and they think that the end of the world is at hand. I'd have given up this nursing business long ago if I wasn't hanging around waiting for a miracle, and some day I hope to see it. And do you know what that is?'

'No,' said Stephen.

'Well,' said Curly, 'it is to come in here some morning and see a big beefy boozer, who religiously insists on his wife becoming pregnant year after year, up there in the maternity ward, waiting to bring forth a baby.'

Stephen laughed uproariously.

'Ah, God,' he spluttered, 'that would be a sight for the

gods and I hope in hell that you're not disappointed, as long as it isn't me.'

'Well, come on,' said Curly, 'and we'll go and seek this Paddy. I have been official amuser for long enough. And besides, I have a date.'

'I'm grateful to you,' said Stephen, 'for having put up with me, and I have also taken all your object lessons to heart.'

'As long as you have,' said Curly, 'I have not wasted my time.'

'And if ever,' said Stephen, 'I am smitten with a disease, I hope that I will be placed under your tender ministrations; only for God's sake, if I do die, pay a little more respect to my corpse when it's swinging on its cheerful way to the morgue.'

Curly laughed loudly then.

'I can see,' she said, 'that all my work on you has been wasted, and I hope that the memories of what you have seen will come back to haunt your dreams.'

'I can see me tossing in the middle of a nightmare now,' said Stephen, 'and thinking that I'm going to have a baby, and you there waiting, rolling up your sleeves with a leering, determined look on your face.'

'Come on in,' Curly laughed, 'before we get too far involved in this.'

They went into the main hall and had just reached it when Paddy came rushing along pulling off a white coat which he threw into Curly's arms.

'Here, Curly, me oul black sole, would you fire this into the quarters? I just managed to get away from that fella now, but I know he's after me again to get me to do something else. So I'm off. Tell him when you see him that I love him very dearly, but that I have an urgent call to bury me Australian cousin. Come on, Stephen.'

He grabbed Stephen's arm and started to rush him towards the door. Stephen looked back over his shoulder to shout at Curly.

'Goodbye,' he said. 'Thanks a lot, and I hope I see you again.'

'Me too,' she said, and waved, before turning into the corridor.

'That's a grand girl that Curly,' he said to Paddy as soon as they were outside.

'Curly is it?' Paddy asked. 'Oh, a grand girl indeed, but too damn independent. She won't play games at all. You have as much chance of getting an oul coort out of Curly as you have of lifting a mountain on one of your palms.'

'That doesn't prove,' said Stephen, 'that she isn't a damn nice girl. In fact it makes her nicer in my opinion.'

'Your opinion, my dear Stephen,' said Paddy, 'is of absolutely no value whatsoever. You and Curly are of a type anyhow, pure spirits. Concentration on the job in hand. That's all mularkey. You might as well have a bit of fun while you have a chance because next week you might be fertilizing a patch of ground measuring six by two, or is it three? I'm not sure because I never attend funerals. Now where will we go for tea, I wonder?'

'You ought to know,' said Stephen, 'but if you wouldn't mind I'd like you to come up and have tea with the lady where I'm staying. She said she'd have tea ready for six, and I wouldn't like to disappoint her the first day. Besides, she's a very nice woman, and I like her. So if you don't mind, we will go there.'

'My surroundings never interest me,' said Paddy, 'as long as I can eat. So come and let us away.'

Stephen did not have much time to look around him as they made their way up the town, because Paddy was talking away about this and that and became impatient if Stephen stopped to ask him about some place.

'What the hell do you want to know what that is for? Isn't it only an oul high wall that was once the jail and has been sold to the Church to build a cathedral by the County Council?' Or, 'That's only the oul Salmon Weir Bridge. What in the name a God do you want to be leaning over looking at the salmon paving the bottom of the river for? We all know it makes the oul poacher's fingers itch to be after them, and you're thinkin' how Michilin'd have a fit if he saw that many salmon all together, but dammit I'm hungry and I want something to eat, so come on for God's sake, and we have to meet this Bishop fella and also I have a surprise for you. Boy, won't you be surprised!'

They reached the digs, to be met at the door by a great smell of frying rashers and Paddy nearly spurted saliva at the mouth.

It took him about five seconds to have Mrs M. wrapped around his finger and in another five seconds he was stirring the extra rashers which she had put on the pan for him, and telling her that although he was really hungry he didn't think he could manage more than four or five sausages and certainly not more than three eggs, but that if she insisted he would give way on the egg argument and have four.

Then when the meal was cooked he made her sit at the table with them and have her own tea, and he had the two of them roaring laughing about this and that, until Mrs M. was completely conquered and vowed that she had never met a young man like him in all her life, and that she hoped he would come and see her often and that the teapot would always be on the hob waiting for him.

And Stephen was glad, because he was very fond of Paddy and he thought that Mrs M. was the nicest woman he had met (not counting Kathleen as a woman) since his mother had died.

CHAPTER TWENTY

It was well after eight o'clock when they reached the street again.

'That was a great meal,' said Paddy, 'and whoever guided you to that good woman knew what he was doing and what he was about.'

Stephen was absurdly glad that Paddy liked the digs and the landlady.

'Where are we bound for now, anyhow, Paddy?' he asked.

'Towards a surprise,' said Paddy, 'and then we must go hunting the Bishop fella. The hunt will, I am afraid, be accompanied by much drinking, but I have been on the tack now for months in order to have my brain free for the exams, so I can afford to relax for a change, and it isn't every day that a friend comes to town.'

They went back through the town again. There seemed to be more people about, hurrying to wherever they were going. Stephen noticed most of the girls were out and about, now dressed in their best and looking very highly polished. When he remarked that he thought there were a lot of pretty girls in Galway, Paddy sat on him with his cynical knowledge.

'My dear young yokel,' he said, 'your first lesson in the big city must be never to judge the book by the cover, and since the recent invention of liquid make-up, and the permanent wave that lasts for two months, the ordinary drab can make herself look like the Queen of Sheba. Boils, carbuncles, black-heads, and all facial blemishes may be discreetly hidden away by make-up, so if you decide to marry a city girl, make sure that you take her and scrub her face first to be sure that she is all that she appears to be.'

All the same, Stephen noticed that Paddy had special smiles for the girls he knew, and that if he stopped for a moment to chat them he gave them of his special smile, and turned on all his entertaining personality.

Stephen remarked on this.

'It doesn't seem to stop you being awful nice to them,' he said.

'Why be cruel?' said Paddy. 'Why should I make their night sorrowful at the beginning, by stabbing them to the heart? Think of the misery they would endure if they thought that Paddy Rice no longer loved them.'

So Stephen laughed and gave Paddy up.

Halfway between the town and Salthill, they turned off the main road and went into what seemed a poorer district. Long avenues of houses, without gardens, stretched away in tidy rows, their front doors opening on to the footpaths.

You could only judge them from their appearance and the appearance of the inhabitants. You knew it was a poor quarter because there were so many children, and they seemed no different from the children in Stephen's street, and their parents were just as inclined to be as passionate and as blasphemous in their defence. Now that their working day was done, there seemed to be more older boys leaning against gable-ends, butts hanging from their lower lips, and they speaking in the slow, flat drawl which Stephen had already come to associate with the Galway people. They looked curiously at the two passing them, and a member of one group would throw a remark after them which would cause the others to break into loud and not very pure laughter. This seemed to annoy Paddy and he would glare back at them. It didn't worry Stephen, because he liked to see and hear all sorts of people.

Some of the houses were very dirtily curtained and some of them were very neat. Sometimes a door would be open and you would see the red tiles on the floors. The tiles would sometimes be dirty, sometimes gleaming with cleanliness. Or you would see the floor almost impassable with the bodies of children, or clothes draped on horses before the open fires. There seemed to be none of the houses without large families the members of which were either coming, or going, or washing, or eating, or shouting, or talking, or crying.

Now and again they would be startled by a door opening, and a mother leaning her head out, and shouting up or down the street.

'Packeen! Packeen!' she would roar. 'Hi, Packeen, come in here or I'll tan your arse! D'yeh hear me callin' yeh, Packeen?'

Packeen never seemed to be available at the moment, and after shouting herself into hoarseness, the poor woman would retire defeated or she would come rushing out of the house with a cane or a piece of stick in her hand, and she would give chase to Packeen. Packeen wouldn't be such an eejit as to be caught that way. He would have his eye on his mother, would judge his time nicely, and when she would have almost reached him he would do a swerve and circle back to the house before her, and you would hardly see his tail for dust.

She would give chase then for a while, but would break into a trot, and pause for a while with her arms folded to have a chat with a neighbour, about how that fella Packeen had the heart scalded in 'er. From which they would drift into other topics, Packeen forgotten, and for all Stephen knew, they would stay chatting all the night. He would have liked to remain to find out.

'Isn't it a great pity,' he said to Paddy, 'that we haven't a lot of people and kids like this in Connemara? I think it makes life real interesting.'

Paddy looked at him with his eyes widened.

'Holy God!' he said. 'Isn't poor oul Connemara bad enough without having that pack of savages dumped on it?'

'Maybe,' said Stephen, 'Connemara wouldn't be half as savage if all those people were living in it.'

'You're cracked,' said Paddy rudely; 'but sure you always had funny ideas, so you had. Here we are now, thank God.'

He stopped at a door which Stephen saw was numbered 97, and rapped smartly with the knocker.

A woman came to the door. She was a thin woman and wore a very harassed look on her face, and no wonder, because she had a pair of safety-pins in her mouth, a white baby's napkin in one hand, and a completely naked boy baby in the other one. The baby had its mouth as widely opened as a young skaltaun after worms, and the most piercing shrieks that Stephen had ever heard were issuing from it.

The woman had to shout to make herself heard.

'Hello, it's you, Mister Rice, is it? Would you hop into the foot a t' stairs there an' give a shout yersel'? I'm givin' me man here his Saturday night bath, an' y'd swear yer solemn oath that I was killin' 'm. Shut up, will yeh!' She shouted this at the child, and then rapped him smartly on the bare bottom with her hand.

The shouts which it was producing before were like the cooing of doves in comparison to what issued from the child after this indignity. The woman retired and plomped it down into the basin of water before the fire, while Paddy, shouting something at her, went to the bottom of the stairs and roared something up them. Stephen couldn't hear what it was, but obviously Paddy couldn't hear what was being shouted back at him, so he turned and glared at the child, and Stephen had never in his life seen such a murderous look on the face of any man as on Paddy's.

This was too much for Stephen, so he walked away, and tried to make his laughing as unobtrusive as possible. Tears of suppressed laughter were in his eyes when he felt a touch on his shoulder, and he turned to be confronted by a smiling Nellie McClure.

He couldn't believe his eyes at first. But there she was, dressed more neatly than he had ever seen her, and behind her was Paddy with a large grin on his face.

'Nellie!' shouted Stephen, and was so delighted to see a familiar face amidst the phantoms of this day's phantasy, that he threw his arms around her and kissed her soundly on the mouth.

There were whistles and cat-calls from the opposite side of the street where the boys were gathered, but Stephen was deaf to them.

'Well, Nellie McClure of all people!' he said, holding her back from him and looking at her with delight in his eyes.

'It's me all right, Stephen,' she said, 'and I was never as happy at seeing anybody.'

'Let us quit this low neighbourhood,' said Paddy, 'until we can look and see and wonder, and . . . speak!' he shouted savagely at the house of the howling infant.

So the three of them continued on the road they were on, and soon came to a long quiet street, with houses on one side, and a wall-enclosed college of some kind on the other. They stopped there.

'Tell me all about it,' said Stephen. 'We all thought that you had gone to England.'

'I did not,' she said, and he was glad to notice that a sparkle had come back into her eyes and that she was nearly the same Nellie that she had always been. She was dressed very well too, cheaply but nattily as far as he could judge. She was wearing a light summer frock which tightened around the waist and clung to her thighs and breasts. 'I came to Galway and I'm working in a factory now and sending money home, so I am. That place where you called for me, she is a relative of my mother's and she is a very nice woman indeed, but you'd want to talk to her without all the children bawlin' all over the place.'

'Didn't I tell you I'd surprise you!' said Paddy smugly.

'But what brings you here, Stephen?' she asked. 'I could a fallen down dead straight whin I saw y'.'

'The same as you, Nellie,' said Stephen. 'I'm lookin' for a job first, an' then I'm goin' to go to Dublin afterwards.'

'And how is Kathleen, tell me?' she asked. 'I didn't even wait t' say goodbye t' her, so I didn't.'

'Oh, she's grand, so she is,' said Stephen.

'What's this? What's this?' asked Paddy, putting in his *ladar*. 'Who is this Kathleen person, and why have I not heard about her before?'

'She's Kathleen Finnerty,' said Nellie, 'and you wouldn't know her, because she has been in England for years, so she has, but she pulled Stephen outa the sea with a rope, and there you are.'

'Aren't you the sly bastard,' said Paddy, 'not to say anything about this to your bosom pal?'

'How could I?' Stephen asked, 'when I've only been talking to you for a few hours, and hardly got a spoke in all that time.'

'You're a lying hound,' said Paddy; 'but come, we will depart to the nearest hostelry and discuss things over a ball of malt.'

So they set off, Nellie having a hand on an arm of each, and she prattling away about the job she had, and the quite good money she was gettin', and how it was Paddy who had got it for her, and she was learnin' all about the machine she was workin' on, and that the foreman was pleased with her and had told her that, if she kept at it, he'd be able to give her promotion and a rise maybe. Paddy interjected here to say that the foreman was probably a wolf, and she indignantly denied this and said that, on the contrary, he was an honest Christian gintleman with a wife and eight children and he went to half-seven Mass and Communion every morning of his life. And Paddy said these were the worst kind, and Nellie said he shouldn't say things like that about people, and that he oney said things like that in order to be smart and it didn't become him at all and he ought to be ashamed of himself; and Paddy said he apologized, that he was sure the man wasn't a wolf but that he wouldn't be human if he didn't like a piece of skirt as well as the next, and then said quickly that he was sorry again, and that he would promise to reform, and henceforward he would speak no scandal about his neighbour, but that if he was a foreman he wouldn't half have a shot at trying to tumble Nellie. Then they laughed.

All this time Stephen was half listening to them and felt as if it was all a dream. Here they were, three of them who had often strolled like this on the Connemara ribbon roads, laughing and talking and imitating the schoolmaster and aping this one and that one. The only difference was that they had no Thomasheen with them. Stephen felt sad as he thought about Thomasheen and tried to fit his figure on the path where the three of them were walking. But he found that the light-hearted, tactless Thomasheen would be out of place here, because now he would be a tall silent man, with the moody cleft between his brows, dropping his eyes when they met your own, and talking through tight lips about things that did not matter in the least, until it was a relief to be parted from him, and doubtless he felt the same way about you. He was going to mention his thoughts to them, but then abstained when he remembered Nellie.

'We'll go Salthill way first,' said Paddy. 'Bish generally starts the night there and ends up in town, or he starts the night in town and ends up there, so we are bound to meet him in between.'

They went into a hotel in Salthill.

Stephen was impressed by the thick carpets, the chromium fittings of the high stools, the modern bar, the glinting bottles lining the mirrored walls, and the polished, beautifully spoken barmaid who seemed to be Lady Something-or-other, stepping from her mansion to take the part of a barmaid for the fun of the thing.

'He's not here,' said Paddy, 'but what'll it be?'

'Would they serve a common pint in a place like this?' Stephen asked.

'It's frowned on,' said Paddy, laughing, 'but they will.'

'That's mine so,' said Stephen.

'I'll have sherry,' said Nellie.

'And mine's the old whiskey,' said Paddy, 'a legacy bequeathed to me by potheen-slugging ancestors.'

He went to get the drinks, while Nellie and Stephen regarded one another with pleased satisfaction.

'It's a bit different from Paddy's father's pub in Killaduff,' remarked Stephen, 'or good old J. J.'s in Crigaun.'

'It is, thank God,' said Nellie.

'Have you no homesickness at all, Nellie?' Stephen asked.

'No,' she said, and Stephen saw she meant it. 'Connemara never meant anything to me but hunger, and a greater hunger for the things you knew other people had, but that you could never acquire. If I never saw the place agin, that'd be fifty year too soon.'

'But how about the mountains and the lakes and things and the kind of place you were born? Surely you can't throw them out of your mind at will,' said Stephen.

'Aren't there mountains on the other side of the bay there?' said Nellie, 'and lakes that you can go up in them in motor-boats if you feel like it, and you don't have t' give a damn, or worry about how the spuds'll do, or the oats, or who you'll get to help you cut the turf without havin' t' pay 'm anythin'? You were always all right, Stephen: your father had money and you never had to worry about where your next meal was coming from. If you had had to live like we had, you would have missed all the beauty that you see in it now. To us Connemara was oney a heart-scald. Why, even with the small amount I'm sendin' me mother now, they're better off than ever they were in their lives before. And then you want me to feel homesick. No bloody fear!'

'I think I know how you feel,' said Stephen.

'No you don't, Stephen,' said Nellie kindly. 'And you never will. Because you were always soft about Connemara, although you never said anythin' to any 'f us about it, so we'll talk about somethin' else, since we'd never agree about that.'

Paddy returned with the drinks then and they drank to one another solemnly, and then burst out laughing because they all felt pleased to be together again.

Stephen got up to get a second round, but Paddy stopped him imperiously and pulled a roll of pound notes out of his pocket.

'Hold on there now!' he ordered. 'This night is on me and on me alone. I won some money at poker yesterday and I got some petty cash from the old man today, besides which whatever dough you have you'll want, brother, before your adventure is established on a sound financial basis.'

'But, Paddy,' said Stephen, 'I'd feel better if I stood my share.'

'You can put your pride in your pocket now, my little boy blue,' sneered Paddy, 'and keep your hand on it, unless you're willin' to stand up and fight it out here in this lounge, and the nice decent upbringing you got wouldn't permit you to do that, so there you are, defeated before you have fired a shot.'

'Let 'm have his own way, Stephen,' said Nellie; 'he'll have it in the long run anyways, or make a show of you.'

'I haven't had it with you yet,' said Paddy meaningly.

'That's different,' said Nellie.

'Who're yeh tellin'?' asked Paddy, signalling to a waiter.

'Where are we going to find this Bishop fella?' Stephen asked, 'and what kind is he?'

'Only God knows the answer to both of those questions,' said Paddy. 'Henry Bishop is the most contradictory person that you ever met in your life; not that you have met many, but if you had met all the people in the world, one after another, you'd still think that Bishop was the greatest enigma of them all. What is he? I don't know. What is he motivated by? I don't know. Is he serious in what he says or is he just kidding you or himself? I don't know.'

'Does he like women?' Nellie butted in. 'He does not!' she answered herself.

'And yet,' said Paddy, 'it wouldn't surprise me to find him drinking with a trollop when we do find him, and yet he's always frigidly polite to nice girls. What a man! That's what I mean when I say that he's a contradiction. Well, here we are again. We'll skip it to another pub after this drink.'

They duly skipped to another pub, and when they finally located Bishop, Stephen felt that he had drunk more than he ought. Certainly he had by then drunk more than he had ever drunk in one night in his whole life. Looking back he could only vaguely remember episodes from the many places they had been.

He remembered one place, just an ordinary undistinguished pub, which reminded him vaguely of J. J.'s. There they had met the admirer of Yeats. He was a short, dark man, in a light raincoat buttoned up to the neck. He was almost incoherently drunk. He would go from one to the other of them, and he would hold up a forefinger in the air, and direct a look at them that was transfixingly blank. After five minutes a kind of a slurred whisper would issue from his closed lips. 'What did Yeats say?' he would ask, as far as Stephen could make out. The listener would look at him inquiringly, and wait. He would also wait. He would waggle the finger to emphasize the question. They never found out what Yeats said exactly because he would obviously say whatever it was the poet had said, in his own mind, and was under the mistaken belief that he had uttered aloud a rolling, dramatic phrase, because he would nod his head then, wag his finger, blow his nose, wipe the tears away from his eyes, and whisper in a broken sob, 'Thass what Yeats said.' Then he would go back to the form which he was sitting on and weep into his beer. They were delighted with this and Stephen thought Paddy would die laughing. Stephen didn't feel like laughing much, because he was wondering about the man's wife and hoped she was an insensitive type who would be amused that her husband was rolling in to her that way every night. He wondered if she knew the answer to what Yeats had said.

He himself had suggested leaving that pub because the man had depressed him.

The next item he remembered was hanging out of the bathroom window of another hotel, whilst the Guards presumably were searching the place for after-hour drinkers. Paddy had shoved up the window and told him to hop out when they had all cleared out of the bar during the first frantic rush after the Guards had knocked loudly on the door. The proprietor had told them in a whisper to clear upstairs for God's sake, and there had been a desperate scramble into bedrooms, most of which were occupied by others, or by cursing guests who woke and blasphemed fluently when the lights were switched on. Paddy and Stephen had ended up in the bathroom, and Stephen, stepping out the window, had missed his footing and it was only the grace of God and the guardian of drinkers that had saved him from falling. He hoped there was a shed or something beneath his feet but he couldn't feel it. He had managed to pull himself back with Paddy's laughing assistance. He felt he needed a drink after this. It was gall and wormwood to go down again and to find that it wasn't the Guards at all but a thirsty reveller who had knocked and shouted 'Guards on Duty' for a joke. He was surprised when the joke didn't seem to be appreciated.

The next clear thing in Stephen's mind was that he had found out all about Nellie and Paddy.

Paddy, believe it or not, wanted to marry Nellie, but Nellie didn't want to marry Paddy. She would go to bed with him, she said, if he wanted, but she wouldn't marry him. Paddy, Stephen gathered, had been not unknown to women before this and spoke about this one and that one that he had been out with on such occasions, but he didn't want Nellie like that. According to him, he had been in love with Nellie since the days when they were coming from school together, the three of them, and all the business he had gone on with about being jealous of Thomasheen had been serious, and not the fun they had taken it for. Paddy was quite emphatic about this, and said that even though he was four parts drunk, it was the truth coming out at last to his friend Stephen; that he had told Nellie about it so often that he was getting carbuncles on his tongue, and it seemed to do no good. They tried to get it out of Nellie, why she would not think of marrying Paddy, and she said that if she was going to marry anybody without loving him, it was not going to be her friend Paddy Rice; and when she was pressed and in a corner she said yes, she loved Thomasheen, she would always love Thomasheen, and if Thomasheen came to her in the morning and asked her to go off with him, she would do so and think that Heaven had been transplanted down to the earth. And Paddy said, 'Holy Jesus, what can a fella say to that!' And Stephen said, 'Don't you know that Thomasheen has changed and that he's not the same Thomasheen at all that was in love with you, and that if you're waiting for a thing like that to happen you'll have long grey whiskers down to your knees?'

And Nellie said, 'I don't care, so I don't. I know well it'll never happen. And maybe it's only me mind, and maybe I'm not really struck about Thomasheen at all, only I can't forget him just like that, and it will be a long long time before I can get him out of me head and the way we used to be watching the sea bashing the end of Ourish, and he holdin' me hand and we wonderin' when or how we'd be able to get married, and watchin' our families and prayin' t' Christ that they'd grow up to hell quick so that they could fend for themselves and leave 's free to do what we liked. And then he marries that oul bitch, and I can see the look in his eyes that night of the hooley, and he havin' no more regard for

her than an oul yoke oo a cow that didn't belong t' you; and
that he should never have done a thing like that and that it
would kill him; that he would get old before his time; or else
that he would get up some night and cut the wan's throat
with a razor, and then he'd hang at the end 'f a rope, and
that'd be a terrible ind for poor nice Thomasheen that was
so innocent and tactless and always puttin' his feet in it; and
here he was now a grown man with a great sadness in his
eyes, and he couldn't even talk to his friends any more.' And
then she pulled out a small handkerchief and started to cry
uncontrollably, and although Stephen knew all the drink
was making her maudlin, he felt that there was a terrible
intent hurt in her. Then Paddy had cursed loudly and had
ordered more drinks. And she had dried her eyes and said,
'I'm all right now, and Paddy, I'm sorry, but honest, maybe
some day if you still want and you don't see any other girl
that you'd like, I would if you still want me, because I know
nobody else, apart from Stephen, that I could live with and
have great gas with into the bargain.' And Paddy had sworn
a mighty oath that if he couldn't have her he'd have nobody
else if he lived to be as old as the old man of the mountain,
and that it would be the happiest day in his father's life if he
could go home and say he was going to marry Nellie,
because his father was afraid like hell that some day Paddy
would descend on him with a painted dolly that'd be afraid
to have a child, and he'd want to be sure that his grand-
children were good stock and conceived on good sound
Connemara thighs like Nellie's. And Stephen laughed, and
Nellie said, 'They's no need to go that far into it,' and they
adjourned to another pub.

As far as Stephen could see, although all the public-houses
were supposed to be closed at half-past ten, they just literally
obeyed the letter of the law and closed their doors; but they
did not stop anyone from coming in as long as they passed
scrutiny, and he became used to having the door opened
carefully by a barman before they went out. The barman
would put out his head, whistle a catch of a song, look up
and down the street to see if there was a Guard in sight, and

then quickly close the door on them. The drinkers were of all kinds, young men, flushed and glassy-eyed and inclined to sing or to leave their hands on intimate parts of the girls that accompanied them. There were many girls, nice well-dressed girls they seemed to Stephen, who smoked incessantly, and seemed to say very little, just gazing at their escorts and listening to them with what appeared to be rapt attention.

Then there were older men, who drank themselves into apathetic stupidity. Their faces, already bearing the blood-pressure bloom of the constant toper, gradually became more purple and red, and their tobacco-stained hands trembled as they raised their glasses to their lips. After-hours drinking seemed to have a solemnity all its own. There was no loud shouting or singing. Everything seemed to be conducted on a subdued note and a word or phrase spoken aloud would attract the look of all the drinkers in your direction, as well as a frown from the barmaid, or the bar tender, or the proprietor. Paddy seemed to possess the open-sesame to any place he wanted to go. A rap on the door and a 'Let's in, this is Paddy Rice' was an infallible key and all doors would open smoothly. Always he would inquire, 'Is Bishop here?' and would be told that he had just left or they hadn't seen him since last night. Finally they ran him down in a hotel at the top of the town. When Paddy said 'Is Bishop here?' the boots who had admitted him said yes, he was up in Number Six, and there was a dame with him. 'We'll go right up to him so,' said Paddy.

They went up carpeted stairs, and Paddy flung open a door. It was a small room with leather-covered couches, some hardwood polished chairs, and a few mahogany tables. The light was on and Stephen saw the couple sitting on the couch.

He was aware of the girl first because she was very exotic and was dressed brilliantly like a bird from a tropic country. She was red-haired and her face was very pale; whether the paleness was accentuated deliberately or not, he could not tell. Her lipstick was scarlet and made of her mouth a seductive gash. Her eyebrows were suspiciously regular and her eyelashes swept her cheeks. Her figure was big and she came out in the right places. Also the light frock she was wearing seemed to show her off to better advantage than a bathing-suit would have done. Her legs were crossed, and the dress was pulled far up on her thighs, so that you could clearly see where the colour she had applied to her legs ended and her own very white skin began.

His gaze shifted to the man then, and he found himself looking into a pair of spectacles reflecting the light and effectively hiding his features. His impression of Bishop after that was always to be a pair of round spectacles reflecting light and nothing else. For the rest of him he saw that he must be tall and thin, and that he was dressed in a blue pin-stripe double-breasted suit, a spotlessly white collar, and a dark tie that was as immaculate as when it had been first put on. For a moment Stephen was startled, because he thought that Bishop was a priest. The white collar and the dark clothes gave that impression. The girl was leaning against him and he had one arm around her. He did not remove this arm when they entered, and remained completely unabashed.

'How do, Bish?' said Paddy, closing the door after them and seating himself on a chair. 'I want you to meet a friend of mine.'

'Won't you sit down?' said Bishop. Stephen got the impression from the careful articulation that the voice was controlled and that what Bishop would say was carefully examined in his brain first. 'Have a drink? Push the bell.'

Paddy got up again and pushed the bell.

'You know Nellie, don't you?' he asked.

'We have met,' said Bishop, not enthusiastically.

'That's the way I feel too,' said Nellie, sitting down.

'And this is Stephen O'Riordan,' said Paddy.

'Hello,' said Bishop, holding out a lean hand.

'Hello,' said Stephen, grasping it, and was surprised at the warm pressure which the other exerted, because he had expected the hand-clasp to be as flaccid and as limp as a dead pollock. He didn't know why, but that was the way he had thought it would be and he was rather pleased that it was otherwise.

'How did you ever become a friend of Paddy's?' Bishop asked.

'We are from the same place,' said Stephen.

'Really?' said Bishop, obviously surprised, 'but how is it . . . no, I won't ask that question.'

Stephen laughed and felt more pleased than ever.

'You're the first one that abstained,' he said.

'What's all this about?' Paddy asked.

'You wouldn't understand, you student-to-be-a-human-butcher,' said Bishop.

'All right,' said Paddy. 'Look, Bish, Stephen here is in Galway to try and make enough money to take him to Dublin, and I thought that if there's any man in town that'll put him in the way of making a few coppers that man is you. What do you say?'

'Why going to Dublin?' Bishop asked.

'To fulfil a plan,' said Stephen.

'I see,' said Bishop. 'Well, I suppose you did all kinds of farm work where you came from. Do any fishing?'

Paddy laughed loudly and slapped his legs.

'Fishing!' he exclaimed. 'Listen, brother, you are now looking at the most accomplished poacher in the Connemara fishery district.'

'Legal fishing I'm interested in,' said Bishop.

'I did a lot of that,' said Stephen.

'Big boats, small boats?' Bishop asked.

'All kinds and sizes,' said Stephen.

'Good,' said Bishop. 'But this is not the time to talk business. I hear our friend coming up with the drinks, so we will drink and chat and forget vulgar commercial pursuits. Before we go I will tell you where I live and I hope you will come and see me in the morning about twelve o'clock and we will talk about what we can do for you. I think I know something that you will find suitable and profitable.'

'Thanks,' said Stephen.

The boots arrived with the drinks then, and they commenced to talk about things which Stephen had no knowledge of, so he sipped his drinks and watched them. Strangely enough Bishop never said to them who the girl with him was. She just sat back against him and let him fondle her, holding the glass loosely in her hands and looking from one to the other of them blankly. Only when her eyes rested on himself did Stephen notice some of the blankness leave them. Her long lashes would leave her cheeks for a moment and she would look at him sleepily like a cat which has been asleep in front of a fire and has been awakened by an opening door. The gaze she directed at him then, made him shift uncomfortably in his chair, because she seemed to look at him all over, and although that was not what she intended, he became conscious of his clothes.

It was very early in the morning when they rose to go. Nellie was sleepily drunk and found it hard to keep her eyes open. Paddy had become garrulous and terribly sincere. He himself felt very muggy in the head. Before they left the room he looked at Nellie and Paddy and wondered if it had been a dream of another life that they had once walked together on Ourish Strand, or if this was the same Nellie McClure who had sat by a Connemara lake while Thomasheen and himself were swimming, and had run away when Stephen had threatened to come out in his pelt. He felt unreal.

Before he went to sleep in the small room of his digs, which he had succeeded in entering without waking the landlady, he thought that he should have dropped a line to Kathleen but that with the help of God he would write to her after he had seen Bishop in the morning.

CHAPTER TWENTY-ONE

It was at eleven o'clock Mass the next morning that Stephen had a good look at the Galway people. As in all the churches in the country, the people, according to their means, were congregated, as if by mutual consent, in different parts of the church; all the better-dressed people seemed to make for the front of the middle aisles. Up there, you could see the backs of sleek bald heads or carefully brilliantined ones, or else the most peculiar and probably the most expensive hats, resting on different-coloured hair which all seemed to have been carefully waved and curled by the same hand. The farther back the seats went, the poorer became the dress of the people, hats and summer dresses giving place to shabby coats and rough scarfs pulled over the hair. At the very end were women completely covered in their black shawls, who were praying devoutly, and sighing at intervals.

Stephen was almost at the very back, and there was a man beside him who was fat, and had a white-hair-fringed bald head. He was dressed in a blue reefer jacket and a dark-blue jersey up to his neck. He seemed to be a great prayerer altogether. He would start off the Hail Mary to himself in a sibilant whisper, and when he came to the end of the first half he would burst forth with a loud 'Jesus Holy Mary Mother . . .' and the rest of it would be lost again. Stephen was startled when he said it first, and other heads were turned as well, but he got used to it, and accepted it as a kind of background to the hushed tones of the priest intoning the Mass. He was a young priest and he was saying Mass very quickly but with a kind of devoted concentration.

Whether it was the night out or not, Stephen couldn't get his mind on to the Mass at all. All sorts of things were running through his head, snippets of conversation which he had heard last night or the memories of people, and then he found himself examining the differently shaped ears of all the people in front of him. It was amazing, he thought, how no two ears were the least bit alike, and he wondered if there was anything in this phrenology business about the shape of the skull shaping your destiny. Or was that phrenology? Then he remembered something he had read about murderers having no lobes on their ears. He wondered if that was true. If so, there were a desperate gang of cut-throats gathered in front of him, because he could see very few lobes. Then he thought how different a person's face would appear if the ears were pressed close to the skull. Ears that stood out straight from the head gave a peculiar look of stupidity to the face, but then he had often seen pictures of very famous people and their ears stuck out like that.

The bell rang for Holy Communion, and most of the people sat up in their seats to scrutinize the communicants. For the most part they were older people, whose appetite, or lack of appetite, would permit them fasting until the eleven Mass; and then the older people were not as given to sins and temptations as the younger ones, so they could go to Communion without Confession the night before. Still, a few young girls were to be seen going to the altar rails too. They were wearing their Sunday best, and for the life of him Stephen couldn't help thinking that Communion on Sunday was a great opportunity to show the rest of the people a new dress or a new hat or a new suit that you had recently acquired, and any sounds of jealousy or dislike that they could have made freely in the open air, would have to be strangled in the Church, and suffered in silence, although now and again you could see the heads of two people coming together, to assimilate and digest the remarks of one or the other. Then you might see the side of a broad smile or a significant look.

Communion over, they remained seated until the priest was ready to read the Gospel. He turned to them, and first taking a handkerchief from under the alb, he blew his nose resoundingly, looked at them defiantly and said, 'I will now read the Gospel.' So everyone rose to their feet. The young priest read the Gospel vigorously but with a hearty country accent which seemed to make it all the more homely. There was much shuffling and coughing and clearing of throats before the people settled back to listen to the sermon. The young priest talked to them about the Sacrament of Matrimony. It was a good enough sermon, except that the priest delivered himself of his young notions along with the canons of the Church, and he was not mellowed enough to hold the attention of the people by the little tricks of gesture and dramatic pause that an older man would have learned. Apart from which, the subject seemed to embarrass him, and his very sincerity made him pause at times to look for a suitable word. Whenever he did this, a barrage of coughs and throat-clearing would ensue from the people, and when he had found his word, he would have to wait until all the noise died down.

When the sermon was finished, there was great shuffling and coughing again as the people went down on their knees, and as soon as they stood up again for the last Gospel, Stephen saw quite a few people rushing for the exits as if they had suddenly heard that somebody near to them was dying. When he was coming down the steps saying the De Profundis the priest looked at the people crowding the doors and a frown came on his face. Stephen thought for a moment that he was going to stand up and shout at them, 'Will ye for the love of God refrain from pushing your way out of the Church until Holy Mass is finished? What kind of heathens are you at all at all?' He didn't say it, however – just dropped to his knees and commenced to recite the prayers after Mass in Irish, 'Se do bheatha, 'Mhuire, ta lan de ghrasta . . .'

As soon as the last 'dean trocaire orainn' was said the rest of the congregation rose and began to make their exit slowly, although here and there you would see a man or woman remaining in their seats, their heads held on one side, as they looked blankly at the Tabernacle, while they told the Rosary beads slowly through their fingers. It always gladdened Stephen's heart to see that there were some saintly people left in the world, because God would take a very poor view of the rest of us, he thought, if there weren't a few really good people around.

Outside the church, men were putting on their hats or their caps, or taking cigarettes out of their packets with greedy fingers and feverishly lighting them, to suck the first puff deep down into their lungs and blow it out again with an absurd look of infinite pleasure and satisfaction on their faces. The girls were waiting for other girls and then going off slowly with them, chatting about things.

Stephen, Bishop's directions for finding his house still clear in his head, directed his feet towards the road that went past the College.

There was a great difference between the Galway of the busy Saturday and the Galway of the Sabbath. All the shops, except the sweet shops, were tightly closed, bolted and barred, and the display of goods seemed shabby and un-attractive in the early light of a Sunday morning. The people who went past in their Sunday clothes seemed to be going somewhere with no definite purpose. Others passed with their faces sunk in the Sunday newspaper. The various corners flourished their quota of young boys and old men, leaning against the walls, some of them well dressed, others with no change of attire except maybe a clean shirt. They were talking and chatting and spitting and laughing loudly, and giving a hilarious greeting to any friends of theirs who might walk past with a girl in tow, taking her to Salthill for a walk, or up towards the lake.

Stephen passed over the Weir Bridge again, and paused to look at the salmon weaving below, pressed together like sardines in a tin. For the few minutes he was there he won-dered how himself and Michilin would manage to get a salmon out of there quickly. The snatch of course would be the proper instrument, but the owner had shrewdly put steel posts some feet apart in the bed of the stream, and connected them with several strands of barbed wire. This obstacle was placed several yards out so that it would be almost impos-sible to get the snatched salmon up on the bridge once you had him. He grinned when he noticed a snatch, caught on the barbed wire and trailing forlornly in the water, attached to a piece of fishing line. He heard a clock striking twelve then, and left the bridge to hurry his footsteps towards Bishop's place.

He reached it eventually. It was a big two-storey house built on a hill overlooking the town. It was surrounded by a neat plastered wall, over which a hedging of macrocarpa waved greenly and profusely. There was a long drive leading up to the house which was backed by tall pine and beech trees. A flight of four steps led up to the door. He mounted them and put his finger on the gadget that said 'Push'. He heard a bell ringing in the house, and almost immediately the door was opened by a small girl dressed in a maid's uniform. She had a stern kind of face and spoke crisply.

'I want to see Mister Bishop,' he said.

'The name, please?' she asked.

'Stephen O'Riordan,' said Stephen.

'Oh,' she ejaculated. 'Won't you come in? He's expecting you.'

'Thanks,' said Stephen, and entered. He found himself in a rather spacious hall. The floor was a wood-block one, which was highly polished and covered with thick rugs. The stairway was about half-way down, and it was painted scarlet and white, with a thick red pile carpet covering the steps. All the doors leading off the hall-way were painted white, the indentations in them being picked out with scarlet. The pictures hanging in the hall-way were prints of modern paintings, some of them startling to say the least of it, and he wondered what effect they would have on maiden aunts of Bishop who might call on him. The girl threw open one of the doors and closed him up in what must be the living-room. The wall opposite the door was pierced with large full-length windows opening on to a lawn, where he could see a tennis net drooping between its posts. The floor of the room was of the same wooden-block business, polished and rug-ed expensively. The fireplace on his right was in the centre of the wall and was low, wide, modern, and useful. He imagined there would be a lot of heat from it.

The furniture was modern too, and strangely enough comfortable when he tried it. It was very well sprung and was covered in heavy Ghaeltacht cloth. The prints on the wall were small and good as far as he could judge from his reading. But it was the books that interested him. They were housed in the modern put-it-together-yourself bookshelves which he had seen advertised so often in the magazines. He looked at the titles and was delighted to discover that the books, in this room anyhow, were all the moderns, and the shelves held most of the books he had never had a chance of reading because they were all banned, and to him in the country therefore completely unobtainable. He saw Hemingway, Steinbeck, Huxley, and one by Sean O'Casey. He was running through this when he heard Bishop speaking behind him.

'Fond of reading?' he asked.

'Yes,' said Stephen, turning. 'I spend a lot of time at it, and most of my spare cash, but I have never managed to get most of the books you have here. How did you get them, when they are banned?'

'Easy,' said Bishop. 'Fortunately there are ways. If you haven't read those before, you may read them any time you like. Take them away with you.'

Seen in the light of day, Bishop was still tall and thin and had a face like a monk, with high cheek-bones tightening the skin of his face, and although he was cleanly shaved his hair was so dark that you could see the outline of his beard. He was looking at Stephen closely.

'You are even bigger than I thought you were,' he said.

'It's the good Connemara food,' said Stephen.

'Yes,' said Bishop. 'Sit down won't you? Here, have a cigarette?'

Stephen took a cigarette from a gold case which the other held out to him and lighted it from what he thought was a very expensive lighter.

'I have thought where I can fix you,' said Bishop, leaning back in an armchair.

Stephen waited.

314

'What do you think I do for a living?' Bishop asked next.

'That's a hard one,' said Stephen, laughing.

'Why?' said Bishop.

'Well,' said Stephen, 'I haven't been with you long enough to make up my mind about you, but as a first guess I would hazard that you were a priest, which is all wrong of course.'

Bishop laughed, and his laughter was free and made Stephen like him all the more somehow.

'You were not far out there,' he said then. 'I was in the way of becoming a priest for many years before I realized that I was not called. So I left before the final deed was done. I'm what's known affectionately in our dear land as a spoiled priest.'

'I suppose,' said Stephen, 'it was your mother.'

'No,' said Bishop, 'it was my mother's sister. My mother died when I was very small. I don't remember her. But my aunt started making Novenas from the day I was born that I'd enter the Church and make it soft for them getting into Heaven.'

'Did your father hold with this?' Stephen asked.

'He was neutral,' said Bishop. 'He was a very hard-drinking man who was scarcely ever conscious, and died like that. My father didn't mind, but if he had had his senses, I think he would have opposed it.'

'Well, anyhow,' said Stephen, 'you're not a priest.'

'No,' said Bishop, 'I'm not, but I don't regret the education I got. It was very thorough and very wide, and I have never regretted that part of it. So now, what do you think I am?'

'It's very difficult,' said Stephen, screwing up his face. 'How about you not doing anything at all? Your father left you money and you're living on it. But no, that won't do, because I can't see you sitting down on your fanny all day and doing nothing.'

'Come here,' said Bishop, walking out through the windows.

Stephen followed him out into the garden.

'Look down there,' said Bishop.

Stephen looked and beheld the City of the Tribes lying at their feet.

'What do you think of that?' he asked.

'It's shining nicely in the sun,' said Stephen, 'but it's probably one of the most haphazard places that ever grew up around a river. It's a funny town that gets a hold on you, I'd say.'

'That's the trouble,' said Bishop. 'When I left the College I was determined to be somebody. I wanted to write and be a poet if I could, or be an artist if I could, or be a writer if I could.'

'Well?' said Stephen interrogatively.

'I still don't know,' said Bishop, 'whether I could be any of them because I have never really tried. I came back. My father was dead and had left a small business behind him, encumbered with debt. So I started in on it, and found that I had an aptitude towards becoming a merchant. So I became a merchant, and a very successful merchant. It's the greatest method of get-rich-quick known to modern civilization. Look down there – factories, houses, and about twenty thousand people. Now, no matter what happens, people have to eat, and sleep, and cook meat in pots and pans, and drink out of cups, and ride on bicycles. That, my friend, is where the merchant comes in. He gets the food and the goods and the clothes and appoints himself as a wholesaler. You get a profit as a wholesaler selling the goods to yourself and you get a profit as a retailer selling the goods to the people. A very sweet racket, my friend. Then when you suddenly find you have a lot of money in hand, you look around and find that such a one will put up a factory if such a one else will put up a little money. So you become a Director of a factory. Everything I touched seemed to prosper because I had one infallible method. I would never touch anything that was not close to the people's bones, because realize this: that wars or revolutions or earthquakes don't matter a damn. The people have to eat food. So sell them food. They have to eat it from something. Sell it to them. Put your money on the people and it will come back to you a thousand-fold, like bread that is cast upon the waters coming back as Christmas cakes with cellophane wrappings.'

They were silent for a time.

'I don't think,' said Stephen, 'that life could be such a swindle or that you could be such a cynic as all that.'

'Isn't it before your eyes?' Bishop asked. 'My dear man, you could count on the fingers of one hand the people that own that town, and I'm one of them.'

'But how about all the small shopkeepers, and the little pubs and things and the barbers' shops?' Stephen asked. 'Aren't they as entitled to make a living too, and you can't turn around and regard them as racketeers because they sell a few fags and things to the people that want them?'

Bishop laughed.

'Never mind,' he said. 'I'm afraid I always talk like that after a night out.'

'It's a terrible thing if that was true,' said Stephen.

'No,' said Bishop. 'Because in a merchants' town it's dog eat dog. You grow rich and then you drink yourself to death, or you don't drink yourself to death, but you die peacefully when you have amassed wealth and you leave it to the sons to drink the business into oblivion. You see, what's really wrong with me is that I'm doing something that deep in my heart I don't want to do at all. I would perhaps be somebody and do something worth while, if I had no money, but now I never will, because I have the taste of money in my mouth and a great fear in my heart that something will happen to take it from me. That's the trouble.'

'But,' said Stephen, 'don't you feel a sense of achievement that you have built up something from almost nothing?'

'No, I don't,' said Bishop violently. 'That was something I never wanted. What the hell am I anyhow, or what will I ever be? A merchant who when he dies will have a large funeral with a large chorus of all the priests in the diocese to sing his requiem, a flower-bedecked coffin in a motor hearse, a plot up in the New Cemetery and a granite head-stone, when his heirs get around to it.'

317

'But God blast it!' said Stephen, 'isn't that going to be the end of all of us?'

'No, it isn't,' said Bishop. 'Some of us will die and will be remembered. I'd rather have been that little man whose statue is up in the square there, a little man who, when he lived, was despised by his fellow men as an idler and a peculiar fellow. But he left something after him. He left more after him than all the riches in this town. He had nothing while he lived but he lived to enjoy life, and he did enjoy it. He had his freedom, and his name will be remembered when I, the Big Bishop with a bigger bank balance, am no longer a topic of conversation in the pubs where I squandered my profits. You, now! I looked at you last night and I saw something in your face. You do something, don't you? You have made up your mind to something, haven't you?'

'Yes,' said Stephen defiantly, and blushing because it was the first time he had ever said it straight out like this, 'I am going to be a writer.'

Bishop smiled then, a cheerful smile, and he put his hand on Stephen's arm.

'I knew it was something like that,' he said, 'but it took a lot to get it out of you.'

'Do you mean to say,' Stephen asked in amazement, 'that all this was just a kind of an act to get me to talk?'

'I wouldn't say that,' said Bishop. 'Maybe some of it was and maybe it wasn't. But I was interested in you last night. I said, Why would he be coming to Galway and why does he want to go to Dublin? I am a man who cannot keep my curiosity in check, and after all, now that we have more or less bared souls to one another, we will be able to talk more freely about things. Come on, we'll walk down the town. I am interested among other things in a fishing trawler. Would you be able to work on one of those?'

'Sure,' said Stephen.

'That's what I thought,' said Bishop. 'We'll go down now and see the skipper. They have been working short-handed for the last month. Of course they won't exactly welcome you with open arms, because it'll mean a smaller percentage for them, but they will have to work less hard and that will probably make up for it. The boat goes out once a week and the average wages per man works out at about five or six pounds.'

'That's good,' said Stephen.

'It should suit you,' said Bishop, 'because I don't know anything else you could do that would bring you in the same money, and if you care to stick it for a few months you should have enough saved to take you to Dublin and back again, if you wish.'

'That sounds better than I had hoped for,' said Stephen.

Bishop collected his hat from the house and they walked down towards the town.

Stephen felt the journey a short one, because Bishop was such an entertaining companion. He seemed to have taken a liking to Stephen, and in fact hinted that he had talked to him more than to anybody else. Bishop's main plaint about Galway was that it was so completely uncultured.

'The so-called aristocracy of this town,' he said, 'are the sons and relatives of shopkeepers like myself. Here there is no striving after culture, and very few seek it in their private lives. They are too busy amassing money and drinking and tarting and playing golf and bridge and all the other pursuits in season. The cinemas will be packed on most occasions except if the picture is a really good one, when it will be as empty as the Protestant Church on the Feast of the Immaculate Conception. The fault of this lies with the town itself I'm afraid, because it is a sleepy town and one that bears the hallmark of Spain. They talk about the Spanish look of the Galway people. That is all my eye and Betty Martin, because you would be hard put to it to find a family in this town that can trace itself back that far. However much it may hurt them to admit it, their early ancestors, and by that I mean their grandfathers or grandmothers, were good farming stock from Roscommon or Connemara who came in here and set up a little business and prospered exceeding well for reasons which I have already told you. But if any mark of

Spain remains it is one that should be written up on the portals of the town, if it had portals, and that would be "Mañana". Because it is the most procrastinating town imaginable, and if you remain here you will find yourself steeped in the same juice. If it is business, OK, we get it done and get it done well; if it's anything to do with broadening the mind or improving the intellect, we say Mañana and put it off until tomorrow.'

'Wouldn't most small towns be like that?' Stephen asked.

'I suppose so,' said Bishop, 'but any man who tries to set a bit of culture going here, would be better off tied in a sack and dumped into the sea from Nimmo's Pier. It would save him a lot of heartache and disappointment. We're going down to the Claddagh, by the way, to meet the skipper. He lives there, although the ship is tied up at the docks.'

They walked down by the canal bridge which Stephen had crossed going out to Paddy. It seemed like a hundred years ago now, and it was only yesterday. He thought that this Henry Bishop was a peculiar individual and that he liked him. It was difficult to find out how much of what he said he believed, and how much was just talk, but it made you feel stimulated somehow, and put you in the mood for talking yourself. They walked down to the many small quays which he had noticed yesterday, above which the masts of the fishing-boats reared their not unshapely tops. Past the church, and they came to the Claddagh houses.

Outside the church wall there were a lot of sailor-men standing and gossiping. Most of them were dressed in the same way – reefer jackets and blue jerseys, and their heads covered with either the peaked sailor's cap or an ordinary check cap. There were some very big men among them, with chests like half-barrels, and all of them looked closely at Stephen as he passed them with the immaculate Bishop. He could almost imagine them trying to place him, and to see if he would be any good in a boat. Bishop stopped when he came abreast of them, and spoke to one of the big fellows.

'Do you know if Pat's at home?' he asked.

'He is indeed, Mister Bishop,' he was answered. 'He's just after lavin' 's now.'

'Thanks,' said Bishop, and continued on.

The houses looked to be frightful monstrosities. They were very narrow seen sideways and were pebble-dashed in two different colours. The railings around the small gardens in front of them were bent and broken in places where the children had probably been trying their strength on them. Here, as in all the poorer quarters Stephen had been, the children predominated, roaring, and screeching, and laughing, but somehow after the other two places he didn't seem to notice them so much. They were probably growing on him.

'What do you think of the Claddagh?' Bishop asked him.

'The houses aren't very beautiful,' said Stephen.

'The stock reply,' said Bishop. 'Mister H. V. Morton deplored the departure of the picturesque Claddagh houses in his book about Ireland. It's a pity he didn't have to live for a year or two in one of the old Claddagh cottages and maybe he would have changed his mind. Sure they looked grand. Lovely yellow thatch, and gleaming whitewashed walls. Not to mention that there were no lavatories or sanitation of any kind and that what were virtually open sewers flowed sweetly between each row of houses. Why the hell shouldn't the Claddagh people be willing to suffer all the diseases known to open drains and congested living, so that people could gasp over their beauty, while they held their noses to shut off the smell, and then go back for lunch to one of the hotels where their feet would sink into thick carpets and the pressure of a handle would carry their excrement to sea, all the time they were talking about the beautiful Claddagh cottages and what a shame and a scandal it was that they were being demolished by heartless Urban Councillors with no soul, and why couldn't the Government do something about it? That is the best thing that ever happened the Claddagh. Nothing became those cottages in life like the leaving of it. I admit that whoever drew up the plans for them should have had a soul, but they are not too

321

bad if you half-close your eyes and look at them from the front.'

Stephen had to laugh at that spate, and he reflected that he was still unsure which side Bishop was on. He said so, and Bishop replied that he was not an observer, merely a reporter of distortions; then he opened the gate of one of the houses and made towards the door.

It was opened before he reached it and a tall, grizzled man was framed in the doorway.

'I seen y' comin', Mister Bishop,' said the man.

'Ah, hello, Pat,' said Bishop. 'I want to talk to you. Can we come in?'

'Sure, sure,' said Pat, 'if you don't mind coming into the kitchen. We were just sitting down to the dinner.'

They went into the kitchen, where a grey-haired woman was just putting plates back on the range to keep them hot.

'Hello, ma'am,' said Bishop, shaking hands with her.

'Hello, Mister Bishop,' she said, wiping her hand on her apron before taking his. 'Everything is upside down, I'm afraid.'

'Nonsense,' said Bishop. 'Oh, this is a friend of mine, Stephen O'Riordan.'

'Hello,' said Stephen, shaking hands with the woman first. He liked her immediately. She had quiet eyes that were inclined to twinkle. Then he shook hands with Pat, who looked at him curiously.

'Won't ye sit down?' said Mrs Pat, pulling out two chairs. They sat.

'Pat,' said Bishop, 'I want you to take Stephen on the crew.'

Pat paused for a while before answering.

'Well, we want a hand badly, there's no doubt about that,' he said carefully, 'and he looks as if he'd be a useful man, but has he any experience?'

'Tell him all about it,' said Bishop, waving a hand at Stephen.

'Well,' said Stephen, 'apart from all the currach fishing, I worked a pucaun all the year round nearly, and then I did eight trips altogether in trawlers from Crigaun.'

'Oh, Crigaun,' said Pat, brightening visibly. 'What k'nd of trawlers were they?'

'Well,' said Stephen, 'one of them was an English steam-trawler that lost a hand through sickness, and they pulled in for a man, and the one I worked mostly on was crude-oil engine. She was small enough but nice and tidy.'

'That seems good enough for me,' said Pat. 'Tell me, how was the herring season over in Crigaun last year?'

'Never better,' said Stephen.

'There y'are now,' said Pat, 'and all last year we didn't see a sign oo a tail a the bastards all the season almost, and I hearin' that they were very lively over that side of Conne-mara and I wouldn't believe it.'

'That's the way they are,' said Stephen. 'Sure there mightn't be one at all of them back there this year.'

'Well,' said Bishop, rising, 'that's that. We'll go now and leave you to your dinner. I'm sorry for catching you in the middle of it, Pat.'

'Ah, that's all right, Mister Bishop,' said Pat; 'it'll be all the better for the waitin'. If you come around to the docks in the mornin' so, young man, you can look around an give 's a hand with the nets. We'll be pushing off on Tuesday mornin'.'

'Thanks,' said Stephen, 'I'll be there. Goodbye, ma'am.'

They shook hands again and departed.

'Well,' Bishop asked when they were outside the gate, 'do you like him?'

'I think I'll get on all right with him,' said Stephen. 'He appears to be a straight man.'

'You can bet your life he is,' answered Bishop. 'The only man that works for me and who is crooked, is myself. Look, come on back up with me and we'll have dinner and then you can take away a few of those books that you were gloating over.'

'I promised the landlady,' said Stephen, 'that I'd be in for dinner.'

'Well,' said Bishop, 'you can eat my dinner first and then

you can go back and eat hers. I'm sure you are big enough for two. Besides I want to find out more about you. We have been talking about me and my impressions all the morning. Now I want you to commence and tell me things about you.'

'It's not a very important subject really,' said Stephen, but he found to his surprise that he could talk to Bishop more freely than he had ever done to anybody before, except Kathleen. He even told him about her, but principally he talked about Connemara and the people in it, and why he wanted to write things, and before he left Bishop's grand house, with a very luxurious meal under his belt, he had promised to show him the one manuscript which he had left out of a lifetime's endeavour, and somehow he felt that he would not be embarrassed by doing so.

CHAPTER TWENTY-TWO

It was on a Tuesday morning three weeks later, and Stephen was walking down to the docks, his bag thrown across his shoulder, containing all the changes of clothing and incidentals which he would require for the three-day fishing trip on the trawler *Enterprise*.

Quite a lot of things had happened to him since he had come to Galway three short weeks ago, and he had not yet ceased to be surprised at many things. He had, for example, been to the pictures for the first time, and had to admit that he liked them very much. It mustn't have been a very good picture, because Paddy, who had been with him, had been groaning during it and making audible remarks. But Nellie had been there too and it had been almost as new to her as it had been to him and they had enjoyed it thoroughly. He didn't remember now what it was about – some complicated story that had taken the good-looking hero from New York to Europe and China and South America. What really intrigued Stephen was the moving glimpses which he got of other worlds and other peoples. He had been very sorry indeed when it was all over.

Also Stephen had received many letters from Kathleen, and he would never forget the flood of an inexplicable feeling that came over him when he saw her handwriting in a letter for the first time. Every word of it had seemed to him to be as precious as water would be to a man in a desert. What she said was simple enough. It reminded him of his mother's letter in its directness. He himself had written her long letters telling her about everything that had happened to him, and he had found great difficulty in forcing the pages into the envelope, they were so bulky. He had written to her regularly; even when he was out in the trawler fishing, he had managed, hunched up in the narrow bunk, to scribble a few pages in pencil.

He was not happy, however, about Kathleen's letters now. They seemed to be just a shade too bright, and thinking back over them, he thought that she was hiding something from him, and he supposed it must be something to do with that Malachai fellow. Just the mention of his name seemed to make Stephen go cold with hatred, and he wondered idly why this should be. He didn't think that his nature was vindictive, and he never remembered hating anybody. He might have had cause to hate his father, but he could never do so. Why, then, he wondered, this flood against Malachai, who never did anything injurious to me? He put it out of his mind, but somehow whenever he thought of Kathleen and the very cheerful letters she wrote, his heart sank a little. It shouldn't, because the words were right. She only said now and again that she was dying to see him and would he hurry up and give her a shout, and that Nora's baby had been born in the short meantime and in a few weeks she would feel herself free to go wherever he wanted her to. Maybe it was what she said about wanting to see him and to leave her brother's place. There seemed to be a note of desperation in it. But that's nonsense, said Stephen to himself; she was always able to handle her brother, and now that he himself was not around, Malachai would feel a lot happier.

The crew were all ready to put off when he reached the docks. Everything was stowed, and they were just waiting for the tide to rise outside the gates to the level of the dock water, and they would be away.

Stephen liked the crew very well. At first they had been resentful of him, but that was natural enough. The profits of the trawler were divided fifty per cent to the owner and fifty per cent to the crew, so that an extra man meant that their 'divi' would be less. When they had seen what a useful man he was in the boat, however, they had changed their minds about him quickly enough, because working a wooden trawler was not an easy task, and Stephen with his great strength was worth two men. He found that they were simple individuals whose lives, contrary to his expectations, were very ordered. All of them seemed without ambition, except that some day in the vague future they might be able to own a trawler themselves and be getting fifty per cent instead of what they were getting now. They would talk about how they were going to save and save, and when they were paid, would go off with their fist tightened over the money in their pockets determined that this time they were going to go home and give it to the wife to put in the glass jug on the dresser.

Alas, they never seemed to get around to it. Going home, they would go into a pub to have just one pint, to take the salt out of their teeth and the smell of fish out of their nose, and then one would lead to another and they would just manage to get home with enough to give their wives to save them from a tongue-lashing, and their children from hunger. He had not yet found out their surnames. The skipper he knew as Pat, the engineman as Taimin, and the other two hands as Mike and Gabriel, and if you asked anyone around the docks or the Claddagh if they knew where Pat or Taimin or Mike or Gabriel were, they seemed to know immediately to whom you were referring, and there was never any need for a surname.

While he never seemed to get terribly close to them, there was a grand air of friendship between them, and he had visited and drunk tea in all their houses, and been introduced as Steve the new trawlerman. There was always an air of reserve about them with him, whether it was because he was not a Galway man or because he didn't speak as they would have liked him to speak, he could never tell.

On the whole, as he had foretold, he was becoming enamoured of Galway and the people. He had never met the richer people much, apart from Bishop, but those he had met had seemed to be friendly and curious about him. The poorer people he had found very friendly and with a keen sense of humour, particularly in moments of crisis or suffering. It was amazing, he thought, how they would crack a joke and laugh uproariously when by any of the ordinary standards they should be silently mooning or wiping red-rimmed eyes.

There was Taimin now, the engineman, a small fellow with a wizened face, a straggling grey beard, who had a sly sense of humour. The week after Stephen had been out with them they had arrived back in the trawler to be greeted by the news that Taimin's eldest child, while playing there, had fallen into the docks and been drowned the same day that the trawler was chugging its way into the bay. Stephen didn't know what he had expected, but it wasn't it. Taimin had heard the news, had looked startled for a fraction of a second, and had then proceeded to clean off the engine with the oily rag which he had held in his hand. All the rest had looked at him with trouble in their eyes, and had then continued with whatever they were doing until he was ready. Then they had trooped off with him in a body.

That was the first voyage Stephen had made, and when they started out on the second trip, Taimin was lovingly coaxing the old engine as if nothing much had happened. A stranger would not have noticed anything at all out of the ordinary, but Stephen noticed Taimin looking back at the docks, as they chugged slowly out, and then letting his eyes wander to where his house was, over in the Claddagh. His oily hands came up then and rubbed his eyes quickly, and Stephen turned his back and started whistling. When he looked again, Taimin was bending intently over the engine.

'Hah, you lazy bastard!' Mike greeted him as he approached the boat. 'Isn't it a nice thing to be holding us up? Waitin' about all the mornin' un'il yer highness rises out oo 's bed.'

'Go on,' said Stephen. 'You know damn well you can't pull out until the tide is up, and you can't tell me that it's up yet.'

'Wait'll the skipper gets yeh,' said Gabriel, 'an' he'll tear out yer guts.'

Mike was very tall, and Gabriel was very small, and they were friends who seemed to be inseparable, although they were always fighting and insulting one another. It was funny to hear them, and funnier still to hear the bloodcurdling threats which Gabriel made, standing up to his giant friend and making remarks two foot up to his red face which would have been a cause of sudden death to another man. Mike always waved his arms and called on all the saints in heaven to help him to hould his timper unless in a moment a wakeness he should batter this little good-for-nothing son of a poodle-bitch into a clot a blood on the fo'c'sle. At which Gabriel would hop up and down like a flea and call on 'm to try it, try it, that's all, an' see what'd happen, what happened t' better min before 'm whin they started anythin' with him, Gabriel. He pointed out that this Mike was just a large lump of wind inflated into a skin-bag be the divil himself, and just let him try, that's all, just let him try, an' Gabriel'd puncture 'm, so he would, like a child stickin' a pin inta a pig's bladder.

This generally happened when they were at their busiest at sea, with the trawl-net out ready to be hauled, and the irate skipper would curse the two of them for a pair a thises and thats and who did they think they were, and were they any better than any other min, and weren't there oney fifty min in the Claddy'd be oney too glad t' get their jobs, and did they think that this was a cruise like they was on in 1918? Did they think this was one a His Majesty's bloody yachts like they were on in the last war? This remark would draw hurt protests from both of them because they had claimed to be fighting on a cruiser in the Battle of Jutland. They would mention this mildly to the skipper, and say plaintively that it wasn't right t' be sayin' things like that and didn't he know how it was their shell that had struck the German battleship and . . . 'All right, all right,' the skipper would say, 'that's enough, that's enough; I don't give a damn if ye sunk the whole bloody German Navy with pickaxes, oney will ye look after the so-and-so this and that net, instead a standin' up there like a pair a eejits that want a slap in the kissers.' Stephen had laughed loudly here, and the skipper had turned on him and asked him why it was so funny, an' did he think that he was at the pictures lookin' at a pair a bloody comics, and wouldn't he be better employed winding the rope around the winch or lookin' after the pull a the shutter instead a standin' up there lookin' like another eejit that wanted a slap in the kisser?

Stephen bent to his work again, saying, 'Yes, skipper,' and the other two grinned broadly and all of them continued with their work, feeling much more friendly with one another after this exchange of pleasantries.

The head of the skipper appeared now over the engine-room hatch.

'Hey, you,' he said, meaning the three of them. 'Climb in, will ye! Can't ye see the gates are being opened? Have I t' wait about all day for ye? D'ye think that it's goin' on a cruise we are?'

They said 'Yes, skipper,' and hurried aboard.

The *Enterprise* was a small wooden trawler which could have been anything up to a hundred years old. She was purely a short-trip boat and there was very little space in her for living quarters. Aft there was installed a rather modern crude-oil engine which also drove the winch for hauling the net. Otherwise the job of hauling in a heavy trawl net with fish in it would have been a job to tax the strength of Goliaths. In the centre was the large hold for the fish, which were packed in boxes ready for shipment to the Dublin agents almost as soon as they were caught. Forrard, behind the mainmast, was the crew's quarters. If the crew had only been a quarter of their own size they would have still found difficulty in squeezing themselves into it. It held a little coke stove with a pipe going up through the deck and covered with a moveable smoke vent. At each side of the boat there were two narrow bunks in which the men took turn about to sleep. The quarters were very crowded, but cosy on a wet night when they were all huddled in there, the ship at anchor, and the hatch closed.

They were not the only boat to be clearing the docks, but owing to the smartness of the skipper and the Providence that made the engine start at the first go of the petrol, they received the ironic cheers of the dock-gate men as they chugged alongside the new wharf. The skipper ignored the jibes of the dock-gate men, but Gabriel subjected them to foul abuse, and cast many reflections on the authenticity of their parents' marriage certificates. This only caused them to laugh all the more, and they cleared Nimmo's Pier, with the laughter still with them, and Gabriel leaning dangerously over the unrailed side, trying desperately to get in the last word.

Stephen had been very taken with Galway Bay from the first day he had seen it, and familiarity with it had not bred contempt. It was completely unlike what he had been used to in Connemara. There, when you went out in a boat, a roller that had probably come all the way from America would hit you in the bow like a blacksmith with a sledge, but here was an ideal landlocked bay, almost. On this side you had the mainland on which the town was built; on the other side you had the Clare hills, which were not high enough to cause any furious eddies, and were just low enough to be right. Then the three islands of Aran were stretched neatly across the mouth of the bay, and their high cliffs on the open side bore the brunt of the heavy battering which otherwise the waters of the bay would have received.

Once you had passed the lighthouse on Mutton Island the town of Galway, so higgledy-piggledy on close acquaintance, even took on a look of order and respectability from the bay. Salthill, with its conglomeration of uglily built and uglily situated houses, seemed like a Spanish village of ancient vintage with the tall tower, white-cemented, standing like a protecting giant over the whole, The tower, as he had found out, was that of a modern little church which was very pleasant, and designed by somebody with a simple and beautiful soul.

Beyond Galway you could see the pier stretching out to form a breakwater at Barna, and beyond that again, the Spiddal Pier hugging in its embrace a grand shelter from a storm, and the Spiddal river where it rushed into the sea, with the salmon leaping at its mouth.

On the other side of the bay there were also many small villages with piers where you could run for shelter, Tawin and Ballyvaughan being the two that Stephen was acquainted with.

They generally started to fish in the Gregory Sound and worked their way back towards the docks. Gregory Sound is that stretch of water between the south island of Aran, Inisheer, and the cliffs of Clare, and Stephen thought that you would be hard put to it to find a more beautiful spot for fishing, if you were not so taken up with the actual job and wondering if you would catch enough to give you a living. When the sea was calm, it was quietly beautiful, but if there was a blow, the sight of the dashing waves mounting almost to the tops of the Cliffs of Moher was enough to put your heart up in your mouth.

All the portents today were good, with the steady breeze coming from the islands. All hands were busy, getting up sail, and minding the engine, which was inclined to be temperamental; getting the net attached to the headline which connected the shutters, hitching the running line to the bridles of the shutters and getting it back to the warp, and then hoisting the whole to the block-and-tackle on the mast ready to cast it when the time came.

The skipper was at the wheel in the wheelhouse, and Stephen had to admit that he knew Galway Bay and its tides and fancies and rocks and shoals and everything about it, better than he, Stephen, had ever known his own fishing-grounds in Connemara.

It took them about three hours to reach the fishing-ground in the sound, and then they were kept very busy getting the net overboard, seeing that footlines, headlines, net, pockets, floats, shutters, bridles, warp, and everything else was in position and working efficiently, because if one or the other was attached with a wrong knot or a twist in a rope, the whole outfit would have to be rehauled and set again, so they held their breaths while it went over and breathed again as the fathom line ran out from the winch. They trawled about a hundred fathom of line and then they could afford to relax for a while, and hope that the net was doing its business down below.

They could see the other trawlers coming closely behind them but well away from their trawl, and out beyond Aran other trawlers were fishing which the skipper said were English steam trawlers, fishing circumspectly outside the three-mile limit. They used the seine-net, and this criminality seemed to drive the skipper to the verge of apoplexy, because he was a seine-net hater, and all you had to do to set him going was to mention its name.

They trawled for an hour or so and then commenced to haul. Stephen wondered why he would always be thrilled at the sight of the bobbing floats on the headline coming nearer and nearer. No matter how often he had fished he had always noticed his pulse beating faster as soon as the net, or the longline, was coming closer to his hands.

They got a good haul this first time, and they were jubilant as they dumped them into the hold. They had some of everything and at this time of the year there were heavy prices for most of them, the black and lemon sole, the turbot, brill, and plaice. There were not many whiting, which they would pick up on the bar of the bay as they were going back, in two days' time.

They sheltered in the little harbour of Kilronan, on the big Island of Aran, that night. Stephen didn't see much of it because it was dark when they pulled in. The lights in the houses were shining on the water and they seemed like will-o'-the-wisps climbing a mountain one behind the other.

They adjourned to the pub in relays. It was like walking into J. J.'s again. It was a small pub, lighted with paraffin lamps hanging from the ceiling, and you sat on a half-barrel or on one of the hard benches that lined the walls.

The people seemed to him to be no different from the people he knew on the opposite shore of Connemara, just that they were more dressed in clothes of their own making than the average Connemara man. The heavy blue shirt and the plaited *crios* had not been worn in Connemara for a generation, nor had the pampooties or the tasselled woollen cap. But the Aran men were mostly fishermen, and spent a greater portion of their lives at sea than the Connemara fisherman, who always ran a sizable farm as well as his fishing-boat. All of them spoke Irish, even the engineer and gangers from the mainland who were building a road in Kilmurvy.

He did not wait there long but got back to the boat, released the others, and hunched himself in the small place to write to Kathleen, and he said in the letter that he had noticed something wrong, and asked her what it was, and appealed to her to write back and let him know if anything was worrying her, and to say that he would soon have quite a bit of money gathered up, and to hell with it, both of them could go to Dublin and chance it and what about it? When he had that done he felt much better and he ran back and slipped it into the post-office on the island, because the Dun Aengus steamer from Galway would be calling at the island tomorrow and would take the mails, which would get there long before they themselves returned.

The first light of the morning saw them away again and they fished all that day off Black Head and Gregory Sound and he could see that all of them were pleased with the catch. The first week that Stephen had been working he had earned five pounds fifteen shillings, last week his share had been over six pounds, and if things kept going as they were now there was a good chance that their share-out this week would be even greater, so they ran at darkness to Ballyvaughan, and celebrated a little, and by early light next day they were beating back the bay with the trawl ready to fish the bar that ran almost the full length of the bay.

They were rewarded at the bar with a lot of small whiting which would be sold locally for a good price tomorrow which was Friday, when all the good Catholic burghers of Galway would be bulling for a fish, since they were forbidden a juicy chop, a leg of pork, or a nice porterhouse steak.

Then they headed for the docks with the tide, and by the time the fish was carefully segregated and boxed and all the gear tidied and stored there wasn't a man of them who was not ready to fall down and die with the tiredness and the lack of sleep. Stephen reflected that they earned their money the hard way without any doubt, even though they only worked four days out of seven. The lack of sleep was the worst part of the business, because even the most hardened mariner found it difficult to snatch four hours in the crowded, uncomfortable, wooden bunks. Stephen hoped that he would not have to work all his life on a trawler, and that he could win his freedom with a pen. It was easy to see how a life like this would sap any ambition you had in you, why it would be so easy when you were so tired to say, Ah, to hell with it, I'll do it tomorrow, and then that tomorrow would become as elusive as the leprechaun with his crock of gold. Even Gabriel of the dynamic energy was silent, and coiled a rope listlessly as the lighthouse fell slowly behind them and they saw the dock-gate in front of them opening its mouth like a hungry whale to gather them in.

Even if it was a whale now, Stephen thought, I would be glad to find refuge in him, which set him thinking about Jonah and what he must have thought when he found himself slipping down that mucous cavern. All of the men, he saw, wore their three-day beards, and their eyes were blood-shot. He put his hand to his own face and found that he was the same himself, and then he smiled to think what a gang of cut-throats they must look, riding this lugger, coated with fish-scales and their clothes probably smelling of stale guts. He looked at his hands wryly and saw that the tar from the ropes was rubbed well into the creases and that he was going to have a hell of a job to get them cleaned. His nails were dirt-encrusted and broken. Well, anyhow, he thought, it's no life for a dilettante, so it isn't. You're not in a job like this for your health, so you're not.

This time as they passed the gates the dock men let them by with a wave; whether they were sympathetic with the tired look of them or alarmed by their ferocious appearance, Stephen could not tell.

They tied off at the quay wall, and then proceeded to get the boxes of fish out, and load them on the lorry which was pulled up beside their berth. When they had almost finished this job the immaculate figure of Bishop appeared. Stephen could not help contrasting the cut of themselves with his polished neatness, and he wondered if Bishop was reading his thoughts when he saw him smiling.

'How did we do, Pat?' Bishop asked the skipper.

'A good trip, I think,' answered Pat, and Stephen noticed how, after every trip, when Bishop duly appeared to put the same question, Pat never called him 'Mister Bishop'. He could imagine how the skipper must feel. Here was he, a man who had spent his whole life at sea, who had learned to fish the hard way, whose knowledge of fish and the bay had been painfully acquired in the teeth of gales, dirt, and hardship, drawing to the yellow sere of his life, and still going out to sea to work the guts out of himself for a sum of money that just gave him a margin of living, while the owner, who had never gone to sea in anything but a rowing-boat and who wouldn't recognize a fish if he saw it with all the bones in it, could stroll down when they came in and calmly pick up more money out of each trip than the whole crew got altogether. The skipper must feel that there was something wrong somewhere, but a night's sleep generally cured him, and he would awaken the next morning quite content with his lot, and completely forgetful of the antipathy he had felt towards the man who was, when all was said and done, as decent an employer as you could get, with an extra pound or two thrown in now and again when they had a good trip, and presents of food and clothes for the wife and kids at

Christmas time. But somehow, after those trips, he could never bring himself to be gracious to Henry Bishop.

When all was cleared up, Bishop, having bade farewell to the skipper and the lads, turned and walked beside Stephen as he made his way back to the digs.

'Well,' he asked, 'has it licked you yet?'

'Not yet,' said Stephen. 'Shaken maybe, but not licked.'

'And you wouldn't believe me when I was talking to you about all these things the first day,' said Bishop. 'I saw you looking at me when I arrived there just now and there was a real look of class hatred in your eyes.'

'No,' said Stephen, 'it wasn't hatred. My mind was just jumping to comparisons.'

'The spider in the web,' Bishop inquired, 'with a silk line attached to the legs of his slave spiders, and every time they catch a fly he takes half of it from them, although he does nothing to earn it?'

'Look,' said Stephen, 'honest to God, I'm too tired to argue social science. All I want to do is get home to the digs and flop on a bed, when I have shaved all this stubble. Incidentally, don't you think you oughtn't to be walking up town with me now? A lot of respectable merchants are regarding you with disfavour, or are they used to you mixing with low society?'

Bishop flushed.

'You have a frightful low impression of me, haven't you?' he asked savagely.

Stephen looked at him in surprise.

'No,' he said, 'honestly. That was just an ordinary remark.'

Bishop was silent for a time.

'That's my careful upbringing,' he said. 'It makes me very sensitive, and I'm sorry that you saw me with that girl the first time. I want to explain that.'

'Really,' Stephen started to protest.

'No, look, please let me talk,' said Bishop urgently. 'You see, I have never met anyone like you that I like so much, and I value your good opinion. It's easy. It's short. When I was a clerical student, I might have been a priest, if it hadn't been for a girl. That finished me. It should never have happened.'

'I see,' said Stephen, slightly embarrassed, but sorry too for Bishop because he thought he could get a glimpse at the twisted psychology of him, which would not let him talk to any girl with a mind above a bit of fun. 'I think,' he continued slowly, 'if you were to talk to, well, to better-class girls for a while . . .'

'No!' said Bishop explosively, 'I can't.'

'Until you do,' said Stephen, 'you won't be yourself. Most girls are nice, if you'll meet them on their own ground, and the nicer they are the less the sex business worries them. It's . . . oh, well, it's your problem, and you'll have to fight.'

For a moment he felt a great impatience with Bishop. Damn it to hell, he thought, why does everybody have to pick on me to unload confidences, when I'm so goddam tired?

'If I have you around here long enough,' said Bishop, 'I might be talked into it. But look, I'm sorry. I know you are tired, even if I am responsible for it. I read "Love's Young Dream",' he said.

This bucked Stephen up momentarily.

'You did!' he ejaculated. 'Well, what's the verdict?'

'I think you've got it,' said Bishop, and Stephen felt from his voice that he meant what he said.

'I'm glad you liked it,' he said sincerely, and felt justified to himself for having overcome his inhibitions and given it to him. If it had been bad, Bishop would have been unable to hide it.

'I want to talk to you about it further,' said Bishop. 'Look, will you come up to dinner tomorrow, when you have slept enough? I'll ask Paddy too, and maybe his girl, what's-her-name?'

'Nellie,' said Stephen.

'Yes,' said Bishop. 'Nellie. She seems a sensible girl too. Look, we'll leave it until after six, hah? That'll give you plenty of time to rest, and we can have a chat. Will that suit?'

'That'll be fine,' said Stephen.

337

'Until tomorrow so,' said Bishop, breaking away. They had reached Eyre Square.

'Until tomorrow,' said Stephen, waving a hand and not halting his stride, because he was afraid that if he stopped he would find great difficulty in getting under way again.

Bishop stood and watched his broad back going away from him. He felt uncomfortable and not himself. He was almost sorry that this Stephen had come into his life at all. He was an upsetting individual with his clear far-seeing eyes and his air of quiet confidence. Bishop knew that what he had set his mind on he would attain eventually, if he had to kill himself in the pursuit of it. That steadfastness of purpose of a young man who was gradually getting to know himself, and who seemed to have inherited a great understanding of other people, made Bishop uncomfortable, and made him long to justify himself in Stephen's eyes.

Though why, he thought bitterly as he turned away, one like me should be trying to justify myself in the eyes of a country boy is beyond me. That didn't help, because Bishop knew that Stephen was no ordinary country boy, and that as long as he was around, this uncomfortable feeling would persist. To hell with it, he thought, and turned into the nearest pub.

CHAPTER TWENTY-THREE

Stephen was not surprised when he reached the digs to see his dinner waiting for him. Mrs M. was a very thoughtful woman and seemed to be blessed with all the perspicacity of the great Jewish judges. She knew the day he would be home so she would look at her newspaper to see the hour of the tides, and she would make an accurate guess as to what time the trawler would pull into the docks. Then she would put an hour on to that time and she would have everything ready when he arrived.

So he ate his dinner, while she fussed around him, as usual loading his plate as soon as he had eaten a bite. He was too tired to talk, so he listened to her prattling away, and enjoyed listening to her. By this time he had come to know most of the neighbours and he found them very nice neighbours and great talkers, and all of them had hearts much bigger than their purses. They always seemed to be running in and out of one another's houses for the loan of an egg-cup a tay, or a few spoons a sugar, or half a loaf, and if one of them went down with a sickness there was always the neighbour who would come in and stay all day cleaning and helping and running out at intervals to do their own work. You couldn't, he thought, have dropped into a nicer community, if you had been trying very hard to do so. Poverty had left them without many inhibitions so that you could talk to them about anything. Most of them were avid readers of the daily papers, with which they seldom agreed, and they always took sides on everything, more, he thought, for the sake of a good heated argument than a belief in the rights or wrongs of a case.

His dinner over, he carried the huge pot of hot water up to his room and poured it into the tin bath which the landlady always had ready for him when he returned. He mixed it judiciously with cold water and then stripped himself to the skin, handing his discarded clothes through a chink in the door to Mrs M., who waited for them with her head averted in case she would be looking at him in his pelt.

He shaved himself first in front of the small mirror, and suffered exceedingly, because even though the razor was sharp, every single hair on his face seemed to come out by the roots instead of being cut neatly. He swore again that he would bring a razor with him on the trawler next time and shave every day. Then he smiled to think what the others would say if they saw him at this foolish business of shaving himself while he was at sea.

He managed to shave eventually, although it left his face feeling raw and tender, and then he stepped into the tin bath and proceeded to scrub himself from top to toe. It took time, and a lot of patience, because he had to go through all sorts of contortions to get at the back of himself, but he managed it, and he felt much better when he stood clad in a clean shirt and trousers. He was appalled at the scum he had left on the top of the bath, but he was always that way. You could believe other people were that dirty, but never yourself. It was the damn fish mostly, and he could see the scales floating on the top of the water and knew that he hadn't succeeded yet in getting all of them out of his hair.

Then, in shirt and trousers, he carried the bath down the stairs and emptied it in the back-yard, and swirled some cold water in it to take off the main dirt.

He retired back upstairs again, pulled down the blind on the window, discarded his trousers, and went to bed. He let his head sink into the feather pillow with a sigh of deep content.

His mind was as blank as the great tiredness could make it, but he still seemed to feel the sideways pull of the boat and the chug of the engine beneath his feet. The trawler was a tub that swung up and down, and varied that by swinging from side to side, so that you wanted to be more of an acrobat than a sailor in order to keep your balance.

He had almost drifted into sleep when he heard a knock at the door. It was a hesitant knock, with the voice of Mrs M. behind it. He knew that if he did not answer she would go away and let him sleep, and that she wouldn't call him until nine or ten the next morning, if he hadn't woken himself before that. He debated with himself. He remained silent, but then his cursed curiosity got the better of his tired limbs, and he knew it must be something fairly important or she would never have called him.

He sat up in the bed and said 'What is it?'

She opened the door then, and came in diffidently. She had two letters in her hand.

'I ought to be shot,' she said, 'for not givin' yeh those whin y' came in. I don't know what's comin' over me at all. They've been here for you since the mornin' yeh wint, that was Tuesday, and here it is now, half-past six on Thursday evenin', an' I forgettin' all about them.'

'That's all right, Mrs M.,' he said, stretching out his hand and taking them.

'I won't let another sinner within a dog's bark a yeh,' she said, 'before tomorra mornin', not if it was De Valera himsel'.' She retired again and closed the door.

The blinded room was dark. Stephen could see Kathleen's handwriting on one of the letters but didn't know who the other could be from. He saved himself a journey to lift the blind by stretching his hand and switching on the light. He looked at the second letter again. The writing was big and unformed as if a child had written it. The postmark was blotted and he couldn't see from where it had been posted.

However, he stifled his curiosity and opened Kathleen's letter.

It was a very nice letter, but somehow the same feeling of depression came over him when he read its very cheerful sentences. Its tone was all right and what she said was all right, and how she put it was all right, but he still couldn't help feeling disturbed, and kind of sad, and he knew that was the wrong way to feel altogether, when you got a letter from a girl that loved you. There seemed to be a kind of a desperate call about all that she wrote. She wrote casually, 'I'd like to see you very much again, and I'm very glad about the good job on the trawler. You should be able to make enough money soon for us to be together again, shouldn't you?' Then she went on to speak of other things, but he still wasn't satisfied. He let the letter drop on the bedclothes and put his arms behind his head. He went over a chapter of possibilities in his mind again, but could find nothing that would account for the feeling he got from her letter.

Then he took up the other letter and opened it. He looked at the top to see the address. There was no address and then he looked at the end of the last page, and there he saw 'Michael Fagan'. That made him sit up higher in the bed, and first he was delighted, but even before he started to read he knew that something must be wrong, or Michilin would never have written to him at all, because Michilin was no writing man. He admitted it freely and said he would rather be dipped like an oul ram in a pool of Cooper's Dip than to have to sit down and go through the tortures of having to write a letter.

It started off baldly:

STEPHEN,

I am taking pen in hand to write to you a line or two at which as you will see and know that I am a poor hand never haven gone beyond the five class at school because I am so much take up with fish and other thins like so. I am sorry when you go stephen and miss you much but that is not what I am saying that is important at all so it isnt and the fact is that something very serious has happened and I think that you are the one to know even if other people dont think so at all.

Your father I am afraid is very sick stephen that one you know who I mean went away last week and we nobody have seen her round the place at all anymore but one of the neighbours who is the mother of thomasheen goes in there and finds the poor man down flat in front of the fire and its said he had stroke whats that, but he is ver sick and in bed now and he has no talk and danny came and is doin about the fields and Thomas mother is helping so maybe you ought to come and see him and what do you think about that.

I wish that was bad but there is more yet stephen for I am sorry to tell you this but think that you should know although I have been made to swear that I will not tell you but what has happen has give me great fright on me oath which is that Kathleen we know who, is going to have a baby for Im sorry stephen, but she tells me some time ago and says that you must not know that you are working hard and that you will be able to send for her maybe and that that will be time enough she says.

maybe so Stephen but now Im afraid that her brother you know who the bastard he finds out and Im sure about this and if so as I am sure I think you should come quick stephen and take her away before anything happens and then you come and see the old man anyhow who is not well at all as I

342

have told you early on in the letter curse it.

I will close now and have no more news for you which is well I think because what I have said is enough and thanks be to the God that this letter is now finished at which I have been busy for a long time on it so I leave down pen now and hope to see you *very* soon because that I am not easy in mind at all stephen because I am old now and would not be able to do what you could do if you were here because you are young and also big.

I am your friend who hopes to see you and that this will leave you as me in great health thank god only all the things that have happen as I show you in this letter.

MICHAEL FAGAN

Stephen leaned back stunned on the pillow, and his eyes were distended, and his breath came very fast. It was some time before the implications of Michilin's letter struck him properly, and as they proceeded to loom, the blood first rushed to his head and then rushed away again from it.

Nothing so personal as this had ever hit him before, apart from the death of his mother, which left him feeling that he had to tuck up his socks and be a big boy, but now there were other people involved in it as well as himself. He lay helpless in the bed and thought about nothing but the tragedy of all this, that had come out of the blue.

He didn't mind his father having a stroke so much, that was to be more or less expected from the heavy drinking which he did, and his highly coloured face which was a signal of blood-pressure, nor did the news that Kathleen was going to have a baby come as an overwhelming shock. When they had made love that was one of the chances they had taken, and he did not feel that it was so very unpleasant except what people would say about her.

It was the thought of Malachai that made his blood run cold.

It was only now, lying back on his bed with a feeling of utter helplessness, that he really saw what Malachai was. He remembered their encounters and the night that Malachai must have been waiting for them to come back and recover their gun, with his fingers ready on the triggers. Stephen knew now that Malachai would have shot him that night with no more compunction than if he had been a rabbit, and he remembered his eyes, and the slow menacing way he talked, and he saw clearly now that Malachai was almost a primitive man, and the fact of his own sister getting that way by an enemy of his own, would be the most unpleasant thing that could happen to him, and only God knew what he would do about it. Kathleen was strong and she could stand up to him, but it was like standing up to a wild beast that would be ever watchful for the slightest relaxing of vigilance, in order to pull you down and tear at your throat. Then he pushed that thought from him, and told himself not to be an eejit.

'What am I going to do?' he asked himself, trying to pull his scattered thoughts into a coherent whole. 'Let me see now. I can't stay here and let things take their course. I have to go back to Connemara, that's the first thing; I will see my father, that's the second; then I will go and get Kathleen and bring her back here to Galway, that's the third; and when I have that done I can start thinking of what can be done after that. That's concrete. That's reality anyhow.' He knew that he had almost twenty pounds with what was coming to him after today's trip. That would be plenty for the time being anyhow. Therefore Connemara tomorrow.

Then he jumped quickly out of the bed as the thought struck him that Michilin's letter had been written on either Saturday or Sunday in order to get to Galway on Tuesday. This was Thursday evening. Holy Jesus, he thought, that's a week ago, and as he thought of all the things that could happen in a week, he pulled on his clothes with feverish haste. No Connemara for him tomorrow; he'd have to go, clear out now, if he wanted to catch the seven o'clock bus. He lifted the blind with a rush and then went quickly to the door and, opening it, shouted out:

'Hey, what time is it, Mrs M.? What time is it?'

'It's quarter to seven, Mister O'Riordan,' her voice floated back to him.

Quarter to seven! It drove him into a frenzy of speed. He pulled on his socks and boots, hurried into a pullover an coat, pulled out Michilin's bag and took his money out of it, stuffed it in his pocket, and then rushed down the stairs.

Mrs M. was staring at him, her eyes wide.

'Look, Mrs M.,' he said, 'I'll have to talk fast now. The letters you brought me, there was bad news in them. My father is sick and there are other things as well. I'll have to go back home for a day or two but I will probably be back here again on Saturday or Monday at the latest. I will probably be bringing a girl back with me. She's the girl I'm going to marry so I'll want you to put her up. Now, I was to see Mister Bishop tomorrow. I won't be able. But I'm sure Paddy or Nellie will call some time tomorrow, so would you explain to them what has happened and why I have to rush off like this. Tell them I'll tell them all about it when I come back. Do you get that, Mrs M.?'

'I get it very clearly indeed, Mister O'Riordan,' she said, and he had no doubt that she did. 'I'm sorry about your poor father,' she went on, 'but it happens to old people like that always, it can't be avoided, and I'll go straight down to the chapel after I've washed up and I'll say a round of the beads for him and another one for yourself that everything will be all right, which it will without doubt, please God.'

'Thanks, Mrs M.,' said Stephen, opening the front door, 'and God bless you, and you better say a fast one now that I'll manage to catch the bus.'

He didn't see her, but she took him at his word and, crossing herself, she looked at the picture of the Sacred Heart where it was hung above the mantel, with a red-globed oil-lamp burning in front of it, and she said, 'For the love of God will You hurry that young man's steps, Lord, and make him in time for the bus, because it is just like them down there to start the bus on the very minute just because a person really needs it, where another day they'd be waiting for an hour maybe, chattin' away there about this and that, before they'd think of going. So will You put Your gracious mercy into their hearts today so that they'll delay the bus a

345

little because I see by the clock that it's almost on the stroke of seven, and if he isn't there now he's sure to be late, and unless he has wings on his heels, he'll never get there in time without Your Divine assistance.' And after that she said a few Hail Marys very devoutly, and then went on with her work because she had great faith in her prayers and knew that everything would be all right.

Stephen couldn't afford to chance it, so he started off running as soon as he left the door of the house. Just then a little boy ran out of a house up the street and Stephen fell over him.

He pulled himself up, holding back the curses of impatience that sprang to his lips, and lifted the little fellow, who was bawling as if someone was squeezing his finger with pincers.

Stephen said to him, 'You're all right now, aren't you? Here, stop crying, you are all right now.'

That should have been the end of it, but the mother of the child came running out of the house and gathered him into her arms and one minute she'd be crooning over him and then she'd turn to Stephen and shout, 'You murderer! Is that the way you go about kickin' over little childer like footballs, more shame to yeh, yeh hulkin' brute yeh!' Stephen tried to explain what had happened, that it was an accident and the child wasn't hurt anyhow. 'What! 'she shouted, 'not hurt, and he's never a one to cry, so he isn't, unless he's hurt deep down in him, so he isn't. Ah, Sweet Jesus, is this the way the world is that great Turks a min can be bowlin' over childer like steam-rollers? And hush, and whist, me darlin', yer mother won't let 'm get yeh. And where are yeh rushin' off teh now, might we ask, an one a me poor childer with one a his bones broken in his body, I'm sure, an' yeh rushin' away like the divil was after yer tail instead a waitin' an' goin' for the doctor?'

'But,' Stephen said, 'I have to catch a bus that goes at seven o'clock and if I don't go now I'll never catch it.'

'Did you ever?' she implored the small crowd who were gathering by this time. 'See how the divil can put the lies

spoutin' out a their mouths like shamrock on St Patrick's
Day, whin the need arises; you wouldn't wait until his father
came home to his dinner, so you wouldn't, and he'd give yeh
somethin' that'd make yeh remimber this day be and . . .
there was I doin' yeh a great wrong, an honest gentleman like
yeh whin the little bastards are always runnin' out under
people's feet like peas that's spilled out oo a packet. Here
you,' she said, shaking the child vigorously, 'shut your
mouth an' don't be bawlin' like a bull. Anywan'd think it
was hurtit you were, the way yer roarin'. Shut up now, and
run after that man gone down the road like a hare and thank
him for the two half-crowns that he slipped into me palm,
and come back then and I'll give yeh a pinny for sweets.

'I must say,' she said then, turning to the curious on-
lookers, 'that this is a quare place. If two dogs takes to havin'
an argumint out in the middle a the street the neighbours
are out lookin' at it like flies around an oul jam-jar. A person
can't have a bite t' ate but they's heads shoved around the
jamb a the dure t' see what people 's havin' for their break-
fasts, an' t' watch the bite goin' inta their mouths. Have ye
nothin' t' do, have ye? Shouldn't ye be at home in yeer
houses, shouldn't yee, tryin' t' cook the slops for yeer husbands' dinners instead a standin' up there and gawkin' at
everythin' that goes on? What kind a people are ye at all?'

A woman in the crowd told her what kind of people they
were and what kind of a so-and-so bitch they thought she
was, houldin' every poor man t' ransom that wint the streets
because he happened t' fall over a little snotty-nosed brat
that should a been strangled the day he was born the way he
was goin' around crawbin' the life outa the whole street.

'Ho-ho!' ejaculated the injured one, 'is that so?' And if
Stephen had been present he might have been gratified or
otherwise by the sizable argument and the undoubted flow
of eloquence which his mishap evoked.

But he was just rounding the corner of the square leading
to the station, where all the long-distance buses were lined
up nose to tail. There were gaps in the line but he couldn't
see from this distance whether the Clifden bus had moved

out or not, so he ran again, keeping a wary eye on any children in his path, determined this time to dodge in time, or to kill one outright in order to stop it bawling, and bringing a haranguing mother on the scene.

He was almost breathless when he reached the line of buses, all of whose engines were throbbing over quietly, with the drivers hunched over the big wheels in the cabs.

He ran along reading the names of their destinations on the front of them, and then he slowed with relief when he saw the Clifden bus, well filled with people, who looked curiously at him as he walked its length. The driver and the conductor were putting bulky parcels on top, as well as bicycles, so he saw that he had minutes to spare. Nevertheless he entered the bus, and sank on to the last seat with a sigh.

He was hardly there when a breathless, dirty-nosed little urchin appeared at the door of the bus and gasped, 'Hey, mister, mister!' With loathing, Stephen saw that it was the child of the mother.

'Well, what is it?' he asked gruffly.

'Me mother says thanks for the two half-crowns,' the child burst out, 'and I'm not hurtit at all.'

Stephen had to laugh.

'That's grand,' he said. 'I can go away now with an easy conscience.'

But the urchin didn't wait to hear the end of it, just pulled back and started running where he had come from, holding his arms out from each side of his body and making a buzzing aeroplane noise with his lips. Stephen, looking out the window, caught a glimpse of him running across the road before the station. Just then a car came the other way, and by some miracle of inspired skill the driver saved himself from killing the child. He stopped the car and leaned out to say a few things which Stephen couldn't hear. The child just turned and stuck out a red tongue and went on being an aeroplane, while Stephen wondered what the mother would have said to the car-driver if she had caught him.

Just then the driver pulled himself into the cab, the

conductor came in, started to don his money-bag and ticket-punch, and paused to ring the bell of the bus twice.

It tinkled, the driver let in the clutch, and they were away.

CHAPTER TWENTY-FOUR

Stephen's mind leaped ahead of the bus, and a surge of impatience rose in him at its frequent stops through the town. There is a great difference now, he thought, between the young man who came wide-eyed and eager into the town of Galway three weeks ago – sweet God, was it only three weeks? – interested in everything, and everybody, new to his eyes, and himself now returning; and his mind's eye automatically filled with lakes and rivers and high mountains, with men standing against the sky.

He felt that he was between two worlds, the Connemara world gradually gaining an ascendancy over this other strange three-week existence which seemed like a dream that had never happened.

His interlude with Bishop and Paddy and Nellie and the other people, he could not manage to bring to reality in his mind at all, and were it not that the petrol fumes made him drowsy now, and forced him to realize how utterly tired he was, he could never have forced himself to believe that he had been fishing on a trawler to make a living.

His trips on the trawler had ruined his love of fishing. It was a much different thing, he thought, to go fishing casually with a strange trawler pulling into Crigaun than to go out on Galway Bay and be worried about the size of the catch, to be doing mental arithmetic every time a net was hauled to see how much was in it for you personally. With the result that the natural liking was taken out of the whole business, and it was reduced to nothing but sordidness, dirt, and hard labour. When I come back again, he thought, I think I will give up the trawler, whether we go to Dublin or stay in

Galway for a while, because the trawler ceases to be a source of inspiration and disorders your mind; and then this constant cursed tiredness, he thought, when he found that his head was nodding and he had to pull himself awake. He looked out of the window, was dismayed to discover that they had not yet succeeded in leaving the town, and he longed to see the last of the buildings and the people.

He looked around at the passengers to try and bury his impatience. They seemed for the most part to be made up of country people who were returning after a day in Galway. One old red-petticoated woman in front of him was engaged in a furious argument with the conductor over a half-bag of flour which she had sneaked into the bus and left at Stephen's feet, when the conductor was up top arranging his load.

'But, ma'am,' he was expostulating, 'don't you know that it's the Company's rules that we can't carry flour inside the bus? You can arg' till yer blue in the face, but them's the rules and we have to abide be them. What kind oo a country would it be if everybody wint around doin' what they like?'

'But, amac,' she said, in a soft persuasive voice, 'isn't it oney a few ounces that's in it, and it takin' up no more room, God save yeh, than a pound a tay in a basket?'

'A few ounces!' he ejaculated. 'For God's sake look at the few ounces, will ye!' and he delivered a hearty kick on the bag. 'Now, look, they's enough there t' feed the 1st Battalion up in Renmore, so there is. You'll have t' get it off the bus, that's all.'

'But,' she wheedled, 'where in the name a God am I goin' t' put it?'

'Y' shouldn't have brought it inta the bus in the first place,' he said. 'The whole lot a ye has the life scalded outa me. Don't ye know the rules better than I do, don't ye? But yer persist in crucifyin' me. Take it now and get rid oo it.'

'But look,' she went on. 'What in the name a God will I do with it now?'

For a moment Stephen thought that the conductor was about to tell her, but then his natural gentlemanly instincts got the upper hand.

'You'll have t' get off t' hell with it,' he said.

'Ah, just this once,' she said, giving him a gummy grin.

'Just this once,' he said bitterly. 'That's what ye say all the time, so it is. Ye do it wance an' ye do it twice, an' before ye know where ye are, ye'll be tryin' t' persuade 's teh stuff a four-year-old heifer into the front seat. Ah, it's not good enough now!'

'Divil a bit a me,' she promised fervently, ' 'll ever bring a grain af it aboord agin.'

'Not half you won't!' he answered out of his experienced knowledge. 'You'll do it agin and agin as sure as yer sittin' on that seat. Don't ye think a me at all? What'll happen t' me if the Inspector comes along an' me cartin' half a flour-mill in the bus with me whin it's agin the regulations? Did ye ever stop t' think a that, did ye? No fear, ye didn't. And suppose I get the sack, what thin? Can I hire a cart and go out to your place with me wife and five kids, for the rest a me days?'

'Ye'd be as welcome,' she said, 'as a few bags a artificial manure which is very scarce at the time, so you would. A Cead Mile Failte.'

'You can lave it there, just this once,' he said severely. 'Just this once now, mind yeh, because the very next time y' do it I'll fire it out on the side a the road, without a word exchanged.' Then he went farther down the bus and chatted to a couple of young girls whom he seemed to know well, and his face was creased with smiles.

The old woman turned to see that her bag was still there and she winked broadly at Stephen.

'He's always like that,' she explained, 'but he gives in in the end. That fella is the nicest man that was ever on the Connemara run.'

Stephen smiled back at her.

It's funny, he thought, how everyone seems to feel sorry for country people in towns, but they are better able to take care of themselves and their interests than any townie who ever lived. He had seen them in the shops in Galway. They never, never paid the price asked for anything. They would say, 'Well how about a bit off now?' or 'What, five shillings for that oul thing whin I was up the town there tin minutes ago and I saw it in me man's shop for four and a penny! Oh, but I did, and if you will come up there now I'll show it to you in the window as plain as I'm lookin' at you there now, on me oath.' Or they would feel the stuff and they'd say, 'Isn't that very thin stuff now, don't you think? I'm not sure that's such good stuff at all at all, and will you look at this gansie I'm wearin' now? D'ye know how much I paid for that, this time three years in Oughterard? Three shillings, as sure as I'm here, and feel the stuff. Can't yeh see the difference between them?' That was a good line, because it planted a suspicion of inferiority in the mind of the salesman. They would be willing to waste over an hour arguing in a shop, and acting away, opening the purse and closing it, walking to the door and walking back again, wheedling, disparaging, being contumelious, haughty, angry, soft, in fact going through a gamut of exhausting emotions in order to get a sixpence taken off the price, and then retiring triumphantly with the article under a shawl or an arm, leaving the assistant tired and perspiring.

They always appeared to win.

' "Appear" is the word,' Bishop had explained to Stephen when he had mentioned this one time they were talking. 'My dear boy, we merchants are not as foolish as we look. Practically all shop-assistants are up to that old gag about the arguing farmer, so as soon as they see one coming they automatically put the price up a shilling or so and allow themselves to be reluctantly beaten down. It's business, and nobody is in business for their health, and if they are they do not be long losing it.'

Stephen had said, 'Isn't that cheating?'

'Who's cheating who?' Bishop had asked. 'Don't they waste precious time for hours, as well as lowering the resistance of assistants? No fear. That's business.'

'But suppose,' Stephen had asked, 'that a man comes in and the chap puts the price up and the man says ,"All right, I'll take it," what happens then?'

352

'Well,' Bishop had said, 'that is what may be regarded as an act of God, and the salesman probably takes the amount off anyhow, and calls it a discount.'

'I think the whole thing is very peculiar,' Stephen had said.

'I told you that, the first time I met you,' Bishop had said.

Stephen had decided that he would never be a merchant or a trader, and with all deference to Mac the cattle-jobber, he would never be a cattle-jobber. He had watched one of the great cattle fairs in Galway. He had been interested in it. The fair was generally held in the square in the open streets, and going or coming to his digs he had to wade almost ankle-deep in cow-dung. It decided him definitely that the Irish nation was a nation of polished actors. Why they couldn't sell a cow in the ordinary way he could not understand. If he wanted a cow he felt that he'd just say How much for that oul cow? and the owner would say so much and he would say All right, here you are, or No, thanks, it's too dear. But it never seemed to happen that way. The sale of a cow could never be conducted without the most extravagant histrionics.

The owner stands beside his cow. He sees a fellow coming wearing leggings on a neat blue pin-stripe suit. You can tell a cattle-jobber a mile away by the clothes he wears. He always seems to sport very good suits and shirts with highly coloured ties. He neglects the headgear, probably because he is out in such bad weather. His hat is always battered and old. He wears leggings over his lovely trousers or he pulls his socks outside the legs of the trousers, and wanders around in heavy, dung-encrusted boots.

So the owner sees a jobber coming, and he looks into the sky and maybe whistles a tune, or hums, or talks to somebody as if he didn't know that there was a jobber nearer to him than the Aran Islands. The jobber walks briskly up to the animal, ignoring the owner, and scrutinizes it closely. Then a look of deep disgust and overwhelming loathing comes on his face. He points disgustedly at the animal and says to the world at large, 'Who in the name of all that's good and holy owns this oul yoke?'

The owner, turning as if surprised that anybody is there at all, says 'What's that?'

'Do you own this bag a bones?' the jobber addresses him directly.

'I own that animal,' the owner says without heat, because, apparently, one must not fly into anger when the baste is insulted, 'and if there's a finer animal than him from here up to the Six Counties I'd like to see him.' 'Look,' the jobber says, 'I'm not interested in this animal except as a humanitarian, and that animal should ha' been put out 'f his misery long ago, so he should, and as an act a charity, I'll give yeh tin pound for 'm.' The owner looks at him with his eyes wide, is silent, spits on the ground and then, turning back to his companion, says, 'Well, as I was sayin', Jack,' or he looks up at the sky and whistles or hums. The jobber gives him a few seconds, and then walks away from him, saying over his shoulder, 'I better go quick before that oul yoke falls dead at me feet.'

Then, apparently, his charitable instincts mounting again, he circles and returns. 'Just as a matter of interest,' he asks, 'what price do you think you'll get for that?' The owner addresses him this time: 'I'll get twenty-two pound for that animal,' he says, 'and I wouldn't sell him under thirty, but that it's a shame t' keep him outa the slaughter-house, he's so prime.' Then it's the jobber's turn to look at the sky. 'Twenty-two pound,' he says, 'twenty-two pound! Holy Jesus, did you hear that? and I'd swear me oath that the man is not a lunatic.' Then he laughs uproariously and walks away shaking with laughter. The owner is unperturbed and waits.

The jobber comes back again. 'Look,' he says, 'I don't know what's wrong with me today, I better get me head examined, but as a favour to humanity, I'll give yeh twelve pound for that thing, and I'll chance 'm fallin' dead before I can get 'm to the station.'

'Twenty-two pound,' the owner reiterates woodenly.

The jobber laughs and appeals to the friend of the owner. 'Look,' he says, 'you appear to be a sinsible man. Will you talk to him and tell him what's wrong with him?' This is the friend's turn to start acting. 'Ah,' he says, 'I don't know him at all, I oney met him today.' 'Well, you're a neutral mind so,' the jobber says; 'can't we talk to him about it?'

And the acting goes on. Sometimes the animal changes hands in half an hour, sometimes he doesn't change hands until late that evening, the jobber waiting to break the other's resistance and the owner determined to bring the animal home rather than give him away. Eventually when they strike a bargain a whole day may have passed with the jobber going and coming and the pantomime continuing again.

Stephen practically became exhausted looking at it, so what must the farmer feel like who had probably started to walk to town with his animal at three or four o'clock that morning? But the whole thing provided colour and noise and filled the pubs to overflowing so that for ever more he would associate the fairs with the mingled smell of dung, porter, and urine, and in his mind a fair would be the Corporation's men that evening cleaning the streets with long hoses that were spouting water from many bursts. Stephen determined that he would take a greater interest in cattle after this, if he was ever on a farm, but that he would never go to try and buy or sell them himself.

All of which didn't help to solve his problems, but every time an image of Kathleen came into his mind, and his heart started to beat with apprehension, he put the thought away forcibly, determined not to bring it to light until he was on the road to Killaduff.

He looked out the window and saw that they were only nearing Moycullen. God, he thought, isn't this terrible, and when I was coming, the journey was too short for me and I thought it would end all too soon. Then he had had things to look at that interested him, but they were now flat and stale to his eyes. And there had been Mac to beguile the time, with his loud talk and his big hearty laugh.

There was the Corrib lake out there, looking big and grey and fitting in with his thoughts. Even from this distance he noticed that it was heavily ruffled and that there must be a strong breeze blowing on it.

He had been up on the Corrib in a boat with an outboard engine attached to the tail of it. When was that? Three years ago, or could it have been last weekend when he had come home from the trawler-fishing? Paddy and Nellie and that nurse girl out of the hospital, what-you-may-call-her, Curly. It had been a great day, and Stephen had been very taken with the lake, except that he found it hard to adjust his mind to the immensity of it after his small Connemara ones. They hadn't fished at all on account of the girls, but he had seen one ten-pound trout that was killed that day, and his fingers were itching to get a line into them. But Paddy loathed fishing, and thought it a great abuse of time. The lake to Paddy was a place where you took a motor-boat, your lunch, and a piece of skirt, and had a good coort in a sylvan paradise, with somebody else to build the fire and make the tea and attend to Paddy's wants as he lay stretched naked except for bathing trunks, on the grass, slapping himself where he was getting added flesh, and remarking what a fine bit of a man he was and what a great comfort he would be to a woman on a cold winter's night.

Stephen had found that Curly was as serious as ever, and that she had forgiven him about the corpse. They had talked about many things, and she had elicited from him that he had a girl in Connemara and she had asked him all about her and what she was like, and he had found that it was a pleasure to talk to her about Kathleen, because at that time he was feeling homesick, not so much for his home as for Kathleen and Michilin and all that both of them meant to his life; and he had wondered then, for the first time, if a man would have to leave the place he was born, and the place that suited him best, in order to be able to write about it. He felt doubts, but restrained them because he thought that it might be the lazy part of him objecting to being uprooted. He had been delighted with his day with Curly. He hadn't known that girls could be so serious, and then he had found a cause for her seriousness. She had been the daughter of a farmer who lived in Roscommon. One day while threshing, both of his arms had been caught in the machine and they had been amputated from the elbows. A fine young man before that, he had become a sour old young man, unambitious, and a confirmed hypochondriac. That was when Curly was very young. Her mother had sold the farm, and they had come to Galway and set up a small business in one of the poorer streets. They had prospered reasonably well, and then her mother had been taken ill with cancer of the womb, and after God knows how many operations which had taken all that they possessed, she had died, uncured, in terrible agony. The father had not long survived her, and Curly had been left in possession of a shop with many liabilities. She had been younger then, and had to leave the secondary school where she was being educated. She had wanted to go to College and be a doctor; whether this ambition had been inspired by the sufferings of her parents or not, she could not say. Eventually she had sold the shop and become a probationer nurse, this being the nearest way to fulfil her ambitions.

He groaned when he saw that they were only stopping now at Oughterard, and that there were thirty-three long miles to cover yet before they reached Clifden. He didn't alight from the bus at Oughterard, remembering how it had depressed him even in the height of his first eager journey. He sat and thought, and counted the long minutes while people got off and people got on, and the driver and conductor argued the toss whether the laws of the Company allowed them to put any more bicycles on the bus. Finally they got out of Oughterard, and Stephen thought surely now we'll get a move on. So they did too, if the bus didn't seem to be stopping at every gatehouse along the road while the conductor alighted and handed in parcels to their destination, and exchanged a few words of badinage with the girls or men who were waiting to collect them. Stephen felt aggrieved that they could be smiling when he was so gloomy, and wondered if people in trouble were always as selfish as he felt now. Those other people in the bus, what about them? Surely were they not all as free from care as their countenances

357

said. Wasn't any one of them in a tangle with fate or trouble of some kind, a father who drank or a husband who was unfaithful, or a son who might be about to be hanged for murder, or a girl who was going to have a baby like Kathleen, with a fierce brother who wouldn't like that, and her man far away from her when he should have been there? God blast it! he thought explosively, she should have told me. I'm not a child, and we could have accepted it reasonably and worked the whole thing out, but to keep it to herself like that smacked too much of cheap heroics which would be inspired by the slushy books with cheap jackets, with their stories of barons' bastards and housemaids' concupiscence.

Then he chided himself, because he knew what Kathleen was. She would have told him if it was for the best. She would never have remained, he thought, if it hadn't been for the sister-in-law's child.

The mountains looming before him left him cold. No longer did he feel that they would be a guardian, a tower of strength to protect one from the outside world; instead they seemed to his red-rimmed eyes to be bleak and bare and frightening, with heavy, dark-tinged clouds rushing past them. And the lakes on each side of the road, with their islands, no longer held any beauty for his eyes. Now they were just long grey stretches of water running by the side of the road, which seemed interminable anyhow, and which in its winding way around the lakes seemed to be infinite. Each lake he passed, it was with gladness that he thought that there was the end of that bloody thing anyhow, and here's another one coming that's longer, if that's possible, and it'll take hours to get by it. Connemara!

He remembered, now, a conversation he had overheard in Galway which, at the time, had made the hair rise at the back of his head, and his neck flush with anger.

He had been in a restaurant with Bishop drinking a cup of tea. The tables were set closely together. There were two well-dressed young men at the table behind them. He had paid no attention to what they were saying until one of them had said in a loud voice 'Connemara!' with a note of great disdain in his voice. Bishop had heard him too and halted what he was saying. They listened.

'Look,' said the young man, 'I worked out there and I know. I was teaching out there in the heart of it for three years. Three years! My God, I thought I'd never get free of it. What is it? I'll tell you what it is! What should be done with it? I'll tell you what should be done with it! If I had my way, do you know what I'd do with it? I'll tell you. You know Maam, where the mountains begin? Well, I'd start there, and I'd build a high wall across the Maam Valley and I'd extend this wall until it met the coast at Furbo, and then I would continue this wall all around the coast of Connemara. It would be no ordinary wall. It would be higher than the wall of China. I would get all the wild animals in the world then and I would put themselves and the Connemara people inside this wall and would seal it up for eight generations. That's what I'd do. But the only trouble about it would be that when you knocked down the wall then to see what would have happened, you would find that the Connemararians had eaten all the wild animals instead of vice versa.'

And the friend had laughed uproariously, and Bishop had smiled to see the fierce look on Stephen's face.

Maybe, thought Stephen now, it was true for him. Maybe we are not half civilized at all. Certainly we accept things like wounding with knives, and ferocious beatings with stones, and sticks, and anything handy, and explain it away by saying that we always knew such a one had a bad temper, so had his father before him, and I still remember the batin' that his grandfather gave to what-you-may-call-'m in 1919. It might be those same romantic mountains that made living fiercer, and that gave small things an importance that would fade if they had been living on a plain with lush grass and deep, swiftly and evenly flowing rivers. Connemara was different to that. Nature in Connemara was turbulent. The mountains were turbulent, and the streams that carved beds into the sides of the mountains were turbulent. The animals on the mountains were turbulent if they wanted to live; the sea was always a menace ready to blow into stormy turbulence. The height of the mountains made turbulent storms out of breezes which otherwise would have been gentle zephyrs. If man copied his own nature from the nature of things surrounding him, then it was no wonder that a man living in Connemara should live a turbulent life, with dislikes fanned into burning hatred by the elements of poverty, hard work, and boredom. Stephen had remembered being shocked by young men whom he had always regarded as quiet, normal young people. They would be their nice pleasant selves one moment, and then let something happen to disturb them deeply, and they became like raging cats, with their lips drawn back from their teeth and a grimace of fury altering completely the shape of their faces.

He supposed that he had a little of that in himself, if not a lot: how otherwise explain the consuming hatred that the sight of Malachai Finnerty evoked in him? Even now, dead tired, impatient, and disturbed as his mind was, rolling along in a vehicle which was in itself civilization, all he had to do was conjure up a picture of Malachai and he felt the hair rising on his neck like a mongrel getting ready for battle.

He rubbed his hand quickly across his forehead to try and wipe out his thoughts.

What am I going to do when I get to Clifden? he thought. I can't get the loan of a bicycle, since there is no one there I know very well. I can't get a lift in the mail-car, because it goes back to Killaduff after the five bus reaches Clifden. Therefore I will have to walk the six miles. Six miles are not a lot when you say them quickly, and after all, I often walked more than six miles of an evening when Michilin and myself were out stalking the wild geese in the winter, which put a picture into his mind of those great birds in a gigantic ragged formation, high in the sky, cackling and circling over the place they were going to land, and then, like cute army generals, sending one or two of their number down to reconnoitre and spy out the land. A bad hunter would have given himself and his hiding-place away by having a quick shot at these scouts, and the circling flocks appeared to be quite willing to sacrifice those of their comrades for the common weal; but the cute hunter let them land and held his breath. Then the lone ones would rise again, and bring a message of hope, and the whole flock would land after more circling, and then, bang, bang, right barrel, left barrel, and the flock would be off again cackling a sort of screaming protest. You would rise from cover, having reloaded with lightning speed, and you would snap-shoot them as they circled for height. Then would come the sight and noise of a heavy body falling through the air, and the dull thump as a lifeless goose hit the ground.

Stephen sighed, and put those pleasant thoughts away from him.

It would be about half-past nine when he reached Clifden, and if he set off towards Killaduff at a moderate pace he should reach it about half-past eleven, see his father, and then get into touch with Michilin and clear everything up this very night. If things looked threatening, Kathleen could come over and stay in his own house, because now, no doubt, the story of her was about, and no further damage to her name could ensue if she slept under the same roof as himself.

The spire of the Clifden church rising in the distance was a great sight to him, portending as it did the end of this journey which he thought would have no ending. The people in the bus started to shuffle, pulling down parcels, and hats, and coats, and bits and pieces of things from the racks above their heads, and half-standing to stretch their cramped limbs, smiling and nodding at one another, as if to say, Well, thank God that's over anyhow.

The bus pulled into the stopping-place and Stephen was the first to alight after the conductor. He started walking quickly towards the road that led out of the town. His legs were stiff, and it took a time for the circulation to get back into them. His head was muggy after the heated bus, and the strong wind that was blowing was a boon to him. Still, his thoughts did not seem to work freely, and he found himself wishing that he could lie on a bed for a few hours before he tackled all the jobs in front of him. If he could do that, he thought, he would feel much more confident. The thought of himself snuggled in the bed in Mrs M.'s room, with the blind drawn and a delightful feeling of inertia descending on him, was one that came back to him again and again. If only she had forgotten those letters. But God, no, don't even think that! If only the letters had arrived before he had left Galway on Tuesday. Then he would have been fit and able to handle them and he would have had time. Now the letters were old and stale and he hoped that events had not gone beyond them.

He could see the road now, which he had cycled in darkness on his way out, but it did not interest him except as regards its length, and the question whether the turn off the main road was around that hill in front or the next one. The hills were loathsome and he cursed them because they made him feel more tired than he was, if that was really possible!

An odd horse and cart being driven past him were the only things to break the monotony, but since they were strange people who passed him silently with just an inquisitive glance, they took him no forrarder.

Eventually he reached the turn off where a bridge ran over a rushing river. It was only then that he felt himself to be nearly home. From here, he knew the road well, each turn and twist of it, and despite his dejection it brought a jerk of speed to his jaded limbs. It must be nearly eleven now, he thought, because it was getting dark, although the high-riding moon was challenging the twilight.

The people in the cottages he passed had their lamps lighted, and he could see their figures moving inside them like the flickering pictures in a film. That was a simile he could use now because he had seen a film. It is strange, he thought, that although we live only a few miles from these people, we know them by repute alone, and hardly any of them by sight.

He met one man he thought he knew. O'Flaherty was his name, and he had seen him over at the strand one autumn when they were digging sand-eels out of the strand by the bucket, under a harvest moon.

He was going to smile at this man, and greet him, when each could recognize the other, but O'Flaherty seemed to stand still for a moment when he saw him, as if he had got a shock. Then he tightened his lips, averted his head, and walked past.

Stephen paused to look after him, and he felt very perturbed. What, he wondered, could be the reason for that? He wondered first if O'Flaherty had recognized him, and was sure that he had. Was it, he wondered, that the story of his father had got abroad, and that they blamed Stephen for the stroke that had hit him?

That was probably it, Stephen told himself, as he walked on with less speed, and feeling more dejected, and, for the first time for many years, feeling lonely, where he had always been self-sufficient. Maybe he was responsible too for his father's stroke. The Connemara people had never been father-beaters anyhow, whatever else they might do; but then, thought Stephen, few of them ever had fathers like mine, or few fathers and sons had as small a feeling of regard between them as Stephen O'Riordan and his father. Or then maybe, he thought, it would be a combination of blaming him about his father and blaming him about Kathleen, whom all of them had a very high regard for.

He turned off the road to avoid the village, and took the rough lane that would lead down to the strand. He could break out from there on to the road leading to his house.

Danny's little cottage was in darkness as he passed it, and he felt sure, with his hand on the latch of the door of his father's house, that Danny would be there before him.

CHAPTER TWENTY-FIVE

Danny was bending over the fire when, having raised the latch softly, he entered the kitchen. There was a bright fire burning. Stephen took a quick look around the kitchen and was surprised that it appeared alien to him. All the familiar things were there, the big dresser with its array of polished delf lined up like soldiers on parade, and the white-scrubbed table under the window and the table along the opposite wall with its load of pots and pans and milk-cans, and buckets of spring water. It was all the same and yet to Stephen it held no glimmer of welcome; the sight of it left him cold, and with a longing to be out of it again.

The noise he made closing the door made Danny look up from the fire.

His eyes widened as he remained in the crouching position, then he said 'Stephen!' in a subdued voice, and came over to him. He stood in front of him for a while and looked him up and down. For a moment Stephen was fearful of what he might say, remembering the way O'Flaherty had turned his head, but Danny put a hand on his arm, pressed it, and said, 'I'm awful glad to see you, so I am.' The words were warm and the feeling was sincere, but Stephen thought that there was something else in Danny's eyes which he could not quite gauge.

'How is he?' he asked in a low voice.

'He's bad, Stephen, I'm afraid,' said Danny.

'How bad?' Stephen asked.

'I don't know,' said Danny, 'but he doesn't look good to me. I'm expecting the doctor back again now any minute. He was here until seven and then he had to go over to a bad case in Leenane in the car, but said he'd be back no matter what time it was, and that I was to keep the old man warm with hot-water bottles.'

'I see,' said Stephen, and wondered why Danny of the transparent honesty was finding it hard to meet his eyes.

'Thomasheen's mother was here with him a lot,' Danny went on. 'But I sent her home about an hour ago to get some sleep and she'll be back again. The poor woman was very good. She hardly left the house at all since it happened.'

'How did it happen?' Stephen asked.

'Well, a few days after you left,' said Danny, going back to the fire and sitting on a chair, 'we were all surprised to

364

see the one that was here leaving for Clifden on the mail-car. She just went, that's all. And then last Saturday, Thomasheen's mother came into the house here for something, I don't know what, and the door was open, and in she walked, an' he was lyin' here stretched out in front a the fire. She thought he was dead, but she saw that his eyes were open and that he was lookin' at her, and movin' his mouth, but he didn't seem able to talk. She got help then and put him into the bed. He has been there since. I would have sent for you but I didn't know where you would be, and I didn't know whether I should or not, even if I did know where you were. How did you hear?'

'Michilin wrote to me,' said Stephen.

'Ah, that's right,' said Danny, keeping his head down.

'Do you think I ought to go back and see him?' Stephen asked.

'Why shouldn't you?' Danny asked in return, looking at him, and Stephen thought that there was a look of reproof in his glance.

'Maybe it'd make him worse to see me,' said Stephen.

'I don't think so,' said Danny. 'Maybe I'm wrong, but it seems to me that he's always tryin' to make your name with his lips whenever I go near him.'

'Oh,' said Stephen, and for the first time since he had heard it, the illness of his father seemed to become personal, and his tired mind said, My God, isn't it terrible that a son should be analysing himself this way with his father probably dying? and without another word, he turned and went through the parlour, and hesitated in front of his father's door. Then taking a firm grip on himself, he opened the door and entered.

He found himself looking into the staring eyes of his father.

It seemed to him that the head made a slight movement, and that a kind of a light came into the eyes. He went over and sat on the side of the bed. The room had been cleaned very well, and the most disturbing thing Stephen found about it was that the bedclothes covering and outlining the body of his father were without a crease in them, and that to Stephen was a horrible shout of the helplessness of the man beneath them.

His father's face had aged beyond anything that Stephen had imagined. The cheeks had fallen in and the temples were shadowed, and purple rings encircled his deeply sunken eyes. One arm and hand that lay outside the clothes was lifeless-looking, and the blue veins stood out like rivers in a plain when viewed from a mountain.

With an effort Stephen looked into his father's eyes.

He could make nothing of the look in them, except that he had a terrible feeling that his father was trying to talk with his eyes, and was putting the effort of his paralysed body into it. His lips were faintly moving, and once he managed to open them a little, but no sound came out of them except a breath that was held, and whistled as it came.

Christ, thought Stephen, this is terrible!

'Hello, Father,' said Stephen, and waited for an answer in his forgetfulness; and then rushing on again, 'I heard that you were sick so I came home to see you. Can't you talk at all?'

Again Stephen got the impression of a great struggle going on in the body of his father. He held his own breath as he sensed it. The struggle seemed to last for a long time, then a look of hopelessness came into his father's eyes. The lids dropped over them and shut them off.

Stephen thought then that maybe his father did not want to have him there at all, and that he was trying to tell him for God's sake to go, get out, and let him die in peace. He rose from the bed. The movement seemed to be communicated to the man, because his lids raised themselves swiftly, and the eyes seemed to look at Stephen with an appeal in them. Unsure of this, Stephen sank slowly to the bed again, and was certain that he saw a look of relief in the eyes of Martin.

That made Stephen think. His father was glad that he was there, and did not want him to go. Holy God, thought Stephen desperately, why must it be this way between a

366

father and a son? He looked at his father and his father was a complete stranger to him, and he felt a great sorrow as he would have felt for any stranger who was as helpless as this man in the bed. Whose fault was it? Stephen asked himself. Was I to blame altogether? He remembered the letter from his mother and the message she had in it about his father. Something on his mind, and Stephen was to try and understand. Stephen had tried to understand. He told himself now that he had done everything he possibly could in order to get to know his father. He had tried to open up a conversation on many occasions but all his attempts had proved unavailing against the wall of reserve and curtness which his father seemed to have raised around himself. Their conversations had never been of long duration and had never consisted of anything else except small talk about the farm or the hired hands or little things like that. The only times there had been any real feeling between them were the times they had been enraged.

What was the secret of the behaviour of this man in the bed, he wondered. Why should he have been such a drinker when he appeared to be so strong about everything else? He had never been cruel, Stephen granted him that. He had never hit Stephen except those two times which had burned themselves into his memory. He had been impersonally kind on many occasions, and looking back now, Stephen thought that he had really been stricken when Martha had died. All the goings-on after that could well have been a seeking after forgetfulness, and a loosening of morals which drink engendered. But he had been drinking before he had met Martha, and she had always hinted that Martin had done something which he wanted to forget. What could it be? Was that the thing, whatever it was, which had coloured his vision and made him draw a cloak over his soul? Stephen couldn't tell, and the more he thought, the more vapourish the whole thing seemed.

All that was concrete was that his father was a shell lying on a bed, who could not talk, and who, unless a miracle happened, would never talk again. What harm? Stephen thought; but if he could talk now, maybe we would have the first honest conversation of our lives, and things could be adjusted. But no knowledge or power that Stephen possessed now could do anything about it. It was too late for regrets, and too late for him to feel any deeper emotion than a kind of dull sadness that this poor creature on the bed should be so isolated and so utterly alone.

'Look, Father,' he said, 'the doctor will be coming soon again now and maybe he would be able to help you. You have had a stroke, you see, but people have had strokes before and they have got better, so maybe you will get better too.'

When he said that, Stephen thought that Martin's eyes seemed to shrink and he couldn't be sure, but he thought the head had shaken itself faintly. What will I take out of that? Stephen wondered. Is it that he doesn't want to get better? Something told him that that was a correct surmise, but then he might be imagining it all, even though the eyes of his father seemed to him to be eloquent pools of light. God, he thought, if he doesn't want to get better, what's the use of telling him he might? He would be better off dead anyhow. Stephen knew that he himself would prefer to be dead than to be paralysed in any part of him.

The bedroom door opened then and Danny came in, carrying two hot-water jars.

'I'll have to put these agin' 'm, Stephen,' he said. 'It's a couple a hours since we put the others in.'

They lifted the bedclothes and removed the still warm jars from Martin's feet and side, replacing them with the hot ones. Stephen was shocked with this sight of his father's body. He had never properly realized his own size and build, but in his eyes his father had always been a towering giant with great shoulders and muscular arms. The body of him now was just a great surge of big bones, loosely covered with flesh. Such decay would nearly bring the tears to your eyes. He felt that he would have to get away from him for a time to try and order his thoughts. Since he had heard from Michilin, he had given only passing thoughts to his father.

Kathleen and himself had been uppermost in his mind, but somehow now, their personal plight seemed very light to him, and one that did not matter terribly, because they had bodies and spirits capable of bearing what they had to bear and fighting where they would have to fight.

When they had him covered again and tucked up, Stephen bent over him and spoke.

'I'm going for a little while, now, Father,' he said, 'but I will be back.'

The eyes of his father remained without meaning for him.

He went out of the room in front of Danny and, reaching the kitchen, he stood in front of the fireplace and gazed into the heart of the burning coals.

Danny left the used jars on the table and turned to him.

'Well?' he asked.

'It's terrible,' he said.

'It's not nice,' said Danny. 'It makes you feel kinda queer, no matter what he was.'

'Yes,' said Stephen, 'it makes you think.'

Danny was silent for a time, and again Stephen sensed a tenseness in the air, as if Danny, too, were trying, as his father had been, to say something that he could not express.

Finally he seemed to find the words for it.

'How did you come?' he asked.

'I walked from Clifden,' said Stephen.

'Did you meet anybody?' Danny asked.

'One or two,' said Stephen.

'Were you talking to them?' Danny went on.

'No,' said Stephen, wondering about this catechism. 'O'Flaherty didn't salute me though.' He turned to face Danny then. 'Does that mean anything?'

Danny looked into his eyes.

Jesus, Mary, and Joseph, he thought with a kind of a desperate prayer, he doesn't know anything about it; and he could feel his heart slowing down, and dropping in his chest. No, don't let it be me, he thought, sweet God, don't let it be me. But it had to be he. As carefully as if he was walking on hot coals, he felt for words.

'Stephen,' he said, 'about you and Kathleen . . .'

'Oh,' said Stephen, walking over to the table to face the window, 'so you know about that?'

'Yes,' said Danny, wishing with every bit of him that that was all he knew. 'I know about that.'

'Well?' Stephen asked, keeping his back turned to him.

'Stephen,' said Danny desperately, 'didn't you read the paper this week? Wasn't there nothin' in the paper this week in the Connemara Notes thing?'

Stephen turned to him surprised.

'No,' he said, 'I didn't see it. The bus I came out on would only have been bringing them to the shops in Clifden then. And I didn't wait in Clifden at all.'

There was a deadly silence with Danny staring at him, and Stephen thought that there was a look of misery and loathing in his eyes. He came closer to Danny then.

'Danny,' he said, 'what is it? What's up?'

'Ah, Christ above, Stephen,' said Danny, 'why in the name a God didn't yeh know? Why do I have t' tell yeh? What were yeh doin' that yeh didn't hear it?'

Stephen felt his breath coming quickly.

'Look, Danny,' he said, 'what is it? What in the name of God should I know?'

'Stephen,' said Danny, and his voice was loud and mechanical, 'didn't you know that Kathleen Finnerty was buried today in Ourish Island?'

Stephen thought that the world had stopped. He could hear the clock ticking and a sod of turf falling from the fire, but he couldn't hear properly what Danny was saying.

'What did you say, Danny?' he asked, coming closer to him, and catching his arm with his hand.

There were tears of rage and pity and self-loathing in Danny's eyes.

He lowered his voice to its normal tone.

'I'm telling you, Stephen,' he articulated slowly, 'that Kathleen Finnerty was buried today on Ourish Island.'

'No!' Stephen shouted at him. 'No!' And he raised a heavy arm in the air. Danny thought he was going to strike him, and he was conscious of the fierce pain in the arm which Stephen was squeezing to pulp between his fingers. He was suddenly afraid.

'Stephen!' he shouted, gazing fixedly into the raging eyes looking into his own. Gradually he saw the look of blankness leaving them, and another look of terribly pained concentration taking their place. Both Stephen's arms fell to his side.

'Look, Stephen,' said Danny, 'you better sit down,' and he moved, and taking a chair from the table, placed it behind him. Stephen sat down on it slowly.

Danny watched him closely. He remained exactly as he was for a long time, then he licked his dry lips with a dry tongue and let his eyes hold Danny's.

'Tell me, Danny,' he said.

Danny sat on the other chair.

'Stephen,' he said, 'I'd rather be anywhere else in the world now than here at this fire talkin' t' you. I couldn't believe that you hadn't heard somehow.'

'I was at sea,' said Stephen. 'I probably left for the bus before the post, or I might have known. Go on, Danny, for God's sake tell me!'

'Tuesday mornin' last, one a the Joyces was goin' up be the Dead Lake. I don't know what took him there or why or what or nothin'. But he went over, and looked into it, and well, he saw her there.'

'You mean,' said Stephen slowly, 'that she was drowned in the Dead Lake?'

'That's what I'm tryin' t' tell yeh, Stephen,' said Danny. 'Joyce found her floatin' there in the Dead Lake and she was dead, and drowned. That was last Tuesday Stephen. They had an inquest yesterday back in the schoolhouse, and they said that she had drowned herself while she was of unsound mind.'

'No! No!' said Stephen, rising to his feet and shouting. 'That's not true, Danny, do you hear? That couldn't be true, I tell you!'

'Stephen,' said Danny, also rising to his feet, 'I'm only

tellin' yeh what happened. She was goin' t' have a baby, y' see, and they said on account a that, that was why she did it.'

'But, God, Danny,' said Stephen urgently, 'that's not true!'

'Stephen, I don't believe it either that Kathleen Finnerty was the kind of a girl to throw herself into the Dead Lake. I don't know why or how it happened. All I'm doin' is tellin' you that that's the way it is, and when the doctor at the inquest told them that she was goin' to have . . . that she was that way, they brought in that verdict, that's what I'm tellin' you. That was the Wednesday, and she was buried today.'

'Oh, my God!' said Stephen, sinking down on the chair again with his head in his two hands.

Danny looked at him, and decided that there was nothing he could do or say. What in the name a God could he say or do, that wouldn't be makin' things worse than they were now? The whole thing was so appalling that there just wasn't anythin' you could do or say.

Stephen rose after a while, and without looking at Danny, he turned and went up to what had always been his room. The door closed behind him and Danny was left staring at it. If only, he thought, I was a holy man that could think of somethin' comfortin', but I'm not even a good prayerer. The only thing he could think of doing was to look at up the ceiling and say, 'Well, Martha O'Riordan, if you are anywhere about now, do somethin' for him, or fix somethin' up where you are, because this is too much for me altogether, or for any other man.'

Stephen threw himself on the bed in the dark room.

It was a long time before he could think. The top of his head seemed to have been pressed with irresistible force on to his brain, and he could think of nothing but a brilliant bursting light that was exploding in front of his eyes. Eventually his eyes saw the darkness.

He went over the story again in his mind to make sure that he had it right. What was it now? That Joyce while going by the Dead Lake on a Tuesday morning had looked into it and seen the body of Kathleen Finnerty in the water. That they had taken her out and she was dead. That was simple enough if you reduced it to fundamentals. What happened next? There was an inquest on Tuesday and the doctor, seeing what was wrong with her, had told them, and they had said that she had drowned herself whilst her mind was unsound. That was the logical sequence. Then the next day they had buried her in Ourish Island, deep, deep in the yellow sand where they had laid his mother.

So Kathleen was dead. She had thrown herself into the black waters of the lake they had loved, and the water had poured into her mouth until she had drowned and died.

Kathleen was dead. Slowly the implication began to dawn on him of what that meant, as it affected himself. This girl that he had found how long ago? Not so long. Wasn't it not so long ago that they had been going back to Thomasheen's hooley and he had left her home and he had kissed her, and found then that something new had come into his life, and something that was as complete as a mountain with purple heather on it, or a river with salmon in it, or a boat with a tall sail on it, or a currach with the four oars on it and two strong men pulling at the water? This had been Kathleen to him. She was the height of his ambition. Now his writing would mean something after all, the big body given to him by nature would find its place in the scheme of things, apart from its pulling oars or lifting hayforks, or lifting a plough over a stone, or pulling reluctant hay from a stack to feed the animals, or lifting a twelve-pound salmon on the end of a rod.

He no longer belonged to himself. The room which he had always owned for his very own became peopled with the images of a woman in different moods – a woman who was smiling, with her body outlined against the sky, laughing as she ran to throw herself on the grass beside the waters of the lake that had claimed her, looking at him with smouldering eyes as he ran his heavy fingers through the electric beauty of her hair, who kissed him fiercely, and said 'I don't want to be alive when you are dead; when we are old I want to die first, so that I will not be left alone to mourn you.' You have your wish now, Kathleen, but not as you had planned it.

You laughed when you talked about the house you would have, and the order that would reign in it, how I would have to remove my heavy boots before I came into the kitchen, and get into slippers even if all the neighbours were laughing at me. And you would have a lot of children and you would be very severe and stern with them one day and spoil them hopelessly the next day, and you would give them hundreds of toys for Christmas since you had never known any yourself. You would walk around London Town with your husband and glare at the girls when they stopped to stare at the fine husband you had, and wondered where that scrawny bit of a girl got a big man like him. You had skipped all that, Kathleen. You had got your wish all right, but you had got it long before the time you had wanted it.

What have I left now? he wondered. Nothing. I lost my mother and I thought the world had come to an end. Now Kathleen is dead and I know the world has come to an end. There was ambition before she came. There would be ambition again if he was not to die too, but it would be like the cold ashes on a hearthstone. Of what use to meet people like Bishop and Curly and Pat and Mike and Gabriel and Taimin, if you were not to know about them too? Of what use to look at them and see what they were made of and why they moved and talked and felt as they did, if you could not have the one whom you could tell about them?

Would a fish out of a river be sweeter because you couldn't know about it, or a bird dropping from the vault of the sky? Did it matter any longer that an old paralysed man who was my father was dying and that I had seen for the first time that there was an affinity between us which I might have helped to destroy? Did it matter any longer if the moon shone or the stars or the sun, if they were to look at a world as empty as the shell of a decayed turnip?

Oh God, he groaned and, turning, buried his face in the pillow of the bed.

There was nothing you could think of that hadn't become

374

pale, nothing that hadn't lost its richness and its taste and its smell and its colour. Why wasn't there some sort of spirit between Heaven and earth that would have told you before you put your foot on a trawler on a Tuesday morning that your girl Kathleen had been found drowned in a dark Connemara lake? How was it that I didn't feel on Monday that there was something wrong? Why should I have been hauling nets or riding the bosom of a ruffled ocean when you were dying and being dead and being buried and no feeling at all come over me to tell me?

He sat on the edge of the bed and rubbed his hair with his two hands.

There was no thought left that you could plumb, nothing else that you could say to yourself that you wouldn't be repeating, except this – and suddenly he looked into the darkness with intent eyes and gripped the bed with his hands – that Kathleen Finnerty did not drown herself, that Kathleen Finnerty would not have drowned herself if she had lived to be a thousand years old, that the men who had said so at an inquest conducted by the State were a crowd of liars, maybe honest liars, who had wanted her to have a Christian burial.

He rose to his feet. His teeth were clenched tightly together. He opened the door and went into the kitchen.

Danny was standing in almost the same spot where he had been when he stared at the closed door.

Stephen didn't remember seeing him there. He made directly for the kitchen door and swung it open.

Danny came over to him quickly.

'Stephen!' he said urgently. 'Where are you going, Stephen?'

The other looked at him with sightless eyes.

'No,' he said through clenched teeth, 'she did not!' and then he walked into the darkness.

'Stephen! Stephen!' Danny called from the door, but was answered only by the sound of determined footsteps.

He remained at the door for a while. Where, he wondered, is he going? What in the name of God is working in his head at all? He was disturbed, unsure, and confused. The workings of his ordered mind and life had never imagined in their most perturbed moments events such as these. He would leave the house and follow him if the old man wasn't there, waiting to die, with nobody in sight or sound. And Michilin. Where was Michilin? He had haunted the place for the last two days to know if he had come. He had written to Stephen on Wednesday, but he had expected him sooner. Even the unconquerable Michilin had looked old and tired and beaten.

Danny was a long time at the door before he came in and left it opened behind him, the yellow lamp carving a cavern of light in the moon-riddled blackness.

CHAPTER TWENTY-SIX

There was a strong wind driving dark clouds across the face of the moon. The night was never really dark, because the clouds were small, and when one part of the land would be buried in darkness, all around it would be lighted by the unobscured moon. If you looked into the sky you would imagine that the moon was moving through the heavens at great speed.

Stephen did not notice the wind or the clouds or the moon or the night.

His feet automatically took him towards Carnmore and ghosts walked beside him. Kathleen had taken her place beside his mother in his mind, and at times he did not know which of them he was thinking about. They had both died suddenly when he had least expected it, the death of his mother being less sudden but not less unexpected. Sometimes he thought he was a boy who walked this road, with his short trousers and his bare feet, and his mother stretching a hand now and again to ruffle his hair and laugh loudly at something he had said. Then he would be grown and Kathleen would be beside him.

The nearer he approached the Dead Lake, the farther

away did the shape of his mother go from his mind, and Kathleen walked beside him constantly. He did not have to look around and see her, but he could feel the warmth of her without turning his head. Her hand was through his arm and the other hand was resting on the same arm, and he could feel the soft bulk of her breast pressing against him. If he looked around he could see her eyes laughing at him on a level with his shoulder, and the blue-whites of her pupils looking up at him solemnly or jokingly or tearfully or hurtfully or worriedly, and each look was a different occasion when she laughed or cried or listened or lectured him about different things.

As he turned off the road and headed for the lake he seemed to leave him and he walked alone. He could hear his boots hitting the stones of the rough road. He could hear a seagull screech high in the wind. He could hear the sea beating, with a magnified roar, as it hurled itself at the cliff below the Arch.

All these things he could hear, but not now the sound of her clothes swishing as she walked beside him, or the warm feel of her breath on his cheek as she spoke up towards him. The nearer he came to the lake the farther away she seemed to go, a frightened phantom, weaving fearfully from the place where she had died.

Stephen's footsteps slowed themselves as he came nearer to it. Something inside himself, or was it outside himself? said No, don't go near this place; turn back and let it be in your memory as it was, and not as it will seem to you now; turn back, turn back. He halted in the middle of the road and looked to his right. He saw the waters of it gleaming in the moonlight and turned automatically towards it, and the nearer he got the quicker he walked, until he had arrived, and was standing on the high bank looking down at it, his breath coming in short gasps and his throat tightening.

Why?

Why?

Why?

She had not liked it as much as he had. Sometimes she had

377

even been fearful of it. Was that because of the old story, the old silly made-up story, of a crazy man and his wife, or was it because something inside of her had told her that some day . . . ?

What did she think of as the water held her for a moment, and then soaked her clothes to her body with greedy fingers? What was she thinking of as she opened her mouth and the dark terrifying waters poured into her lungs? Was it of himself she was thinking, or had terror encompassed her soul and her mind, so that she thought of nothing until the peaceful lassitude of the murderous waters wrapped her round?

He sat down on the grass and let his feet dangle over the water.

I must become reasonable, he thought. I must work all this thing out the way it happened. It is only that way that I will become sane and ordered again. He dropped his aching head in his hands and tried to compose his thoughts.

We will take first things first.

We will start with what men say.

What do men say?

Men said, in solemn conclave, that Kathleen Finnerty was going to have a baby, and because that was such a horrifying, shameful, and unbearable thought, she had come to the Dead Lake, where she had so often met the man who was responsible, although nobody knew for sure, and in a fit of remorse she had drowned herself there.

He knew Kathleen.

Would she do that?

Kathleen found she would have a baby, and it would not have been a shameful thing to her. No, it would not, because she knew that she loved Stephen O'Riordan and that he loved her. She would have been glad. The thought of what the neighbours would think would weigh no more with her than it did with him, which fact she knew very well. It was happening every day in Connemara. It was happening every day all over the world that people had given rein to love without thought of consequence. Then that had happened, and if everybody that it happened to thought it such a shame-

378

ful thing that they would have to kill themselves, there would be millions of suicides every day. So it was not shameful, and that would be the only reason she would have for doing it.

Suppose she had thought so?

She came down here at night, when the people were asleep, not because it was the place where she and Stephen had met so often, where she could recapture memories, and think of the day when memories would be realities: she had come down, and she had looked at the dark waters, of which she had ever been fearful, and she said, I can't put up with this shame that's on me. I will drown myself in the lake because I can't go on. So she had jumped into the water.

What happened then?

She was an excellent swimmer.

She had told him about the indoor swimming baths in London where she had often gone, of the green chlorinated water that tasted so terrible when it got into your mouth, of the black-painted swimming-lines on the bottom of the bath, of the cubicles where you undressed, and the metal key which you wore around your wrist.

So she had thrown herself into the water and kept her hands close to her sides, had she, lest some last reflexes would force her to swim to save her life?

No, he said to himself, slowly and emphatically, Kathleen Finnerty did not drown herself, because she wasn't the kind of girl to drown herself, and because she had so much to live for, and because she had always liked doing things for people, and if it was only for that reason, she would have liked to remain alive.

If she didn't drown herself, what happened?

Slowly the blood mounted in Stephen's head and he felt his pulses hammering. I'll tell you, he said! Kathleen Finnerty didn't drown herself, so somebody else must have drowned Kathleen Finnerty.

For a time he couldn't think any more as the possibility, no, the certainty, beat its way into his brain.

He remembered the letter from Michilin, and the one

sentence in it which had sent him rushing from his bed and the town of Galway like a fearful mother. Michilin had said that Malachai knew.

Malachai!

There could be no other answer.

Malachai, who hated Stephen. Malachai, who hated everybody. Malachai, who was a cruel and primitive man. Malachai, who, people said, must have a screw loose somewhere or he wouldn't be as different to normal people as he was. Malachai, who would regard Kathleen's lapse as a real shame, that would start people talking about him, Malachai. Malachai, who seemed to be so sensitive about what the people were saying about him, and at the same time such a setter-aside of what the people thought. Malachai had done this thing. Malachai had killed his sister as sure as there was a God up in Heaven, and if he had done so, then he, Stephen O'Riordan, would kill Malachai as sure as he was standing up on the bank of the Dead Lake, with his blood hammering, and a great rage of sorrow and anger in every bit of him.

As clearly as if he were looking at it on a screen, as he had seen in the picture-house, he saw it happening.

Sure, Kathleen had come to the Dead Lake, but she had come to it so that she could get away by herself to the place where both of them had always gone to get away by themselves. This time she had not been alone, because Malachai had come after her. What had happened in the house, what Malachai had said to her when he had found out, how he had found out, all these things flashed through his mind in quick succession, formless but real and terrifying. Perhaps she had been afraid, and that was why she had fled to the Dead Lake. Perhaps she had, at last, seen something in the eyes of her brother and she knew that her days of standing up to him were numbered. Perhaps she remembered too vividly the days of their youth when Malachai had made such a business of drowning the kittens.

She had come to the lake. There would have been a moon shining then too.

She would not have known that her brother followed

behind her, because Malachai was like an animal that could stalk a bird or a mouse or a fish with stealth acquired from long practice.

She looked around and there was her brother behind her with this thing in his eyes.

Did she scream?

Did she shout?

No, she wouldn't shout. Being who she was, she would have prepared to fight and to sell her life very dearly.

Had he spoken to her? Had he addressed her and told her that she was a common bitch who had disgraced the bones of her dead father?

There couldn't have been much of a struggle or the doctor would have seen the marks on her body.

No. Malachai had pulled her to him with one hand and had hit her on the temple with a closed fist. That would have been enough. Then he would have raised her in the air, and with a cry of fury he would have flung her far out, as he would do with something loathsome.

Malachai!

Malachai!

Malachai!

The last time Stephen said the name aloud to the night, and he felt tears forcing their way through his eyes, not tears of sorrow, because he couldn't feel sorrowful then, but tears of anger and hopelessness that she had been alone when she should not have been alone. Where was Michilin? Stephen had told him to keep an eye on her. Where was the great poacher Michilin, who could walk in the night anywhere as if he were wearing the fur of a silver fox nailed to his boot-soles?

Somewhere, some time, there would be an explanation from Michilin.

Not now, because first things came first. And the first thing would be Malachai, even if you had to go deep in hell to find him.

Something percolated through the hammering thoughts of Stephen's mind. It was like a light touch on his shoulder, or a finger touching him gently on the back of his neck. It was an effort to pull himself back to his surroundings, but he did so, and remained as still as an otter by the side of a stream.

There was something behind him.

He thought furiously for a moment of what he would do.

He turned quickly with his whole body, jumping around on the balls of his feet.

Malachai Finnerty was behind him, towering against the sky, his two arms raised high in the air and the moonlight glinting on the wet rock which he was clutching in his hands.

Stephen looked into his eyes.

Before the rock flew towards him, in that split second, Stephen knew that he was right, and that Malachai was the murderer of his sister. And as their eyes clashed, Stephen knew that Malachai knew that Stephen knew. There was more than hatred and a great rage in the eyes of Malachai. There was a kind of terror and a sadness and also there was a glint of fear.

If it hadn't been for that glint of fear the night might have ended differently. Because Stephen knew that no man would do what Malachai had done unless he were more than mad, and if Malachai had been mad, he would still be mad, and what he had done would have made no more impression on his soul than would the eating of his dinner.

But Malachai was afraid.

To Stephen, that said that Malachai was not mad, that what Malachai had done he had done cold-bloodedly, as you would wring the neck of a chicken or drown a kitten in a calm pond.

The heavy rock brushed his dodging shoulder and, deflected, dropped with a great splash into the lake. With a great splash, such as a body would make when it was hurtling towards its suffocation.

For a few seconds they stared at one another and they might have been in another age, in a different world. The clothes they wore were merely the trappings of civilization. Their fast-beating hearts were the same as the hearts that had beaten just as fast behind the skin-covered torso of the primitive man.

Their bodies clashed like the beating of a great drum.

Over Stephen's mind there came a veil, and what happened after that clash was just a confused jumble in his mind. He felt himself go cold, and the creeping hatred of Malachai came into his heart, but that hatred was tempered by many other emotions, of which the predominant one was that this man had deprived him of Kathleen, and when he struck he struck with all the great emptiness of the years ahead stretching like a grass-grown road into a barren wilderness.

They clutched one another for a few moments, and they breathed like prehistoric beasts on one another's face, but no word was spoken because what was between them didn't need any words.

There were several breaks in the fight that followed which Stephen remembered. He didn't remember getting hurt himself then, although he must have, because he could hear his own agonised groans when a fist or a boot or an elbow belonging to Malachai landed on his body, or sank into his flesh. Once he felt Malachai's nails tearing their way down his cheek. He used his arms and his fists and his head and his knees to batter his enemy. There came a pause when he stood over him, and Malachai was lying on the ground.

Stephen stood back then, not out of pity for Malachai, but to gain a breathing spell and to allow one to his enemy, so that the fight could go on.

Malachai raised himself slowly to his knees as if in great pain, and then he suddenly straightened, and he ran.

Stephen followed him.

Malachai didn't pause when he came to the road, but sped across it and headed towards the sea and the Arch in the break of the land.

Stephen followed him.

Arrived there, Malachai paused and turned around.

Even to Stephen's confused mind the reason was clear, that Malachai wanted him close to the cliff, so that by some means he could get him over it and look at his body being battered by the waves against the pointed rocks.

He didn't care, because he was not afraid to die, and he closed again with Malachai.

What happened after that was confused too. He remembered once being held on the ground with sinewy hands at his throat and the feeling of the spray drenching his hair held out over space. How he got out of that he did not know, but he must have risen to his feet and fought again.

He must have fought until there was no more fight to fight, because Malachai was limp in his hands like a poisoned dog.

The next thing Stephen remembered was himself holding the body of Malachai high in the air at the full reach of his arms, as he had seen Malachai holding the body of Kathleen in his own, and hurling him over the cliff. There had been a second when reason had returned to him, and something or somebody had said, You must not do this, but the thought of dark hair floating on the waters of a lake and sightless eyes turned to the sky with the water flowing out of them, gave the heave to his body and the push to his arms, and he remembered seeing Malachai turning slowly two times in the air, before the sound of his hitting the rocks was muffled by the pounding waves. The moon was shining brightly, and he had once seen the brass stud in the front of Malachai's shirt glinting.

His mind became a dead thing then, and it was some time before he turned and dragged his feet after him as he walked back the way he had come.

If his mind had been functioning he would have seen the two men who were running towards him from behind. He would have heard the shout that one of them emitted as he stood in the moonlight with the body of Malachai held high in the air. His mind was shut to all those things and he neither saw nor heard.

The lake was no longer of interest to him and he walked past it.

It was Jack and Tim Finnerty who had stood and watched the death of their brother. They were too far away to do anything and it was the younger Tim who had shouted, in the hope of averting what was happening in front of his petrified eyes.

Horror held them in its grasp for a long time. Stephen had turned and walked away, and was well down the road when they came to themselves and silently rushed over to the Arch.

They went to their knees and looked over. The moon was hidden behind a bank of cloud and they waited until it would shake itself free.

They had been worried about Malachai and when he had come out that night they had followed him.

The Finnerty house for the past week had been a place of hidden and open emotions, and terrible things which were left unspoken.

It was Nora who had found out about Kathleen. Being so close herself to pregnancy, she it was who had found a reason for Kathleen's sudden sicknesses, lassitude, and changing appearance. Tim had wished that she had kept her big mouth shut and had told her so afterwards whilst he was beating her soundly. But Nora had never liked Kathleen, even when she herself was lazing and watching Kathleen doing all her work.

Nora it was who had told Malachai.

Malachai had risen from his chair with a terrible blackness in his face.

'Is this true!?' he had asked Kathleen.

Kathleen had looked at him.

'Yes,' she said quietly, 'it is true, but we will be married as soon as I get out of this house, and I'm going out of this house by next Tuesday.'

Malachai hadn't said another word.

He put on his hat and walked out, leaving more feeling behind him in the kitchen than if he had delivered himself of a long tirade.

Jack had looked at Kathleen with grim eyes, and had followed his brother.

Tim, who was the one of them to feel less deeply about these things, had looked at his wife and said:

385

'Come on up to the room, I want to talk to you.'

And Nora had looked at him with apprehensive eyes.

The house had been unbearable after that, until the Monday night. Malachai had spoken to none of them.

When he was in the house he just looked at Kathleen all the time.

Once she had burst out with a 'Stop looking at me like that, can't you! If you have anything to say, say it!'

He just kept looking at her until even Tim felt a cold chill running up and down his spine.

Kathleen had gone out on the Monday night and she had never come home. Malachai had gone out shortly after her with the gun under his arm as usual, and he had come back with the gun under his arm.

It was very late when Tim had ventured to say, 'I wonder what's keeping Kathleen?'

Malachai looked at him and said, 'Maybe she's not coming back,' and Tim had thought that there were terrible things in his face, and Malachai had gone to bed. Tim thought, for the first time, that maybe Malachai wasn't all right in the head.

Then had come the news the next morning of the finding of his sister's body, and after the first shock all of them avoided one another's eyes.

They spoke little at the inquest, just to say that they had all gone to bed early on the Monday night, and hadn't known about Kathleen's all-night absence until they awakened in the morning. No, none of them had left the house all night. Their tacit cloaking of Malachai's going-out was in itself an admission of what they felt, but what none of them dared put into words.

Ever since, they had been disturbed by the behaviour of their brother.

Tim and Jack had taken to following him at nights. Sometimes he walked and walked and that was all. Sometimes he would throw himself on the heather and wild inhuman sobbing would be carried to their ears on the night air.

They followed him tonight, and were afraid when they

saw him walking towards the lake where Kathleen had been drowned. But the land leading to the lake was very open, and they were afraid of Malachai seeing them, so they stayed far, far, behind him.

We shouldn't have stayed so far behind, said Tim to himself, as a shaft of moonlight showed the body, darker than the rocks, rising and falling and disappearing under the white-foaming waves.

Jack rose to his feet and turned slowly to look along the road Stephen had taken.

'Come on,' he said.

'No,' said Tim with a strangled cry. 'Hasn't there been enough?'

'Come on!' shouted Jack.

Tim looked at him, and then looked down at the body of his brother. There is no other way, he thought, there is probably no other way.

'All right,' he said, rising to his feet.

They padded along the road which Stephen had taken.

CHAPTER TWENTY-SEVEN

Danny rose from beside the bed where he had been sitting when he heard the kitchen door opening, and looking at Martin in a sort of explanation, he hurried down.

He halted, petrified, when he saw Stephen looking into the fire.

The side of his face which Danny could see was torn and bleeding. The left sleeve was almost completely torn away from the coat. There were ugly bruises on his face and his hands were bloody.

He approached Stephen quietly.

'Where were you, Stephen?' he asked.

Stephen looked at him, but it was some time before his eyes lost their blankness.

'I was out,' he said.

Suddenly he felt a great weariness coming over him and he might have fallen, if his hand had not automatically found the back of the chair. He sank into it, with his head drooping.

Danny felt that something was terribly wrong, but he also felt that he should not speak or ask questions. All sorts of possibilities, one worse than another, chased themselves through his mind, but he was afraid to formulate them properly.

'The doctor hasn't come yet,' he said.

Stephen nodded.

'I wouldn't be sure,' said Danny, 'but I think that he is not as bad as he was. Just something a little better I see in him.'

Stephen nodded again.

'I think maybe,' said Danny, 'that it was the sight of you that did it. Maybe you ought to go up and see him again.'

Stephen raised his head and looked at him. He gave a shrug of his shoulders to indicate the state he was in.

'That's all right,' said Danny. 'I'll go first and pull back the lamp so that it will be behind yeh, and he won't notice nothin'.'

With an effort Stephen raised himself, and followed Danny out of the kitchen, striving to bring his mind back to reality, and never quite succeeding.

Danny entered the room first and shifted the lamp from the small table beside the bed, and put it on the ledge of the window, shading the light with his own body until Stephen had entered and stood behind the bed. The lamp behind him threw a gigantic shadow of him on the wall. Stephen looked at his father.

Even to his mind it seemed to him that a change had come over the face looking up at him since he had left before. The eyes seemed to be clearer, and the hand on the coverlet was moving, the fingers crooking and uncrooking a fraction of an inch, and the gleaming eyes seemed to be directing his attention to this.

Stephen was without words. It seemed to him that he was no longer part of his own body; that he himself was floating around in his mind, separated from his frame; and that he was looking at a person called Stephen O'Riordan, who was passing through a dream that was as unreal as a story about fairies which he had heard from his mother.

The things that had happened to this Stephen could not be real. Maybe he had never left Connemara at all. Maybe he had never been born and this was a sort of fantastic nightmare. It could never have been he who had gone in a bus to Galway with his pulses flushed like a child on its first visit to the zoo. Was it he who had placed himself on a trawler in Galway Bay, had brought him back to Connemara again, had told of drownings and suicides and murders, and put into his vision a body turning slowly with the moonlight glinting on a brass stud, or was it a figment of his imagination?

Was it really he himself who was looking down at this strange man in the bed with the gleaming eyes, and if it were he, what in the name of God was he doing here at all?

This man is my father, something said to him, and a rush of memories tore at his aching brain: this man who had never been a happy man, who had closed himself up like an oyster in a shell, afraid of something that would hurt him from outside, when all the time he was being lacerated with a memory.

What kind of memory could that have been? and with fear Stephen noticed that his mind had thrown off its outside influences again, and become its hated analytical entity.

He tried to, but could not stop it following this thought to a conclusion.

Martin O'Riordan had been in America, in New York, when he was a young man, and one day he had come home and he had a mysterious source of wealth. According to his mother, Martin O'Riordan had been working as a barman. Where had his money come from? Why was he always afraid? Stephen tried to stop himself thinking this way, tried to think of anything else at all, but any other avenue he explored sent him back again with feelings of hatred or sorrow or horror, and he had to go on with this.

Would it have happened like this? Was the son like the father? Was he, Stephen O'Riordan, a chip off the old block. Suppose his father had been in the bar this night in New York, and it had been a dark night outside with a heavy mist rolling up from the wide river. The place would have been dimly lighted with gas then, because this was a long time ago before that American succeeded in putting the light into a glass bottle.

Would a man have come in to his father for a drink or two then? What kind of man would he have been – small, or big and rough with a beard maybe? No, he would be small, and hearty and jolly and innocent, and he would have shown his father a large roll of bills which he had got for something. What? Anything at all, but something. And maybe his father had said, 'You better hide that, and not be showing it around.' And had the man departed to his hotel or where-ever he was going, and had Martin O'Riordan followed him?

Would this have happened near the river? Most pubs seemed to be near a river or a sea or a canal. Stephen saw a picture of a small man walking along whistling maybe, and the mist wrapping him around, and cloaking the man who followed him with long steps and stealthy ones, which he had learned from nature, because he had often in his youth followed sheep on a Connemara hillside.

A blow, a stifled cry, a deadly pause, and then the splash of something falling into the river. A man dead, unnoticed in the teeming millions. Another man left on the side looking at the water, trying to pierce its mist-swirling depths. With regret in his heart and a great fear, and the memory of a face looking into his own with horror-stricken eyes, and a look of wonder that any man could do this to him for the sake of some bits of paper printed at little cost by slaves.

This thought took hold of Stephen and he found himself shaking. Fiercely he searched the eyes of the man beneath him. He wanted to catch him by the shoulders and shake him into talk, to shout at him, Is this thing true that has come to me now? Is this how it was? Was it the memory of a dead face that haunted you all those years, that made you cold to your son in case you would one day see the same look in his eyes too, and know that you had handed down to him the brand which you carried yourself? He wanted to shake him and shout at him and make him say that this thing was not true, because if it were true that it so happened, then he, Stephen O'Riordan, was a murderer, because when he threw the body of a man over a cliff so that it turned twice slowly in its descent, he did not do this because he really loved his girl who had died, but because there was something inside of him that made him want to kill, a fester that would not have him lower his arms when he should have done. This would make him a murderer, who had killed because he had wanted to kill to assuage an emotion. Was this true? he shouted silently at the man in the bed. Was this true? he shouted silently and savagely.

Stephen shivered and sat on the edge of the bed. God, he thought, what is to become of me at all, at all? What am I, or where am I, or who is there left that will be with me? Can I go through life too, haunted by the memory of black hair floating on water and a body turning over twice casually before it squelches on sharp rocks? Am I to make a murderer of my father in order to fit my own ego?

He rose to his feet slowly, and forced words out of his mouth. He could not make himself smile, and he knew that he would find it hard ever to smile again.

'I have to go out for a little while now,' he said, 'but I will be back.' And to his amazement the head on the pillow nodded once and a look of something came into the eyes which Stephen was too tired to read. He walked out of the room quickly. Danny followed him.

Stephen turned in the kitchen and looked at Danny.

Danny thought he had never seen anyone in his whole life with such a look of inexpressible weariness and sorrow on his face.

'Danny,' he asked, and his eyes were burning, 'how did Kathleen Finnerty die?'

391

'Kathleen Finnerty,' said Danny firmly, 'did not drown herself. I think that Malachai Finnerty did that for her, and I'm not the only one that says that.'

'That's what happened, Danny,' said Stephen. 'Tonight I met Malachai. We fought and Malachai is dead.'

'Sweet God!' ejaculated Danny, and felt himself shrinking, because of all the possibilities that came into his head, this had not been one. A blanket seemed to come down on the world for him. Stephen was looking at him all the time, watching his reactions, waiting for him to speak.

Danny spoke.

'That's not good,' said Danny. 'One murder should not breed another one, and no man should take the law into his hands. But if it had to be you or him – that's the way it was, isn't it?'

'I think he would have killed me,' said Stephen, after thought.

'No man can blame you so,' said Danny.

'No,' said Stephen bitterly, 'no man can blame me except myself. And maybe there was a time when I could have stopped.'

Danny couldn't find anything else to say.

'I want to see Michilin,' said Stephen. 'I want to ask him a question, and then I'll call at the post-office and I will ring the Guards and I will tell them what has happened.'

'Are you sure that is the best thing?' Danny asked.

'There is no other way,' Stephen answered.

'They won't come over for you until the mornin',' said Danny, and wondered if this could be himself talking so quiet-like about a thing that should have the life frightened out of him, and even as it was, he could feel his heart sinking like the lead weight at the end of a fishing line. 'I'd stay with himself inside for as long as you can. He seems to like having you there with him.'

'I won't be too long,' said Stephen, and walked with the drag and pace of a very old man to the door.

If only, he thought, opening it, I weren't so tired. If only I could lie down somewhere for an hour even, and sleep away this nightmare feeling that is on me. If only I could have slept before I came, if only I could ever sleep again without dreaming.

Danny stopped him at the door.

'Stephen,' he said, and there was a new fear in his eyes, 'keep away from the Finnertys!'

'I will,' said Stephen, and left the house behind him.

He turned up the road.

Where the road from Stephen's house joined the main road, the two Finnertys crouched behind the wall. They had been unable to catch up with Stephen when he had left the lake, so they had hidden where they could watch the house and hope for him to emerge again; or if he didn't emerge for a hundred years, Jack Finnerty would have waited until he did, holding his weaker brother to his side by force.

He nodded now with satisfaction, when he recognized the figure walking slowly towards them.

'We will wait,' he whispered, 'to see what road he takes and then we will get ahead of him.'

Tim nodded.

They watched silently, holding their breath.

Stephen came closer to them and turned off to the right on the road leading to Crigaun. They gave him plenty of time, and then they pulled back from the road and circled away in a crouching run. The road came out in a great loop to avoid a low hill that had blocked its path, so they got behind this and ran faster. Where the road came around the far side of the hill and turned away again, they took up their position beside the wall, sheltered by overhanging blackberry bushes.

Stephen could not get speed into his footsteps no matter how he tried. Why was he going to see Michilin? Because Michilin was the only man he had ever talked to properly, and the only man who with his shrewd mind might know more about him than he knew himself. He would tell Michilin and he would see what Michilin had to say. Michilin would not lie to him. He was certain of that. And even if he did lie, Stephen would be able to see his face. Also he would like to ask him why he had let that happen to Kathleen, and if he had written or wired or what had he done to let Stephen know that it had happened.

The shades of the dead did not walk beside him now, nor the near memories of them. They seemed as if they had been gone a thousand years, and left in their place a great loneliness which was overwhelming him, so that he found it hard to breathe. There was no daylight to illumine familiar things so that he could get a grip on those, and say that the mountain of the Brooding Hen is real and is there in all its granite strength. Or that is Shandra Lake which I fished how many centuries ago, and on such a day we took a two-pound trout out of it over there near the bushes. Or this is the road I walked with my love when the sun was high, and the heat on my face and the smell of the decaying heather was being wafted in front of the breeze.

There was no aid to reality now. The moon had shaken itself free of the clouds and beaten them with its light, so that they lay low and fearful on the horizon. And the moonlight glowed with a further sense of unreality, so that familiar things assumed the shape of dreams, as they hid themselves in unfamiliar shapes which were too unreal and grotesque to the eye, to be even of the stuff dreams are made of.

Will I have to walk this road for ever, he thought, surrounded by fantasy? Will this be what I have to endure as well as everything else? Am I walking, walking, and getting nowhere at all? Doesn't that bend of the road seem to be as far away now as it was when I came here several hours ago, or was it years? Is this what is going to happen to me? Am I to walk, and walk, and walk, on a moonlit Connemara road until my boots fall off and I become old?

The thought hurried his footsteps. His eyes widened frantically and he kept them riveted on the turn.

He rounded it and paused, and a great flood of relief came over him.

I came to the bend, he thought, and that is real.

Then a stone struck him on the side of the head and he fell to his knees.

The blow returned him to reality, and the instincts of years of poaching, and watching for birds and fish and men, came to his aid. He was no sooner on his knees than he was up again and facing in the direction from which the blow had come. The blow seemed to have cleared his head of the ache that was in it, and to have cleared his brain of the fog that was bemusing it.

With clear eyes he recognized the Finnerty brothers closing in on him.

They paused when they saw him looking at them, but they did not pause for long, because no matter how big a man he was, they were big too, and there were two of them. They got added courage from that unspoken thought, and also from the fire that was burning in Jack. Even Tim's shrinking soul, now that it had come to the point, felt that this man who had killed their brother in front of their eyes should be punished or destroyed.

Stephen felt that if they had been any other two, he would have been able to deal with them.

But not the Finnertys, God, he thought, not the Finnertys! His mind, which had been so clear a second ago, became listless. Maybe, he thought, this is a better way out of it. Maybe this is to be a retribution. His hands sank to his sides and his shoulders dropped.

Jack hit him on the mouth with his closed fist.

Tim hit him on the temple with his fist.

Stephen came out of himself unconsciously, and his soul revolted against the whole thing. If I am to die, he thought, then I will die fighting and I will not let them hit me until I am limp and useless.

So he struck with his right hand and Tim went flying back against the wall. He would never again show two of his front teeth in a smile.

Stephen could not avoid the kick of Jack's heavy boot on his knee and as he bent with pain, he could not save himself falling to the ground from the blow delivered to his already stone-battered head. He fell in the dust and hugged it for a time.

Jack drew back his foot to kick him in the face, but Stephen blocked it with his arm, and reaching out his other hand, caught Jack's foot and pulled him down and beneath him. Then he raised his right hand and brought it down on the face beneath him. He raised it again, but before it descended a bright light seemed to flash in his brain, as Tim hit the back of his head with a pointed rock, which he had picked up as he lay on the ground.

Stephen's unconscious body sprawled across that of his antagonist.

Tim pulled back, breathing heavily, watching the bright blood on the back of the head below him, and letting the stone fall slowly from his hand.

He saw Jack pulling himself out from under Stephen. He looked at him, and then turned him over on his back. He looked at the lifeless face for a moment, and then reaching into his pocket, he took out a penknife and opened it. It clicked gently as it opened.

'No!' said Tim, the sound bursting through his lips.

Jack paid no attention to him.

Dropping on one knee, he went to work with the penknife.

Over the Three Parishes, high in the air, borne on the wind, and seeking its pockets, a seagull soared and sank, and shrieked a shrill protest.

Below him were the lights in a few houses, the rest blanketed in darkness.

The moon was bright, and below him the roads lay like green ribbons criss-crossing a black curtain.

Stephen regained his senses with the cry of a seagull echoing in his ears.

His head was turned outwards and he could see with one eye. The road was on a level with his eye and he saw where it rose in the middle. He felt that his face was wet and wondered if it had rained or if somebody had been beating him across the face with a thin whip.

Then he remembered the Finnertys and he tried to get up.

He was unable to get up and fear struck at him. Why, he

wondered, can I not rise to my feet? With a great effort he raised one of his hands, leaving the elbow resting on the ground, and brought it in front of his eye that could see. It was wet and shining. He was looking at it for a long time before he realized that he must be looking at his own blood. His head felt as if it were separated from his body and waves of weakness were flowing through him. Still using his elbow for a fulcrum, he brought his hand up to his face. He knew then what had happened to him and he let his hand fall. He had seen just once before a man who had been penknifed in Connemara. He had lived because somebody had found him in time. But he could never look at himself again in a placid stream without a shiver of loathing, and the wonder if this face with a thousand crinkled scars could really be his own.

Stephen wondered how long he had been lying there by the side of the wall, hidden from human gaze by the overhanging bushes. I am going to die, he thought, and the thought was not unpleasant. A clearness as bright as a noonday sun had come to him, and he went over in his mind calmly the things that had happened in the past few hours, and now to him the hours were not distorted. All that had happened appeared to him to have been as inevitable as the coming of the swallows in the springtime. Because he found it so hard to move, he knew that he must have lost a lot of blood. A great lassitude was descending on him. This, he thought, is what Kathleen felt before she died, this, that I am feeling now. He relaxed himself even more, and thought how little pain he was feeling. He could imagine himself lying on a feather bed, sinking into it. It seemed like that to him, this grassy verge at the edge of the boithreen.

He was feeling this for a few seconds when something said to him in a strong voice, You do not want to die. He fluttered open his eye that could see and he drew back from the voice, because to die would be so easy; there would be no further effort required from him, no need to stir his body now, nor to watch the ashes of the dead being stirred and distorted in the eyes of men. No, he shouted to himself, no! The voice had not 'spoken' to himself but clearly it had rung in the night air and come back to him, and the strength of it hardened his flagging will. He said aloud to himself then, 'I do not want to die,' and he thought of what he had to do. Maybe he would never do it. Maybe he would never be allowed to live to do it, but he couldn't afford to die. He didn't want to die.

If he were to live he would have to get out from his soft bed and the cover of the bushes that were waving over his head. He could lie here until many suns had burned the hillside and he would be invisible to all eyes except the goats and the sheep that wanted the gift of speech.

He turned on his side, and thought that hooks had been pulling and tearing at the flesh of his head and face. He felt nauseated, and remembered a day long ago when the sea had almost got him, and he lay puking at the feet of a girl with black hair. He turned on his stomach and pulled up one of his arms, and placed his head on it.

He rested then.

After some time, he tried to pull himself to his knees, but such blinding pain shot through his head that the embryonic movement collapsed.

He lay and suffered.

His mind told him that he would have to get to the middle of the road; that the only hope for him was that he would be discovered soon by somebody who would help him, bind his wounds, and stop the flowing of his blood, if all of it had not drained out of him already. His mind reasoned it out and he saw there was only one way. He would have to roll on his back and then roll on his face, and each time he did this he would gain the width of his own body. Also, his mind said to him, you better do it now at once, before your brain becomes clouded again.

Two turns of his body, aided with elbows, hands, and knees, found him almost in the centre of the road. The effort proved too much for him and he felt his senses going from him again.

Before he lost consciousness he heard the seagull above him scream, and a vision came to him of a ten-year-old boy lying on a hill-top waiting for the release of his friends from school, while another gull sported in the sky. He said to himself, if by chance this is not the end of Stephen O'Riordan, some day I will write about all these things, and I will remember that seagull. I will say this:

'CHAPTER I

The seagull soared in the sun-misted air, high, high over the village of Killaduff . . .'

Then his senses wavered and were gone.

The seagull still circled and soared.

Shortly, the moon was challenged by the gleaming headlights of a car travelling the road where the strange shape lay huddled. It was driven by a fuming old man, who cursed the day he had ever thought of becoming a doctor, who hoped that Martin O'Riordan would not have died until he reached him. It was only the skill of long practice that enabled him to bring the car to a stop with screaming brakes, inches from the head of the man lying in the road.

The seagull, startled by the lights and noise, squawked protestingly, and swept widely towards the rocks lying like dark islands in the yellow immensity of Ourish Strand.

Fiction

☐	**The Island**	Peter Benchley	£1.25p
☐	**Options**	Freda Bright	£1.50p
☐	**Dupe**	Liza Cody	£1.25p
☐	**Chances**	Jackie Collins	£2.25p
☐	**Brain**	Robin Cook	£1.75p
☐	**The Entity**	Frank De Felitta	£1.75p
☐	**Whip Hand**	Dick Francis	£1.50p
☐	**Secrets**	Unity Hall	£1.50p
☐	**Solo**	Jack Higgins	£1.75p
☐	**The Rich are Different**	Susan Howatch	£2.75p
☐	**The Master Sniper**	Stephen Hunter	£1.50p
☐	**Moviola**	Garson Kanin	£1.50p
☐	**The Master Mariner Book 1: Running Proud**	Nicholas Monsarrat	£1.50p
☐	**Platinum Logic**	Tony Parsons	£1.75p
☐	**Fools Die**	Mario Puzo	£1.50p
☐	**The Boys in the Mailroom**	Iris Rainer	£1.50p
☐	**A Married Man**	Piers Paul Read	£1.50p
☐	**Sunflower**	Marilyn Sharp	95p
☐	**The Throwback**	Tom Sharpe	£1.50p
☐	**Wild Justice**	Wilbur Smith	£1.75p
☐	**That Old Gang of Mine**	Leslie Thomas	£1.25p
☐	**Caldo Largo**	Earl Thompson	£1.50p
☐	**Ben Retallick**	E. V. Thompson	£1.75p

All these books are available at your local bookshop or newsagent, or can be ordered direct from the publisher. Indicate the number of copies required and fill in the form below

5

Name_____

(Block letters please)

Address_____

_____

Send to Pan Books (CS Department), Cavaye Place, London SW10 9PG
Please enclose remittance to the value of the cover price plus:
35p for the first book plus 15p per copy for each additional book ordered
to a maximum charge of £1.25 to cover postage and packing
Applicable only in the UK

While every effort is made to keep prices low, it is sometimes necessary to increase prices at short notice. Pan Books reserve the right to show on covers and charge new retail prices which may differ from those advertised in the text or elsewhere